CARBON RUN

CARBON RUN

◆ ◆ ◆

A novel

J.G. Follansbee

©2017 J.G. Follansbee / Fyddeye Media
All rights reserved.
ISBN: 0984905448
Print ISBN-13: 9780984905447
Ebook ISBN-13: 978-0-9849054-5-4
Library of Congress Control Number: 2017912177
Fyddeye, Seattle, WA

Seattle, Wash., USA
Cover art by Christian Bentulan
http://coversbychristian.com/
Edited by John Paine
http://www.johnpaine.com/
Proofread by Edith Follansbee
For Grandma Thelma

SOME POOR DEVIL DOWN-VALLEY'S GOING to have a carbon ticket in their com if they don't douse *that fire now.* Anne Penn dismissed the thought before turning back to the male Klamath magpie. Pushing hair the color of fresh-sawn pine from her oval face, she was so intent on the bird she was observing from her blind that she didn't notice the disappearance of the sun as charcoal clouds skulked east. The bird grasped the carcass of a dead tree with its needle-like talons, the yellow band on its left leg visible. He belted out a *screep-screep-screep.* Anne hoped a female answered. If it didn't, the sub-species was doomed to extinction, another victim of the Warming.

Anne, what do you want for supper? The com message from Anne's father blinked in her visual field.

She clicked her tongue impatiently. Wait a minute, Dad. He always managed to break her focus at the wrong time. Something's happening.

Can't wait long, my dear.

Another rumble rolled down the valley toward their ranch a half-mile away. Anne crouched in the wildlife refuge where she had watched a colony of the magpies since her fourteenth summer. For five years she had worked as a volunteer observer, following the instructions of government scientists. That first summer, the ornithologist called her "swiftie," a comment on her keen, if immature mind, which bounced from subject to subject, turning on a dime like the swifts he studied. Last summer, one of the young biologists, a cute, bookish boy, claimed her elegant, streamlined shape compared well with the swift's.

The awkward compliment made her laugh. She thought the word "lanky" was enough of a description. Her mind was more disciplined now.

The male bird called again, and Anne heard a whoosh overhead as a drab female Klamath magpie swooped onto the nub of a broken branch. The male called again, showing his blood-red throat patch. The lady bird lingered. The male spread his wings in an invitation. They tussled.

Anne was elated at the mating. This population of Klamath magpies, the last known on earth, just might make it through another year. She yawned, tired from the long day, and she grew hungry in anticipation of her father's basic, delicious cooking.

Coming home, Dad.

I broke out a jar of my pasta sauce. Pasta's boiling on the hot plate.

Bill Penn made gallons of Anne's favorite Italian sauce from the tomatoes they didn't sell at the farmer's market, but the smell of smoke drowned out her anticipation. Two fixed-wing aircraft roared overhead up the valley. Anne called up the Brier Valley news chan, and she found live images of a forest fire 10 kilometers upwind under attack by the tankers. The images broke up in her minds-eye display.

Anne, I've got a problem. Her father's message broke into her minds-eye. "Anne, are you there?" *He never uses that voice unless something's wrong.* "Anne, answer me."

"Switch to voice," Anne commanded the com stud in her ear. "I'm here, Dad. What's wrong?"

"Call 9-1-1. I've got a fire in the kitchen. The extinguisher is exhausted." His voice was calm, if clipped.

"Did you say 'fire?'"

"I'm rigging up a hose. I need you here."

He spoke in his sailor's voice, the one he used to give orders, the one that gave others confidence. "What about Maxie? Where is she?"

"I don't know where the dog is. Get down here now, please."

She scrambled across an old stream bed and ducked under a fence. Despite his even tone, she heard impatience, and it magnified her anxiety. Her house was a hundred yards away, and a thin plume of black smoke rose from behind it. She'd lived there all her life. Everything she owned was there. *The woodcut. Please God, no.*

Anne remembered her father's order and directed her attention to her com. "Emergency numbers. Call 9-1-1."

"McCall County emergency services. Can we help you?"

I can handle this. "My house is on fire. It's in the kitchen." A tremble in her voice betrayed her fear.

The emergency dispatcher confirmed Anne's coordinates sent to the dispatcher when Anne made the 9-1-1 call. "The Penn ranch, William Penn?"

"Yes, that's right. Hurry, please."

"Fire units on their way, ma'am."

Anne ran to the far side of the house. Her father was spraying water from a garden hose into the kitchen though an open window. An electric pump labored, drawing water from an aluminum horse trough, but the stream was weak. *That will never put out the fire.* Sparks curled up over the eave and landed on the roof. Anne felt useless as the water hissed off the shingles. *If I can save the woodcut, I don't care if the whole place goes up.* She approached the kitchen steps, putting her hand up to block the heat.

"Stay away from the kitchen," Anne's father bellowed. "Damn this piece-of-shit pump. I'm going to start the gasoline pump."

The thought of rescuing her father's precious gift vanished. "No, Dad. You can't do that. The cops—"

"To hell with them. I'll do what I have to do." Bill Penn headed toward the shed where they hid the obsolete engine. His intricate tattoos shone through his water-soaked t-shirt. In the shade of the outbuilding, Maxie whined. The ranch's old basset hound was frightened, but unhurt.

"No, Dad, you can't risk it. What if the cops show up? You know what the judge said."

"Screw the judge. This is all I have." He pointed at the burning house. "It's all *we* have."

Fear for her gift returned, even as flames licked the walls of her home and threatened everything else she owned. Her father found the woodcut in an antique shop in Port Simpson a year after they stopped hearing from her mother.

It was a page in a book of poems published in the 1820s. Frayed, yellowed, but preserved under glass, the print showed a vigorous English sailor and a girl child of four or five reaching out to embrace each other. To Anne's eye, the sailor looked exactly like her father: pleasant face, strong arms, rough around the edges. The gift marked the moment her anger toward her mother began to fade. For 15 years, the artwork hung in the kitchen, above the table where father and daughter ate their meals. More than two hundred years ago, an artist had captured their love and respect for each other. The thought of losing the image tore at Anne.

Bill knocked down the tongues of flame, but two sprang up in their places. Convection currents carried embers over the roof and out of sight. Soot stung Anne's eyes like tiny insects until it obscured the minds-eye display for her com. Messages came in from her loop as friends picked up her emo-sigs of distress but the smoke made her eyes tear up, and when she wiped the tears away, her hand distorted the shape of her eye and the display went fuzzy. Dirty sweat trickled down her neck along a gold chain with almost microscopic links that held a thumbnail-sized crucifix next to her skin. Her control over her fear slipped as it mixed with the stink of burning insulation and decayed tar paper. She heard her father's voice, but couldn't see him.

"Anne, where are you?" her father screamed through the surging blackness. "Call 9-1-1 again. The fire's spreading."

Anne updated the dispatcher, but it would take ten more minutes for the trucks to arrive because the Penn place was so far up the valley. Her rising terror emerged as frustration when he repeated his plan to use the gas pump. She grabbed the dribbling hose. "You're always breaking the rules. Is that why the fire started?"

The accusation brought her father up short. "What are you talking about? I need your help, not a lecture. Help me with this pump."

"I'm sorry, Daddy. I'm scared." She rushed to the back of the building, guilt and thoughts of rescuing the woodcut and a few belongings driving her. A window shattered from the intense heat, discouraging her. She called out to her father again but he didn't answer. She wished he would get one of the new augmenters. Adding him to her c-tribe would give her a better sense of what he was thinking and feeling, even when there wasn't an emergency.

"Dad, I'm in the back."

Most people over thirty didn't get the concept of c-tribes, anyway. Like her dad, they were still using old-fashioned slow jack-in's. *They might as well be using cell phones.*

Her father came out to the back porch and Anne pointed to the sky. "There's smoke coming from the roof, Daddy."

"Get some water on it." Fear pitched his voice high as he handed her the garden hose. For the first time in her life, she saw raw horror in his face. It was the opposite of what Anne knew. There was the time Maxie confronted a rattlesnake when she was a puppy. The snake coiled to strike, and Bill crushed its head with a shovel. He was always calm in a crisis, but this one was getting away from him, and it frightened Anne.

He coughed as he held a cloth over his mouth. "I'm going to move the truck. We can't lose it."

The decision bolstered Anne's confidence. *If I could just get inside the house for 30 seconds.* Mentally, she listed holo-pics of dead ancestors, trophies and ribbons from school, her prom dress, the signed t-shirt from the Hindu Mistress concert, the only time she'd ever seen a live music performance by a pop band. Bill had taken her.

A bark from Maxie brought Anne back to her job: get water on the roof. Mist from the nozzle soaked her denim overalls. Water dripped on the rockery by the front porch and boiled away. On the roof, flames danced among the shingles.

Anne heard the whine from the old truck's electric motor pitch up and the *churrr churrr* of the gears as her father tried to find reverse. They couldn't afford to take it to the repair shop. Despite their poverty, he had bought her the minds eye for Christmas after she had begged for months. Everyone in Brier Valley owned one. Everyone she knew, at least.

Helpless as she and her father waited for the firefighters, Anne's thoughts flashed to that birthday. She went with her best friends to the mall in Medford and the com company booth with the gift certificate in hand. She was not one to buy gaudy electronics, and she picked out a head appliance styled like an ordinary silver stud, if larger than average. She had it installed at the top of her left ear, which was the fashion at Brier High. She had to settle for one without the imager, because of the cost, so she wouldn't be able to share stills and vids. It would take her months to save for the imager add-on. The sales tech tuned the appliance to the wave frequencies of her occipital lobe and limbic system. She squealed with delight as she looped herself into her friends' tribes and created her own tribe.

Her digital memories were safe with the com company, but when a corner of the porch collapsed, she despaired for her other memories, the ones she could hold in her hand. *They're all gone.* Pieces of her life were slipping through her fingers. Bill managed to get the truck moving, even as the fire's heat blistered the paint off the hood. A gust of wind lifted an ember and it floated like a feather in a breeze. The wind carried it to the woodland next to the ranch. As if she had second sight, Anne saw the future.

"Oh, god. The refuge."

The wisp of fire landed in tinder-dry brush and flared. Her fear turned to panic, but not for her home. Her matted hair flying, Anne ran past the lurching truck carrying a tin bucket. Bill yelled as she flew by. The house no longer mattered. She dipped the bucket into the half-empty horse trough and splashed the water onto the blackening grass. It wasn't enough. Within seconds, the offspring of the house fire raged into the pines. The fire jumped from tree to tree like a mad demon. Anne made another call to 9-1-1. "Where are you? Are you coming? Please hurry!"

As if in answer to a prayer, a fixed-wing aircraft arrived first. Anne heard the drone before she saw it. *It's about time.* Several of the big tankers were always somewhere over the Cascade Mountains twenty-four hours a day, seven days a week during the dry season. Their pilots waited for orders at workstations in the western states fire suppression center. Anne had taken a tour of it for her junior year environmental defense class. The tour guide said most of the pilots were veterans of the Three Degrees North War.

Anne ducked by instinct as the initial sorties dive-bombed the forest around the refuge at tree-level. It was now a war against destruction. She prayed for every strike. Experienced pilots were as precise as raptors. They could hit a single tree with their water payloads, leaving the tree's neighbors dry as a bone. She leapt for joy at each hit. She messaged her c-tribe in jubilation and the Hurrahs and Yays came back within seconds. Thousands of gallons of fire retardant and water carpeted the blaze, but the flames defied the aircraft like rioters. More sorties attacked the fiery stragglers. Messages in her minds-eye warned her to stay clear, but she thought she saw the magpie nest with the newly mated pair, unharmed. *Stay in the nest. You'll be fine.*

The sun glinted off the silver wings as the planes banked to avoid the mountains. As soon as they turned, the fire flared again, marching in patches up the hill, heading straight for the refuge and the birds. Anne was running up to the blackened, still burning forest when her father texted her.

Anne, where are you? I can't fight this by myself.

She hesitated, torn between the birds she had come to love like a family and her father, the only family she had. More tankers roared overhead. I'm coming.

When Anne returned to her father's side, gray ash covered his face like a shroud, highlighting the shock in his blue-green eyes. The entire house was engulfed in a roaring cacophony of fire. A helicopter slinging a full bucket of water hovered into position over the house. A thousand-gallon deluge dropped onto the house's remains.

All the flames at the house died, leaving charred wood, twisted aluminum from the window frames, and a concrete set of steps that led nowhere. White steam rose from the debris. A puff of brown smoke escaped from the stove pipe. The wood stove was one of the few pieces of the house left over from the original building, which her father said was built a century ago, long before the development restrictions of the 2020s made the appliance illegal. The stove kept Anne and her father warm in the high-country nights. Its blackened carapace chilled her.

"Oh, god. Oh, god." Bill clasped his hands on his head, as if protecting it from the devastation. Anne had never seen him in a state of shock. *Was this how he looked when Molly left us?* They walked into the corpse of the house. Heat rose from the ashes. Grit choked the air. She searched for the woodcut, but found nothing, not even the glass case. The only fragment she recognized was the cooked blob of her pistol marksmanship trophy. Bill lifted a metal picture frame, which still held a seared, soaked image of Anne's dark-haired, fair-skinned mother. He dropped the photo among the scorched fragments of two lives—mementos of his sailing days, melted plastic toys—and he keened as if his heart had been torn out.

Anne wished the photo had burned. It had the opposite meaning of the woodcut. The photo sat on the shelf for her father's sake, not Anne's, a reminder for her of abandonment, not love. All she remembered of her mother was her anger, which flared into rage in dreams or the occasional argument with Bill. Her father sometimes fell into dark moods and glared at the photo. Why he kept it was a mystery to Anne as a child, though as she grew into a young woman and noticed the young men around her, something about her father's need for the photo became clearer. He was lonely, and some of his memories of Molly were happy ones.

Daughter wrapped her arms around her father, guiding him like a child, pulling him away from the carnage, ignoring the sweat and caked dust on his body, her own tears mixing with the dirt and water that saturated his shirt and jeans. Her c-tribe posted dozens of messages trying to soothe her and tell her she wasn't alone and that the community would help. She heeded nothing aside from her father's grief, her own disbelief at the destruction of her life, and the cadaver of her home. It was the end of her world.

The world around Anne kept going. Two fire trucks, one a red pumper from the local fire district, and the second a fire-suppression unit from the state Department of Forestry, roared up the pitted dirt road that wound through the Penn place's forested ravine. The pumper peeled off across a field to the front of the ruined house. A firefighter, his face streaked with sweat, dragged over a hose to soak the coals. He impressed Anne with his fearlessness.

The suppression unit pulled up to the rear near the equipment shed, its electric motor straining as it climbed the steep driveway. It drove to the blackened edge of the trees that bordered the refuge. Hydraulic levers lowered a squad of four-legged robots to the ground. Each robot had two huge tanks on its back. They moved like enormous, headless bulldogs. The machines climbed straight into the trees and up the hillside into the flames, as if they were fireproof goats.

A wailing aid unit stopped on the dry grass that was once the Penn's yard. A McCall County sheriff's helicopter, the size of a wren, hovered twenty feet over Anne's head. A patrol car, lights blazing, kicked up dust as it parked next to the aid unit. A well-built man, wearing body armor and a pistol, trotted up to Anne and her father.

"Are you and Anne alright, Bill?" the officer said.

Anne's father was weary and red-eyed. "I can't say I'm glad to see you, Gary, but was I ever glad to see you?" Anne's father shook as adrenaline rocked his body. She was jittery herself. The EMT led them to the back of the aid unit. He draped each with a thermal blanket, despite the ninety-five-degree temperatures.

"I don't remember a single time, Bill," said the officer. His name was Lieutenant Gary Schmidt. He was responsible for the scattered farms and homesteads in this part of the valley. Schmidt was one of the few cops Anne trusted. "I'm not going to ticket you this time, Bill, even if you deserve it again for that wood stove."

Bill lowered his head into his heads, as if hiding from the horror around him.

"Do you need anything, Bill?"

Anne's father shook his head. She clung to him in a way unlike any since her mother said goodbye. Anne's eyes—which her father said were the color of fertile loam, like her mother's—stared toward the remnants of the house. Neither she nor her father was physically hurt, and the fact of their material losses did not feel real, despite a hollowness in her chest. *Are the magpies gone too?* She remembered the single nest, untouched by the fire as the tankers fought it. She raised her eyes to the refuge, and she watched another small remote-controlled helicopter buzz over its smoldering remains.

CHAPTER 2

DEPUTY INSPECTOR JANINE KILEL TRACKED the surveillance drone out of the corner of her eye as it hovered over the blackened landscape of the refuge. She sat in the front seat of her forest-green cruiser, its doors emblazoned with the shield of the Bureau of Environmental Security, going over intelligence reports on her highest priority case, an oil-smuggling ring operating on the west coast of North America. As the one available case officer in the region, she was sent to the fire scene when BES monitoring stations picked up the emergency calls. A screen showed the refuge from the drone's perspective, but Kilel's attention was on an analysis of the smugglers' conjectured routes. The pigeon-sized copter's AI maneuvered among the blackened pines and halted the aircraft at each stump of wheat grass, sedge, wild sunflower, and yarrow.

A tiny beep interrupted Kilel's focus, and the drone's camera showed the ash-covered corpse of a bird, its feathers burned off. Taking control of the camera, Kilel sought out a yellow band on the leg, but the bird appeared to be a juvenile, rather than an adult banded by the biologists who monitored the refuge. Kilel touched a key, instructing the copter to search for similar objects, and the aircraft found two more dead chicks.

Kilel recalled the copter, and she opened up the local fire district database via her tablet. She found the preliminary report on the fire. It pinned the cause on flying embers from the fire at the neighboring property, which belonged to a William Penn. There was a link from the name in the fire district report to the county sheriff's database, and she read a summary of his case file. A driver's license photo showed a man in early middle age with short-cropped hair, kind eyes, a roman nose, and thin lips. She noted numerous carbon breaches, though the penalties were slaps on Penn's wrists. Penn was an ongoing problem, and Kilel wondered if law enforcers in these parched Oregon counties would ever understand the seriousness of environmental crimes. *It doesn't matter. It's in my lap now.* She pressed the accelerator, and the car's electric motor whispered.

Kilel saw the mailbox at the gate to the Penn property before she made out the burned-out house, eddies of smoke rising from the ruins. The lights of the pumper truck and the aid unit flashed as the firefighters and the paramedics packed up. She edged the cruiser past the scene to a spot closer to the refuge. The state fire-suppression unit was mopping up near the ridgeline.

The inspector was tall, athletic, with bust and hips proportional. She wore office-style attire, standardized for the Bureau. The com stud in her ear was functional, without the decorative flourishes some women preferred. Her blond hair was cut in a plain manner and she wore little makeup. She didn't need it. Her father described her as pretty, but not girlish. She had a voice the color of fine dark bread, and lips as smooth as nectarine skin. She was a woman unafraid of her own power.

Walking a quarter-mile up a trail that wound through the desolation, she found the corpses of two adult birds, a type of magpie, near a dead chick in the remains of a nest. She bent down to the victims, resisting the urge to touch the evidence in a crime scene. Kilel grew heartsick as she imagined the adult birds, torn between escape and protecting their offspring, overwhelmed by the speed of the fire. *How many other times will this drama play out, as the Spike continues to devastate the natural world?* All the efforts to protect wildlife for future generations undone by the thoughtlessness of one person. She had joined the BES to defend nature and her planet against such people.

The birds were dead, but the ID chips in the bands still transmitted species, sex, banding date, and ID number. Kilel noted the codes as she tapped into the biologists' database. Only twenty-nine nesting pairs remained in the wild. Walking through the open graveyard, Kilel found fifty-two more dead adults. She guessed that all the chicks were dead, or soon would be. All the nesting pairs lived in this refuge. No signals broadcast for the remaining four known adults. She imagined them flying off in terror; it would be up to the biologists to find them in the follow-up investigation.

Kilel tipped her head back and opened her eyes to the sky, where a pair of turkey vultures circled overhead. She offered a prayer for the deceased birds.

The inspector returned to her car, and she drove into Penn's driveway. She recognized him from the driver's license photo. Next to him was a young woman whom Kilel deduced was his daughter Anne. Her arm was woven into her father's. A sheriff's patrol car obscured Kilel's view, but she watched them through the car's glass, as if peering through layers of time. An unwelcome memory stirred: a grieving father at the bedside of a dying mother. Brushing the memory from her mind, Kilel glanced in the rear-view mirror, her mahogany-colored eyes seeking out the robot in its locker, which took up half of the rear compartment. A ready light glowed green.

"Security, deploy."

The robot left the car, and Kilel followed, smoothing out the dark green fabric of her BES uniform. The color matched the green paint of the car. A small gold tulip was pinned to the collar of her blouse, the color of malachite. Kilel approached Penn, the girl Anne, and the deputy, her robot a step behind her.

The girl glanced back to the refuge, which was smoking like a vision of hell.

"No, you can't take him." Anne shook her head, in denial of facts she knew to be true. "It was an accident."

"William Penn?" Kilel ignored the girl and addressed a man with a dirty face and stained t-shirt. Her voice was even and smooth. The sheriff's deputy stepped back.

"Yes." Penn's eyes widened with fear. *Fear is good.*

"My name is Kilel." Her BES badge reflected the lights of the emergency vehicles. "I am an environmental crimes investigator. This is—was—your house?" Kilel saw his pulse jump, belied by the throbbing carotid artery in his neck. If he ran, the security robot would hunt and stop him.

"I'm sorry for the loss of your house, Mr. Penn." Kilel's feeling was sincere. "A preliminary investigation of this incident has found that the burning of your structure led to the fire at the wildlife refuge."

"It was an accident." Anne's blond hair hung limp against her face.

Penn broke in. "I was cooking dinner when there was a spark——"

"Before you say anything more," Kilel said, "I advise you that this conversation is being recorded, and your words and actions are evidence."

Penn swallowed.

"I must ask you to turn around and place your hands behind your back."

He complied, as if it were a habit. Anne shouted and tried to push Kilel away, but the deputy restrained her. "Anne," Penn said, "don't make it worse. You know the bessies will, if they can." Penn's face tensed with rage.

Kilel ignored Penn's assessment and the "bessie" insult. She tightened the handcuffs around his wrists. "You are under arrest, Mr. Penn, for destroying protected habitat of an endangered species, unauthorized killing of members of that species, and violations of the Carbon Acts."

CHAPTER 3

MARTIN SCRIBB'S BEGGING BOWL YAWNED empty for three hours before the colonel dropped in his business card.

The clunk of paper on brass echoed around the dun walls of the town square. Waves of April heat rose around Martin into a sky the blue of a gas flame. The scrubby foothills beyond the town reflected the heat back to the square and added a new load of dust. *How many years has it been since April was a pleasant month in northern latitudes? Twenty? Thirty?* Martin's thought was an attempt to distract himself from the card. The attempt failed.

The bowl's rim glowed a poppy red when the card hit the metal. A second later, it glowed amber, instead of the usual green.

Martin bowed to the colonel as he did to every alms-giver or petitioner. "I apologize, sir, but my bowl isn't reading your card."

"I wouldn't expect it to." The colonel was on his haunches in front of Martin. "Give the card to your abbot. It has a message."

Martin's stared at the card, which was embossed with the tulip of the Bureau of Environmental Security. Martin reflected on the simple three-point beauty of the stylized flower, and the terror it provoked. The tulip mirrored the brand above his left eye, just below the hairline.

"Thought you were done with me, eh, Brother Martin?" The colonel winked. "Never."

Martin felt as if something in the air had ignited and engulfed him. He held the folds of his dirt-brown woolen habit against his chest.

The colonel stood over Martin as he sat cross-legged in his customary place in the center of the square. His vows of penance compelled him to sit far away from the slivers of midday shade, but the colonel's shadow covered Martin, reminding him of his sins. *My alleged sins.*

"How did you find me?" Martin whispered the next words. "I am dead."

The colonel spoke into the beggar monk's ear. "Not easy, even for me, Brother Martin. I supervised your disidentification, after all." The colonel resumed his full six-foot plus height. The black faux-leather of his shoes shone so brightly that Martin spied the overhead disk of the sun in the uppers. "The Bureau is skilled now with erasing an existence, though it was so much simpler in the old days, before the squeamish ruled the world." Martin raised his tonsured head and torso from his obeisance, and he saw a grin on the colonel's face. "The authorities killed miscreants. A couple of injections, bury the corpse, and call it a day."

Yes, physical death would've been easier, Martin thought, remembering the worst day of his life. "Our sentence of identity obliteration is too good for the defendant," the judges on the Environmental Crimes Tribunal announced. *If I don't exist in any human record--digital or otherwise--am I alive? Or am I a damned soul in a living hell?*

Martin visited a library a few weeks after his sentence, and he found not a single hit about himself. Nothing on web pages, news groups, or com nets. No images, moving or still. He wasn't in the government databases. His birth certificate was gone. Because he hadn't been "born," in a manner of speaking, he didn't have a death certificate either.

Before the Spike, a person would find hundreds of thousands, maybe millions of hits about Martin. The whole planet knew who he was.

Despite his lack of ever existing—officially—Martin had a tombstone. It had no name, year of birth, or year of death. It was raised like a penny-sized monument out of his forehead, reminding all of his sins, telling all to treat him as non-existent.

This is what happens when someone bears false witness against you.

The colonel regarded the disidentified man. "Even though you're dead to the world, you might say, there are always traces. I dug them up, and here I am."

The colonel moved back a step, letting the sun pound down on the monk again. "The Catholics have this concept of 'limbo,' Martin." The colonel taunted him. "I think that's where you live."

Martin found limits to society's twisted tolerance. One rainy winter day, he took a poncho from a sporting goods store in full view of everyone—he never hid his intent—and left the store. A block away, the manager, his badge flopping on his chest, ran up to Martin and took the poncho from his hand without saying a word and ran back to the store. Martin was elated, as well as disappointed. The manager's behavior was a silent and reluctant acquiescence to the physical fact of Martin's existence, if not the social fact.

"The Penitents of St. Francis took me in." Martin blinked at the colonel. "Father Gonzales found me after I had sat at a bus stop for three days. I'm a lay brother now."

"Penitents? As in penance? As in forgiveness?" The colonel shook his head, as if looking at an abstract painting titled with a person's name. "Is that what you want now, Martin? Redemption?"

The colonel loved to dangle the prospect of a slate wiped clean in front of Martin, always before he asked for something Martin was sure he would never give, and did anyway. The thought forced beads of sweat to seep onto Martin's forehead, as if the colonel were squeezing his skull like a damp sponge. Taking his time, hoping to hide the terror in his trembling hands, Martin gathered the card and bowl, placing them in his shoulder pouch. He kept his eyes down as he got to his sandaled feet and put on his tattered straw hat.

"You won't find what you want in this hellhole," the colonel said.

Martin adjusted his habit to maintain some dignity. He glanced upward. The colonel's familiar face was in shadow. The eyes, though, were backlit by contempt.

"I have some of what you want, Brother." The colonel's pattern was repeating. "Remember your days in parochial school?"

Martin did remember. The severe, though loving stares of Sister Sabina. The boredom of First Friday mass. The soaring echoes inside the archdiocese's cathedral.

"The old nuns said that once you had confessed your sins and received absolution, your soul would be like a fine linen sheet, spotless. I can do something like that in the real world. I can resurrect you." The colonel laughed. "You'd have a fresh start, at least in this life. What your god does to you afterwards, I can't influence."

"I ask for nothing, sir, except for what people may put in my begging bowl to help my brethren."

The colonel sneered. "How pious."

It was true. It was the begging bowl that brought Martin back from physical death. Father Gonzales cleaned him up, dressed him in a habit, and set him down, back at that bus stop, with the bowl. There's something about that open, silent request, made by someone who does it with a purpose larger than himself—in Martin's case, supporting a religious community—that leads people to act. Despite the official ostracism, he'd never forget the joy he felt when the first coin dropped into the bowl.

The colonel, the man who, for all intents and purposes, had put him to death, was back in his life, wanting something more. Martin made a 180-degree turn, hoping to leave the BES officer behind, resigned to knowing he would follow him until he got what he wanted.

"Where do you think you're going?" the colonel said.

"I have my devotions."

"Devote yourself to this, Brother." The colonel chuckled. "Molly Bain. It's time to give her up, Martin Scribb. To me."

Martin stopped mid-stride. A death certificate for Martin, if one had been issued, would list the cause of death as Molly Bain.

Father Alberto Gonzales was at the front door of Martin's house saying goodbye to a guest when the beggar monk returned home. The priest was a dark, demanding man who bathed irregularly. He was forty-one years old and the abbot of the community.

"You're back early, Martin. Something wrong?"

The lay brother told him about the colonel's visit.

"Did he force you to leave the square?" Gonzales said.

"No, Father. I was afraid of him."

"You should not have left an hour before your scheduled time."

"Father, I..."

"Brother Martin, do I need to remind you of your vows? Four hours a day begging in the square. In full sun. In any weather."

A grizzled monk walked between Gonzales and Martin carrying a well-thumbed Bible, the screen scratched and the casing chipped. Like the other monks, he glanced at Martin, but offered no other connection.

"Come to my office." Martin followed the abbot through the reception area with its out-of-style, tattered furniture to an interior door. A life-size marble sculpture of St. Francis of Assisi guarded this private entrance, which led to the community's cells and living areas. Lay people—except lay brothers, such as Martin—weren't permitted beyond this door.

Once in the hallway, the temperature fell ten degrees, due to the construction of the house, which imitated the old adobe haciendas of the colonial Spanish. The style had crept north as the local climate dried out, even before the Spike. The architect wanted to install air conditioning, but the Franciscan builders a century ago didn't like artificial cooling, because it increased their carbon footprint, as people used to say. The plain, clear windows were small, and artificial lights few, so the house had a close, airless quality. A few devotional paintings hung on the walls. The air smelled of just-snuffed candles.

In Gonzales' office, the abbot gestured for Martin to sit. Gonzales switched on his holo-console. One of the abbey's benefactors was the wealthy, retired president of a pre-Spike, eco-boom company who liked gadgetry.

"Brother Martin, I've been thinking for awhile that we ought to review your place here." The changing reflections of light in Gonzales' concentrating face suggested he was looking for something. "Here it is, your record. You've been here since—"

"March 16, 2053."

"A little more than four years," the abbot said. "You were one of the youngest men that we've accepted. How old were you?"

"Twenty-seven."

"It's rare enough that a man your age comes to a vocation. It's even rarer that one agrees to vows of penance."

Martin contemplated his folded hands.

"You're an unusual case. Penance was certainly called for."

"I've kept the penance candle in my cell lit day and night, Father." Martin laughed. "I must use the most chem-dle's in the abbey."

"Don't boast," Gonzales said, "but yes, despite today's lapse, you have kept your vows."

"I've done my best so far. I am sorry for my deeds, and I want to show the world."

"I believe you, Martin, but your breach today must be addressed. Let me think on it." Gonzales paused, moving his hand in front of the console. "I see that you did not take in any donations today."

"No one was out because of the heat."

"This is puzzling." Gonzales' brow creased. "There's an error message, something about 'unreadable data', just before you left the square."

"That must be the business card."

"Whose card?"

"I did get one visitor, as I said."

"Give it to me."

Martin handed over the card. The abbot placed it on a reader near the console. The light on his face shifted, and he turned the display around for Martin.

The colonel's face was angular, like an unfinished stone sculpture. The image spoke. "Good afternoon, Martin. If my avatar is not mistaken, I'm also speaking to your Father Abbot. Good day to you."

Gonzales didn't acknowledge the greeting. He knew of Martin's history with the BES.

"Father Abbot," the colonel's avatar said, "some of the material I have for Brother Martin is sensitive."

"I am his confessor, avatar. Martin would be required to relay this information to me anyway. Secrecy is frowned on in my abbey. It makes no difference if I hear what you have to say now or later. I will keep what's said in strictest confidence, according to our rule."

Martin was struck by the cordial affect of the colonel's virtual self, which was so different from the bullying corporeal version in the square. Perhaps the avatar was programmed to be deferential to authority.

"As you wish, Father." The avatar turned to me. "Brother Martin, I want you to disappear."

Martin's heart skipped a beat. Gonzales shifted in his chair.

"I want you to leave the abbey and head north, without anyone knowing about it, except Father Gonzales, of course." The avatar's voice contained a hint of disappointment in that final phrase. "I'm sending you to Bežat, in Russia."

Gonzales wrinkled his nose. "What interests you or Brother Martin in Bežat, if I may ask. I've heard that it's a haven for prostitutes and deviants, if it even exists. It seems to be more legend than fact."

"BES does not concern itself with fringe behavior, Father. Our mandate is protection of the environment, not morals."

"Bežat is said to be in the Arctic Free Economic Zone," Martin observed.

"Or near it," the avatar said. "Believe it or not, BES does not have its exact location in 'The Wild North,' but we've learned that you have a reputation in Bežat and the surrounding area among people who question our carbon control laws and policies."

Martin was taken aback by the avatar's statements. "If what you say is true, I'm ashamed of it. I'm ashamed that a few people have praised me for my past actions, even if the actions were well-intended. I don't understand why they have overlooked the consequences."

As always, some people refuse to adapt to new realities. Oil rebels and coal criminals were a staple of news chans and the primary targets of BES investigators. Both were ruthless, but the BES was fighting for a sustainable future, while the miscreants fought for a profit-driven past. At least, that's what the BES propaganda claimed.

"These misfits exist, nonetheless, Martin. We have reason to believe they are more dangerous to the earth than we originally thought. We think some of them are the leaders of a carbon smuggling ring, a very large one, with global reach."

"Smuggling?" Gonzales said.

The avatar addressed the priest. "Raw materials. Crude oil. Coal. Sometimes refined materials, like kerosene. We think Bežat might be a center of these activities."

"Why are you sending me there?" Martin said.

"Our agents have never been able to penetrate the organization, but we think you might get in, given your reputation. We want you to get information that will prove their guilt, and then we will destroy their facilities and arrest the ringleaders."

"What if I don't want to go?"

The avatar ignored Martin. "Detailed instructions follow this message."

Gonzales raised himself in his chair. "I believe I have a say in this matter—"

"Father, let me say that you do not. As you know, you are technically in violation of an authenticated disidentification warrant by helping Mr.—Brother— Scribb. I've overlooked this because of Martin's potential usefulness to BES. I could notice this problem at any time. Do we understand each other?"

Gonzales swallowed, and agreed.

"Martin, if you are successful," the avatar said, "I will personally usher a decision through the agency and the Environmental Crimes Tribunal to restore your identity. That would include a new name. You would be a legitimate person again."

"I've never heard of this," Gonzales said.

"It has been done in exceptional cases of service."

"Why should I believe my executioner would resurrect me?" Martin's puzzlement went further. *Why has your avatar said nothing about Molly? Today in the square, you were interested only in her.*

Gonzales wiped sweat from his forehead with the palm of his hand. "Martin, you must learn more gratitude. BES doesn't have to give you anything. This is a generous offer."

"I suppose I don't have a choice, do I?" Martin said.

"We always have choices." The avatar sighed, as if it regretted something. "Some choices have more utility than others."

The message ended, and Gonzales closed the console window. He gave the business card back to the monk. "You have another vow, Martin. Obedience to legitimate authority."

The vow referred to the abbot, in an ecclesiastical sense. In this case, the intimidated Gonzales also applied it to secular authorities.

That evening, Martin served the abbot's sentence for leaving the square: a night in the 40-degree heat of his cell, instead of sleep on the roof of the community house under the stars with the other brothers. It would be 30 up there at midnight, and down to 25 by dawn. *Was the room any cooler before the Spike? Yes.*

Father Gonzales sent Martin to the abbey barber, who trimmed his hair and beard, and shaved his tonsure down to the scalp. The barber avoided the skin that grew over the brand at Martin's hairline. The DNA of the bone cells had been altered to grow it, never to be removed. *The colonel promised...*

He prayed for an hour at the *prie dieu* under his tiny window and a crucifix.

That night was the last Martin spent in his cell.

An hour before dawn, Martin rose, donned a homespun robe, straw hat, and rope belt, which hung on a wooden peg in the adobe wall above his pallet. The colonel's card, with its instructions, waited by his stoneware water cup.

Martin ate breakfast with the rest of the community in the dining room, savoring the sourdough bread famous throughout the region. Gonzales announced Martin's departure from the community after the Gospel reading. The abbey rule forbade speaking during meals as a sign of reverence for God's bounty. Martin had learned to read these silences, and he sensed the monks were happy he was leaving. After the meal, Martin returned to his cell and studied the colonel's instructions. Gonzales came to say goodbye, and he gave the lay brother a gift: a new pair of sandals.

"Thank you, Father, but my current pair is still in good shape."

"The most important thing a traveler needs is a good pair of shoes." Gonzales handed him the faux-leather footwear. "Go with God." He smiled as if relieved of a burden. "You are still bound by your vows, though I can't supervise you.

Remember that I'll know something about what you're doing by your bowl's automatic reports. I still expect you to bring in money for the community."

One of the friendlier brothers had once remarked to Martin that the abbot had his own special omniscience.

Martin placed the sandals in his pouch with his bowl, religious ID card, abbey debit card, and com link. The ID card, not strictly legal, was a convenience in case Martin was challenged by local cops. As a former businessman himself, Gonzales trusted Martin with money, thus the debit card. Martin's share of donations to his bowl was transferred to the debit card for living and travel expenses. Perks such as frequent flyer miles were forbidden, but earned individual carbon offsets were encouraged in light of the Penitents' mission of prayer for the earth's healing.

Gonzales walked Martin to the front door. Martin turned to shake his hand in goodbye, but the abbot averted his eyes from the lay brother. "Is something wrong, Father?"

Gonzales folded his hands beneath his mantle. He coughed. "Martin, I must tell you something. The colonel threatened our community in his message."

Martin feared Gonzales' next words.

"I'm not sure we can welcome you back here."

"Father, this is my home now. You are my family."

"Yes, but——" Gonzales cleared his throat, his eyes askance. "——just make sure you do what you have to do."

CHAPTER 4

BILL PENN'S HOLDING CELL ON the fifth floor of the McCall County Courthouse smelled of chlorine bleach. The acrid, gassy odor nauseated him, and he clawed at the collar of his blaze orange jail jumpsuit. Bill had breathed jail air before. Vagabond young men and women with no ties and the vaguest sense of the future got drunk and fought with each other for no apparent reason. *That cage in Vladivostok was fit only for rats and carbon dealers.* The next day, they went back to the ship and shared a fo'c'sle and climbed aloft as if nothing had happened. Bill had nothing to lose in those days, which meant a level of freedom he missed occasionally as he worked the Brier Valley ranch. Once, when he was sick of digging post holes to replace an old fence line, he was nearly overwhelmed with an urge to run back to the sea and freedom. Aware of his frustration, Anne brought him a jug of flavored ice-water—*orange, my favorite*—and his desire to escape evaporated as he remembered why he had given up the sailor's life. From the moment Molly's midwife handed Bill the tiny, mewling, pissed-off-after-being-squeezed-into-life Anne, Bill had only one purpose: caring for this child. Now, for the first time since Molly went away, they were separated and kept apart by iron bars.

The refuge fire and the BES threatened the unthinkable—losing Anne—but he had no idea what to do. He imagined a tiny spider that crawled up the wall next to his head as bewildered as he was. Surrounded by a featureless sea of concrete, with no landmarks to guide it, the arachnid was adrift and uncertain. *No, it's figuring out its next move.* He remembered his training: When shipwrecked, panic kills. Stay calm, take stock, make a plan, have a goal. *Get back to Anne.*

He had no idea if his daughter would be at his hearing before Judge Parker or even if she knew about it. From the moment he stepped off the special elevator for inmates in the custody of Gary Schmidt, he lost touch with Anne. The jail blocked all com signals. No texts, no voice, no emotional signals, though Bill couldn't run the emo-sig package due to his obsolete jack-in. *I need you there, just so I know you're alive and well.* His gut twisted into knots.

The spider crawled a few centimeters, stopped, and lifted its head as if discovering Bill's presence. *Maybe the spider is a BES surveillance bot. Let them see the fear in my face. I don't care, because, God damn it, I'm afraid, and I'm not ashamed of it. It'll keep me alive.*

"Bill Penn! Are you there?"

Bill pressed his face to the hand-sized, bullet and staser-proof window on his cell door. *Twelve cells in all.* The arrangement brought to mind the stalls of the dairy barn on his parents' farm. *Long-dead, long-gone, thanks to Raleigh.* "Vassy! Is that you?" Vasily Petrov was an occasional hire at Penn's ranch.

"*Fu*, I thought I was dreaming when they brought you in last night." Vasily was Russian, but his accent was almost gone. The other cells were quiet.

Hearing the ranch hand's familiar voice cheered Bill. "Why are you here?"

"Water overuse. Second strike. Too many showers at the shelter." Vasily's back was strong, his mind sharp, and his ambition minimal.

Bill itched his scalp at Vassy's mention of bathing.

"I'll soon be granted the honor of career criminal status." Vasily laughed. "What is your heinous crime, boss? Forgetting to compost the cantaloupe rinds? I thought you left your vices at the bottom of the ocean."

Bill's chest tightened. He didn't want to list the accusations against him, as if saying "species genocide" out loud would make them true. He'd worked hard to build a life for Anne, though his compulsive habit of forgetting the details of the rules of living in a world damaged by the Warming and the Spike got him into trouble. He recounted to Vassy how he fought the flames destroying his home. He left out the feeling of total helplessness, the utter loss of control as the inferno consumed everything he owned. The memory of his reaction as he surveyed the ashes embarrassed him. He mentioned the refuge in passing.

Bill grasped the stakes. The loss of his house was the least of his troubles. *If the bessies blame me for the refuge fire, Anne would be alone.* "I'm not guilty of anything, Vassy."

"Of course, you're not, boss. No one in jail is."

Bill denied the doubt in Vasily's observation. "I'll fight them, just like I fought the house fire." *I'm not going to lose control again.*

"Yes, well, you lost that battle, didn't you?" The ranch hand hacked. "Boss, you're a tough guy, but don't fuck around with the Bureau. Maybe you can work something out."

"Not a chance in hell. I won't let them wreck my life a second time, not after what they did to my family." *What Raleigh did to our parents.*

"There's Anne to consider—"

"That's what I mean. Anne is my life." Bill's eye was drawn again to the spider on the wall. He put his thumb over the bot, ready to crush it, then changed his mind. *What if it's a real spider and not a bot?* He laid his thumb in the path of the spider, and it crawled onto his nail. *A bot wouldn't do that, would it?* He carried it to the slit in the cell door. The spider jumped off and ran out, disappearing over the lip. Bill smiled. *Don't worry, shipmate. I'll be following you soon. I just need to—*

A jangling interrupted Bill's thoughts. "Penn! It's time for your hearing." A heavy man in a uniform approached Bill's cell. "Back away from the door."

"Hey, boss," Vasily called out as the guard put Bill in cuffs. Bill glimpsed Vassy's grizzled face through his cell's window. "Give 'em hell, okay?"

After a short ride down the jail elevators, Bill was listening to the judge interrogate Inspector Kilel. Anne was not in the courtroom. His bravado in the cells ebbed.

"Inspector, please come to the point." Judge Ezra Parker was a gnarled man who stooped over even when he was sitting down. "I've already read through your report and I know the facts, such as they are. Tell me what you want."

Bill sat on a plain metal chair within reach of Kilel's security bot, which was ready to stop an escape attempt. Bill wished it would step forward, so he could put his foot out and trip it.

"Your Honor," the inspector said, standing at an aluminum table similar to Bill's, "I'm asking the court, in its capacity as the judicial representative for the Environmental Crimes Tribunal in this circuit, for authorization to take the accused into my custody, permanently."

No, I can't abandon Anne. Bill caught Parker's eye. "Judge, I..."

"The accused will remain silent." Parker's gaze was soft. "I'll give you a chance to speak, Bill. Be patient." The judge spent three days a week hearing small claims cases and presiding over trials involving shoplifted coats, failure-to-recycle tickets, and graffiti citations. Today, Kilel made a case to Parker for taking Bill into the byzantine world of the ECT.

Kilel inclined her head toward a tablet. "If you will allow me for the record, Your Honor, to recount the facts. On Thursday the 23rd, a fire destroyed Mr. Penn's house."

"Yes, yes, go on." Parker rested his chin in his right hand.

"Investigations by the local fire marshal and my own investigation show that the house fire led to the refuge fire, which killed twenty-three of the twenty-five nesting pairs of the Klamath magpie, along with all of their chicks."

Bill was bursting to speak, but he kept his thoughts to himself. When he got the flyer from Anne's school about the citizen observation program, he promised to help her build the blinds. It reminded him of how his parents cared for the wetland next to their farm. *Anne and I knew our wetland was the magpies' last home.*

"The number of deceased birds is approximately eighty-nine percent of the entire population of this endangered species." Kilel touched a stylus to the tab. "I have an affidavit from the managing biologist at the refuge that says this loss has a ninety-three percent chance of causing the extinction of this species. In other words, the species is no longer viable and will likely disappear from the face of the earth within three years."

Thoughts of Anne and his lost home crowded out the ritual playing out around Bill. *Where is Anne? Does she know I'm here?* More than anything, other than seeing his daughter, he wanted to go take stock of what was left from the fire, salvage anything useful, and start over. He'd managed to save a couple of items from the house, a few memories. The outbuildings weren't touched. *I've got all of my farm implements. The AIs might need some upgrades. A year or two from now—*

Kilel drew herself up. "As you know, Your Honor, the charges the State will bring against Mr. Penn are capital offenses."

Bill snapped up his head. *Social death?*

The judge spoke as he studied Bill. "Has the accused been advised by an attorney?"

"Your Honor, in light of my ongoing investigation, I've elected to postpone review of Mr. Penn's case by a defense attorney. I need more information from the prisoner before I can allow that."

Parker scrolled through Kilel's report on his tablet. "I see here, Inspector, that Mr. Penn has cooperated with your investigation, though by your notes—" Parker touched the screen with a stylus "—he's not given you anything useful."

Bill lifted a corner of his mouth in a half-smile. After his arrest, Kilel peppered him with questions, but he didn't need a lawyer to tell him to keep his mouth shut. Anne said nothing either. *Good girl.* The BES may be the most powerful law enforcement agency on the planet, but it still had to follow the principle of innocence before proven guilty.

Kilel shifted on her feet. "I consider his reticence uncooperative, Your Honor. The accused has a long record of flouting the law. The violations of the Carbon Laws due to the burning of the house alone are Class A felonies. They carry automatic prison terms of several years each."

Bill regarded Kilel in profile and felt a flash of awe.

"I expect my investigation to take several weeks, perhaps months, to complete. Once I am ready, I will allow counsel to interview Mr. Penn. I don't want his evidence tainted by discussions with others."

Parker grunted, then turned to Bill. "Do you understand the spot you're in? What do you have to say for yourself?"

Bill's wrists were bound to a linked steel chain that encircled his waist, and his ankles were shackled. He blinked as he turned back to the inspector. The shade of her suit was responsible for the sobriquet "green shirts," whispered whenever rebellious-minded people spoke about BES and the regime it served. He addressed the judge. *What can I offer him?*

"Don't let her take me, Ezra," Bill said, speaking to the judge as if he were an old friend. "I haven't seen Anne or heard about my house or anything." He hoped that Parker, who had presided over Bill's occasional run-ins with the law, would sympathize. "You know me. I make mistakes now and then, but I've always paid my fines and tried to do better."

Parker knocked his finger on the table. "Bill, how many times does the sheriff have to ticket you before you understand that it's against the law to burn wood for heating or cooking or any other reason? The atmosphere can't afford the carbon."

Bill returned to a more formal tone. "I wasn't using the stove. I was using a hot plate. The wiring on the house was old and I guess it caught. I don't have the money to buy the new stoves."

Kilel made a note on her tablet.

"I can't afford to rewire the house." Bill held out his hands in supplication. "Prices for my produce never seem to be high enough to pay the rent on my leases, much less buy nice things. Is my daughter supposed to eat a cold supper every night?"

"There's assistance to buy the approved cooking stoves and upgrade wiring," Parker said.

"Those are loans, Judge. Loans. I don't want to be in debt. I pay my taxes and I pay them on time. That's enough."

Parker was growing irritated. "What about the fire at the wildlife refuge? This is serious, Bill. The inspector here says it's your fault."

"My house caught on fire, Judge. How could I have prevented an ember from drifting over to that brush? I helped the biologists with their work. I know the magpies were endangered. I'm as heartsick about the refuge as anyone."

"The law is very strict on assigning responsibility for these incidents when they involve protected species. Someone has to be held accountable."

Even when they are hard-working people suffering bad luck? Is mercy completely forgotten? "It's not my fault, Judge."

"The fact that you have a history of burning wood illegally is an aggravating circumstance. Even a fire caused by faulty wiring which results in excessive carbon emissions is a serious offense."

Has Parker turned against me? "I'm sorry, Judge. It was an accident. I didn't mean to hurt those birds."

Parker sighed. "I don't have much choice but to grant the inspector's request. Do you know what that means?"

Bill's imagination ran wild: Anne alone on the property, no money, her father in prison or worse, the shame of her father's environmental crime hanging over her. *She'd be able to take care of herself for a while, but people are cruel. She'd be defenseless.* He remembered his vow to fight the charges, for her sake, if not for his own. "I'm innocent, Your Honor."

Parker's voice went low. "It could be a long time before you're released."

"Ezra—Your Honor—please listen. I have only one thing I can offer you..." Bill glanced at Kilel. "...and the BES. It's my promise that I'll stay in the valley and cooperate with the investigation. I only want to go home and protect my property and Anne."

Parker's expression changed from scowl to grin, as if he lay his fingers on a solution. "I don't have to decide today whether to hand you over to the inspector. This is a complex case, and I think I should take my time."

"Your Honor, I'm not sure..." Kilel said, suspicious.

"Bill," the judge said, "if I release you, will you promise to go right home, and stay there?"

"Your Honor—"

Bill interrupted Kilel. "Yes, sir. I swear to God, I will." He grasped at Parker's offer like a lifeline. "I need to get back to Anne. Please, sir, I'd be so grateful."

"How much is your promise worth, Bill?" A hint of certainty in Parker's face faded into indecision.

Bill swallowed and tried to encourage Parker. "Sir, my life is here. Everything I love is here. Why would I run?"

Kilel's voice signaled alarm. "Your Honor, this is very unusual. These requests are always granted with immediate effect. You can't—"

Parker's face turned red as a morning sunrise before a gale. "Don't tell *me* what I can or cannot do, Inspector." The judge pointed at Bill. "I know this man. You don't. I've known him since——Bill, when did you move back here?"

"Twenty-forty-nine, Judge."

"You grew up around here, correct?"

"My parents had a place over by Eagle Point, before the bessies shut it down——."

Parker held up his hand. "Never mind that. Remember that ropes course at the high school?"

"Yes, sir, I do."

"This was two years ago, Inspector. No one but an experienced sailor would've noticed the problems with the rigging. Without him, some kid might have been hurt or killed. He worked for a week to fix that course."

I wouldn't let Anne within a mile of that death trap.

"Bill Penn is an upstanding, if imperfect member of this community. He has integrity, a rare thing in my experience. I believe he's entitled to some consideration."

Kilel's voice dropped a half-octave. "Your Honor, may I remind you that we are under a global state of environmental emergency. The average global temperature is up five degrees in the past century. The Arctic ice cap is gone. The western part of Antarctica is ice-free..."

"Don't lecture me, Inspector," Parker said, annoyed.

"...species extinction rate is still climbing. The Klamath magpie is going to be another..."

"Tell me something, Inspector." Parker's voice was firm but smooth. "How does a state of emergency last a dozen years? How long do legal rights have to be suspended before the emergency is over?"

For Bill, the contempt in Kilel's face reflected everything people feared and hated about the Bureau of Environmental Security. Protecting the earth had evolved into an arrogance that corrupted the agency.

"You've no doubt noticed that I am an old man." Parker's tan had faded into splotches, reminding Bill of a military camouflage pattern. "I was once a defense attorney. When I graduated from law school, we had a constitution people respected. The government followed it, most of the time, anyway. Legal rights mattered. They don't seem to matter anymore." He fixed his eyes on Kilel. "While I am a judge in this county, what I say, goes, in my courtroom. Therefore, I am releasing Mr. Penn, trusting that he will keep to his word."

Bill drew in a breath, but kept to his seat. *Stay cool and calm. Stick to the plan.*

Kilel's face grew florid. "He is a flight risk. He will run."

"You just heard the man make a promise, and I believe him." The judge took up his stylus and wrote on the tablet. "He's a non-conformist, and he gets himself into trouble, but he's not a liar. I'm letting Mr. Penn go, on condition he remain on his property, until I can review his case in more detail. We'll reconvene Tuesday at 9 a.m."

"Your Honor, I insist."

"Insist all you want, Inspector. My decision is made." The judge rose, and Bill followed suit in his restraints. Parker waited until Kilel rose, reluctantly.

The courtroom's main door opened. "Dad!"

Bill twisted around, his restraints jingling. "Anne, where were—" The guard tugged at his arm.

"I just heard about the hearing, Dad. The bessies never tell you anything. Where are you going?"

The guard led Bill away. "Don't worry, sweetheart. I'm coming home."

CHAPTER 5

THE LOUNGE SERVBOT SET THE glass of 2054 Château Ste. Michelle Columbia Valley Sauvignon Blanc before Molly Bain. She sat alone at a table in the bar of the New Ocean clipper *Aurora Borealis*. Molly sipped, her coral lipstick leaving no trace on the crystal. A short, gray-haired man in a business suit took a seat at another table a few feet away. Acknowledging him with a glance, she fingered her 24-karat gold necklace, drawing the man's attention to her smooth neckline and her full décolletage.

"I admire your choice of wine." The man had a Scandinavian accent. "The art has fallen on hard times."

Molly turned up the corners of her full mouth a millimeter. Molly had an oval face, skin the color of polished beech, and her auburn hair was arranged in the current fashion of East Indian traditional styles. A length of small diamonds covered the lighter skin beneath her part from her crown to a point below her hairline, forming a sparkling widow's peak. "It's amazing that the wines produced in the lower continent are still this good. The Spike has destroyed wine-making everywhere else."

The man moved from his table to Molly's. He was short, but well-built, and drunk. "May I?" His voice quavered. Molly sensed a hint of awkward teenager in him, though he was in his fifties. She indicated the mahogany chair with her slender hand, the sapphires in her com-bracelet glittering. He set his own wine on her table. "Allow me to introduce myself..."

"She knows who you are, Nordland." The interrupting voice was an animal's snarl grafted onto the baritone of a man who dominated others. Molly knew the growl, but Nordland did not, and he lifted his eyes in a mixture of horror and disgust.

"What's the matter, Nordland? Never seen a pussy cat before?"

"You know who I am, but I've not had the pleasure."

"Kapitan Gregori Ilyenevich Gorov, at your service." He fixed his golden eyes with slit pupils on the smaller man, and Molly thought for a half-second that Gore, as the world called him, would sink his seven-centimeter canines into Nordland's neck. The captain's face was close enough to Molly's that she spied his skin. It confirmed for herself that the colors of a tiger's skin matched the stripes of its pelt. She resisted an impulse to pet Gore. She had done it before, but a bar, even one as elegant as the Bear's Den was not the place, and this wasn't the time..

"Gore." Nordland wrinkled his nose. "I've heard of you, I'm sorry to say."

"I know many, many things about you." Gore's eyes glistened.

Molly huffed. "Kapitan Gore, you've broken the mood." She sniffed the wine. "It's part of the game we cyprians play."

"Game is the right word." Gore grimaced, an echo of a non-modified human smile. "The question is, Nordland, which game are you playing?"

"I don't play games, Gore, no more than you are still a human being."

Slaver collected in the corners of Gore's tawny mouth. "I have a tiger's stealth and a human's cunning."

"You and your kind are nothing but mutants. That makes you less than human in my mind." Nordland snapped his fingers.

"Boys, stop your posturing. Neither of you impress me." Molly allowed herself the lies. In fact, she felt a surge of desire similar to one on the day she saw Gore for the first time all those years ago. His DNA tattoo had taken hold, and the thing she remembered was the way he stalked her at the party in the New Victoria Underground. It was in plain sight, among hundreds of people, like a hunting cat in a trembling, mist-obscured forest of arms and legs. Nordland, on the other hand, was a business partner, and she decided to confess her fib later and say his lack of fear in front of a bully made her wet. Men liked to believe such things.

"I've changed my mind, Nordland." Gore relaxed and placed a paw-like hand on the chrome surface of the servbot that had arrived to take his order. "I won't kill you now." He drew his hand across the chrome, and a screech broke through the murmur of the low music and muffled conversation. When he stopped, five deep gouges scored the bot's case. "I may kill you tomorrow."

Nordland's face was flushed. "You're a vandal, as well as a ruffian, Gore. Check your bill in the morning. You'll find an extra fee."

Gore eyed Molly. His face softened, and Molly swore she heard the creature purring. "I'll pay a visit to your cabin and we'll discuss old times."

Molly brushed the sleeve of Gore's tux. "I'd like that."

Gore hissed at Nordland and left the bar, the eyes of every patron on his broad back and gliding gait.

"That man, that *thing,* is dangerous." Nordland swallowed the rest of his wine. "Anyone who splices animal DNA into that which God gave him should have his head examined."

"He's more snarl than bite." *Another lie.*

"He's a pirate too," Nordland.

Molly laughed. "You're being ornery."

"You haven't heard the rumors, then? The BES is sniffing around a lot of the Arctic ports, more than usual. Gore's name comes up. So does Bežat."

"Bežat is its own rumor. Oil refining? After the Warming and the Spike? It's crazy."

"Maybe so." Nordland shrugged. "Alright, enough of Gore and carbon scandal, Ms. Bain."

Molly half-listened as Nordland prattled about *Aurora,* his new luxury liner. Gore's musk lingered, a mix of sweat and the coat of a predator, and that held her attention. Even with her wide experience of males, nothing matched Gore's style and poise when he was at his finest. That was why she fell in love with him. Like the solitary tiger in India, before it vanished forever, he moved on to other prey, other mates. They crossed paths on rare occasions, and if she was made the choice, the reunion left her exhausted. *I loved Bill Penn first. Did I love Gregori Gorov best?*

Nordland's tinny voice brought her back to the *Aurora*'s bar. "Allow me to say to you again that your idea was brilliant, Ms Bain. To bring all the principals together aboard the *Aurora* for the final rounds. Here, surrounded by such beauty—" Nordland swept his eyes around the lounge, accented by Italian leather and Turkish copper, settling on her face. "—agreement is certain."

"Don't get ahead of yourself, Kristian." Molly tilted her head as she studied another couple ensconced in a booth. "We have a few issues to work out before we reach Dudinka. Fee scale details, security..."

"Now that we have taken on our last passengers, I have a feeling we'll close our business long before we reach Russian waters."

Rain splattered against the picture windows, distracting Molly. She made out the lights of Churchill as *Aurora* prepared to head north out of Canadian waters. She also saw Nordland's reflected profile, and she found herself running various negotiation scenarios with the executive through her head, as if she were writing an AI subroutine. He was a key vote in the consortium she and her partner had bargained with for eight months, and the next days would make or break her plan to dominate the Arctic market.

Nordland placed his hand flat on the table. He swayed with the ship's mild roll. "Once we conclude our business, perhaps we can find more ways to work together. Who'd have thought that sailing vessels might be a growth business again? That's just one opportunity the Warming has given us in the Arctic. You still have a worldwide reputation for artificial intelligence software, despite some of your history."

"History?" Molly knew what Nordland meant, but she wanted to explore his attitudes.

"The technology community knows about your role in the methyl hydrates disaster, though no one blames you. It's understandable that you dropped out of sight afterward, but you haven't fooled anyone by publishing some of your research under a pen name."

A compromise made to survive. No one would publish Molly's work after her conviction, but the government successfully pinned the primary blame for the Spike on Martin Scribb. *Where it belongs, as far as I'm concerned.* First one editor, then another, turned a blind eye to Molly's part in the Spike affair, because they recognized her brilliance. It wasn't enough to restore her reputation in the AI community, but it salved the wound. *If Martin hadn't pushed so hard to launch, we could've found those bugs and I wouldn't be making deals with a lecher like Nordland.*

A tone sounded, and a feminine voice came through the public address system. "Your attention, please. *Aurora Borealis* crew is required to inform all passengers that our departure from the Port of Churchill, Manitoba places this vessel under the regulations of the International Arctic Free Economic Zone. Thank you."

Nordland gulped his wine, eyeing Molly. "I've known you up to now as the president and founder of your Association, but your professional reputation in AI science, and now in your current line of business, is widespread. Everyone sings your praises...in both realms."

Molly listened, pleased by his compliments and the confidence in her intellect.

"I'm curious." Nordland's voice quavered again. "We've departed Churchill. Are you, um, working?"

"Thank you, Kristian, for the compliment, but I'm very busy. You know, reviewing proposals, answering emails, com calls, and so on."

"That work is in your capacity as president of the association. Perhaps I could persuade..."

Molly considered Nordland's proposal. He knew every port authority executive and C-level leader among the shipping companies that had taken advantage of the new trade routes through the Arctic Ocean. He was the best connected man in the AFEZ. Another business deal with him raised the prospect of significant dividends down the road. "I have no appointments this evening." Molly ran her fingers down the stem of her wine glass.

Nordland grinned. "Your fee, if I may be so direct?"

"Standard A-1 rate on the Cyprian Association updated scale. Hourly or for the night?"

Nordland swallowed, as if anticipating his favorite dessert. "I'd like a companionship contract."

On the other hand, Molly thought, a liaison with someone on the opposing side of the bargaining table might complicate matters. Some sort of balance was required. "I'm sorry, but my availability is limited tonight. I'll be off duty, you might say, until the association agreement is signed."

"Just so." Nordland was crestfallen. "I agree to your terms. One private evening with you is worth a week with the best elsewhere." Nordland cleared his throat. "Shall we go to my cabin?"

Molly directed her com to run a high-level background check on Nordland, looking for arrests, convictions, media reports, or other hints of violent behavior. Results were negative; he didn't even have outstanding surplus trash or recycling tickets. A scan of his health records in her private database showed nothing worrisome. "Sounds lovely."

The New Ocean executive offered his hand, and they left the bar. He had trouble putting one foot in front of the other, more due to the wine than the ship's roll, which was muted by dampeners. They descended a companionway into a passage. "Here we are." Nordland spoke his name, the cabin door opened, despite his alcoholic slur, and Molly followed him inside.

CHAPTER 6

BILL PACED AT A MUNICIPAL bus stop in front of the sandstone courthouse, frustrated that he could not reunite with Anne right after the hearing. Gary Schmidt's son—*Mike?*—told her the hearing had started and she rushed to the courthouse. After the judge's ruling, the sympathetic guard took Bill to a room where he could get a com signal.

Bill to Anne: There's a snag in the paperwork. That's what Kilel says.

Anne texted: I'll wait for you as long as I need to.

I think she's looking for an excuse to hold me.

The judge said you could go.

I'd feel better if you were away from here. Bill imagined Kilel arresting Anne as an accessory. Didn't you have to work today? I want to get back to normal.

I'll tell my boss I'm sick.

It'll take months to get back on our feet. Bill didn't need the emo-sig interpreter in his minds-eye to see her anxiety. *I can barely hide mine.* I'll see you at home.

Five hours later, the sun was within a moon's width of touching the hills separating Brier Valley from the rest of Pacific West. The humiliation of the hearing intensified his anger at the BES and Kilel. *I'll talk to Anne about what she thinks we should do.* The bus was empty, save for him, a dark old woman with a cart of groceries, and the driver, who was a middle-aged, frumpy white woman wearing a loose vest over a sleeveless shirt, wraparound sunglasses, and fingerless faux-leather gloves. The bus route passed near the cutoff where the gravel road to his property branched off the two-lane highway. Above his head in the slot where the advertisements go, a public service announcement urged riders to text suspicions of illegal fuel burning to the BES. *Finking*, Bill's old shipmates called it. *Informing.*

The bus jerked to a stop and let off the old woman. The robot cart following her like a puppy. Sitting near the bus's door, Bill glanced over to the driver, who put a thick finger to her ear, as if trying to hear something better. *An old reflex from the time before jacks?* A rush of torrid air from the driver's open window ruffled her hair. The bus passed through the outskirts of town and rounded a curve, accelerating. About 150 yards ahead, a young man in blue jeans and a t-shirt stepped out from a privy-sized shelter, a signal for the driver to pick him up. The bus blew past the rider as if he wasn't there.

"Hey, driver, I think you missed that guy." The young man ran after the coach and gave up.

The driver ignored Bill. The low whine of the motor grew louder. The tires thrummed against the asphalt. A black car passed on the left and changed lanes in front of the bus. Bill glimpsed the tulip shield on the passenger side door. *Shit.* Alarmed, Bill saw a stop ahead and sent the stop request via his minds-eye over the local network. He heard the plaintive *ding*.

The driver flew past the stop.

Fuck, they're coming to take me.

Bill's heart beat faster when he saw the flash of the black car's brake lights and the right turn signal. The car slowed and eased onto a dirt road, stirring up dust like fog. His eyes fell on the red emergency door handle protected by thin glass. A millisecond before he reached for it, the bus's brakes squealed. Bill's hands gripped the handrail as the vehicle threatened to topple over from the force of the turn. The bus bounced over a pothole as it followed the black car's lead into a dust cloud.

How in hell do I get out of this?

Unexpected grit flying into the open window made the driver gag. She eased off the accelerator, losing the black car's brake lights in the cloud. Seeing his chance, Bill grabbed the steering wheel of the bus. He forced it into a weed-choked ditch. Saplings snapped in two and gravel flew into the brush. The bus halted nose down, throwing Bill and the driver into the dash. Bill tumbled out of the front doors, leaving the driver struggling to unlatch her seat belt.

Bill clambered up to the road from the ditch. His steps kicked up more dust as the air started to clear around him. He stood up to run and a searing pain tore into his lower back, like a kidney punch. His knees buckled and he fell face first into the dirt. The razor-sharp edge of a basalt fragment from the surrounding cliffs sliced his cheek and dripping blood turned the fine soil into a soup.

Inspector Kilel's security robot, its gun-like weapon deployed, stood over him. A bolt of fear coursed through his half-conscious mind. The shiny black robot reminded him of a headless, neckless, de-feathered ostrich. He had seen the robots run 40 klicks an hour. A man on horseback couldn't beat them.

"At ease," said Kilel, and the robot stowed its weapon. Bill blinked as the woman came into view. She was dressed impeccably in her dark green suit, the sun glinting off her tulip pin. *Not a mote of dust on her. She's inhuman.* Behind her was the bus driver.

"Mr. Penn, I'm sorry we had to bring you down like that," Kilel said. "I meant to take you into custody with less fuss."

Bill tried to get up, but his legs buckled underneath him.

"My superiors have given me permission to transport you to the nearest Bureau facility," Kilel said. "I hope you will be cooperative."

"The judge... He said..."

"Parker is a relic, and he is misguided," Kilel said. "He does not understand the need for swift action in carbon law and species protection cases. Justice delayed is justice denied. The hearing was a formality we can dispense with."

"Is shooting me a formality" Bill's words slurred. "What have you done with Anne?"

"I don't know what you're talking about. Your daughter is fine."

Bessies always lie. Bill rose to his knees. Every joint in his body felt like soft rubber. *Gotta get home to Anne, figure out how to beat Kilel.*

The inspector turned to the bus driver. "Thank you, Mrs. Hill, for assisting me. Citizen help is essential for our work. I'm sorry about the damage to the bus."

Kilel addressed the robot. "Security, attention." The bot stepped forward.

"Mr. Penn, you've experienced the effects of a staser at quarter power. You don't want to experience full power, do you?"

Dizziness rocked Bill when he shook his head.

"Good. This way, if you please."

Bill propped himself up with his hand and tried to stand, but he fell back on his butt and nearly passed out. "I'm... my head..." The world lost focus.

Kilel lowered herself to her haunches and studied Bill's dirt-encrusted face. "Mild concussion, and that cut is deep." Kilel rose and turned toward her car. *Is she letting me go?* The robot didn't move, and Bill heard the trunk lid close. Kilel returned with a first-aid kit. "Here, chew this." The BES officer handed Bill a mist stick. "Drink some water."

Bill sipped a plastic bag of filtered water. The tasteless liquid revived him. The mist cleared his vision. *I know this road.*

She ripped open a package. "This will hurt." Bill smelled alcohol and antiseptic. Kilel's touch was gentle, practiced. "Hold this dressing to the cut."

He pushed Kilel's hand away. "I don't want your help."

"You're bleeding badly."

Bill grabbed the dressing and pushed it against his cheek. "Go to hell."

"Refusing my assistance only hurts you, Mr. Penn." Kilel stood up and waited. "Are you well enough to walk?"

Bill tried his feet again, and he recognized the trail that led up the slope. *It goes about a hundred meters, then branches, one to the north, the other west to my place.* The trio of people and the robot walked past the wrecked bus toward Kilel's car. Mrs. Hill sat on the bus's sagging bumper, eyeing Bill with a frown of contempt. *Bitch. That's the last time I catch a ride with you.* His trudging feet kicked up dust. *The gravel on the edge of this road is pretty loose.*

The robot was a single pace behind him, its pneumatics making a tiny hiss with each step. The robot walked on the firmer, grassier edge of the road, next to the ditch. On the opposite side of the road, a steep pitch of rubble from rust-brown rock cut out of the hill to make way for the road rose from the road bed in a steep slope.

Time to get pushy.

Bill spun around and rushed the robot, shoving it over into the ditch, where its stick-like legs flailed. Bill scrambled up the rubble on all fours toward a break in the cliff. On the other side was a gulch and heavy woods.

He heard Kilel shout "Pursue! Full power!" He glimpsed the robot getting to its feet. Bill had a head start and the robot lost its footing on the loose rubble. Bill was frantic as he climbed. A staser at full power fried victims from the inside out.

Bill reached the break and pulled himself over the edge. He tumbled down the other side into bramble, which scratched his skin and tore at his shirt. Crouched low, he pushed his way through the thorns, hearing Kilel call after him. Her voice grew faint, and he heard no sounds from a pursuing machine. He broke through into a grove of manzanita trees, his shoes crunching the dried leaves.

He avoided the trails he had hiked over the years with Anne, preferring to follow animal paths that led toward his property. He stayed in heavy cover for fear of the aircraft searching for him. Once he thought he heard the buzzing of a remote-controlled mini-copter, but it was a hornet's nest. He had one goal: home.

He came up over a rise and saw his place. The terror and helplessness of watching his home of twenty years burn replayed in his mind. All that was left of the house was ash the color of frost, peppered with charred timbers and twisted metal from the duct work. The fireplace chimney, unused for its original purpose since the passage of the Carbon Laws, had toppled over, a final punch to his gut.

For a moment, Bill forget Kilel's pursuit. Up until now, the fire was part dream, part reality. He knew that the house had burned, but he hoped something substantial remained to salvage. The dark hole of the cellar snuffed his fantasy, leaving pain that choked him, tightening around his throat. It was the same feeling he had in jail, that the fire had consumed all the oxygen of his life. In that century-old house, he and Molly had created a family, which more than compensated for sacrificing the sailor's life he had loved. The light of Anne's intelligence and drive replaced that darkness after Molly's decision. Together, Bill and Anne filled a thick log of memories: Chapter books read to every school night before bed, her standing on a stool at the kitchen counter to slice vegetables at mealtime, cold beers (soda for Anne) with Vassy in the parlor after a hard day, and later, Anne writing up the refuge observations on the kitchen table. *Nothing now on my land except a wound.*

A screech distracted Bill from his worry. *It can't be. They're all dead.* A flapping wing caught his attention, but he couldn't see what made it. *Ornithopter drone?* The prospect reminded Bill that Kilel was near. His anger at Kilel and the BES returned, fueled by memories of the injustices against his parents. *No time to dwell on what can't be fixed.* He worried about the present. *Am I bringing Kilel down on Anne? Maybe I should stay away.* He ran through his limited options, and nothing jumped out as a workable idea.

He emerged from a line of shrubs behind the barn. The heat from the house fire blistered the barn's red paint, which looked like frozen fizz of a soda drink. Nothing stirred inside the barn, but all was as he had left it: the hulking tractor, the rusted blades of a old wind generator, a derelict robot seeder. He stepped out into the dusty yard, between the remains of the house and the barn, when he heard a rustle.

A ground-hugging shape shot toward him. The creature bellowed, a wet tongue licked Bill's whiskered face, and he laughed.

"Hold on, Maxie. I'm happy to see you too."

Dog and master sat together, though a part of Bill's mind nudged him to be wary. "Have you seen Anne?" The hound bellowed again.

"Dad? Daddy!"

Bill's heart burst as Anne raced to him from behind the chicken coop, her tall, lithe form trailing dust. Her long, flaxen hair flowed, her delighted squeal like music, and she held out her arms. Bill's mind flashed to a time twenty years earlier, when Anne's mother ran to him in the same way. Bill wiped away a tear.

"Daddy, why are you crying?"

I have to be strong for her. "I'm happy to see you. I thought I might not see you for months or years."

"Where did you come from? I was waiting for you down by the road. What happened to your face?"

Bill told her the story of his escape. His anxiety eased, but the new danger stood out. "Kilel's probably following me. She might even think you helped me." *I can't stay.*

"Dad, what are we going to do about the house?"

He stepped over to the ashes, which were as cold as the dead.

"I salvaged a few things, Dad. Some dishes, tools, and...wait." Anne entered the two-man tent set up under the black oak. She found a small box and brought it to Bill. "I found a few photos and a holo-pic."

Bill held the scorched picture of his wife. When he spoke of her to Anne, the girl's mood darkened. Many years in the past, he decided to cling to the positive memories of Molly. He also examined a photo of Anne, about ten years old. "Can I keep these, sweetheart?"

Anne's face twisted in confusion. "Well, sure, but... what do you mean? Aren't you staying?"

Bill turned to the storage shed, where he and Anne stored extra food and equipment, including their backpacking gear.

"Dad, tell me what you're thinking."

Bill fumbled about in the darkness of the shed and found his pack, which still contained stuff from their last trip: wool clothing, a first-aid kit, a mess kit, a small tent, canned and freeze-dried food, a fire shelter, a large water bottle, and an xGPS. He grabbed more food from the shelves and threw it in the pack. He slipped a leash on the dog and staked her near the water trough. He didn't want the dog to follow him. Sitting on a salvaged kitchen chair, he changed into a spare set of hiking boots.

"Dad, talk to me."

Bill glanced at the glow left from the sun as it sank below the hills. *West. To the ocean. Anne can't know. Kilel will pull it out of her.*

The decision relaxed Bill. He had a semblance of a plan, or at least direction. He patted Maxie's black rump. "You remember when Maxie ran away?"

Anne sat on the brown grass near her father. Maxie slobbered a bowl of water. "It broke my heart. Stupid dog." The latter comment was ignored by the basset hound.

"You were about 11 or 12, and Maxie was maybe a year old."

"A rescue dog, always getting into trouble. Mike Schmidt told me about the family that couldn't take care of her."

"You made me look for her."

"You wouldn't let *me* look for her." Anne folded her arms, still defiant. "I could hear you calling her name. When you came home without her, I swore to hate you the rest of my life." Anne looked sorry for her oath.

"She came home. Remember?"

Anne's smile beamed, as if Maxie had returned from another sojourn.

Her father laughed with her. "She brought us a present."

"The idea of eating that rabbit after what it had been through was ridiculous. I'm proud that I nursed it back to health. I haven't eaten rabbit since."

"The point is, Maxie disappeared and we thought she was lost, maybe even dead. But she came home, safe and sound. She even brought a gift."

Anne scratched the dog's ears. Her face darkened. "What are you going to do?"

The relived joy of Maxie's miraculous reappearance faded. "I don't know. Get a job on a ship, maybe." Bill said. "I'm sorry, baby. I'm so happy you were here. Now I have to say goodbye." Tears filled his eyes again and he covered his mouth to hide his chagrin.

"Why don't you stay here and fight the charges? The BES will listen to reason. Maybe they're not as strict as people say."

Anne's plea echoed her grandmother's, Bill's mother, though he barely remembered the details of his parents' clashes after his father's deceit on the environmental monitoring was discovered. No amount of reasoning and apologizing swayed the bessies from following through on their threats to close and liquidate the farm. *I won't risk that kind of humiliation for Anne.*

"They want me. If I go away, Kilel might leave you alone. You'll have to trust me on this."

Anne wiped away her own tears. "I know, Daddy. I love you, but I know you have to go. They'd just put you in jail for something that wasn't your fault."

Bill lifted the backpack to his shoulders and tightened the straps. Maxie bellowed, as if she knew what was next.

"I'm coming back, Anne," Bill said. "Don't you worry. Hey, I almost forgot." Bill reached up to a shelf near the barn door and removed a cloth-covered object. "I rescued this before the fire got it. I know how much it means to you."

Anne's face lit up as she unwrapped the object and found the woodcut, the one with the English sailor and the little girl, protected by a plastic sleeve. Bill never got around to framing it.

"Read the caption, Anne. Tell me what it says."

Anne covered her mouth with her hand, tears welling again. The words fought their way out. "*A fair wind and a following sea, so that thou may return to me.*"

After a mile or so of determined, fast-paced hiking, Bill heard the buzzing of the heat-sensing mini-copters. He donned the inexpensive night vision glasses sold by the outdoor equipment stores to help people lost at night find their way to a road or a settlement. The goggles magnified the stars into green punctures of light in the dome of the sky. Bill used the starlight to run further into the pine and oak woodland. He hoped the copters would have trouble seeing the heat of his body through the forest canopy.

The buzzing intensified and he heard a voice, which he recognized as Kilel's.

"William Penn. This is Inspector Kilel of the Bureau of Environmental Security. Surrender and no harm will come to you." The message repeated as texts in his minds-eye, but the repetitions did little to persuade Bill to alter course. He avoided every path, walked on rocky ground, doubled-back on himself, took a path for a few yards and got off, all to confuse trackers, human and bot. One thing could hide his tracks: fire.

He picked up his pace toward a new fire he noticed back home. He smelled smoke, and the goggles picked up the glow of flying embers, like lightning bugs. Kilel's voice echoed in the woods, making honey-sweet promises of a bath, a warm meal, and a reunion with Anne.

He heard the roar before he saw the flames. The fire was below him on a steep slope, and the rising heat carried the embers up the hill. The brush and dead grass was so dry it exploded when the heat reached the combustion point. The whine of the fire-fighting aircraft drew Bill's eyes skyward as they swooped over, but no water or retardant fell. They were attacking another point in the fire.

Fearful the fire would overtake him before he found shelter, Bill searched for a break in the brush, a small meadow, or a large rock, something with little fuel that would burn in the fast-approaching fire. He spotted something better. A jumble of rocks had formed a tiny natural shelter. He ripped away the dried grass and debris from the narrow entrance. The tiny cave smelled like animals.

Nothing attacked Bill, but he glimpsed other creatures bounding away from the fire, and a part of him begged to follow. He had faced other storms and survived, and he stayed calm. The fire climbed the hill fast. The flames were so bright that Bill took off the night vision glasses. Flames swooped up into the crown of a pine tree. The crackling sounded like a thousand tiny toothpicks breaking in half, and Bill threw his backpack off his shoulder. With the fire yards away, he found the portable fire shelter, and opened the package, shaking out the spring green fabric like a blanket. He pulled the cover over his head, praying the fire would not consume all the oxygen around him as the raging blaze passed over.

CHAPTER 7

MARTIN SCRIBB SAT IN THE train station for hours with his empty bowl before the truck driver spoke to him. No one else had said a word to him, though he had collected a few coins.

"Where're you headed, father?" The driver was unshaven, about forty-five years old with a paunch that spilled over his belt.

"I'm sorry, friend, I'm not a priest," Martin said. "I have a mission, a job to do. I'm headed to the Arctic."

"I've been there. There's not much to see, except a lot of crazies."

Martin glanced at his bowl. "A small gift would help me pay my way there."

The driver bent down, his knees cracking, and he dropped a €10 credit token into Martin's bowl and walked away. It was the biggest gift Martin had received in weeks.

The driver returned to Martin. *That's odd. I'm sure that he saw I am disidentified.*

"I'll take you as far as the Canadian border." The driver beckoned and headed to the exit.

Martin ignored the flash of anxiety in his gut and slipped on his sandals. People never gave him free rides. For the first hour or so, Martin watched the driver, ready to defend himself from an attack. Most people thought of the dissed as fair game for an easy robbery or a sexual assault, and they were right, as far as the law was concerned. Yet the driver kept his eyes fixed on the road, his paunch jiggling when the truck hit a bump. A figurine of the Virgin Mary was glued to the dash. On the dry hills flanking the road, robot-like, spidery towers taller than the abbey's bell tower marched two-by-two like monstrous soldiers on the way to some battle. Power lines sagged between the towers.

"So how'd you get that?"

The driver's voice woke Martin from a doze. "What?" The driver had said his name was "Raul."

"The mark." Raul touched his forehead. "Environmental crime, eh?"

As a tumbleweed rolled across the truck's path like a skeletal beach ball, Martin's mind played back the entire story, from the beginning. Martin felt again that surge of optimism, even hope, at the start of Project Algid. He would go after the last great reserves of fossil fuels, to give people some breathing room while the new energy sources came online, and relieve the suffering of those who couldn't heat their homes or cook their food.

We were so committed, almost fanatic. Young men and women. Engineers, financiers and academics. Full of themselves. Arrogant. With Martin as the "visionary." Everyone knew where the energy sat, untapped, but no one knew how to get it out. Martin and the Project Algid team solved the extraction problems. Geologists thought disturbing the methyl hydrate deposits might release catastrophic levels of methane into the atmosphere, increasing global temperatures at a stroke, but the Algid techniques proved themselves safe in test after test. Success meant enough clean energy for a hundred years. *Molly so promised, and she stabbed me in the back.* Martin would make sure Algid was safe for the earth, that it wouldn't affect a climate already damaged by the Warming. He'd step back, the job done, the earth carbon-free, easy as pie. Everything was ready. All over the globe, Martin's friends waited for his go signal. Stations on every continental shelf watched him. The whole world waited. *What a show it would be, unsurpassed in history.* A turn of a key, and the Hydrate Era would begin.

A new era alright, but not what Martin imagined.

The painful memories pressed against Martin's temples. "Yes, an environmental crime."

Raul waited, as if expecting more details. Martin shook his head. He was not ready to reveal the entire story to a stranger. The truck's AI swerved to avoid a dead animal in the lane.

"My brother was dissed, too, but he was framed."

Martin feared a connection with Raul, because it exposed the driver to legal jeopardy. "What happened?"

"It was the Crash of '35. He was a currency trader in New York West. I don't get the details, but I guess he sold when he should've bought." Raul's huff was a mix of pain and recollection. "They put an 'Au' right here." He touched his forehead in the same place where Martin had his tulip.

"The chemical symbol for gold." Martin stifled a laugh at the International Monetary Reserve's idea of a joke.

"He didn't do it," Raul said. "He was at the trading desk, but one of his partners pulled the trigger. That's what Juan always said, anyway, before he passed." Raul crossed himself.

The phrase opened a new floodgate of memories. *I was in my office, when she pulled the trigger. Molly Bain was the trigger man, not me. She's the one guilty of attempted murder of a planet's biosphere, not me.* "Your brother, he took the blame."

"He took the fall, indeed."

I took the fall for her crime. She pushed me into this pit of Hell. The brilliant AI scientist is a demon who spawned a bug that nearly killed everyone with a global belch of methane. "I'm sorry, Raul. Perhaps Juan has found justice in the next life."

"I doubt it."

Raul remained silent for the next few hours until the truck came to a roadblock. A message was posted on the public net saying that an emergency repair crew was fixing a washout after a flash flood. Raul pulled the truck over to a parking area. Martin exited the cab, and his ears were assaulted with a hiss, which blossomed into a muffled roar as he came to a old concrete platform. It jutted out into space at the lip of a cliff, and a rusted railing ringed the outside edge. Squat sagebrush and bunchgrass struggled in the cracks. Martin peered down into a canyon.

Stretched from one wall of the canyon to the other, maybe a full mile, was the remains of a gigantic concrete structure. The masonry was recent, but something had happened to the structure. It had been cut in a step-like fashion on each end, down to the river bed, leaving a thousand-foot gap in the center. Millions of gallons of water flowed through the cut, the spring snow melt pouring through it as if pouring over the spout of a giant pitcher. A huge eddy received the water, which churned white for several hundred feet downstream.

Martin remembered. The structure was once a dam, one of the biggest in the world, built during an economic disaster in the 20th century. The dam generated electric current before the Warming, before the wind farms and solar arrays. In their ignorance, the builders had destroyed an ecosystem. It wasn't until the salmon disappeared that people decided to redeem their mistake. *All the dams on the Columbia River were breached.* The fish never returned. Mother Nature killed by a human dream, like Project Algid.

Molly Bain fired the bullet, not me, but no one listened.

The roadblock lifted and Raul motioned Martin back into the cab. Two hours later, Raul pulled over. The truck and double-trailer raised a cloud of choking dust. The border crossing was a half-mile ahead. "I have to let you off here. I can't be caught taking you across the border."

Martin exited the cab. "God bless you for your kindness, Raul." Other semis and cars flew past. Raul didn't fit the stereotype of the long-haul trucker. He was too gentle, too well-spoken, and he struggled with more than a lost brother. Martin smelled guilt. Raul was the partner who sent Juan and the world into perdition.

"Most people turn their backs on me when they see who I am," Martin said.

"Driving truck, you think a lot," Raul said. "We failures have to stick together."

CHAPTER 8

ANNE PENN LAY QUIET, RELAXING her neck and facial muscles. A trapped mosquito bounced against the mesh door of her tent. Through the nylon veil, she gazed at the devastation of her home—the blackened bones of her house, the scorched earth that surrounded it, the carbonized truck, the outbuildings that had survived intact, and in the middle distance, the remnants of the wildlife refuge. The English woodcut hung from the zipper pull like a talisman. She touched it, believing it still warm from her father's touch, though he had left the evening before.

She unzipped the mesh and waited for the mosquito to exit. The spare refrigerator and large freezer in the storage shed still worked, and she grabbed a couple of brown eggs. They crackled in the iron skillet on the solar-powered camp stove, and she added a spoonful of diced onion and red pepper from the garden. After her meal, she went back to work modifying the chicken coop.

The simple and repetitive tasks soothed her. Hammer on nail. Saw through wood. Anne relaxed and focused on the readouts from her minds-eye. She lost herself in the postings of her Brier Valley friends and com acquaintances all over the world. Her father's avatar was marked "offline" and hued a pale gray. *Like death.* The gray-out meant one of two things: He was not within sight of a com tower, or he'd switched off, which the police discouraged, especially if you were hurt or injured and they had to find you. Only criminals, hermits, and Luddites switched-off, but her father did not want to be found. Bill didn't like the com culture much. He and Anne shared only text because he never upgraded from his old-fashioned jack-in tech. *Too much sharing and not enough thinking, he'd say.*

She was disappointed that Mike Schmidt's avatar was labeled "inactive." Just knowing he was on the net brightened her day sometimes. He was the image of his father, the deputy sheriff who had shown kindness after the disaster that had destroyed her life. Mike's features had more angles, and his hair was a deeper brown, cut in a layered style that reflected an interest in life outside his isolated community. His gray eyes had a gentleness that Anne had always found attractive. They'd known each other since primary school.

He was the only man she knew that made her want to try deep sharing. She had the basic limbic system extensions for emo-sigs, but she couldn't afford the expensive gear that allowed individuals to share complex emotions or long-term memories. Or carnality. *A few more months and I'll have the money to buy them.* The basics, though, let her feel and experience the texts, as well as the holo and 2-D pics and vids, shared by others. They faded in and out like dreams, enhanced by the sigs that colored them to communicate the poster's emotional attitude. The com company offered hundreds of pallettes based on the traditional hues: green for envy, crimson for love, beet red for hate, blue for sadness.

Mike Schmidt's avatar changed from "inactive" to "available," haloed with the color of anticipation. Anne smiled inwardly.

Mike sent: < I saw you online. Just wanted to say hi. >

< Hi back. >

< Have you heard from your dad? >

Anne wasn't sure how to answer. Rumors flew constantly in the c-tribes about police snooping.

< If you don't answer, no problem. > Mike's amended question was painted with understanding.

Anne checked her emotional filter settings to keep her emotional expressions low key in the tribe. < I'm fine, in case you're wondering. > The color was correct, if vague. Mike's avatar abruptly grayed-out, which usually meant a lost carrier from the com company towers, a constant problem in mountainous rural areas if you didn't stand in one place. She watched his avatar a moment, hoping it would come back quickly.

The rest of her c-tribes provided plenty of distraction as she measured lumber and tightened wood screws on the coop. She joined c-tribes on subjects she cared about: birds, environmental science, the pop band Hindu Mistress. She kept an eye on the *BES Watch* c-tribe and its citizen journalists, because they exposed the agency's abuses. *They might mention Dad.* Sometimes, she let the stream of data flow over her like water.

< ...warmest temps for Moscow ever recorded... >

< ...uncle can't reach the vets agency. Does anyone know... >

< ...Paris artists are way too political these days. The Louvre... >

< ...grabbed my boob and I slugged him. Knocked out his tooth, ha... >

When Anne got her first com set, Bill insisted she set the filter defaults to exclude the racier c-tribes, though she sneaked in. Once she turned 18, she blocked his monitoring. *He threw a fit, but got over it.*

Mike's avatar turned "active" again, and Anne was conflicted on whether to contact him as she labored to position a two-by-four of found faux-wood. Like many of her friends in the aftermath of the fire, he had offered to lend a hand with cleanup or rebuilding, but she politely said No to all the offers. She preferred to fix problems herself, a trait her father respected while noting that no one ever achieved anything important by themselves. She shared her thoughts and mental images about her chicken coop, though she had to keep secrets about that project as well. *If I decide I need help, I'll ask Mike first.*

Her miracle, as she labeled it in her own mind, kept her going. Shortly after the fire, as Anne watched a dragonfly cruising along the heads of overgrown grass, she heard a rapid-fire *screep-screep-screep*. At first, she thought she was in that state between sleep and wakefulness, when some people dream that monsters lurk at the foot of their beds. *Could the fire itself have been a terrible nightmare, and the refuge as lush and alive as before?* She heard the sound again, faint, but clear.

How could anything have survived the fire? The blaze had crowned every tree in the 20-hectare parcel, turning them black as matchsticks. She ducked under the crime scene tape and paced forward with slow steps, listening. The still air carried almost no sound, and the cloying odor of burnt pine sap irritated her nose. Small flags marked the bodies of dead magpies.

Anne heard the call again, stronger, from the western edge of the refuge. She knew where to go. A few individuals of the Klamath magpie had an odd nesting behavior for the genus Pica. Instead of building domed nests made of mud and sticks, Klamaths liked to find a hole in an old tree and build the nest there. One of the nesting pairs had done just that, the same one that Anne had watched before the fire. When she reached the gnarled and twisted pine growing out of a clump of basalt boulders, she saw that the fire had skipped it. *Perhaps the robotic firefighters had stopped the flames before they reached it.* She jumped for joy when she saw the male Klamath magpie deliver a fat grasshopper to his mate. Anne put her hand to her neck, touching the crucifix on the thin gold chain.

A part of Anne wanted to call up her c-tribe and trumpet the news, but she held back. C-tribes were much like small towns or tight city neighborhoods; everyone knew everybody's business. *What if my discovery could somehow be used against Dad?* She wouldn't take the risk. On the other hand, she understood the fragility of her find and its importance. The birds she now watched more intently than ever before might be the only nesting pair left in the wild, or anywhere. They needed protection, at least until the chicks fledged. *What if they didn't, or a predator found them?* She rejected the idea of telling her biologist contacts, again fearing the information would somehow be used against her father. She remembered a story from environmental history: In the mid-20th century, scientists had saved the California condor from extinction by collecting all the wild eggs and making sure every egg hatched and every chick survived to adulthood. The species was saved from extinction, at least until the Spike.

The law proscribed lengthy jail terms for unauthorized interference with the life-cycle of an endangered species. As she finished the modifications to the coop, Anne thought little of the legal consequences. She wanted to make right what had gone wrong. She stuffed a handful of straw into an egg carton and loaded it into her backpack. She dragged out a six-foot step ladder from the shed, and trudged back to the refuge with the ladder balanced on her shoulder. The ladder wobbled as she climbed to the hole in the old tree. The male magpie screeched as he attempted to drive Anne away, and she felt the pecking of the female through her heavy gloves. Anne felt seven eggs and removed six so the male and female wouldn't abandon the nest. Even if all seven hatched, only one might survive. The others might be killed or die of malnutrition as the strongest sibling out-competed them for food. It was possible the female might reject the egg left behind after Anne's invasion. Magpies were intelligent, even crafty birds, and Anne hoped they would give her a pass. Cradling the pilfered eggs as if they were precious jewels, she placed them in the egg carton.

Returning to the coop, Anne set the magpie eggs in one of the nesting boxes. A week before, she and her father had slaughtered the chickens, most of whom were old and had stopped laying. Their plucked bodies were frozen in the shed, waiting for the stew pot. In the nesting box, Anne had set up a heat lamp to keep the eggs warm, though she didn't know the optimal temperature for the magpie eggs to mature. An access panel at the rear of the box let her feed the chicks once they hatched.

Her preparations complete, she brought a rusted folding chair to the coop and sat next to the nesting box, watching the mottled green-blue eggs for signs of life. She researched magpie habits on the net, and she settled in for a long wait. *It could be days or weeks.* She left her spot to stretch her legs or prepare a meal. She tended the large garden, weeding around the rows of drought-resistant corn and tomato plants, and examining the apple and pear trees for pests. With the chickens slaughtered, she had no animals to tend, other than Maxie. She and her father couldn't afford the methane licenses for horses or ruminants, though they sometimes boarded horses for wealthy people who kept second homes in the valley.

A notification in her minds-eye stopped her cold. Her father's avatar ungrayed. The location reference put him halfway across the mountains to Port Simpson. *He's moving fast.* She nearly dialed in a voice call, but she hesitated. *If I call, will the bessies see it or hear it?* The last thing she wanted to do was expose him.

Dad, are you okay? Anne couldn't keep herself from sending a text, though a wave of guilt washed over her. She waited, but he didn't respond. That wasn't unusual. It all depended on the com signal strength. *Would he text back if he could? Yes.*

Bill's avatar grayed out again. Anne was relieved. She didn't have to worry about whether she was giving her father away to Kilel.

A few seconds later, Mike's avatar lit up. The signal was strong. He was in Thomasburg at his job.

< Sorry that I lost you earlier. Com signal's terrible right now. There's another fire, on the other side of the valley. I heard it hit one of the towers. > His emo-sig showed remorse. The sig for yearning faded. *He missed me!*

Anne took the bus into Thomasburg the next morning for supplies. She'd heard nothing from her father since her one attempt to text him, and his avatar never activated. Her worry lingered, but lessened as time passed. Her heart quickened when the Applegate Feed and Seed came into view. Mike worked at the supermarket., which hugged the outskirts of town, keeping the name of its ancestral business and little else. Discreetly, she scanned the check out area where Mike worked, but he wasn't in sight. Anne breathed out, surprising herself, because she hadn't realized she was holding her breath.

The fire destroyed all the food in Anne's house, including the canned preserves she and her father had set aside from the previous year's harvest. Blessed with meat in the freezer, she needed flour, salt, and sugar, not to mention personal items, over-the-counter meds, and cosmetics. With her robot basket following her like a mute servant, she prowled the aisles, picking things by habit rather than plan as her mental focus caromed between the unhatched magpie eggs in the chicken coop and wondering if Mike was in the store. The inventory system transmitted the prices and a running total to her minds-eye, keeping track of suggested retail prices and the sale prices and noting whether a purchase qualified for special deals. She had to limit her purchases to what fit in her pack.

Anxious to get back home, she led the basket to the checkout, and she stood aside while it docked and the store computer confirmed the secure connection to her com, relisted her selections, and rang up the totals, including tax. With a thought, she accepted the total and her minds-eye displayed a cheery "Thank-you! Come again!" message. With all the distractions, she failed to notice Mike as he placed her items in her pack until he had said "Hello, Anne" twice.

"What?" Anne glanced upward and brushed a handful of pale gold strands from her eyes. "Oh, hello, Mike."

"You okay?" Mike bent down, trying to catch Anne's attention. He was tall and his hands and arms bare as he packed Anne's purchases. She compared the strength in his hands and forearms to her father's: a good match, though Mike's were less sinewy.

Anne folded her arms against her chest. "I'm fine. Just tired."

"You look a little tired." His face twisted. "I mean, you look great, but it must be hard." He put more items in Anne's pack. "I'm sorry."

"It's alright. I never know what to say when bad things happen." Something in Anne swelled, a kind of emotional zeppelin that lifted her off her feet, and she felt a sudden urge to spill every emotion that swirled inside her. *I can't keep it all to myself. He thinks Dad is at home. He doesn't know about the magpie eggs. Who can I trust with the truth?*

"If you need anything, let me know. Okay?"

"Thanks, Mike. I really... Shit!" Out of the corner of her eye, through the store windows, she saw her bus trundling through an intersection toward her stop. Mike had barely pulled his hand out of her pack after loading the last item when she grabbed it and ran off. The pack's weight surprised Anne and she stumbled, recovering as the store's automatic doors opened. The bus halted, then pulled away. Anne yelled at the driver, but he accelerated.

Mike came up beside her. "I know that driver. He never waits."

"The next bus isn't coming for hours." Anne sat on the bench next to the bus sign. The schedule readout in her minds-eye confirmed the two-hour wait time for the next coach.

Mike sat next to Anne. A whiff of a breeze stirred the dust on the pavement of the parking lot in front of the store and the small businesses of the adjacent strip mall. Anne realized she would miss a scheduled feeding of the magpie chicks, but there was nothing she could do. Now she had two hours to kill.

Mike cleared his throat. "Well, my lunch break is in about ten minutes. Do you want something to eat?"

Anne admitted to herself that she had an appetite, in spite of the disgust she felt at missing her bus. "Sure."

"Great. I'll meet you over at the Squeeze." Mike waved in the direction of a small restaurant. He smiled and went back into the Feed and Seed.

Anne yanked her backpack onto her shoulder and entered the restaurant, whose full name was the "Squeeze Inn." A bell tinkled, announcing her arrival. A radio somewhere in the kitchen played Asian country. All ten of the tables and booths were empty, and she picked one of the booths.

"Hello." A plump woman wearing an apron come out of the kitchen. "What can I get you?"

"I'm waiting for a friend. He'll be here in a minute."

"No problem. Just order when you're ready."

The restaurant's menu popped up in her minds-eye. The fare consisted of variations on vegetarian burgers and Szechuan, all with reviews and recommendations from patrons, and the restaurant remembered her last order of a vegetable stir-fry. Anne glanced at the clock.

The bell over the door tinkled and Mike came in. He spotted Anne and beamed. He had removed his work apron and combed his curly hair. A com stud sat high on his right ear. His shoulders were broad and neck thick but not disproportionate; He had played football in high school. For an instant, she forgot the burdens of the last few days, and she smiled back at Mike, taken aback at her own response to him.

"Sorry I took so long," Mike said.

Anne noticed that he was pleased, despite his polite apology. "I was just going to order a stir-fry."

"Let's see." Mike paused. Anne knew by the look on his face that he was logging in and checking the menu. She switched to her c-tribe readout and saw his current activity noted as "lunch." She updated her status to the same, but didn't mention Mike's presence. *If someone noticed us at the same location, well, two plus two equals...*

Mike drew a breath. "Stir-fry looks good. I'll have that too."

In each of the patrons' minds-eyes, the restaurant noted their orders and gave a list of ingredients, estimated cooking time, and estimated delivery time.

The waitress brought out two iced colas. "Here you go. Your orders will be out in a jiff."

Anne took a sip of the cola, and her mind wandered back to home and the magpie eggs.

"Something wrong?" Mike's concerned face was disarming.

"I was just thinking about a project that I'm working on, back home."

"What's your project?"

"I found some bird eggs in an abandoned nest. I don't know why, but I couldn't leave them there, so I'm trying to hatch them." *I won't say they're from an endangered species.* She explained the set-up in the coop.

"That's amazing. I mean, with the fire and everything, you're still doing that." Mike grinned, showing perfect teeth. "I think I'd be going crazy."

"It's pretty important to me."

"I heard your dad took off." The statement came out like a bullet from a gun.

Anne straightened. "He did not...take off. He wouldn't abandon me."

"Oh, hey, sorry. I didn't mean, didn't say that he just took off..." Mike coughed. "I mean, he's gone, right?"

"How do you even know about that?" *Did I give it away somehow? Is Mike spying on me?*

"My dad's a policeman, remember? Everyone's out looking for your dad. He's been missing almost two days."

Anne glanced away, embarrassed.

"I was just thinking that it must be hard without him, right after the fire and everything." The words came out staccato, as if Mike was trying to erase an earlier mistake. "I mean..."

Anne regretted her assumptions about Mike's statements. *He's only being sympathetic.* She took another sip of her drink. "Yeah, he left." Condensation on the glass dribbled to the table. "He had to find work."

"I know what that's like."

Anne was uncertain about Mike's meaning, but before she asked, the serving robot rolled up to the table. On smelling the spices and the steamy warmth, Anne's appetite spiked, and she dug in. Mike followed suit. After a few bites,

Anne found herself studying Mike's face with its roman nose, hint of stubble, and occasional acne scar, the modest tattoos on his upper arms, his t-shirt—clean, if faded—and his soft eyes.

"I had to find a job, too." Mike poked his fork at his food. *Is he upset?* "Dad needs me. Mom's getting worse, you see." Mrs. Schmidt had an inherited genetic disease that destroyed her brain. The disease was terminal. *At least Mike knows his mother.*

The scorched photo of Anne's mother flashed in her mind. Her father said it was taken a few weeks after they were married. Psychiatrists had the power to erase memories with pills and nanobots. *Can they wipe the images of my mother from my mind?* Anne didn't allow herself to think of her as Molly Penn, her father's wife, even though he still had feelings for her. The woman was not a real wife to her father, and she wasn't a mother for Anne. *Molly never wanted to be either of those people, or she wouldn't have abandoned me and Dad.*

Anne bit down on a slice of carrot in her stir-fry, her resentment hot as the oil in the kitchen's wok. She glanced up at Mike, ashamed of her anger in front of her friend. "I'm sorry about your mom."

Mike's face brightened. "Hey, I meant to tell you. I'm working on a novel. It's about life in the Valley, my friends, and...well, things." He fidgeted and caught her eye. "I'm almost done."

"How come you didn't tell me before?" Anne knew he liked to write. She saw his byline on local sports news blogs. "Can I read it?" Anne was months behind on her book list.

Mike's face flushed and he cleared his throat.

Anne was alarmed. "If it's not ready, I mean, don't feel like you have to, just for me..."

He lifted his brows, making it even easier for Anne to lose herself in his eyes, which promised comfort, if Anne asked. She chided herself for imagining anything beyond mild interest in Mike. He lifted a hand in reassurance. "No, I'd love to show it to you. I was about to send a note to my c-tribes looking for alpha readers. You'll get the first copy."

"Does it have a title?"

"I was thinking *How Brown Was My Valley* or *How Scorched Is My Valley*, but..."
He laughed, and so did Anne.

Mike paused, and Anne recognized again the minds-eye stare. He spoke
up. "Crap, I'm going to be late to work. I'm sorry. I have to go, Anne. Wait
one..."

A notification appeared in Anne's minds-eye. He paid the lunch bill.
"Thanks, Mike."

"No problem." He grinned. "I'm glad you missed your bus."

"Me, too." The words came out of Anne's mouth before she realized
it. "Wait a minute. I'll walk you over." Anne slipped the pack over her
shoulders.

The powerful sun forced the pair to squint as they headed for the Feed and
Seed. Anne noticed two black cars jump away from the curb on the far side of
the store. They raced toward her and Mike and she slowed her pace to watch
what was unfolding. They stopped in front of the pair and four green-shirts—
two from each car—exited the vehicles and surrounded Anne, pushing Mike
out of the way. The cars had BES logos on the doors. They didn't bother to
deploy the security bots.

"Anne Penn?" The question came from a sturdy man with a buzzcut.

"Yes?" Anne was frozen in place.

"You're under arrest. Please come with us."

Mike spoke up, challenging the bessies. "What for? She hasn't done anything." A second man put a huge hand on Mike's chest and pushed him away.
"Anne, don't go with them," Mike yelled.

Before Anne protested, a third man removed her backpack. He tossed it
into the open trunk of the first car. The first man had her by the biceps of her
left arm and directed her to the open rear door on the passenger side of the first
car.

"Stop!" Mike's yelling irritated Anne, because it was useless. The car door
closed on her, and all sounds from the outside halted. She saw Mike's mouth
moving as one of the green-shirts pushed him back. The BES cruiser sped
away.

Panic flooded Anne's mind. She was squeezed between the green shirts, trapped like an animal. She wanted to scream. Instead, she gasped for air. Thoughts raged. *What have I done? What about the magpie eggs? Have they caught Dad?*

CHAPTER 9

THE TRUCKER WHO PICKED BILL Penn up on the highway above Port Simpson dropped him off at the docks. So much had changed that Bill hardly recognized the area, but the anticipation and excitement of salt water was the same. Old habits, memories, and routines came back to him as if his twenty-year hiatus from the sea was twenty days or twenty minutes. He counted a dozen wind ships of various types and vintages tied up at a vast new terminal. He wanted nothing more than to jump aboard the first ship and cross the bar, partly to escape the BES, and partly to feel the freedom of going aloft to unfurl the huge sails. He filled his lungs with the tangy salt air, and he let the ancient sea wall guide him to Yesler City, the oldest neighborhood of Port Simpson.

Worry for Anne was never far from his heart. *Leaving her behind was the best thing I could do for her.* Fearful that BES might track him via his jack-in, he let the battery die. *It's better she not know where I am so the bessies can't pull it out of her.* He tried not to think of the moment when the forest fire's hot wind sucked the air out of his lungs as he hid in the animal den. At that instant, a tanker soared overhead and dropped water and retardant on top of the den, snuffing the fire, and giving Bill a second chance. His luck astounded him, and he raced to the west, leaving the useless fire blanket behind. He force-marched himself overnight, stopping in the morning at a stream where he washed off the retardant. He slept under a rock outcrop, then hiked down an ancient, overgrown logging road to the coastal highway. He hitched into Port Simpson, looking like another vagabond victim of the Warming and the Spike.

Two decades after Bill's last visit, the sidewalks of Yesler City had more cracks, the streets more potholes, and the walls of the decrepit brick and sandstone buildings tilted further outward over the whole scene. Though he recognized landmarks and street names, he couldn't shake a fuzz of disorientation that resulted in a collision with a tattered, hunched-over wreck of a man, triggering a psychotic outburst.

"Help, oh god, help me," the derelict screamed. "The bessies are taking me again. Again!" An aura of mold enveloped the creature.

"No, no, I'm sorry. I'm not BES." Bill's eyes darted. He feared a local cop or security bot might hear. "It was an accident."

"I'm dying," the man sniveled. "I need my oil. My oil. Oil to keep me warm." The grizzled derelict bawled, tears streaming down his tanned cheeks. "I'm freezing to death. Can't you see?" He grabbed Bill's coat like a madman. "You know where it is, don't you? You know who has my oil?"

Bill tugged at the man's arms, desperate to get away. "No, I don't."

"That freak, that animal. The Tiger. He'll kill you for your oil. He'll rip you neck out. He'll snap your spine, like a pencil."

Bill feared the old man's grip would break his arm. He had no idea what the crazed man was talking about.

The derelict yanked Bill's face close and whispered, his breath polluted with cheap mist. "Do you know what fuels the fires of hell? Do you?"

Bill shook his head, the pain in his biceps tearing through his frame.

"Captain Gore's farts." The old man cackled. He released Bill, and Bill left him sobbing and mumbling his incomprehensible laments in a doorway. Rubbing the incipient bruises from his upper arms, Bill stopped at a tiny cobblestone square and counted the last of his euros, keeping the bills close to his body. He bit his lip. With his com dead, he couldn't withdraw any cash from a bank. *The bessies would trace me. At least Anne has enough to get her through the next few weeks.*

He found a flophouse just off the main drag that ran along the shoreline. The lobby floors of the Henderson Hotel were clean and the duct-taped furniture dusted. Once inside, Bill smelled bathroom cleanser and wet wool. The audio of a television and the accented English of a Chinese game show host echoed down a hall. Bill stood at the desk, nervous that no one was on duty. "Is anyone there?"

A chair scraped the floor, and a short, dark woman waddled out of an office. Her uniform was faded by dozens of washes.

"Yes?" She scratched the inside of her ear. Her name tag said "Lin."

"A room, please."

"Tramps stay at the shelter." She pointed to the door. "It's a block over."

I must look like hell. "I've been in the mountains. I have money."

The woman reassessed her prospective guest. "How many nights?"

"I'm not sure. I'm looking for work. Could be a day, could be a week."

"One-fifty a night." The woman's voice was crusty. "Checkout at eleven."

Bill pulled out his thin wad, counted out the bills one-by-one, and handed them to her. She counted them also, but with her eyes.

The online register displayed in the glass counter. "Sign in."

Because his com battery was dead, the register wouldn't get a signal and couldn't access his ID. He wasn't even sure he wanted to sign in. BES computers watched net traffic for traces of wanted criminals.

"Sorry, I left my charger back home." Bill shrugged. *My lies better be convincing.* "Been on the road and haven't time to buy another one."

"I've got a spare I could loan…"

"No, ma'am." Bill smiled. "I mean, thanks. My com, um, my com is a new model. Different battery type. Not many out there."

The woman was skeptical. "Law says I gotta have your digital sig in case someone comes around asking questions."

Bill breathed out, trying to stay calm. *Maybe something extra would help.* He reached into his grimy pants pocket and placed a 10-euro coin on the counter over the electronic register. "I'm happy to register in the old-fashioned way."

The clerk studied the coin for a second or two, and she reached under the counter. Bill tensed, wondering if she was somehow alerting the local police or even BES. Instead, she showed a yellowed registration card. She took a pencil from her hip pocket.

"Put a name and address on this." The coin disappeared into her apron pocket. "It'll do 'til you're back online."

Bill wrote a fictitious name and the address of a bar in Churchill. He sighed, feeling the weight on his shoulders growing heavier. *How many lies will I have to tell before this is over?* He hoped the clerk wouldn't ask for more details.

She handed Bill an object that reminded him of a playing card. "You'll need this since you're com is dead."

"What is it?"

"Wave it in front of the lock."

"Okay."

"Second floor, hang a left."

Bill found the room, and after a few passes with the card, the lock clicked. He peeked around the door, half-expecting an occupant. The room had the usual furnishings. A stink of decaying vegetables and grease drifted through the open window. The towels on the shelf were clean, if threadbare. Bill shared a bathroom with the other ten rooms on his floor. His tight shoulders relaxed. He emptied his pockets, which contained nothing more than a few bills, coins, and his favorite holo-pic of Anne. She was angelic in her first communion dress. Bill's family was Catholic, and he felt the need to at least introduce her to the traditions, even if he was not a religious man.

He undressed, wrapping himself in one of the towels.

On his way to the bath, a banged-up cleaning robot announced itself at the door of another room, and a gruff female voice demanded that it go to hell. Bill almost tripped over the robot as it reversed to turn toward the next room.

Bill couldn't buy the bar soap and shampoo in the hotel's vending machines because of his dead com. However, a kind person had left a used bar and half-filled shampoo bottle in the two-person shower stall. He punched in his room code, programmed the shower temperature, and luxuriated in the soap and water, careful to rinse before the stream stopped flowing. He used up his room's five-minute daily allotted time, or perhaps the ten gallons allowed by the government. He wasn't sure. Either way, the shower gave him a jolt of new energy.

All Bill's clothes burned in the ranch fire, and what he wore reeked. A card on the dresser said the flophouse had a laundry room. He wrapped his damp towel around his waist and draped a second towel over his shoulders. Carrying his wallet, sheathed rigging knife, com recharger, and dirty clothes under his arm, he took the elevator to the basement. Modesty was his habit, strengthened by the presence of his daughter, and he was glad the elevator made no stops.

When the elevator halted, Bill hesitated at the open door. *Where would I run wearing a pair of towels?* No one was in the laundry, which had two washers and dryers, newer models than his at home. *Mine are scrap now.* Bill cursed when he saw the readout on the washer. Like the bathroom vending machines, the washers and dryers only took electronic payments, but there was a scratched-up machine that changed paper and coin euros, American dollars, and renminbi. He fumbled with the coin feed. *I haven't done this since my last time on the beach.* Bill punched in the code for the first washing machine, along with a soap purchase. Water and detergent poured into the washer, showing that he hadn't used up his water allocation, and Bill stuffed in his clothing. He bought twenty minutes of dryer time as well.

With his body clean, his clothes fresh, but his stomach empty, he counted his remaining cash. Three small bills and some change. He left the hotel, checking up and down the street for anything that might signal police or BES. *Kilel could be on top of me in five minutes, or five days.* His palms sweat, in spite of the chill. Nearer the water, the air temperature was lower than inland, and he pulled a wool cap tighter over his short haircut. Thick clouds moved in overhead, and Bill smelled rain, though none fell on this street. Chandlers, brokers, branch offices for shipping lines, union halls, bars, and the occasional tourist trap lined the avenues and narrow lanes first laid out in the 1850s.

Bill headed for a sailors' hangout, the Brass and Canvas, on a narrow side street. Water from a previous rain shower glistened on the broken asphalt, which revealed older bricks underneath. A neon sign glowed over the bar's entrance.

The place hadn't changed. Its generic intimacy was comforting and strange at the same time. The bar was dark and narrow, squeezed between two ancient brick buildings like an afterthought. Faded color photos of old oil-burning cargo vessels gathered dust on the walls. He thought of his first job as a cook's helper. He was fifteen, but passed for eighteen, a few years after the first carbon laws. The shipping companies were desperate for labor to man the sail training ships and big sailing yachts pressed into cargo service. A young man with experience around boats could get a berth easily.

Bill took a seat in a booth. A woman with hanging jowls and no eyebrows came up to him. "Afternoon," she said. "What can I get you?"

Bill now assessed each person he met as a possible threat, and it didn't help that he couldn't be pinged by servers for payment types he preferred or stored preferences for food and drink. His lack of electronic availability was a red flag, but the waitress didn't say or do anything that signaled a problem. *She sees off-the-net shellbacks every day. They're like stray dogs.*

"I'm kind of hungry." Bill watched the waitress's face. "Anything special on the menu?"

"We've got a veg burger, fries and a Pepsi."

"Can I substitute a Hanoi Dark?"

"Sure, for a couple of extra bucks."

Bill added up the cost in his head. It would clean him out, but he needed some cheer. If he was desperate, bread was free at the shelter the desk clerk talked about. He dismissed the thought, feeling sure that he could get a job in no time. *I'll take anything. I'm doing it for Anne.*

"Alright then."

The waitress touched the order into her notepad. She returned with the beer. Bill took a thoughtful sip and hoped to see a familiar face. *Would I recognize anybody after twenty years?* He wanted to work his old channels, keeping away from the mainstream, meaning the unions and the shipping companies themselves. It was easier to stay in the shadows that way.

Bill spied someone through the window. *Micah?* He left the table and ran out the door. "Micah Panang?"

She patted a salt-and-pepper dog tied up at the entrance and looked over to Bill. She wore a vest over a t-shirt, a clue about her attitude toward the weather. Her woven, graying ponytail looped twice at the nape of her neck. Her face brightened. "Bill!"

The two embraced, but Bill was shocked at the change in her. The skin of her face and arms was still the same sun-cooked, leathery brown it had when he first met her in Honolulu, when she was bosun on the *Artful.* The lines and colors of her tattoos were blurred by age, and a frostbite scar marred her left cheek. When she smiled, her perfect white teeth punctuated the air like the Cheshire cat's, though without the feline's guile. *I learned everything I know about tall ship sailing from her.* "You're looking pretty fit, I have to say." Bill admired her powerful shoulders. He would lose a wrestling match if he challenged her.

"You're looking the same. Ugly as ever." She punched his shoulder.

Bill laughed. *God bless Micah, an old friend.* "How are you, really?"

"Been working a lot. Just got in after two months at sea. Won't be here long. How long have you been here?"

"Just got in myself."

"Wow. Seaman's luck."

"Come inside." Bill beckoned her into the bar. *I need some luck. Maybe Micah's it.* "I'm getting a burger."

The waitress delivered Bill's food. Micah rested her bare arms on the table, and Bill noticed faint bands of dark and light pigment on her skin. *A new kind of body art? Micah always liked that craft.*

"Anything for you, ma'am?" the waitress said.

"A Hanoi would be good."

Bill gestured at his plate. "Have a couple of fries, Micah."

"Christ, it's been forever, Bill." Micah munched on one of the fat fried potatoes. "I never imagined we'd run into each other."

"This place is swabbie central."

"What are you doing here? God, it's like the years have disappeared. Didn't you quit the sea, right after you got married? Got a farm or something for you and your kid, um——"

"Anne."

"Yeah. What about Molly? What happened to her?"

Bill put down his burger and sipped his Hanoi. He weighed whether or not to lie to one of his best friends from his youth. He once depended on her for life and limb. They were both much younger then with no ties and fewer cares. He realized, as he noted the sadder, wiser cast to Micah's obsidian eyes, that she had changed in ways he couldn't know. *Can I trust her?*

"Last I remember, you and Molly had some trouble and you split up."

Bill was surprised at how much pain Micah's remark caused. It was an innocent statement; she was trying to catch up. *I shouldn't keep things from Micah.*

She was my mentor, my best shipmate. That was twenty years ago. Anne was all that mattered now to Bill. "Some things don't work out."

"Sorry to hear that, Bill. You were head over heels."

Micah's comment brought everything back about Molly, his only serious love, starting with the moment Bill saw her on the *Chelsea*, a hulking 35-meter brig. Molly was an experienced mariner who didn't think much of Bill at first, but he tried to be nice to her, help her with chores, do an extra watch so he could speak with her. One night, he was coming off watch at midnight, and on the way to the crew mess, Molly found him, led him to a storage locker, and... Bill smiled inwardly at the memory. *She was the most beautiful woman on the planet. Chelsea* arrived at Singapore and the chief engineer declared the mainmast cracked. It would take two or three days to repair. "Molly and I found a room and we didn't leave it until the blue peter went up. I asked her to marry me that day."

"How did you know it wasn't just a fo'c'sle romance? Did you really love her?"

"I did. I think so." After two decades, Bill wasn't certain. "She married me, didn't she?"

Bill sipped his beer as he told Micah more of the story. A few days after the couple arrived at Port Simpson, Molly discovered she was pregnant. She was troubled by the news. She had planned to go back to school to finish a master's in computer science. She was only a few credits from getting a degree, but she had to go back to maritime work to earn the money to pay for the schooling. Bill had no plans. His parents had died, leaving him enough for a down payment on a house. Molly could finish her degree with online courses, and they agreed to buy the ranch in Brier Valley. They married at the courthouse, and Anne was born about seven months later.

"Things were fine until she finished her degree," Bill said. He took care of Anne while Molly earned high praise for her work on artificial intelligence, and her thesis was published as an article in a scientific journal. Then she got a call from Algid. It was Martin Scribb himself."

Micah gasped. "You mean *the* Martin Scribb?"

Bill nodded. "Algid offered her a job doing advanced AI work." *Damn Scribb to hell.*

The family would have to move to Seattle, but Bill wasn't up for it. "I don't feel comfortable with over-educated types and their grand ideas." In the end, Molly would go to Seattle, see how the job went, and if she didn't like it, she'd come home. They'd use her earnings to pay off debts for farm robots and BES fines they'd run up getting started.

Six months dragged on to a year, and two years. Molly came home whenever she could, and Anne and Bill went up to Seattle a couple of times, and they talked on the com almost every night, at least in the beginning. Anne was too young to understand that her mother was far away. *I was her only parent, as far as she was concerned.*

"One day, Molly didn't come home." Bill lowered his voice. "I don't know where she is now, or what she's doing."

Why is truth so painful? After they met, no one else existed in the world for Bill than Molly, at least until little Anne came along. *If I had understood what Molly wanted for herself, to be more than a shellback, to make a bigger mark on life, I might not have asked her to marry me, and she might not have said Yes. She did, regretted it, and moved on. I've never regretted it. I wouldn't have my daughter if Molly had said No. Maybe that's why the whole mess still hurts after 20 years.*

"I'm sorry." Micah said. "How do you feel about Molly now?"

Bill raised the glass to his lips, but stopped short, considering an answer. Embers of anger still glowed, but so much time had passed. "I don't dwell on it."

"What would you do if you saw her?"

How possible is that? Bill snorted. "I probably wouldn't ask her to marry me." *How would I tell her about Anne?*

"What about Anne? Tell me about your daughter."

The request was another stab at Bill's heart, but his reaction was protection, not bitterness. "Anne was the best kid a dad could have. Never any trouble." He dug into a pocket, pulled out his holo-pic of Anne, and switched it on for Micah.

"A beautiful girl. You should be proud of her."

"I am." *Here I am, abandoning her, like her mother. I don't deserve her loyalty.* He cleared his throat to change the subject. "Look, I need a job."

"I see." Micah draped her right arm on the top of the bench. Bill saw the tight tendons of her forearm. "What sort of job?"

"I've renewed my AB papers every few years, just in case I needed them."

"You had more skills than that, I think."

Bill considered how much to say. He had to trust someone or risk starving. "Nothing special. I'm familiar with AI cargo-handling. Programmed some nav AI, though I don't have a ticket for that. I was thinking maybe one of the container ships. Or a bulk carrier. I've done the wheat runs from Australia to Vancouver. Do you know of anything?"

"What was your last ship?" Micah searched Bill's face.

She's sizing me up for something. "The *Edward T. Parson*, out of Everett."

"You've been on the beach awhile. She went aground off the Queen Charlotte's eight years ago. Five lost. The skipper too. I watched her slip under."

"Sorry to hear it." *How much else have I missed? Twenty years worth.*

Micah cocked her head. "What's going on, Bill? I know something's wrong."

"I suppose you could say that." Bill sighed as he dipped a fry in soy sauce.

Micah touched his arm. "You need to get away from here, fast, is that it?"

"I need work. I'm out of money and I've got a room for one night. After that, I'm on the street."

Micah slid over to the wall, and rested her foot on the bench.

"You're wearing shoes." Bill marked her feet with his eyes. "Last I remember, you hated wearing anything on your feet, unless it was fifty below."

"I lost half my toes in the Arctic a couple of years ago." She pulled off one of the shoes and showed Bill three robotic grafts. "They cost me half-a-year's pay. Don't want to lose them."

Bill's appetite waned as he recalled his own brushes with Arctic gales. The reality of his decision to run from Kilel hit him. He might have to take jobs or sail on routes a man his age who'd stayed in the maritime business could avoid and still make a good living. Perhaps it was a fantasy, going back to sea, living in an uncomfortable fo'c'sle, going aloft in rain and snow, even if he was still physically capable after two decades of working a ranch. Micah had changed, and he imagined other things had changed as well in ways he didn't understand. He could lose a limb or worse, and he might not see Anne or talk to her or even text her for months or years. Maybe never again. He was fugitive of the BES, and Janine Kilel was as relentless as they come. *I can only do this if it's for Anne.*

Micah rubbed her chin with a wiry hand. "I know a ship that's looking for crew. The captain doesn't ask a lot of questions. Interested?"

"I don't have a lot of choices." The longer he stayed, the greater the chance Kilel would catch up to him.

"Meet me here tonight." Micah's eyes twinkled. "I'll take you to it."

CHAPTER 10

"WHERE ARE YOU TAKING ME? What have I done?"

Anne pleaded with the driver and the agent seated next to her for information. Anne tested the door, but it was locked and the locks were controlled by the driver. The car slowed for roadblocks set up by the local sheriff and fire departments.

"Are you still looking for my father?"

The agent's stone-faced response knocked Anne's emotions from pillar to post. *Dad is dead! No, think it through.* Ninety percent of escapees were caught within a day of running, she'd heard. The rest were found within days. If her father had died, not even BES would've taken her off the street. After a storm of worry, the silence of the agents made her believe that her father was alive, but missing.

"If you think I'll help you, you're wrong."

Even through the filtered air of the car's A/C, Anne smelled the dankness of wood smoke mixed with vapor from the water and retardant drops. Another forest fire. The sheriff's deputies waved the car she was in through, and Anne passed other people who would have to wait for hours at the side of the road. Red Cross workers under a stand of Douglass-fir trees handed out coffee to people whom Anne guessed had lost their homes to the fire.

All through the drive, she received pings and texts from her friends, Mike included, but her attempts to send messages generated errors. The agent beside her wore sunglasses and scanned the road, as if looking for threats. "I can't talk to my tribe," Anne said. "I mean, my net link is blocked." The bessie remained tight-lipped. The agents' reserve enraged Anne more than frightened her.

"I know this road. It goes to Eugene. Are you taking me to the BES office there?"

They entered a broad valley and Anne recognized the Eugene skyline. A sign announced the BES entrance a mile ahead, but the driver turned onto a narrow blacktopped road marked "Government Vehicles Only." Anne made mental notes of the facility. *I might need to run.* Razor wire topped fences that disappeared into the trees on each side of a gate. The car stopped at a modern three-story office building with darkened windows and no landscaping. It was so nondescript, that it was perfect for hiding people. *Like Dad?*

At a side entrance, the driver opened Anne's door and a female green-shirt cracked a smile. The woman took her by the elbow. The mild pain dampened thoughts of escape. An automatic door clicked and opened into an atrium big enough for her and her guard.

"Place your hand on the pad, please." The guard rested her eyes on a dull gray slab.

"What is…"

"Your hand on the pad, please."

Anne obeyed and she felt a slight suction. The device's screen lit.

The green-shirt spoke. "You are Anne Eileen Penn, born October 1, 2040, in Coos Bay, Oregon, Pacific West?"

"Yes." *It's a DNA sequence identifier. It's how they tag suspects.* Anne was puzzled as much as afraid. She turned to the guard. "Please tell me why I'm here. If you're looking for my dad, I don't know where he is."

As impassive as the agents in the car, the green shirt led her down a short hallway to another door, which opened into a small apartment. The guard closed the door behind Anne, and the lock clicked. In mild shock, Anne stood in the semi-darkness, unsure what to do next. She took a half-step forward, leaning ahead as if expecting someone or something to jump at her. The place was silent, except for the hum of a refrigerator compressor and a breathy hiss from the HVAC system. Natural light filtered through curtains covering a window. Gaining confidence, Anne explored the suite, which had a queen-size bed, a dresser, a small table with two chairs, a large bathroom, and a kitchenette. There were cold drinks in the refrigerator and food in the cupboards. Anne relaxed a little. *Too nice for a jail, but not exactly homey.*

Anne pushed back the curtains from the ground floor window and searched for a latch to open it. It was solid. She switched on the TV and cycled through the channels. They were all there, even the hottest new programs from China. Anne's Mandarin was decent. Her father insisted she do well in her language classes. They'd watch the Chinese cop shows and he would turn off the subtitles and tell her to translate so that she would practice. The thought of cop shows made Anne wary. She thought of cameras, but they were practically invisible these days, as small as mites and spiders. *No cobwebs in the corners.* Perhaps the bessies were watching her right now.

The apartment was missing the most important thing, besides her father: connectivity. For an hour, Anne tried to loop herself in her c-tribe and other tribes, but her minds-eye always returned a "networks unavailable" message. The one available network was labeled "BESSecureHolding." She logged in and found a menu limited to outgoing pings and texts to other users. It confirmed what she'd already figured, despite the comfort. She was now an inmate, and it was more than a jail of the body. A wall had virtualized between herself and her social circle.

She was cut off. De-networked. Un-networked. It was as if an arm or a leg had been torn off. The shock of sudden isolation from a community she had known for years left her missing a part of her existence, like someone close had died. She felt half-alive. She lowered herself to the floor at the foot of the bed. A pounding in her head increased. *Too much is happening.*

Anne was alone until someone knocked on the door and it opened. It was Janine Kilel, and she was carrying a tray of food. "Hello, Miss Penn." Her pleasantness aggravated Anne's immediate dislike. The inspector had arrested and jailed her father, stasered him, and tried to kidnap him. Nothing would soften those facts. Kilel lay the tray on the table, as well as a tablet, the newest 财富精神 (Wealth Spirit, Cáifù Jīngshén) model. "I'm sorry about all the trouble of the past few hours. We've compounded the loss of your home and family by bringing you to a strange place with no one to talk to. I brought you some kiwis, star fruit, some Montana pineapple, a French baguette and real cheese, fully licensed."

A peace offering? Anne did her best to avoid looking at the colorful food, but she couldn't avoid the smell of the bread.

"Eat whenever you're ready, Miss Penn, but the food here is very good."

Anne's hunger pangs intensified. She got up from the floor and climbed into a chair at the table opposite Kilel. Anne couldn't help reaching for a slice of honeydew melon, but she distrusted Kilel's kindness.

The inspector took a chair at the table. "You're here for an important reason, Miss Penn. A serious environmental crime has occurred and we sometimes have to detain witnesses. It's completely routine."

"How long?" Anne tore off a bit of the baguette with her thumb and forefinger and ate it. It was still warm.

"A short time. I have questions for you."

"Don't I need a lawyer or something?"

"I don't think so." Kilel grimaced as if she had tasted something bitter. "That would slow things down and we want to get you back home as soon as we can."

"Sorry if I don't believe you."

"Why would I lie?"

"Are you serious? You're a bessie. No one trusts you people."

Kilel folded her hands on the table. "Nonetheless, I'm not interested in keeping you here longer than I have to."

Anne avoided Kilel's gaze, and picked off a bit of cheese, which was delicious. "How come I can't connect to any of the networks?"

"Too distracting. We like our guests to focus on answering questions. You'll be home sooner if you do."

"Guests?" Anne mocked Kilel with the word. "You've put me in jail, just like you put my dad in jail, for no reason."

The inspector pushed the plate closer to Anne. "Why don't you eat some more? You must be starving."

"I had a big lunch." Anne thought of Mike. Somehow, the image of him in her memory was more vivid than one in the cache of her minds-eye, as if she summoned him, like a magician. He stood next to Anne, defending her as Kilel bribed her with food. Anne brought her feet up to her seat, her knees against her chest, and placed the crumb of cheese in her fingers back on the plate.

"Perhaps you prefer butter to margarine. Let me get some." The officer rose and spoke to the refrigerator, which delivered a small wrapped dollop of butter. The fridge doled out just enough so that nothing was wasted, and no unnecessary packaging. Kilel brought it back to the table. Anne ogled the luxury spread.

Kilel sighed. "Let's get down to business, Miss Penn. Tell me about the fire."

Anne decided to say nothing.

"Listen to me, Anne..."

"Don't call me 'Anne.'" Anne put her hands to her temples. "I want to go home."

The tablet's screen blinked off as it went to sleep. Kilel's silence forced the seconds to pass for Anne as if they were minutes, and the muscles of Anne's neck tightened. Kilel's eyes narrowed before relaxing, as if she was running through a list of questions to ask Anne, rejecting some or accepting others. It was different than the minds-eye stare; Kilel was playing back a memory, or a dream, interpreting it in light of new facts. Kilel rested her left hand over her right and drew a breath.

"Anne, you love your father, don't you?"

"Of course I do. Why would you ask such a thing?"

"What would you sacrifice him for?"

The question shocked Anne. "Sacrifice? I don't understand."

"As in giving him up for something greater, something larger than yourself."

"Are you saying I should just rat him out? To you?"

Kilel pressed on Anne. "The sooner you cooperate, the sooner you can leave. It's a simple as that. You're not under investigation for a crime, but failure to answer lawful questions from a police officer are grounds for holding you longer than we both want." Kilel lifted her right hand, and studied it, as if it were a weapon used in a murder. "Anne, I admire your closeness to your father. Maybe I envy it, but there are larger things at stake, more important things than your love for your father."

The question reminded Anne of one of the few conversations she and Bill had about Bill's family. Anne was 13. She was doing homework on the outdoors picnic table while Bill hammered nails into loose siding on the house. Bill had spent his early years at his parents' farm outside Eagle Point, but they had lost the farm when he was six. He said little else, and when Anne asked him more about her grandparents, he only said her father had died when he was eight and his mother died when he was 18.

"It was a dairy farm, right, Dad?"

Bill pressed his lips together. "Mmm, hmm."

"They told us in school that all the dairy farms in the valley were closed down because the cows were passing too much methane into the air."

Bill said nothing, but his hammering was insistent.

"Teacher told us that the BES helped all the families find new jobs that were more sustainable. It was hard, but everyone was happy."

Bill pounded a nail so hard that it made a round dent in the wood.

"Daddy, what's wrong?"

Anne's father fought to control himself. "Anne, I'm only going to say this once. The bessies break families. They destroy families. They make sons turn against fathers, against mothers, against brothers. Don't ever forget that. Ever."

In the detention center, an older Anne chewed her lip at the memory of her father's fury. "What could be more important than my family, inspector?"

Kilel paused, and Anne's sense of Kilel playing back her own recollections returned. "The air we breathe, the water we drink, the land we live on. If our family is hurting these things, we owe them nothing."

What is she telling me? Anne picked up a finger-sized wedge of melon and put it in her mouth. She weighed her options, even as a knot of anxiety in her stomach wound tighter. *I'll give the bitch the bare facts, nothing more.*

Anne swallowed her bite and recounted the story of the house and refuge fire in short sentences and Yes or No answers to the inspector's questions. Kilel highlighted points in a rolling transcript of the conversation on her tablet.

After an hour or so, Kilel ended the conversation. She rubbed her eyes.

"Can I go home now?" Anne said.

"Soon." Kilel placed the tablet in a sleeve.

Dad was right. They always lie. "I've told you everything. I don't know where my father is, or where he's going."

"I appreciate your cooperation, Anne, even if you are...terse. You're telling the truth, according to the stress analysis. I believe you." She brushed invisible dust motes from her uniform. "It's getting late. You'll be staying the night here."

Kilel left the apartment.

Anne restrained her panic. All her bodily needs were cared for: the green-shirts even brought her stylish, if simple, clothes and sandals. They weren't enough. She needed to connect with her friends, but all her attempts to loop-in failed. Her heart fluttered. Kilel's questions had the side effect of raising Anne's curiosity. The BES believed he was alive, but it had no idea where he was. Anne was sure of this, or they would have told her he was dead. There was no reason to keep that a secret. It was logical that he would go west, probably in the direction of Port Simpson. *Back to sea?*

After darkness blanketed the compound, sleep refused to come. If she were traveling, she would've packed her own pillow, a habit since childhood. The smell and texture fooled her mind into thinking she was at home in her own bed. *It was burned in the fire.* After many hours in the apartment lying awake in the dark, she finally slept.

The next morning, a green-shirt came in with a plate of fresh fruit and bread. The isolation from her c-tribe drove Anne mad, and she begged for a few minutes out-of-doors to check in. Nothing persuaded the green-shirt. It was torture.

At least Kilel was right about the food. Anne's anxiety didn't interfere with her appetite, and she explored the cupboards and refrigerator. Cereal, milk, eggs, juice, and toast for breakfast. Whole-grain quinoa bread with avocados, sprouts, vine-ripened tomatoes, and fresh spinach. The veggie lasagna and pizza were heavenly. The food brought to mind meals with her dad with the old woodcut tacked to the wall behind his usual seat. A mental picture surfaced: Mike and her dad sharing breakfast with her. The fantasy warmed her.

As Anne puzzled over a laughable old sci-fi show on a vintage TV channel, Kilel walked in. She didn't knock this time. Anne got up from her slouch, embarrassed that she was in a terry robe and hadn't brushed her hair. *They never give you any warning.* An older man followed Kilel. He wore a similar uniform, a cross between a business suit and military dress. He had two pips on his collar, as well as the BES tulip.

"Miss Penn," Kilel said, "this is Colonel Raleigh Penn. He's the commanding officer for the Pacific West district."

Colonel Penn offered his hand in greeting. "Miss Penn."

Anne balked, from surprise, not fear. "Penn?" The shape of his face, the thinning hairline, the low-slung ears, and the length of the jaw made his face too much like her father's. *A cousin? Dad said something...* The gray tinge of his skin contrasted with her father's healthy tan. She returned his greeting, feeling the mild dampness of his palm and the weakness of his muscles, the opposite of her father's.

"Yes, Anne." Colonel Penn took one of the chairs at the table. Kilel remained standing. "Did your father ever mention a brother?"

Anne's eyes were locked on the colonel's. He was far older than her father, and his eyes were the wrong color, that is, they were the same rich loam of Anne's own eyes. He was telling the truth, as far as she could tell, but bessies were knee-jerk liars. "Maybe. I don't remember."

"I haven't spoken to your father, my brother, for almost 30 years."

"You're my uncle?"

"We've never met, Anne. Bill sent me a video of you after you were born, but that was all I knew about you."

That has to be a lie. All it takes is a five-minute search of the net to find everything about me. He's full of shit.

The colonel interlaced the fingers of his pale hands. "Once I heard about the fire, and your detainment, I decided it was best that I bring you the news."

"What's happened? Is my dad alright?" Anne draped her right arm across her chest, as if protecting herself from a coming blow.

"Your father has escaped custody. He ran into the mountains toward a forest fire. We found a fire blanket that didn't belong to the fire crews."

"Are you saying he's dead?" Anne forced back her tears, wanting to stay strong in front of this stranger who said he was her uncle.

Kilel offered Anne a tissue. Anne ignored the woman who had caused her so much trouble.

"We don't know." The colonel unlaced his hands.

"Do you recognize this?" Kilel showed Anne a close-up photo of the fire blanket, dirty and charred. It was one of the blankets her father had bought in town before the hiking season started. The photo showed a yellow tag with the word "EVIDENCE" in block letters.

"Yes." *Say nothing.*

"Did your father own blankets like this one?"

Anne nodded. The photo showed charcoal and ashes around the blanket, but it was odd. *No body or any of his hiking gear.*

"We aren't sure, but we think your father used the fire as cover for his escape," Kilel said. "Because he had a fire blanket, he likely had other backpacking equipment. We think he's still alive in the mountains, but he's eluded us so far."

It's true. They've lost him. A strange joy coursed through Anne's body. Bill had eluded the bessies for more than two days. He had beaten them, at least up to this point. The joy gave way to terror. *If he's hiding, he could also be badly hurt, in pain, and dying.* The lack of any detailed information ripped at her.

"We want to find your father, almost as much as you do," Kilel said. "We need your help."

Anne wanted to help her father get away from Kilel, but the worst outcomes gnawed at her. *What if he's alive, but horribly burned? Who will take care of him? I can't do it alone. Can I?* Anne shivered, as if freezing, and she ran her hands through the hair at her temples.

"I've studied your records, Anne." Colonel Penn's voice was gentle, sympathetic. "You loved that refuge since the day you arrived in Brier Valley. Your science project in eighth grade was on the magpies that nested there. Every year you've done something for those creatures, volunteered, reported problems. A good partner to the earth."

Kilel breathed in, then out. "Anne, the magpies are gone. The species is now gone."

No, they are not. The inspector's voice was like sandpaper on Anne's skin. "I need to connect to my friends. I'm going crazy. I miss them. When can I connect?"

Kilel stepped back and folded her arms. "Colonel, sir, a word?" The two BES officers huddled in the kitchenette and spoke in whispers. Anne watched them, curious at how Kilel spoke to the colonel in hushed tones as if she were a student, or an acolyte.

Could that man really be my uncle?

The colonel agreed with something Kilel said. The inspector turned to Anne.

Queued c-tribe messages flooded Anne's minds-eye. A kind of bliss flooded her heart. *I am alive because I am shared.* Everyone she knew tried to reach her after she fell offline, and the virtual touches and words of concerns made her laugh. Mike sent the most texts and messages, cc'ing everyone in town, including his father. Without opening any other message, Anne composed a response to him, but the "send" command was grayed out. As fast as it had materialized, the connection vanished. "No." Anne shook her head and faced Kilel and the colonel. "No. I need to talk to them. Please."

"Anne, when you help us, we'll restore all of your net capabilities." Kilel returned to her chair. The colonel followed suit.

Fury replaced the blissful emotions. *It is torture. They might as well put me on the rack.*

Kilel took Anne's hands in her own. Anne recoiled, as if the inspector's fingers were gloved in slime.

"My job is to protect wild things." Kilel didn't notice or else ignored Anne's visceral reaction, but the inspector's face was within millimeters of Anne's. Her breath was warm, but odorless. The younger woman's stomach churned. "We have to hold someone to account for the refuge fire. People can't get away with this kind of destruction anymore."

Anne glanced at the colonel, whose gaze was on Kilel. His own doubts about Kilel were thinly masked. *Is that also fear in his eyes?*

Anne shook her head no to Kilel's statement, not because she agreed with her philosophy of accountability, but because she knew her father's capture might be the first step in a road to a kind of living death. She knew about disidentification, its horrors, the scarification, the erasure of everything about a person, and the shunning. *If Dad's alive, he couldn't live that way.*

"You understand, then," Kilel said.

I do, but not in the way you think. How could she help Kilel find her dad if it meant he might die to the world? And she might never see him again.

"Perhaps you could say a prayer." Kilel's tone bordered on unctuous.

"What?"

"The cross on your necklace."

"A crucifix."

"It's unusual for teenager—a young adult—these days to wear them."

"Dad gave it to me." Anne wanted to spit into Kilel's eye. "He said we had to pay attention to what we couldn't see."

"A sailor's superstition, eh?"

"No. No!" Anne got up from the chair. "You watch yourself. My father is smarter than you, ten of you, a hundred of you people. You're chasing him for something that wasn't his fault. It was an accident. We're all tired of you people. We're tired of your harassment and your secrecy. Why don't you leave us alone?"

Anne shoved away the plate of leftover breakfast, and it flew toward Kilel. Juice-laden fruit and cheese and crumbling bread spilled into her lap. She sprang up, surprised, and stared at the spreading stain on her tunic.

"You little bitch." Kilel lifted her hand, and Anne blinked in self-protection.

"Inspector!" The colonel's voice filled the room. "Control yourself."

Kilel twisted her head toward her superior, her arm cocked to land a blow.

"Get out. Go clean yourself up."

Kilel took a breath, and the rage left her face. Her forehead and jaw muscles relaxed, and she brushed off bits of food from her tunic. She backed up a step, turned, and left the apartment.

An automated cleaning bot slid from a closet and set to work on the spill.

Colonel Penn ignored the bot and interlaced his fingers again. "Will you help us, Anne? Your father is a resourceful man. His merchant marine record shows it. His work on the farm shows it, despite his disregard for the law. If your father's alive, and Inspector Kilel and I think he is, he'll be worried about you. He'll want to find you. We can reunite you with him, if you'll help us."

The more Anne studied the colonel's face, the more she believed he was her uncle. The two millimeter gap between the front teeth and the shape of his fingers was exactly like Bill's. As she accepted her relationship to him, speaking to him became easier, unlike speaking to Kilel, which grew more painful with each word. *If you are my uncle, why have you stayed hidden from me and my dad? And what happened to keep the two of you apart?*

Kilel returned to the apartment, wearing a fresh tunic, though it didn't fit as well as the first. She had borrowed it from someone, perhaps one of the guards. The interruption gave Anne a chance to change the subject. "Why don't you just trace his jack-in sig through the net. You'll find him instantly."

The inspector's anger had disappeared, or it was suppressed. "Pings to your father have led us nowhere. Even these days, some remote places don't have network services, and I suspect he'll switch off his net link, or wait until the battery dies in a few days. He'll be cut off from the world, and we'll be cut off from him."

Anne's father was always forgetting to recharge his netlink battery. *Kilel has run out of ideas.*

"I'll help you," Anne said.

"Very good, Anne," the colonel said.

"I'll help you, colonel. Not her." Anne refused to look at the uniformed woman. *I almost said "uncle."*

"Very good, and thank you." Colonel Penn glanced at the inspector. "You'll have to, um, tolerate her, Anne. She's my lead investigator, and I'm a busy man."

Kilel picked up the tablet. "Let's talk about where your father might go."

The colonel lifted his hand. "A moment, inspector, if you don't mind."

"Sir?"

"Anne, I would like to ask another question, before we continue the... conversation."

Interrogation, you mean. "Something about your brother?"

"No, Anne. Your mother."

"My mother?"

"Do you know where she is?"

The bus pulled away from the head of the long gravel drive that led to Anne and her father's property. The summer crickets were in full throat, as were the tree frogs. Overhead, the sky was a thick purple, with the brightest stars peeking through the manzanita and pines. Anne's booted feet kicked up dust, her mind entangled in memories of the interrogation, and her belief that more had happened than she was aware. The strange holo-vid stumped her. When she was dropped off at the bus stop in Eugene by the same men who arrested her, her network access returned as if nothing had happened. She reveled in the digital welcome of her friends. After it died down, she spotted the video file in her com's personal private folder, which the com company claimed was triple-encrypted against intrusion. She played the file in her minds-eye, and it showed a young man, a young woman, and a newborn. Anne had seen hundreds of these kinds of shared images in c-tribes; new parents loved to show off their children. Anne was indifferent to most of these vids, but not this one. The couple were her parents, and the child was her, days after her birth.

Anne rejected Kilel as the source of this personal history. *Colonel Penn said he first heard of my birth through a photo sent to him by Dad.* Anne speculated and discarded a dozen reasons for the gift, including the simple desire to make a connection with a niece the colonel had never met before the encounter in the detention facility. The familial emotion she felt in the colonel's presence had already faded. *It's only a video of a new family, like billions of others. It must mean something else.*

As full darkness settled on the valley, Anne arrived at the ranch's gate. She followed the path around the remains of the house to the outbuildings and the coop. She smiled when she saw the warm red glow of the heat lamp. *At least the eggs haven't died of cold.*

Anne noticed another light, an ice-like, whitish glare, too bright to be natural. It was an LED lamp. She hadn't left any lamps on besides the heat lamp when she had gone to town. Someone was in or near the coop. She halted and switched off her flashlight. Her mental map of the property was accurate down to the centimeter, and she stepped to keep distance between herself and the intruder.

Has Kilel come looking for me? Are the bessies back to take me away for more questions? During the interrogation, she said nothing to Kilel about the magpie chicks, assuming any survived while she was gone. She guessed her plan was illegal under the endangered species laws, and she didn't want to place her father in any more danger because of what she was doing on his land.

Anne's heart pumped hard as she circled around to a point behind the light. He, or she, or it, was next to the modified nesting box with the eggs. Anne had no weapon and no cover but the darkness. The intruder held still for several minutes, and she crept toward the light. The person was male, with his back toward her. The figure turned around. Anne recognized him.

"Mike?"

Mike Schmidt squinted in the dimness, uncertain about the visitor. "Anne, is that you?"

"What are you doing here?"

"After the BES people took you, you dropped off the com net. I got a little... worried. I didn't know what to do. I got off work, and I remembered the eggs. I came up here to see if you were here. But you weren't. I found the eggs... and so I waited for you..."

"You've been here the whole time?"

"Not the whole time. I had to go to work. I've got my bike and camping gear. Where have you been?"

Anne didn't answer the question. Instead, she walked up to Mike and embraced him.

CHAPTER 11

BILL RETURNED TO THE BRASS and Canvas after dark, and he found the place packed with raucous sailors and longshoremen, male, female, trans, and andys. It was a Friday night, and a band called Shanghai People's Outlaws stuffed the chords of the latest Sichuan rockabilly into the narrow bar. The hot, smoky air vibrated with the music and hazy recollections of alcohol and mist-fed all-nighters ashore in his youth. He bought a Hanoi with the last of his paper euros, but he was not looking to satisfy his nostalgia. He squeezed into a corner near the front window to watch for Micah.

An hour later, she touched him on the shoulder, startling him; she hadn't come through the front door, as he expected. Micah smelled of sweat from a run.

"Are you ready?"

Bill couldn't hear Micah over the music. "What?"

The sailor was agitated. "Do you want a job or not?"

Something held Bill back. He was wary after his near-kidnapping and escape from Kilel, but he couldn't put his finger on his doubts. "I want to know more about the job first."

"You've got to decide now. I'm not taking you to the ship unless you want the job."

Bill didn't like Micah's demand for an answer. "What's the name of the ship?"

"Forget it!" Micah started to leave.

"Wait." Bill grabbed Micah's arm. He hesitated, feeling a warning in the thick atmosphere. *What other choice do I have?* "Fine. I'll go."

She beckoned Bill to follow. "Hurry up."

Bill pushed his way through the crowd, getting a return shove once or twice. Years ago, he might have pushed back, but he had no time for stupidity.

"Come on," Micah urged.

Bill heard a siren. Two dark cars with blue-green lights entered the narrow street. Kilel's BES cruiser racing through the Brier Valley dust flashed in his mind.

A bouncer at the front door yelled "Cops!"

Scores of people poured out of the door like cattle let loose from a pen. They tore down the sidewalk away from the police cars. Micah plunged into the crowd. Bill lost sight off his friend. A wave of disorientation derailed him, and for a half-second, he imagined Anne carried away as the crowd split into pieces and spread onto the adjacent streets. He blinked and the desolate apparition disappeared, but Micah was not in view.

Bill snatched a look over his shoulder, and he saw two green-shirts near the bar's entrance pushing men and women into the wall. Another pair of BES officers took up positions outside the front door. A patron slumped against the glass, taken down by a staser. Bill's pounding heart skipped a beat. Janine Kilel was in the face of the waitress who had served him.

Micah waved. "Over here."

Relief at the sight of a familiar face other than his nemesis drove Bill toward Micah. Another dark car screeched to a halt. It disgorged a security robot. Bill dragged his old shipmate behind a composting dumpster. "Help me move this before the tin can gets here."

The insistent robot moved toward Bill and Micah, avoiding parked cars and fire hydrants.

"What's the point of hiding here? Let's run," Micah said.

Bill's heart thumped. "No. We need time." He heard the muffled steps of the robot's rubber-shod feet. There was a clicking sound. The robot deployed its staser. Phantom pain from the memory of his staser hit coursed through Bill's lower back.

"Ready?" Bill said.

The robot's staser swiveled to the pair.

"Heave away!"

The pair pushed the dumpster, half-full of garbage, into the path of the robot, smashing the staser against a brick wall. The fugitives bolted into the alley.

Micah surprised Bill with her speed, cyborgian toes and all, and he almost lost her again when she turned a corner. Micah came back. "Come on, damn you. We're lucky the green-shirts haven't caught up."

The pair jogged down a cave-like, brick-paved alley, leaping over passed-out derelicts. Micah pounded on a back door, with Bill close behind. The door was opened a crack by a young woman wearing a bra and panties in the ruddy light. Micah pushed her aside. The woman pushed back. "Micah, what the fu—"

"Sorry, Beth. Bessies on our tail. You'd better close the door behind us."

The woman didn't argue as Bill brushed past. "Excuse us."

"Of course."

The fleeing pair trotted through the hall into a lobby with a few upholstered chairs and a leather sofa. Two men and a woman sipped glasses of wine at a table. Micah stopped at the establishment's front entrance, checking the street, Bill presumed, for bad guys.

Bill's curiosity was piqued. "Do you know those people?"

"Friends from a long time ago. I drop in now and then." The neighborhood was dark and quiet. "Cops'll be here any minute. We need to get to the ship."

Micah marched into the darkness, compelling Bill to trail her. Micah followed alleys and side streets, heading in the general direction of the water. A sense of disorientation returned to Bill, though not as frightening as the seconds after the raid. Keeping one eye on Micah, he picked out a mist gallery, a seafarer's mission, and a lawyer's office. Only the god-house was familiar. After a quarter-mile, the pair came out to a thoroughfare, empty of traffic, except for an automated trolley trundling toward them.

Micah halted near a trolley stop, keeping to the shadows. "I think we're safe enough now."

Uncertain whether to believe Micah, Bill scanned the area. When the trolley was within a hundred feet or so, Micah stepped over to the pickup zone, and the machine slowed to a halt, its wet brake pads screeching. *Christ! Every green-shirt within ten miles heard that.* Micah dropped a couple of renminbi coins into the fare box.

"Destination, please." The disembodied voice came from a speaker in the box.

"Terminal 53," Micah said. "For both of us."

"Please take a seat." The trolley's voice was friendly, if impersonal. "Would you like a narrated tour of the sights as we travel, ma'am? I entertain many visitors like yourself. Does your com have visual enhancement features? I can show you some interesting images as I narrate. Port Simpson is very historic and has many interesting shops and entertainments. I note you speak English. If that is not your first language, I can deliver narration in Chinese, Japanese, Urdu, Hindustani, Arabic, Russian, Polish, Swedish, Inuit…"

"Belay that."

The voice paused a half-second, as if translating. "Yes, ma'am."

Bill stifled a laugh at the nautical order given to a bus. For a moment, he felt as if he'd come into a temporary safe harbor.

Micah nudged Bill, eyeing a plastic globe in the ceiling, reminding Bill of the danger. "The cameras. Cover your face." Bill pulled his coat hood over his head. He eyed the graffiti-marred windows, looking for other travelers in the reflections. The trolley was empty save for the fugitives. The clack of the trolley wheels marked time and distance. An overhead light flickered, casting shadows as bolts of lightning would in a storm.

"Terminal 53." The trolley announced the stop as it ground to a halt.

They exited and Micah led them back the way the trolley had come.

"Wait. There's no ship here." The empty berths rattled Bill. "Where are you taking me?" *Could she be working for BES?*

"Relax. We're backtracking." Micah pulled Bill by the arm. "Someone's going to review that recording and know where we stopped. The ship is back a ways toward town."

Bill regretted his obsessive doubting. *Micah was always cautious ashore and aloft.*

Huge automated cranes loaded containers onto wind ships. The cranes' winches whined in the cool marine air. Robots—smaller, more benign versions of the BES models—patrolled the inside of a fence. The popped in and out of view as they passed under the security floodlights. Bill didn't see another human until he turned onto a concrete pier. At the end of the pier was another ship, and Bill's heart swelled. The lights from the pier shone on the sweeping hull of a big three-master, like something out of the nineteenth century. The new wind ships took in their masts and yards to make cargo loading easier. Before the new designs took hold, a few companies, hoping for a competitive edge, brought back the older style.

Bill forgot his troubles as he cast his eyes along her flowing lines. Red and green navigation lights marked port and starboard. A white lamp shone at her stern. Another white lamp, paired with a red aircraft warning lamp, blinked at the head of the main mast. Bill remembered pride in similar vessels he had crewed two decades past. *I wish I had brought Anne here more often to admire these beauties.* Awed by the vision, Bill followed Micah, feeling his way up the aluminum gangplank.

A human voice, rasping and whispery, from a man restraining himself from screaming at the top of his lungs, pierced the night. "Panang, where in hell have you been." It grew louder as the owner drew near. "You're hours late. We've missed the tide. If it weren't you, I would've sailed."

"Sorry, Jay." Micah displayed a respect Bill didn't remember from the old days. "We're one step ahead of the green-shirts. The tip we got was right."

A bearded man at least six-foot-three and a hundred kilos, maybe more, in his late forties, stood at the head of the ramp. The cap and coat made him look twice as tall and heavy. "Who on God's green earth is this?"

"This is the seaman I told you about."

"Damn you, man." The officer addressed Bill with a commanding directness, but his tone was friendly. "Are you signing on?"

Bill wondered if a decision to stay would mean worse trouble than he was already in. Then he remembered Kilel's face back at the Brass and Canvas. "I am, sir."

"Fine then." The officer extended his hand. "I'm Captain Jaydon James McMadden. Welcome aboard the barque *Aganippe*."

CHAPTER 12

MOLLY RETURNED TO HER CABIN aboard the sailing liner *Aurora Borealis* at midnight—earlier than usual when she was working with a high-powered client—though Nordland was happy to fall asleep after his drinking and their session. She was glad for the extra hour before her usual bedtime, though she took a moment to enjoy the twinkling lights of Churchill's northern suburbs on the western shore of Hudson's Bay. The ship was well on its way to a passage of the Arctic Ocean and the new Russian ports. She had to prepare for the next day's meetings. All that remained of the Cyprian Association negotiations with Nordland's company and the other big players in the AFEZ was crossing the t's and dotting the i's, as well as the final signatures. All her work since her conviction at the Spike Trials was within a few strides of the finish line. *I wonder what Martin Scribb—that devil in a business suit—would say? He was always chintzy with praise.* Despite her confidence, anything could derail her dream, and preparation was the best defense.

She slipped off her dress and jewelry, except for her com-bracelet, which she preferred over the ear studs fashionable among young people. She was two decades past that hormone-ravaged time.

"Service: Bath, temperature 104 degrees Fahrenheit. Salts, lavender, a quarter cup, English measurement."

The room servbot lifted itself from its bay in the wall and navigated to the bathroom on its three legs. Its glossy, cerulean finish over its humanoid body echoed the New Ocean logo in the corner of the Egyptian cotton linens and towels. *Nordland may be a drunkard, but his hirelings have good taste.* Molly heard water flow into the tub.

Molly donned a red silk robe and logged in to one of her Swiss accounts. With a satisfied grin, she verified the €12,500 deposit from Nordland. She normally verified deposits before a session, but Nordland had proved trustworthy. She also arranged the transfer of €6,250—New Ocean's cut—from her account to the company.

"Safe: Bain Cabin 114. Open." The room safe's door clicked and she placed her jewelry and Nordland's $1,000 cash tip inside. *A true businessman.*

A dozen emails and newsloop notifications had arrived since her last check. News headlines: a spate of out-of-control forest fires in Pacific West; a cargo ship captain sentenced to 25 years for petroleum smuggling; a march on Ottawa by veterans of the Three Degrees North War; the launch of the world's largest sailing cargo ship. A few referrals by regular clients. Most of the email was from Ginny Magante, her second in the talks with the Committee of the North, which managed the International Arctic Free Economic Zone. The impatient called it the AFEZ.

"Coffee, madam?" The servbot waited for Molly's response. The machine's eyes—a hollow black and ringed with polished chrome—stared ahead. Its voice was male and deferential.

"Hmm?" Molly said. "Oh, no, chamomile tea, please." The servbot walked to the kitchenette. "Put the tea in the bathroom, and then you may un-deploy and shut down."

"Madam."

Molly called up her minds-eye address book from the com and selected Ginny as she tested the bath water. The bracelet linked into *Aurora's* net. Her friend's location was noisy. "Where are you? Can you talk?"

"I'm on the dance floor."

"Are you working, too?"

"I'm a workaholic." Ginny sounded sharp and energized.

"Can we talk about the latest from the Committee? Go someplace private."

"Give me a sec, Mol." The background noise died away. "What's up?"

The women went over each of the Committee's final points and they decided how to respond.

"Gut check, Gin. You're my best friend. Tell me the truth."

"Mol, this is it. It's what they want. Another island of stability and predictability after the war. The Wild North a little tamer. It's what *you* want."

"A monopoly on personal entertainment services in the AFEZ. It's what the Cyprians want." Molly rose from her seat and paced the floor of her cabin. "Fair treatment. Good wages. Good conditions. Good benefits. Pensions. Medical. Never been done before for sex work on this scale."

"You know it, Mol."

"Not to mention dignity. Respect. For us. It's been three thousand years since we've been taken seriously."

"Mol, I also got a call from the Committee staff about an hour ago. They want to close the deal when we get to Pole Station. Two of the reps are leaving on the helo right after the signing."

"What's the rush?"

"Some of the government reps are getting nervous about the politics." Ginny said. "Signing contracts with ladies of questionable reputation is unseemly to voters back home."

"Their leaders were happy enough to turn a blind eye to the traffickers before the war." Molly turned off the bath faucet. "The New Valleys in Greenland were full of debt-bonded women. It took the war to stop it, but the demand is still there. We're offering a preventive solution."

"What if these guys get cold feet?"

"I'm not worried." Molly slipped off her robe. "Kristian Nordland said he'd play Pied Piper, if needed."

"Why would he help?"

"He's a smart guy," Molly said. "His company just launched a big new sailing cargo ship. The other lines are scrambling to catch up. He's also planning another new port in the AFEZ. He needs to keep his employees happy. Six months of cold, dark winters are tough."

"I'm being hailed, Mol. Call you later." Ginny closed the connection.

Lowering herself into the tub, Molly lay still as she let the water's sloshing subside. The surface tilted a few degrees to starboard, reflecting *Aurora*'s heel as her sails embraced the freshening Arctic breeze. Collections of bubbles floated like icebergs in the bath. Tiny wavelets ruffled the water, kissing Molly's skin where it broke the surface.

Molly closed her eyes, waiting for that juncture when her body temperature matched the temperature of the bath water, the point where she melded with her corner of the universe. Random images and thoughts flowed through her mind: Nordland's praise of her trim, athletic body; code fragments from forgotten projects scribbled on whiteboards; her client's compliant agreement to her demand of orgasm first; chapters and paragraphs and subparagraphs from the Committee contract; the booming music in the background of Ginny's call; the beautiful face of a young man she had loved once and married.

At first Molly thought Bill Penn was full of himself, too proud to know Able Seaman's papers were just that, paper, and the thing that mattered was whether he was brave enough to go aloft in a force ten storm and come down alive. Three days after they met on *Chelsea*, he volunteered to climb to the main royal yard and clear a fouled block. She watched him in his blaze orange rain gear and harness head up the shrouds like a monkey, managing the ship's 30-degree rolls as if the sea were flat as glass. Her breathing quickened as he edged out to the end of the yard, cleared the tackle, and gave a thumb's up. When he dropped to the deck in front of her and gave her a huge smile, she had to fight for the customary emotional distance cultivated with all her shipmates. *I wanted him right then and there.* She kept much of her true self to herself, knowing that friendship in the foc'sle did not always carry over to life ashore. An unwelcome voice told her it would be harder with Bill Penn. The next day, they were lovers. *Leaving him was the smartest thing I've ever done.*

Molly brushed her face with a water-soaked hand, as if washing away a thought that led to unpleasant recollections. She was in a good mood, and memories of Bill were likely to ruin it. A musky fragrance encouraged her good feelings.

The perfume was too strong to be a fantasy, and she lifted her face over the rim of the tub to find Kapitan Gorov standing at the door to her bathroom, his tux tie loosed and his shirt open. He stroked his chin with his hairy hand; the resemblance to a house cat grooming itself striking to Molly. "Gore, you might've knocked first."

"I did, but you were talking to someone. I let myself in. I'm not a patient man."

"Can you still call yourself a...man...after what you've done to yourself?"

"My heart is still a man's, and other parts of me function the same way as before."

Her face flushed as she let his desire cast its spell. "Hand me my wrap, will you?"

Gore lifted a thick terrycloth robe from a hook and handed it to Molly. She stepped out of the bath, aware that she was allowing him a glimpse of her. The Mother of All had blessed her with a body that opened doors and gave her command of powerful men, and a few women. As she pulled tight the robe's belt, Gore stepped forward and wrapped his paw around her wrist. His grip was firm but not painful. She remembered that touch as if his last touch were yesterday, and it lit a fire in her. When she let go of the belt, the robe fell open. Gore's slit eyes roamed over her.

"You are the most beautiful woman in the Arctic, Mrs. Molly Bain." Gore's growl was comforting rather than frightening. "Every centimeter of you should belong to me."

"I thought you wanted to talk about old times."

"I want you to join me in my universe. The treatments are not painful, and you can't imagine the sense of power they give you."

Molly knew what she wanted, and that wasn't part of it. "I'm building a life of my own in the AFEZ, Gore. Let's be friends for now. Maybe business partners in the future."

Gore's voice took on a new hint of aggression. "I will have you."

Molly let a laugh escape as she dropped the robe. "Maybe for a little while."

Gore followed her into the bedroom and took her, like a tom. A half-hour later, he was gone.

Yes, that's what I wanted. Nordland was a client. Gore was a lover, and one of a few men—*creatures*—who could sate her. Her mind drifted as the sheen of sweat from their lovemaking evaporated. Only one other man came close to Gore, Bill Penn. He was better in some ways. Molly and Bill's passion was closer to the surface, innocent of the calculation that comes with experience. Like the moisture on her skin, however, their passion dimmed after their marriage, and it disappeared after Anne's birth. Molly touched her belly, remembering the sickness and difficulty of pregnancy, and her satisfaction when she had the stretch marks removed. She knew of other women who had given up their children. They pined for them, but not Molly. *I am mother to no child. I am mother only to myself.*

CHAPTER 13

THE SKIES OVER PORT SIMPSON opened up as the first milky morning light touched the three masts and white hull of the *Aganippe*. Donning foul weather gear, Bill wondered if the light rain might move inland and ease the forest fires in Brier Valley and the eastern slopes of the Cascade Mountains. He convinced himself Anne was safe, though he had no way to knowing and couldn't go on the net to find out. He and the other two dozen crew of *Aganippe* loaded the last boxes of food and supplies, lashed down crates of ionic nanotube batteries in the engine room, and stowed the mooring gear after the ship cast off. Bill found Micah at the arms locker, cleaning the barrel of a high-powered rifle. "Do you think we'll need that?"

"If the sea lions get nasty," Micah said casually. She had been a sniper in the Navy. Bill knew that worse animals prowled the Arctic Ocean as well, and self-defense was often the last recourse for a cornered ship. *What would I do if Kilel cornered me? Could I kill her?* He dismissed the idea as senseless.

Bill checked in with McMadden. His ship's nav AI nursed *Aganippe*'s twin props and bow thruster, and the ship crawled like a slug. If the skipper could whip the marine electrics like pack animals to spur them, he would, Bill sensed.

"God give me a bootlegged diesel that could get me somewhere before I die of boredom," the captain swore.

Bill watched the lights of the pier flicker on the river's rainy chop. "What's your rush? Not that I'm interested in hanging around."

McMadden's sneer in the cool light of the instruments made him look demonic. "This place stinks of green."

A man carrying a tablet so dirty Bill thought it had sat on the bottom of the river for several days called to him. "You there. I'm Stubbs, the mate. You're the new crewman. I need you to sign this."

Stubbs had a five-day beard, a deep tan, and a receding hairline. His face belonged to someone who had heard a thousand life stories, most of them bullshit. The tablet displayed the ship's articles, Bill's employment contract, which made him a topman, like most of the line crew. *Lowest paid, hardest working.* He used the same alias as for the hotel. *Now I know why officers always think crew are liars. We sometimes are.*

"You're on 'A' watch, along with Panang over there."

Micah gave Bill a thumbs-up, and he realized she had some say in the matter.

"I need some clothes. All I got is what I have on and my knife." Bill had left everything else back at the Henderson Hotel, belongings he'd never see again. He didn't mention the com.

Stubbs didn't bother raising an eyebrow. He'd seen it all before. "Slop chest opens when the captain says it's open. Turn to now and fast. Panang, come over here and lend the new man a hand."

The work tying down the lifeboat gave Bill a chance to learn more about the voyage. "What are we carrying, Micah? Where are we going? Judging by the amount of supplies, we're going to be at sea for a while."

Micah eyed Bill, as if judging his trustworthiness, or his intelligence. "Let me tell you something."

He matched her whisper with his own cautious voice. "Is something wrong?"

"Remember I said the captain doesn't ask too many questions? You shouldn't ask a whole lot of questions yourself."

"If you mean I should be grateful for the job, I am, but..."

"If you can't control your nosiness, call up the paperwork on the net. The basics are there, if you can believe them." Micah's grimace confirmed Bill's growing suspicions. *She knows the truth.*

"Why don't you just tell me?"

"If you haven't figured it out by now, it's too late."

Why doesn't she trust me? Something nudged at Bill's ankle. At his feet was a robot about the size and depth of a sauce pan. Its once-white casing was stained and chipped, and a section was missing over one of its brushes. It sprayed soapy water in a corner and extended a brush in dire need of new bristles.

Bill moved out of its way. "That swab-bot has seen better days."

"Pain in the ass, always underfoot." Micah nudged it impatiently with her shoe. "At least *we* don't have to scrub the deck."

Aganippe's mate returned with a grim look that Bill guessed was his standard expression. The rain had stopped, and the eastern horizon was showing the first hints of dawn. "You two, aloft to your stations and shake her out. We'll make sail as soon as we're over the bar."

Without warning, the mate flinched. The swab-bot had sprayed his ankle, like a dog marking a tree. "Damn." He kicked it, and the machine landed upside down under the rail. It righted itself, like a turtle, and it continued its never-ending cleaning routine.

A few minutes later on the foremast yard, Micah elbowed her watch mate.

"What?" Bill said, struggling with a tight lashing on the sail.

"The nav AI says we've got company. Patrol boats."

Bill's mouth went dry. "How many?" He scanned the horizon.

"Two."

"Aloft there!" McMadden yelled from the deck. "Do you see them?"

"Not yet," Micah yelled, looking back toward the Oyehut River bar. Micah and Bill hurriedly finished with the sail and dropped down to the deck beside the captain.

"Damn them. They aren't using their ID transponders." McMadden put his fists on his hips. "They have to be military, or worse."

Bill had a good idea they were worse. He had to figure out a way to hide without being too obvious.

Stubbs came over from the wheelhouse and handed binoculars to McMadden.

"God's ass, it's worse." McMadden studied the craft. "Bessies."

Stubbs put his finger to his ear. His com was a ring that hung from the lobe. "They're ordering us to heave-to, Jay. What should we do?"

"I don't suppose we can outrun them." McMadden laughed. "Bear away and clew up, for chrissakes. Let's not give the green shirts any cause for alarm."

"Helm up." Bill understood the order was intended for the AI navigator.

"All hands! Clew up tops'ls and t'gallants." That order was meant for Bill, Micah and the other topmen.

As they started climbing the ratlines, Stubbs laid a hand on Bill's forearm to stop him. He handed over a banged-up com with a ear appliance that had known far too many wearers. "It's one of the ship's spares. Don't lose it. It only works on our ship's net. Your netlink ID is 'Agatha.'"

"Works for me," Bill said as Micah laughed.

McMadden strode to the rail and studied the oncoming patrol boats, their sea-green superstructures and titanite hulls angled and fierce. The boats slowed off the *Aganippe*'s beam, their all-seeing, never-sleeping radars on constant watch, like the eyes and ears of hungry predators.

Bill's hands sweated with the fear of trapped runaway. He did not want to admit his guilt, on the chance the patrol boats were making a routine inspection stop. He also reckoned *Aganippe* was special in some way, a bad way.

Still, maybe McMadden would help him. He had nothing to lose. "Captain, I've got to tell you something."

"What the hell?" McMadden glanced sideways at Bill. Stubbs leaned in to listen.

"I think they might be coming for me."

"For you? What for?"

"I escaped BES' custody a few days ago, and I'm sure they've been tracking me."

For a second, Bill thought McMadden was going to dispute his story. "You've got a high opinion of yourself, Penn, to think BES would send two patrol boats after you." His eyes darted toward the approaching craft. One had peeled off toward the *Aganippe*.

"They'll be here in a few minutes," Micah said urgently.

"Captain, help me hide." Bill was too proud to beg, but he was damned close. "A judge told them to let me go, but they ignored him."

"I don't think you have anything to worry about, Penn." McMadden watched the lead boat through the binoculars.

Stubbs wasn't so sure. "Jay, we don't want to give them any excuses to force us to turn around. If they see him here, they might."

McMadden lowered the binoculars and gave Bill a look of appraisal. Bill didn't act like a criminal, and that wasn't the way the captain was regarding him. "Any ideas, Penn?"

"They'll be looking for com sigs. My com's dead," Bill said, trying to be helpful. He searched skyward, eyeing the rigging. "The foresail is still half furled. How about I climb into it and Micah can roll me up in it, like a carpet."

"I can't think of anything better. Panang, you and Wong"—the captain pointed at another crewman who was listening—"get Penn ready. Quickly now."

With the BES craft a half-mile away—far enough that Bill hoped they wouldn't notice the unusual activity on the yard—Micah and Wong wrapped Bill in the foresail. His head happened to come to rest near a torn seam on a patch in the sail. The break was wide enough for him to view a portion of the deck below him, though he viewed the scene at an angle. The dense, heavy canvas smelled of salt spray and mildew.

Bill heard shouts and a metallic bump on the hull as one of the BES craft came alongside. He had seen them operate before; one of the boats would let off one or two people, the other would stand off a hundred meters or so, or it might do a slow circle around the *Aganippe*, making sure nothing was happening out of sight. He caught glimpses of movement through the sail's open seam, and sometimes a face or a uniform. It was like trying to watch a vid through a straw. He heard the clop of hard-soled shoes on the teak deck.

"I'm looking for Captain McMadden." No mistake, Bill knew that voice.

"That's me." McMadden stepped forward.

"I am Inspector Kilel, Bureau of Environmental Security."

Bill licked his cracking lips. He spied McMadden through the seam, and he was shaking Kilel's hand, though he wasn't enjoying the greeting.

McMadden's tone was all-business. "This is my first mate, Stubbs. May I offer you coffee?"

"No, thank you, captain. I'll only take a few minutes of your time." Bill heard slow steps. Kilel was walking along the rail. "I assume you're aware of the carbon-smuggling ring operating in this area? Oil, in particular."

Smuggling? Bill thought it had been stamped out years ago.

"I've heard rumors about it, yes."

"To be sure, Captain, rumors are all we hear as well, but we take such things seriously. One of the rumors concerned traditional sailing ships operating on this part of the West Coast."

"We have no interest in breaking the carbon laws, Inspector."

"No one is accusing you of doing so," Kilel said crisply. "You know, Captain McMadden, I've developed an interest in ships like yours. A professional interest." Bill adjusted his head, and she came into view through the torn seam. If he weren't so afraid of her, he'd describe her as a handsome woman in her green uniform and tulip emblem. As it was, she was worse than a demon. "You don't use the modern wind ship design. I'm not a sailor, but I see natural fiber ropes, ordinary steel for the masts, steel hull, a wood deck. Why not modern materials?"

Bill realized he might be creating a long bulge in the canvas. He prayed the fabric was thick enough to hide his prone outline.

"The original owners of our line were the first to realize that wind power was again important for trans-ocean shipping after oil was banned as a fuel." McMadden sounded like a CEO instead of a ship's master. "They revived traditional designs and technology. A return to tried and true ways."

"Ah, the 'New Age of Sail' with electric motors and nav AI. Very romantic but short-lived. The new wind ships came along, correct?"

"Yes." McMadden's voice had a touch of contempt. "Big, ugly, with about as much spirit as that thing." He pointed at the swab-bot.

Bill regarded some of the newer wind ships as graceful, even lovely. The captain had to defend what he had, though.

"I take it, Captain, you're a traditionalist yourself."

"The old ways did not bring on the Warming, or the Spike."

Kilel's voice took on more of an edge. "Just so, but how do you compete?"

"Passengers, though none this trip. Training voyages for students. Small cargoes. Specialty cargoes. Cargoes no one else will carry."

"Nothing forbidden, I'm sure."

"I'll admit our customers are not always honest with us."

"How is business?"

McMadden spoke in a measured manner. "Inspector, and I mean this respectfully, I don't have much time for a chat. Do you want something?"

Bill made out the details of her stony face. "We've reviewed the manifest that you filed with the Port Simpson authorities. We'd like to conduct a spot check." She gestured toward a husky BES marine with a holstered automatic pistol on his belt.

The captain was not fazed in the slightest. "Please do, Inspector. Panang, please show the man our hold."

Micah's voice was polite and terse. "Follow me." She led the marine toward the ship's waist and the main hatch.

Kilel motioned to a second man dressed as a sailor, a thin man in glasses. He pulled a small device from a shoulder pocket and gave it to Kilel. She waved it in the captain's direction. "This can detect the presence of crude oil from a kilometer away. The aromatics, you know. Hard to get rid of, even if nothing is spilled. This will even tell me which well the oil came from. You don't mind if we sniff around, do you, Captain?"

"Please take your time."

Kilel handed the device back to the thin sailor, who wandered aft, his eyes studying the readout.

"Always a pleasure to work with a cooperative citizen." The inspector glanced at the watch and the off-watch, which had come from below. "I see that you've gathered your crew for ID checks. Is this your entire complement?"

Bill held his breath. Kilel scanned the faces of the crew members, mostly younger men and women, attracted to the challenge of the old-style sailing traders.

"Yes, ma'am." McMadden had lied again, this time for Bill's benefit.

Kilel shifted a half-step, and Bill saw her tablet. "The port records say you have twenty-six souls aboard. I count twenty-five, including you. Where is the other person?"

The captain's weather-bitten face didn't give away a thing. "One of the crew never showed up. We don't wait for stragglers."

"Are you certain, Captain? Why haven't you updated the manifest?"

"It's on my list of things to do."

Kilel was unmoved. "We ran a spectrum scan as we approached, Captain McMadden. We found twenty-six active coms. Let me ask each of your crew their netlink IDs." She went through each one. "Agatha seems to be missing."

"Stubbs!" McMadden barked, never taking his eyes off Kilel.

The mate was behind McMadden. "Aye."

"Didn't you tell me just now that Agatha was lost somewhere in the hold a couple of days ago?"

Stubbs swallowed, also putting on an act. "I looked long and hard for it, Jay, but it's nowhere to be found. Maybe it's in the bilge. The battery will die in a few days."

McMadden lifted the edge of his mouth. "There, Inspector. Mystery solved."

Kilel's irritation showed. "You seem to have an explanation for everything. Was this the man who failed to board?" Kilel showed the tablet to McMadden.

McMadden made a show of looking at it. "Could be. Some of these hard luck types, it's hard to tell one from another."

"His name is William Penn."

McMadden maintained an innocent, if impassive, face. "Does he have something to do with carbon smuggling?"

"No, not that I know of. He's wanted in a species extinction."

"Shocking," McMadden said, deadpan. "I'm sure glad he never showed his face."

Bill heard more steps on the deck, and he spied Micah's shoes. The sailor sent to the hold had returned.

"You found nothing, I take it," Kilel said.

"The hold is clean, ma'am. The cargo tags match the manifest."

"What about you?"

The sailor with glasses came into Bill's field of view. "Nothing, Inspector."

Kilel tapped the tablet with her stylus, weighing the pros and cons of something. "My compliments, Captain. I find no infractions, for now."

McMadden was silent.

"I will let you go on your way, then." The inspector handed the tablet to the marine. "Safe travels to you" —she stole a look at the sails— "and your crew."

By the sounds of the Jacob's ladder on the *Aganippe*'s bulwarks, Bill knew when Kilel and the BES men had departed. He heard the whine of an electric motor and the whoosh of water parting before a bow. A few minutes later, Bill heard Micah's whisper. "Bill, are you all right? They're gone. Almost over the horizon."

"Get me out of here."

Micah loosed the ties and set Bill free. When he was back on deck, he thanked the other crew members for not saying anything, but something was wrong. McMadden strode down the deck, pissed off. Bill extended a hand. "Captain, thanks—"

McMadden threw a right, a sucker punch, striking Bill in the neck under his left ear, knocking him down.

Taken by surprise, Bill scrambled up and lunged at McMadden, but Micah held him back. "Let me go. I don't take shit like that from anyone."

"Who the fuck are you?" McMadden demanded.

"I'm Bill Penn, that's all."

"You came within inches of getting my ship confiscated, you asshole." McMadden's ruddy face was swollen with anger. "I thought maybe you'd cut down a couple of trees or took some fish without a license, but you're a fucking species killer. I should've handed you over."

"Why the hell didn't you?" Bill felt the crew's eyes on him and McMadden, waiting for a fight.

The master took a breath, regaining his composure. He spat overboard.

"I need a full crew, even shitheads like you."

McMadden's reaction surprised Bill. The skipper risked his master's license and his business by harboring a fugitive.

When McMadden ducked into the main cabin, Bill went up to Stubbs. The first mate was staring out to sea in the direction of the BES boats. Sweat drenched his hair and his flannel shirt. His hand shook as he put a mist stick to his mouth. Bill realized Stubbs' state had nothing to do with his near brawl with the captain, or Bill's status as a fugitive. "Stubbs, are we carrying? Do we have—"

"Shut up, Penn." Stubbs tossed the spent stick over the rail. "Shut the fuck up."

At Penn's feet, the swab-bot sprayed liquid into a crevasse between the deck planks and scrubbed. A bubble, dancing with iridescence, reflected the rising sun.

THE SUN SHINED INTO MARTIN Scribb's empty begging bowl as he lingered on a slatted bench in Osoyoos, British Columbia. His saved-up food had run out on the morning of day three in the town. The yawning cavern that was his stomach filled his every waking hour like a disease. He distracted himself by thinking of his mission: Go to the Arctic Free Trade Zone and find Molly Bain. Martin had only a few weeks to accomplish his goal, though the colonel did not explain the urgency of his task.

Once he found Molly, the colonel had directed him to report her location and stay with her, nothing more. The order was simple on its face, but laden with unpredictable consequences for Martin. He planned and re-planned ways to react to her when they met. The scenarios ranged from calm indifference to rage. *How do you greet someone who sent you to hell to save her own skin?*

When Martin awoke at the first lightening of the sky on his fourth day in Osoyoos, hunger strangled his last shreds of dignity. He rose to his feet, unsteady and dirty. His hair flew off in all directions. Flecks of dried spittle stained his beard. If he hadn't known the brute reflected in the broken windows of the hamlet's abandoned storefronts, he would've thought the person had lost his sanity.

Creativity is insanity under rein, and Martin hatched an idea, hoping his non-status would generate indifference. The last holdout of the local economy, a desultory convenience store, doubled as a bus station. According to the schedule, the next coach was due in a few hours. He had noticed a working faucet behind an empty café. He removed his monk's habit and he washed his body in the filthy water, not knowing if he was exposing himself to an escaped genetically modified bug. *Maybe if I looked more like a sojourner than a survivor of the Warming Famines, I might have less trouble.*

When Martin returned to the bus stop, several people stood under the sign. He had not seen them come in or vehicles drop them off. A sleeping child was draped over a woman's shoulder. An old East Indian man sat on a portable stool, his hands resting on a cane, a day-bag at his feet. The old man and mother had open com signals.

A couple, perhaps in their thirties, showed nothing on the open net. Both had set their com sigs to maximum privacy. The woman regarded Martin with suspicion, her drawn face signaling recent grief. A plain yellow dress was draped loosely on her heavy, though powerful body. Her long, stringy, blond-ish hair needed brushing, as though she had abandoned the most basic personal habits. The dark-haired, haggard man who stood beside her in a brown t-shirt and canvas pants was an inch or two shorter than his partner, and he was just as disheveled, though more from habit than circumstance. She whispered something to him, and he cocked his head, as if listening closer to a strange sound. The bus arrived in mid-afternoon, the hottest part of the day. In contrast to the surrounding decay, the bus gleamed as if freshly washed.

"Welcome to Greydog lines," the AI said in a pleasant, ethereal female voice. "Please place your luggage into the cargo bay. Please be respectful of other people's belongings. Once you have loaded your luggage, please approach the passenger door."

The suspicious couple threw their luggage into the cargo bay and pushed their way onto the bus. The old man climbed on next. Martin helped the young mother load her bags. Because he was dissed, she did not say "Thank you." In the same way as the other passengers, she held her com near a reader by the passenger door. A red indicator light turned green. The mother and child boarded and disappeared into the vehicle. "Next, please."

Martin's heart beat hard. He lifted his foot to the first step and put his hand on a short railing. A sharp chord sounded.

The pleasant voice chimed. "I'm sorry, I'm not reading your com. Please hold it closer to the reader." The AI would not let Martin aboard without checking his identification first. He held his pouch next to the reader. The light turned yellow.

"Stand by, please." The AI's voice was amiable. "Please wait."

The cool air of the bus's A/C cascaded down the bus's steps like a waterfall onto Martin's face, drawing him closer.

"Stand by, please, or authorities will be called." The AI sounded as if it were an airline attendant asking Martin if he needed an extra pillow.

A minute or two ticked by. Someone from inside the bus dipped his head into the short passageway that led to the seating area. He turned around and said something Martin couldn't make out, but he did hear a collective groan.

"We apologize for the delay, Brother Martin." The boarding light turned green. "Please enjoy your ride aboard Greydog."

Curiosity got the better of Martin. "Thank you. May I ask the cause of the delay?" His voice sounded cancerous.

"The security status of all passengers is reviewed at boarding. Further information on your status denied."

Martin puzzled at the explanation. BES was tracking his progress somehow, likely through his com sigs. Perhaps the colonel had purchased a ticket for him. He had no way of knowing. Martin's heart sank. He would never escape the colonel's power over him.

The monk found a seat on the lower level of the articulated coach, in front of the private cabins. As he stepped into an empty row, the mother and her child exited a cabin and moved toward the rest room at the back. She squeezed past the suspicious woman, who eyed Martin with disgust. Though he was used to this sort of look from people, she was angrier than most.

The coach pulled into Yellowknife eleven hours later. After a pleasant announcement by the AI recommending restaurants and an upcoming music festival, a handful of passengers departed. Martin had slept in the coach's coolness the whole trip. He had left his begging bowl in the seat next to him, and someone gave him the remains of a sandwich, which he devoured when he woke. Martin wanted to continue north, but a security officer came aboard and stood at the end of his row. Martin understood the message and exited.

Outside, the air was colder, and he wrapped his habit around himself like a cocoon. He had no socks on his feet, and the chill was invasive. A shelter for destitutes was across the street, and it had a clothing exchange box. Martin found two socks, of different sizes and colors, stinking of fungus, but both were wool. He also found a heavy flannel shirt, too large and threadbare. He had nothing to leave in exchange.

The bus station was located near a park on the edge of a large lake. Tentative clumps of white and purple crocus decorated the otherwise dormant flower beds. The bus had reached the town in the early evening, and darkness would fall within the hour. Huddled at the base of a war memorial, Martin was comfortable in his wool habit over his flannel shirt. No one in authority bothered him.

"Don't move." The female voice came from behind the memorial, a life-size statue of a soldier. Despite her order, Martin turned his head.

"She said not to move," a man hissed, "unless you want a hole in your head."

Martin's mind raced to think who they might be. "I will give you all I have, but I have almost nothing."

"We're not interested in your money, dead man." The woman's voice sounded as if one of her vocal cords was paralyzed.

Away from the abbey, since his disidentification, Martin had spoken more words to AIs than to humans. The gifts in his begging bowl were a form of communication, of acknowledgment, but they never came with words, much less the anger, even hatred, in this woman's voice. "What do you want, ma'am?"

"I haven't decided yet, but you're coming with us."

"There's nothing to be afraid of, Mr. Martin Scribb," the man said. "She promised me she wouldn't kill you."

Martin gasped, though not because of the threat. No one, except the colonel, Father Gonzales, and the other brothers in his abbey, ever called him by his name without the appellation "Brother." He moved his eyes, snail-like, to see the threat. The woman and man were the suspicious people on the bus.

"Get up," the woman said to Martin. "Harry, lead the way back to the truck."

"Okay, Millicent."

"Our guest will walk with us like we're old friends, so we won't draw attention. Right, Mr. Scribb?"

Harry and Millicent. Do I know them? The monk drew a breath. "I don't think we've met. How do you know my name?"

Millicent growled. "We've never met, but Harry and I know you well enough." She turned to her partner. "Take his com."

"Give it to me." Harry held out his hand, wiggling his fingers. Martin gave it to him, and he gave it to Millicent, who put it in her shirt pocket. The top of the com peeked out of the pocket like the cap of a pen.

Millicent coughed. "If you try anything, you're a dead man, a double-dead man, in a manner of speaking."

"Hah, that's a good one, darling." Harry showed yellow teeth, with the left upper canine missing.

Millicent pushed Martin into a grove of trees, which shielded the trio from the eyes of the few passers-by. Martin followed the woman's instructions like an automaton, terrified she would shoot him if he did anything to displease her.

"Tie his hands," Millicent said.

Harry lifted a length of twine from his pants pocket and turned Martin to face him. "Put your hands together like you're praying." Harry wound the twine around Martin's wrists and made a loose knot. They approached a mud-covered, dented pickup truck at least twenty years old. Millicent waved her com at the driver's side door handle and the lock clicked.

"Get in, Scribb, slow and easy." Harry had already climbed in the cab. Martin sat in the center of the bench seat. Trash cluttered the floor of the cab, which reeked of rotting fruit.

"Harry, that is the damnedest knot I've ever seen. Hold this." Millicent handed the gun across Martin to the man. "Don't drop it. It might go off in Scribb's lap." Martin froze when he saw the gun. He knew nothing about personal weapons, but he recognized the lines of an automatic pistol. The safety lever was in the "off" position.

Harry said "Whoopsies!" and pretended to drop the weapon. Martin started, and he caught his breath. Harry chortled. "Sorry about that, Mr. Scribb. Millicent's always going on about my butter fingers."

Martin sat still as a stone, not wishing to offend with that gun in such close quarters. He couldn't call for help. He had no idea where they were going, and he didn't know what the couple wanted.

Millicent finished retying the knot on the twine. She started the motor, put the truck into reverse, and they bolted out of the parking spot. Martin braced for the crunch of a collision. She switched into forward and punched the accelerator. The motor whined and Martin smashed into Harry as Millicent turned hard left into the quiet street.

"Don't get too cozy with my man."

Harry giggled. "That's my wife for you. She's the jealous type."

Martin swallowed. "What do you want from me? I don't have anything to give you."

"I want you to suffer, like I suffered," Millicent said.

"What did I do to you?"

"You don't know, do you?" Millicent gave Martin a sidelong look. "You, of all people. Fuck. I ought to kill you just for your ignorance."

"Millicent, you promised." Martin couldn't tell whether Harry was sincere or sarcastic.

"Shut up, Harry. I'm driving."

The truck passed the edge of town into the surrounding countryside. The two-lane road wound into the hills, and the air in the truck's cab grew colder, despite the vehicle's heater, which was set to max. Millicent reached into a pocket on the driver's side door and removed a paper sack. She pressed her knee against the steering wheel, while she unscrewed the top of a bottle and drank.

"Oh-oh." Harry tsked. "That's not a good sign, Mr. Scribb. She drinks when some of those old memories come back."

The smell of liquor filled the cab.

"Please," Martin pleaded. "I'll do whatever you want."

"You've done enough already, Scribb." Martin smelled the cheap alcohol on Millicent's breath. "You've done enough to me and my family." She took another drink and screwed on the cap while managing to steer the truck. "You and your plans. Your plans killed my daddy."

"I'm sorry. I'm very sorry." Martin had no idea what the high-strung Millicent was talking about. He was looking for any way to keep her calm.

"You should've thought about that before your grand scheme. Did you really think you could save the world?"

She's right. I did think at one time that I could save the world. Martin remembered back to the months and years before the Spike, when he and his investors believed they could satisfy the world's energy needs and make a profit, at least until the newer technologies were advanced enough to take over from fossil fuels. The methyl hydrates were there to be taken and used. *We decided to do it, and we thought we could do it safely.*

"The Warming was bad enough." Millicent's voice slurred as she worked at keeping the truck steady. "Grandpa and Daddy got through it. Lost everything, though. The droughts killed every fruit tree they owned. They tried again, failed, and tried again. They managed, and they always had the forest property. They owned those trees. Kept the family going through the tough times."

"I always liked your dad, Millicent," Harry said. "Too bad he's gone now."

"It was the Spike that killed him," Millicent said. "The Spike caused by Mr. Scribb."

It's true, but it's not. If Molly hadn't...

Millicent took another drink, and the truck swerved across the center lane before recovering. Martin flinched at an oncoming car. Harry did not react.

"Harry, darling, do you remember when we were first going out, and I took you to our land, and we camped there for a weekend?"

"Oh yes, a fine weekend." Harry chuckled. "I don't think we left the tent."

"That grove, that meadow, the waterfall, it's all just a pile of ashes now. The Spike, it changed the weather. Didn't rain there for years. Dry as bones. The Warming made it sick, but it was surviving. Still pretty. Still peaceful. It burned to cinders. All because of him." Millicent glowered at Martin.

Harry pouted. "It's a sad thing."

Martin said nothing to defend himself. He didn't cause the fire that destroyed Millicent and Harry's forest. It was true that the Spike shifted some weather patterns. *If I could change the past, I would, but hadn't I paid the ultimate penalty: identity death?*

"When they found Mr. Scribb hiding out in the mountains and arrested him, I was ready to break into that prison in California and murder him." Millicent licked her lips from another pull on the bottle. "I had to let the law take its course, like everyone else. Somehow, the dissing didn't satisfy me."

"I remember how angry you were." Harry winked at Martin. "She gave me a black eye."

"I never thought I'd get a chance for revenge." Millicent took her eyes off the road and stared at Martin. "Then I saw you get on the bus. I'm supposed to ignore you, like you don't exist. A living death, because our society's so civilized, but there's times when you have to grab for your opportunities, and here we are."A car honked and Millicent returned to her lane. Soon she turned onto a long gravel driveway, and parked near a rundown ranch house. Several dogs barked in unison.

"Home, sweet home," Harry said.

Millicent leaned toward Martin, until he could smell the remnants of her strawberry-scented shampoo. Terror kept him from moving unless told. She stepped out of the cab and pointed the gun at him. Her breath formed a light fog when she spoke. "You, come out and stay in front of me. Follow Harry into the house."

Nothing except the porch light over a sliding glass door broke the pitch blackness. The thousands of stars and the sliver of a moon shed no illumination. The barking of dogs was strong but distant, as if they were in a kennel or fenced in on a nearby property. Harry opened the house's sliding door. Millicent pushed Martin inside and turned on a light on a ceiling fan. The secondhand, torn furniture contrasted with the tidy kitchen, as if the cook of the house wanted to maintain a semblance of dignity in one small corner of the occupants' lives.

"Stay put," Millicent said.

Martin was left stranded in the center of the room. *I could run, but where would I go?* Harry had disappeared. A clanking came from the kitchen as Millicent rummaged in a drawer. She took one of the four chairs at the kitchen table and set it down next to Martin. "Sit down." She held a long kitchen knife.

Martin whimpered.

"You'd better be afraid." Millicent cut the twine that held his hands together. Like the blood cut off from his hands, relief flowed into Martin, but the emotion was short-lived. "Put your hands behind the chair."

Martin obeyed her.

"Harry, where the hell are you?" Millicent's hoarse vowels rasped at Martin's ears.

A toilet flushed. "Taking care of business, darling." Harry returned to the living room.

Millicent pointed her knife at the gun, which was in her jeans pocket, and she thrust her hips out. "Hold this thing on him while I tie his hands again."

As Millicent bound Martin's wrists, Harry held the gun as if a sticky residue covered it. "I'm not a violent man, Mr. Scribb. Just a supportive husband."

"Give me that thing." Millicent snatched the gun away. "Get out of the way."

Harry plopped on the couch and dropped his feet on a coffee table. Millicent growled at Harry, and he shifted his feet to the carpeted floor. As she faced Martin, her breathing deepened, as if something in her was building pressure, like a balloon filled up too far. "WHAT THE FUCK WERE YOU THINKING?" Millicent pistol-whipped Martin, arcing the barrel across his face, opening a gash under his right eye. Martin felt no pain at first; his mind registered the blow with a detached interest that something bad had happened to his cheekbone. The pain rose in earnest after a second or two, then shot up like a rocket. A sound came out of his mouth, but he didn't hear it because of the pain.

"What the fuck were you thinking?" Millicent repeated the question at a lower volume, but with as much intensity. "Everyone said you were stupid to do what you did, before you did it, to try to get that methane up, burn it in power plants."

Martin couldn't defend himself, not morally, but he felt compelled to say something. "We thought we were doing the right thing. We needed—"

"SHUT UP." Millicent whipped Martin again, this time with a forehand any tennis pro would admire. The barrel caught Martin on the temple, and stars swam before his eyes.

Harry propped up his head in his open hand. "Darling, be gentle. He's a guest, you know."

Millicent ignored her husband. "Instead, it started burning, tons and tons and millions of tons on fire, like the ocean was on fire. What didn't burn evaporated. We watched it. Everyone watched it on the netlinks. Can you imagine what we felt, once we knew what was happening?"

Martin knew. He watched it himself, disbelieving that the engineers' worst-case disaster scenario, which no one believed was possible, was playing out. Almost nothing traps heat in the atmosphere like methane, and millions upon millions of tons were vented into the air.

"It was the end of my world," Millicent spat.

In her frenzy, Martin's com fell out of her pocket. The net light glowed green. It was live.

Millicent's eyes filled with tears. "We could've survived it. The family could've made it. Even after the forest burned down, thanks to you. We wanted to replant. We ordered the seedlings, but the government clamped down. Everything stopped. We had to get permitted and reviewed, and even when we did, they said no until there was further studies."

Martin's head reeled with the memories of his own terror on that day more than a decade past. *What had I done?*

"We decided to plant the seedlings anyway. Someone found out. The bessies stopped us before we even left the house. Arrested my dad, threw him in fucking jail. How could planting trees hurt the earth? The world had gone insane."

Martin shook his head, as if saying no to the reality around him. He stared at the com with its green indicator. The augmenter was still on his ear, but he needed to touch the com to activate a connection to the net and maybe send a call for help.

Millicent had not tied Martin's feet, but he had to touch the com with his skin so the DNA reader would know him as the owner. Martin wheeled his tormentor, looking for an opportunity to move. "It's not my fault. The engineers, they failed me. It was their fault."

"You're to blame. It broke Daddy—jail, the government rules, they broke him. It killed him. Everything he worked for was for nothing. It was gone. All because of your stupidity."

Martin got to his feet, pulling the chair up with him.

"Where the hell do you think you're going?" Millicent cocked the gun's hammer, and Martin heard a round go into the gun's chamber.

"Not my fault."

"The world is damn near extinct because of you." Millicent whipped Martin again. The barrel came down on his temple, but he managed to direct his fall, pointing his face at the com. He hit it with his forehead above his left brow, and he yelped in pain. Streaks of white light swirled in the back of his eyes. He succumbed to a numbed state, like the instant before a dream. Martin eyed Harry, whom he imagined for some bizarre reason was dressed in an Italian suit, and around him were the Algid Project engineers, the programmers, and Molly Bain. Panic twisted their faces and the skin between their fingers was purple with the pressure, and they argued like a flock of chickens. *Who ordered the changes... No one tested these... Molly was the last to review the subroutines... The commands came from her net ID... The government wants answers now... We'll all be dissed...*

The connection light came on in Martin's visual field, and his mind cleared. "Anyone. Anyone. I'm hurt." He sent a message in his half-conscious state. "It wasn't my fault."

"Get up off the floor." Millicent ordered. "Get up before I shoot you."

"Darling, remember your promise."

"Shut your trap, Harry."

The woman grabbed Martin by the loose folds of his habit and pulled him up. Her rage powered her like a dynamo. As she lifted Martin back into the chair, he saw his com, blood smeared over its anodized surface. To his horror, the activity light had gone dark. Either the battery had died, or he had damaged it with his skull. Blood from his forehead streamed into his left eye, and he blinked as the salty liquid stung.

Harry started laughing. "Are you winking at my wife?"

"Harry, I just can't stand that this man is alive, so soon after I buried my daddy. I just can't stand it. I buried my daddy not two days ago, and here's his murderer. What am I supposed to do?"

"It is an unusual situation, darling."

Martin was lost. His call for help had failed. He had no means to escape, nowhere to go, and he thought another blow would kill him.

"Harry, I'm afraid I'm going to have to break my promise."

"Oh, no."

The woman stepped around to Martin's right. He felt the cold barrel of the automatic on his uninjured temple. Tears caused by the stinging blood and his own misery flowed down his face.

Millicent hissed, like a monstrous reptile. "Mr. Scribb, now you'll know what a real execution is like." Maniacal rage appearing like a mask over her pained features.

Martin heard a crash. Millicent gaped, and her head evaporated.

Harry had time to scream "What—" and then his chest imploded, as if a huge, invisible weight crushed it, driving his body into the couch. He was hit again, and his body somersaulted backward, landing on a dining table.

In shock, Martin turned toward the crash. Standing in front of the remains of the glass door was a robot, black as night. He discerned its shape by the reflection of the weak light in the room. It stood on two legs, like an ostrich, and some sort of weapon was sticking out in front. The gun retracted into the egg-shaped body. The robot stepped backward through the door and turned. Martin watched it move down the steps, and in the yellow glow of the porch light, it broke into a loping run, disappearing into the evening.

Martin couldn't move. His captors' sudden deaths froze time for him. One moment he was at the end of his life, and the next, their lives were gone. He hadn't seen them before they boarded the bus in Osoyoos, talked to them before they kidnapped him in Yellowknife, known anything about them until they brought him to their home. They were dead now.

The weight of his guilt for causing so much pain in the world rose from his gut like a worm, eating him alive, and he cried out in a prayer to Heaven for mercy. *I have brought untold misery to the world, and now I have caused two innocent people to die horribly.*

The smallest voice in a corner of his mind he had learned to ignore spoke up. *No, it was not your fault.*

An hour passed before Martin calmed down enough to think. Flies collected on the gory remains of Millicent and Harry. He saw the kitchen knife on the coffee table, and he stepped around Millicent's body, going down on his knees, turning around so as to pick up the knife in his stiff fingers. He managed to turn the blade on his bindings and cut them.

His habit was spattered with blood and brains. He went into the bathroom. Purple welts rose around the cuts on his face. He opened the sink taps and threw water on his face, washing off the blood. He massaged his wrists where the twine had rasped the skin.

Martin reflected on how the robot found him. *Was the colonel watching over me?* He remembered the puzzlement in Millicent's face just before her head disappeared in a red mist. He vomited into the sink and collapsed on the floor.

Martin awoke when he heard a com ring, not his own. The sun peeked through the windows. He realized if the owner—Millicent or Harry, he don't know which—didn't answer, the caller might think something was wrong. Martin had to leave fast or face the prospect of a police call and arrest on suspicion of murder. They would never believe a story about a robot. Martin couldn't go back to Yellowknife looking like he had just committed a mass killing.

Martin took a breath and held it. He left the house through the smashed door and saw the truck. Inside, sitting on the bench seat, was his shoulder bag. He got in, and realized the truck would not start for him. The biometrics were keyed to the dead couple, and maybe others, but he didn't have the override code in case they loaned the truck to a friend.

His com was still in the house. He went back to the living room, which resembled an abattoir. He found the device, net light still off, covered in his blood. He wiped it with a cloth folded on a kitchen rack. He caught his blood-soaked, distorted reflection in the clean chrome of the range hood. He was a butcher gone berserk.

Praying for forgiveness, he found the couple's bedroom and a clothes hamper. He stole a pair of jeans and a t-shirt from Harry, who was about the same height and weight as Martin. He found socks and a pair of heavy work boots. He also took a winter coat from the mud room, stuffing his filthy habit and shoulder bag into a light backpack hanging on a peg. His begging bowl fit into one of the coat's pockets.

When he returned to the living room, he saw something that brought up the little that was left in his stomach. A round white object, with pinkish sinews hanging off of it like threads, and a thicker, whiter string leading from one end, lay in a corner. It was an eyeball, thrown aside when the robot destroyed Millicent's head. Fascinated and repulsed, Martin saw his chance. Fighting revulsion, he picked up the lifeless globe by the optic nerve, dangling it before him like a child's toy.

A com rang again. Time was slipping away. Martin paced to the truck, holding the eye in front of him like a charm against evil, and he climbed into the cab. He prayed for deliverance, and maneuvered the unseeing organ in front of the biometric camera. He pushed the truck's start button, and the dash came to life. He stifled a yelp for joy when he saw that the batteries had a full charge. *Harry must have plugged in the truck before coming into the house.*

Martin tossed the useless eye onto the crabgrass. He unplugged the truck, drove to the highway, and turned north.

CHAPTER 15

JANINE KILEL CONFIRMED THE INSTRUCTIONS to her auto's AI as it turned up the gravel road to the Penn ranch. The AI navigated the twists and turns of the road, which followed a wide, shallow stream. Cutthroat trout patrolled the eddies and pools, ready to pounce on unwary prey. The fish were free from the worry they might be fooled by a fly fisherman's sleight-of-hand with thread and feathers. BES had banned the sport as cruel.

The car found the ranch and rolled into the dirt drive. The dust and heat of the afternoon blasted Kilel, and she scanned the property: charcoal remains of the house, intact outbuildings, grass in the yard the color of electrum, two tents at a makeshift campsite, crime scene tape flapping in the distance at the boundary of the wildlife refuge. Kilel noticed an enclosure about the height of a man and the length and breadth of her car, made of rough-cut wood and chicken wire, with a wooden shed inside. The loose feathers and manure on the floor identified it as a chicken coop, but no birds scavenged for a meal inside or out. An orange outdoor extension cord snaked to an outlet on an outbuilding. The coop end of the cord ended in a lamp that gave off a thin, reddish glow.

"Can I help you?

Kilel spun around.

"Inspector Kilel. I'm sorry if I startled you." Anne Penn stood about fifteen feet away. A basset hound barked and ran up to Kilel. The inspector stiffened, and the dog sniffed around her ankles.

"My apologies." Kilel bowed. "I should've warned you I was coming." *A deliberate oversight on my part.* Kilel glanced behind Anne.

"This is my friend, Mike," Anne said.

Kilel raised her eyebrows, assessing their relationship. Without moving her attention from the young man, Kilel's gaze followed the path behind the pair. It merged with the edge of the burned wildlife refuge. "Well, Anne, I hope you've recovered from your ordeal."

"What does it look like to you, inspector?" Her tone was defiant.

Kilel shrugged. "No, I don't suppose you have. I was trying to be sympathetic. I know it's been tough."

"I don't need your sympathy. It's because of you that I've lost my dad."

Kilel expected Anne's resentment, but she wasn't sure why Mike Schmidt was with her. *The second tent. A lover? A protector?* Kilel clasped her hands her at her back. "You know that's not true, Anne. Your father broke the law. He ran. It's my job to bring him in."

"It's an unfair law." It was Mike that spoke. *He's here to support Anne, probably because he's in love with her.* They did not touch each other, or even stand very close to each other, in the way lovers do.

"Bessies like yourself are nothing but thugs." Mike's voice pitched higher, breaking like a teenager's.

Kilel was experienced enough not to rise to Mike's bait. In her earliest days at the Bureau, she might have argued with the young man, pointing out that the BES was given power by the national legislature and the UN to enforce the carbon laws and the updated species protection laws after the Spike magnified the effects of the Warming. After a few of these informal debates degenerated into shouting matches, Kilel learned to let insults such as "bessie" roll off her back.

Anne stepped closer. "Why are you here?"

"I'm investigating a crime." Kilel peered toward the refuge. "My prime suspect has escaped. I haven't found him." *I was close. I know it.* "You were the last person to see him, Anne. You know him best. Can you help me with any ideas on where he might have gone?"

"I don't understand," the young woman said, anxious for any word of her father. "I told you everything I know when you held me in Eugene."

Kilel told Anne about Yesler City and boarding the *Aganippe*. "Someone was missing from the manifest. Was that your father?"

"I've never heard of that ship. I don't know where my dad is going. I haven't heard from him since the fire."

Kilel knew Anne was telling the truth. BES intelligence showed no calls or other contacts from Bill Penn to his daughter since the refuge fire, though she had tried several times to reach him. He was either dead or off the grid. More likely a broken or lost com.

"I've gone through his records while he was a sailor, before you were born. He's been to fifty ports or more. Did he ever talk about a favorite, where he had many friends?"

Anne didn't pause to think. "No."

"Did he maintain any contacts in the shipping industry after he quit the merchant marine?"

"No one came to visit, if that's what you mean. He kept his papers up-to-date, I know that much."

"Why would he do that if he'd given up that life?"

Anne stiffened at the implicit accusation. "He was very proud of his time at sea. I guess he always thought he could go back, if he needed to."

"I think he's done exactly that. I wonder if he'll come back."

"What are you saying? Of course he'll come back. Everything he has is here." Anne turned sadly toward the black pile of ash that was once her house. "Or was."

"Sailors are fickle," Kilel said, as if instructing a child.

"When they are hounded by police for something that wasn't their fault."

Kilel ignored Anne and stepped toward the chicken coop. "Do you mind if I ask what's going on here?"

"It's just eggs," she said nervously.

"I don't see any chickens."

Mike flexed his hands.

"We lost all of them because of the fire, but they left fertile eggs. We're trying to hatch them."

"I see. Very... resilient of you." Kilel moved another step toward the coop. *She's lying. Why?* A notification displayed in Kilel's minds-eye. It told of new video feed in the area, which was not noted during the initial survey of the crime scene. "Excuse me."

Anne and Mike glanced at each other, both uneasy.

An automated signals monitor on a BES satellite sent Kilel more information via her minds-eye. A live video feed was operating on the edge of the wildlife refuge. The monitor gave a GPS location, and Kilel scanned the refuge in the direction of the coordinates. The video feed was set to update on a new priv-chan, hiding the images. Kilel ordered a scan of com company records, and the scan reported that Anne Penn had purchased the priv.

Kilel cursed under her breath; the com companies were in a constant battle with BES over encrypted private channels. Enterprises bought them to protect trade secrets and negotiations. Individuals purchased them to hide everything from illicit affairs to criminal conspiracies. BES regarded the channels as subversive and a nuisance, though they were legal, provided they weren't used for banned activities. Abuse was rampant. The channels were also expensive, and Anne Penn wouldn't have spent so much money unless she had a reason to cover up something. *She's lying about communication with her father. Why else would she buy a priv?*

Kilel fired off a question at Anne. "What's going on in the refuge?"

Anne swallowed. "What do you mean?"

Kilel struggled to keep a wave of contempt from showing on her face. She headed for the GPS coordinates of the video feed's origin. Anne and Mike followed. A dusty haze hung a inch or so off the burned ground of the refuge, still marked with small evidence flags. Kilel followed a path of beaten grass. Movement in a tree on her right caught her eye. She gaped as a male Klamath magpie with its red breast patch flew across her field of vision, screeching in alarm. "What in hell..."

"It's the male from a nesting pair," Anne said, "the pair that survived the fire, though we think there might be a second pair."

Kilel's heart leapt in gladness. This was why she did her job, to protect these helpless creatures. Not that she minded confronting scofflaws. "Do the refuge biologists know about this?"

"I don't know. I haven't seen or heard from them since the fire."

Kilel's step quickened. *The last remaining nesting pair from an endangered species. More precious than all the gold on earth.* She ignored the puffs of ash that settled on the legs of her crisp uniform. Her minds-eye kept track of her progress toward the source of the video feed until she came to the snag of a dead pine. A ladder was propped against the snag.

Kilel turned on Anne. "Is this yours? What are you doing?"

"Nothing," Anne said defensively. "I know these birds. I've watched them for years."

Kilel ignored Anne's pleading and climbed the wobbly ladder. The male magpie stooped over the BES agent as if she were a predator. As Kilel neared the nest opening, the female screeched, though she was not visible. The male swooped closer to Kilel's head, but the agent ignored the animal. Her eyes focused on a fingernail-sized camera at the top of the nest's opening. "What in the Mother's name is this?"

"It's just a video camera." Anne was frantic. "There's an egg in the nest. Mike and I wanted to watch it."

Mike piped in, "It's the only magpie eggs left from the fire. We're trying to help the family."

Kilel was livid. "Knowingly interfering with a natural process in a protected area without permission is a crime." She rarely caught environmental criminals red-handed, and finding an illegal wildlife camera so soon after a devastating fire unhinged her. She tore the camera from its mount and held it out to Anne. "This is why the earth is in so much trouble. People like you have no sensitivity for nature. You never let anything alone. You never let nature take its course. When will you stop trying to make nature into something it's not?"

"It's just a camera," Anne said, not understanding Kilel's rage. "We've done nothing wrong."

Kilel regarded the tiny device as if it were a weapon. So much death and destruction in the last centuries. If only oil was never refined and the internal combustion engine was never invented, then we wouldn't have the carbon problem and the Warming. If only Martin Scribb and Algid hadn't caused the methane spike. If only, if only, if only...

Kilel did not voice her rage. Her professionalism kept her from spitting at Anne Penn for the girl's interference with nature's order. She reached into her breast pocket and pulled out a small manila envelope imprinted with the word "Evidence." She dropped in the camera and returned the envelope to her pocket. She realized she had more leverage over Anne than before. The girl was liable for an environmental crime. She would not arrest her, for now. Perhaps the threat would loosen Anne's tongue about her father.

Kilel walked back toward the ranch house, then made a sharp turn to the campsite. She opened the flap to the nearest tent.

"Hey," Mike said. "That's my property. You have no right——"

Kilel saw a sleeping bag and a lamp. She moved on to the other tent, presumably Anne's.

Anne spoke with resolve. "I'll have to ask you to leave."

Kilel continued to rummage through Anne's tent. She had a few books, and a box with scorched items salvaged from the fire. Kilel took the box outside. "Let's see what we have here."

"How dare you!" Anne reached out to grab her things, but Kilel moved away, like a child playing keep-away.

"Get off my property right now."

"Or what? You'll call the police?"

"Anne asked you to leave. My father is a police officer." The younger Schmidt exploded in anger. The basset hound barked as if agreeing. "This is why we hate you. You don't care anything about the environment. You're nothing but a fucking bully."

Kilel carelessly tossed the box on the trampled grass. "You forget that I'm investigating an environmental crime. No, a series of environmental crimes on your property, Anne. I'm perfectly within the law." A good lawyer would challenge her search of the campsite if it ever came before a judge, but Kilel needed more information from Anne, and a judge's wrist-slap was nothing. "Anne, I've tried to be reasonable, but you haven't been very helpful."

"What are you talking about? I told you that he might go to Yesler City and find a ship. That's what he did. You said so."

"True, but it wasn't enough. I think you know more. I think you know where your father is."

Anne shook her head, disbelieving.

"And once I find your father," Kilel said, eyes blazing, "I'll deal with you."

CHAPTER 16

THE FIFTY-THREE STORIES OF THE David Maynard Medical Center towered over Colonel Raleigh Penn like a gigantic doom-predicting stele, intensifying his foul mood. The indecisive Seattle weather reversed itself from spring sun to winter rain, and the prospect of poking, prodding, sampling, and interminable waiting for a doctor—even the best one of his specialty on the planet—irritated him like a splash of raindrops down his back.

A call from Kilel irritated him further. "You found nothing?" The tires of the colonel's car squealed as the AI turned the vehicle into the medical center's underground parking garage. "The information I gave you is extremely reliable."

"We may have missed the target."

"What about the sensing equipment?" The colonel rubbed his eyes against the throbbing in his skull. "It's brand-new and cost half my equipment budget. I expect it to work."

"We analyzed the samples again and the data is inconclusive." Kilel sighed. "We didn't have enough to justify a further search."

"We've seized property and arrested people on less evidence, Inspector."

"I believe petroleum was on board, somewhere, but I can't prove it."

The auto's headlights reflected off a concrete wall. "I asked you to take on this investigation because you get results. You need to be more aggressive, Inspector."

"Sir, with respect, you asked for my help only a few weeks ago. I can't be held responsible for sources I don't know."

"*My* sources are the best." The colonel's voice was edgy.

"*My* training, sir, requires me to find evidence, then act." Kilel spoke her next words with care. "How would it look if an inspector, just assigned, acted on impulse, made an indefensible arrest, and you were blamed?"

The colonel had to grant that option was a bad one. Kilel impressed him with her fearlessness. Years ago, when he came across her name on a list of candidates for recruitment, he had noticed a methodical approach to problem-solving, coupled with a relentlessness that was awe-inspiring. She once donned an atmospheric diving suit to get a firsthand look at the ancient remnants of an oil well blowout in the Gulf of Mexico. If he convinced her to join BES, she had the potential to crack the most difficult cases of environmental crimes. She had one weakness: a temper. Janine Kilel was an angry woman.

"Kilel, I didn't realize you were a politician as well as a police officer. I'm grateful for your foresight," the colonel said. "Keep an eye on that ship."

"I have other information, Colonel." Kilel cleared her throat. "Your niece, Anne Penn, said Port Simpson was the most likely place where her father, your brother, would turn up. One of our contacts reported a man fitting his description had checked into one of the Yesler City flophouses."

"Apparently, you didn't find him, Inspector."

"The *Aganippe*'s crew manifest was not in order. He may have been on that ship."

"All the more incentive for you to keep it in your sights." *Bill may be on that ship.* "It would be interesting if he were connected to the smuggling."

Venom flecked her voice. "It would compound his crimes."

"The one is a small thing compared to refusing to obey the laws against the transportation and consumption of earth-destroying fuels."

The colonel closed the connection. He doubted his brother had anything to do with the smuggling ring; Nothing about his record suggested reckless-ness. However, Raleigh knew his brother marginally. When he had left home at eighteen to join the military, Bill was six at the time. They had never really known each other; it was differences with his parents that had driven Raleigh away. For most of his career, Raleigh kept thoughts of his brother at bay. His illness broke down these defenses, and regrets snuck up on the colonel like an unwelcome secret.

For her part, Anne intrigued, disturbed and surprised the colonel. She was a bright young woman who might have been his daughter in another life. *Are blood ties that powerful?* The decision to deposit the video file in her com account was an impulse borne on an instinctive trust of her. *Could she be an ally, even a friend?* She would accept the file as an odd gift from a distant relative, and not even BES techs would think to look there for notes and scraps of evidence embedded among the pixels of an innocuous family holo-vid. Instincts honed to needle-sharpness warned Raleigh that he was a layer or two from the center of a petroleum conspiracy that could wipe him from public memory. *They'd find a way to disidentify me, just like Martin Scribb.* The laughing images of Bill, Molly, and the infant Anne were his insurance against failure.

In the Medical Center's lobby, Colonel Penn removed his raincoat, and he attempted to ignore the ever-present pressure deep in his head, like a gagged demon. The pain was a reminder that in this building, he wasn't a powerful law enforcer who made his own rules and had the power to pluck anyone off the street if they so much as littered. Instead, Colonel Raleigh Penn was a test subject, no different than the caged rats and mice from the days of animal experimentation.

Furthermore, the colonel resented his dependence on the godlike—from the rat's perspective—Dr. Maureen Pierson, the most brilliant cancer researcher and treatment specialist of the century. She was why the colonel was in Seattle. His doctors referred him to Pierson after they had exhausted all the other treatment options for his terminal illness. The researcher's experiments offered the colonel hope of survival, but it meant handing over control of his life to a stranger in exchange for a promise of time. After months of treatment by Pierson, Colonel Penn suspected the specialist may have lost the razor-sharp scientific mind attributed to her.

In Pierson's office, the colonel sat in a plush, stained chair in front of the doctor's desk. He imagined the faint spots on the upholstery as the dried tears of those who had lost hope, or had found it. Ten minutes passed. Fifteen. Pierson walked through the door, and after a handshake, the doctor wrote a novel's worth of notes on her tablet, pushing the colonel to the edge of madness.

Pierson removed her glasses. "So, Raleigh, how are you feeling today?"

"Fine, apart from the fact that I've got a brain tumor."

"Sarcasm isn't helpful, Raleigh." Pierson returned her glasses to her nose. Her hair was gray, and she carried herself in a way that resembled Italian renaissance portraits of powerful matrons. "Your general health is good? Apart from our problem?"

"Yes, Doctor."

Pierson made a note on her tablet. "Your meds. Are the novo-opiates working for you?"

The colonel glanced at the patch on the flesh between the thumb and forefinger of his left hand. The headaches had warned him something was wrong. He never caught cold and never took a day off, but the pain was crushing, the way he imagined the depths of the Arctic Ocean would compress his body to the size of a rice grain if an enemy sub in the Three Degrees North war took out his boat. No amount of drugstore pain pills or Siskiyou sensimilla deadened it. "Yes, they're working. At least I can get up in the morning."

"I see you've reported no seizures since we saw you last."

The colonel flashed back to his first seizure. An hour before seeing someone for the headaches, he was in a routine meeting. In the middle of a sentence, his mind went blank, and he woke up in an emergency room. The ER doctors said he had suffered an atonic seizure and had fallen off his chair, hitting his head on the edge of a table.

Within days, he was diagnosed: glioblastoma multiforme, the worst kind of brain tumor. The surgeons pronounced it inoperable; too deep and spread out. The good news: he'd hardly notice it—except for the headaches—until his last weeks or days. How much time did he have left? Six months, maybe seven. Four were gone. He had told no one, apart from his doctors. "The anti-seizure meds seem to be working, too."

"Very good." Pierson touched her stylus to the tablet. "You had your last chemo treatment three months ago. No effect." Her speech slowed as she read and talked at the same time. "The DNA modification therapy is in the final stages, and again, no effect, I'm sorry to say."

"Why are we wasting time with these treatments that didn't work for me before?"

"Because our human trials protocol requires us to keep trying, in case they begin to work, even during our tests. Perhaps our nanobot and AI treatment will be the weapon that works on a weakened tumor."

The colonel acquiesced.

Pierson brightened. "I see your blood work has come in. Will you give me a minute to look it over?"

Fidgety, the colonel got up from his chair. He was drawn to the Ivy League diplomas. "Tell me, Doctor, how did you wind up here at Doc Maynard's?"

"Seattle has always been the place to go if you want to be on the cutting edge of anything in medical or intelligent tech." Pierson turned from her tablet. "This place is future-oriented. The city survived the Warming and the Spike because of that."

Seattle's two-hundred-year-old traditions of environmental awareness and activism had nurtured the colonel's world view, that the earth's biosphere was sacrosanct, and Raleigh was proud of Seattle's engineering prowess, which was known world-wide. As sea-level rose, and the Puget Sound estuary threatened to overtop the seawall, the city lifted the streets nearest saltwater ten feet. Dozens of other coastal cities around the world had followed Seattle's lead.

The colonel tapped the doctor's engineering degree. "You got your software engineering degree just a few years ago from the Delhi New School. Mid-life crisis?"

Pierson chuckled. "The Spike caused a lot of people to reassess their lives, and I needed the background for my AI work."

Pierson's mention of the Spike relaxed the colonel. The event had become a common excuse for people to share their personal experiences.

"What's your Spike story, Doctor? Where were you when you heard?"

"You mean heard about the incident?" Pierson recalled the time. "I was driving home from defending my dissertation. It was on AI applications for nanobots. I flipped to a chan with a report about a catastrophic methane release. I knew enough about the Warming to have a terrible feeling in my gut, terrible as in 'terror.' What about you?"

"I was doing some policy work on the first carbon law proposals. The teevs were on in a conference room." The colonel paused. "Usual chattering, but there was a crawl on the bottom of the screen saying something about a methane release in the Arctic Ocean. No details, but I remember my stomach turning."

"You mean, you saw the future?"

"One of other teevs was set to our special video feeds from the surveillance satellites over the Arctic. I was amazed and frightened at the same time. The ocean boiled like enormous pots of water on a stove, these huge bubbles bursting. They were miles across. Some of these, well, cauldrons—I don't know a better word—were on fire, like something out of a children's book on witches." The colonel sat down in the chair in front of Pierson's desk. "The predictions came in: more warming, almost at one time. A nightmare was coming true."

"It changed everyone's life."

"My work was no longer theoretical. The carbon laws were approved. The final drafts made my first drafts look like rules for a grade school. BES was created. The Tribunal was established. I was put in charge of the BES investigation of the incident. Special Inquiries' first job. I prosecuted the case."

"The pressure must have been enormous."

Memories flooded the colonel's consciousness. "We had to hold someone accountable. The obvious choice was Martin Scribb."

"The CEO of the Algid Project, as I recall. He was as arrogant as they come."

"That's an insult to arrogance, doctor." The colonel's smile was thin. During the probe, the colonel came to know Molly Bain, and learned of her brilliance as an AI engineer. The investigators determined that one of her software robots had gone on a digital rampage, setting off a chain of events that culminated in the disaster. It was enough evidence to disidentify her. No one had heard of her, though, and Raleigh wanted to take down a giant. He offered her freedom for Scribb's virtual head. He knew she was Bill's ex and Anne's mother, but it mattered little.

The colonel revealed nothing of these details to Pierson, instead saying, "I watched the executioners burn the brand into his forehead."

Pierson breathed in and returned to her tablet. "Well, I see that the nanobot replication rate and saturation ratios are fine. Decay rate is within expected range as well. I'd like to schedule another appointment next week to check on your progress."

"I'm running out of time, doctor. I don't have a week."

"I understand perfectly, Colonel, but it's important that we stick to the protocol. Yours is not the only life at stake. We have to think of the future patients who might benefit."

Without this treatment, I have no future. Raleigh was tempted to order Pierson to proceed with whatever next steps his protocol demanded, but he decided patience was the best strategy. *Molly Bain is my trump card, if only Scribb can find her before it's too late to play it.*

CHAPTER 17

MOLLY BAIN WAS JUBILANT. THE Committee reps voted with no dissent to award the Cyprian Association—her association—a monopoly on personal entertainment services in the Arctic Free Economic Zone. The deal was done, and it was time to celebrate. She was throwing a party in *Aurora Borealis'* parlor. A black silk, off-the-shoulder, ankle-length gown hugged her trim figure. She adjusted the colors of the holo-tattoo on the left side of her neck where the jaw line curved upward. On her bare shoulders, she touched the stopper of an aphrodisiac fragrance.

On her way to the casino, acquaintances and strangers reached out their hands in congratulations. Her eyes followed the winding teak rail of a spiral staircase, past a twisting water sculpture and through the clear overhead glass set in a gossamer, oyster-colored lattice of titanium. The ship's navigation AI spread all of *Aurora's* snow-white, square-rigged, ultra-thin canvas, as well as the three jibs above the bow, to take advantage of the easterly.

As a former tall ship sailor, Molly enjoyed the measured pitch and roll of *Aurora*. Sunlight glinted off the hull and two maintenance robots, shuttling around a spot fifty feet from Molly's position. A thin black streak led away from the clustered bots. One scurried from the other, following the streak, grasping the embedded handholds. It sat on the streak, making it disappear. *That's odd. It's not red, so it's not rust.*

Inside the gambling hall, she was enveloped by the percussion of samba drums, thick cigar smoke, clanging bells from floating one-armed bandits, perfumed air made languid by sex hormones, and the press of men and women whose aim in life was making the next deal. She stopped at each booth, touching the greeting light first so as not to interrupt a moment of intimacy.

A glance at her accounts showed the rising total of the evening's revenue, despite the discounts offered as a courtesy to her new business partners. In the AFEZ, sin was not sinful. She found her business partner Ginny, dazzling in a diamond-studded backless gown, laughing with an overstuffed Russian. Molly begged everyone to enjoy themselves before the signing ceremony planned at Pole Station tomorrow. The room of two hundred or so applauded with the enthusiasm of the rich who are about to get richer, and their gratitude and fondness for Molly was genuine. She was a businesswoman who kept a bargain.

The evening became the wee hours ship time, and Molly strolled to the observation deck. With her were Kristian Nordland, Ginny, and the Russian businessman, who introduced himself as Vladimir. The Arctic sun shone as bright as it had at noon ship time. A servbot trundled by, holding a half-dozen glasses of champagne. Molly picked up one and sipped. Her eye fell on an antique sailing ship cruising nearby, a barkentine with customized rigging, by the look of her. A number of mounted telescopes had been emplaced for spectators, and Molly aimed the lens of one of the scopes at the ship.

"Molly used to work on boats like that," Ginny said to Vladimir, who was building new container yards at Archangel.

"Twenty years ago," Molly said.

"An adventurer. That explains many things." Vladimir slurred his words.

"Can you see the name of the boat, Mol?" Ginny sipped her champagne.

"The *ship*'s name is…" Molly adjusted the focus. "*Aganippe*."

"Aga-what?"

Nordland peered through the window. "*Aganippe*. A Greek naiad who inspires poets."

"Aga-nipple." The drunken Vladimir stared rheumy-eyed at Ginny's full breasts. "*Ya vdokhnovennyy*." He grunted and tripped on the leg of a deck chair.

Molly ignored the Russian's antics. Her mind flashed to days when she was ordered aloft to loosen gaskets, letting the sails fly…

The ship held station off the port beam, heeled over a bit much, in Molly's opinion. *The wind is rising. I'd shorten sail, if I were her master. A reef would put her in perfect trim.* As if the captain read her mind, figures crawled up the shrouds to the t'gallant and topsail yards. Molly imagined hearing the orders from the deck, despite three layers of glass that separated her from the forty-degree temps outside. Setting her champagne glass on the narrow ledge of the window, she adjusted the telescope, following the foremast to the fore-tops'l yard. She made out the faces of the sailors as they reached down to reef the canvas: a bull-necked Asian, a middle-aged woman with a tanned face, and a forty-ish man with powerful forearms and broad hands who reminded her...

No, it can't be.

Molly stepped back, making an awkward twist in her stiletto heels. The telescope swung off kilter, knocking over her champagne glass. It shattered on the deck, splattering the fizzy liquid on her dress. Ginny rushed over, but Molly pushed her aside and stumbled, not from drink, but from shock.

"Molly, wait!" Ginny called, but her partner tore off her shoes for better purchase on the carpeted deck, and she trotted forward in her hitched-up gown; running was impossible. Drunken Vladimir held up her companions, and Molly struggled with the com code to unlock her cabin door. The image of Bill on the *Aganippe*'s yard floated in front of her, ghostlike.

She took refuge in the need to change clothes. She picked a fresh gown from the closet. She picked up a lipstick, then dropped it into the sink. Her hand was shaking, as if she were freezing or terrified. She willed herself to regain control, gripping the counter, taking deep breaths. She picked up the lipstick again and touched it to her lips, not daring to apply it, for fear her trembling hand would smear the cosmetic.

Knocking on the cabin door morphed into a pounding, and she heard Ginny's voice. Molly opened the door, allowing Ginny in but leaving Nordland and Vladimir in the passageway.

"What's wrong, Mol?" Ginny was alarmed and insistent. "I've never seen you like this."

"I saw him, Gin. With the telescope."

"Saw who? Was there an accident? Did somebody fall?"

"I never thought I'd see him again. I didn't want to see him again."

"Who? Who are you talking about?"

"It's Bill. I saw him."

"Bill who? Who did you see?"

"Bill Penn. He's here."

Ginny was taken aback, then spoke slowly. "Bill Penn. You mean *the* Bill? The man you told me about? The one you married?"

"Yes, he's here."

Molly sat on the edge of her bed, her hands in her lap. She didn't believe her own eyes, but she knew it was Bill on the yard, reefing the sail. Ginny pulled over a chair and took both Molly's hands in hers. "Mol, listen to me. Are you certain it's Bill?"

"Yes."

"Do you think he knows you're here?"

Molly, dazed, shook her head.

"Okay, listen. If he doesn't know you're here and the boats just sail together, there's nothing to be afraid of."

"I'm not afraid of him."

"Fine. That boat isn't going to be there very long. It will go off somewhere. Right?"

Ginny's face was framed by golden curls interwoven with iridescent silver thread. *She always has a level head in a crisis.*

"Stop worrying and come back to the party," Ginny said.

Molly didn't move. The image came back of Bill's face: older, more lined, perhaps with worry, perhaps with loss. Feelings from a life given up long ago reappeared in Molly's mental vision, irritating her, resisting her attempts to push them away.

What about Anne?

Ginny, attuned to Molly's moods after years of working together, gathered herself. "I think the night's over for you. Maybe it's best you turn in."

Molly fought back tears and nodded to her friend, whom she loved like a sister.

Ginny sighed. "I'll make your apologies to the guests. I'll tell them something, last minute details on the agreement. You're going to be one hundred percent tomorrow, right?"

"Of course."

Ginny kissed Molly on the cheek and departed the cabin. Molly sat for a long time, wondering what she was going to do.

The electric-powered longboat *Dawn* slipped from its berth below the *Aurora*'s broad fantail and took up a northerly heading. The air was clear and the sun intense. The wind had died to almost nothing, and the sea had grown quiet. The longboat's clock in the enclosed cabin read 11:44 UTC. Molly, about a dozen of her guests—including Ginny and Nordland—and an equal number of entertainers, made small talk in the *Dawn*'s cabin. *Aurora*'s AI furled the liner's entire suit of sails. A skeleton of yards and masts remained. They had gentle curves to take maximum advantage of the wind's energy when the sails were deployed.

"It's the curves that give sailing ships such feminine majesty. Do you agree, Kristian?"

Nordland followed Molly's curves with his eyes.

"Your logic is impeccable."

"So tell me, Kristian, are you making money with her?"

"Enough. Thank god for government subsidies of green power."

Aganippe kept station nearby, her sails stowed. The shock of seeing Bill had worn off, and Molly was embarrassed at her schoolgirl reaction. None of her friends said a word, and she reassured Ginny that she was concentrated on the signing ceremony.

"Ladies and gentlemen," Molly said, "we'll be arriving at Pole Station in a few minutes. Please prepare to disembark."

When the *Dawn* was secured, Molly and her guests entered an elevator, never feeling the freezing outside temperature. The huge station resembled an oil-drilling platform. It floated on six hollow pylons, each anchored by a half-dozen cables to the sea bed fourteen thousand feet below. The station's lower level was manned year around by an international team of scientists who monitored the atmosphere and the sea. Above the observation deck was a mast that soared upward a thousand feet. Hundreds of radio antennae, microwave relays, satellite dishes, radars, and anemometers studded the length of the structure. At the top, six powerful strobe lights flashed together once a second.

The appointments of the foyer, lounge and the enclosed walkway on the observation deck that encircled the station were like those of a good quality airport terminal. The lounge was filled with men and women in business wear. Gold pen sets adorned a linen-covered table on a dais. Buffet tables were set with slices of Fairbanks apples, quartered Newfoundland oranges, wild Scottish salmon, Greenland veal, and Australian beef from that continent's last working ranches along the south coast of Victoria State. Molly noticed a bronze plaque on the wall. A relief of a man's bearded face was framed by the ruff of a parka's hood.

At this location, the North Pole, on April 6, 1909, Robert Edwin Peary, USN, and four Inuits, Ootah, Seeglo, Egigingwah, and Ooqueah, became the first human beings known to reach the top of the world.

"So much has changed in a couple of hundred years," Molly said to Nordland. "What do you think he'd say about what we've done to the Arctic?"

"He's past caring."

A servbot offered Molly a tray. "Champagne, madam?" Molly took a glass as Ginny arrived.

"We're still waiting on the U.S. rep," Ginny said. "The *Dawn* has to go get her. Thirty minutes, max."

"We have a short delay, my friends," Molly called out. "There's a time-honored tradition for visitors to Pole Station you may have heard of. I'd like to invite you along. We'll be stepping out of the lounge, so it will be chilly. A servbot will hand out wraps and collect them when we return."

The machine laid the service tray on a table and pushed a wheeled cart with two dozen parkas through the crowd. About half the group, including Molly and Nordland, donned a parka.

Molly took Nordland's arm again, and beckoned people to follow. They passed through a door into another section of the corridor, open to the Arctic air, starker and Spartan compared to the lounge, with rust stains on the steel under the windows and on the doors. The pair strolled, as if on a seaside path, making a slow circumnavigation of the platform. She smiled at Nordland. "Technically, we're circumnavigating the globe."

Nordland leered. "There's another *Pole* Station tradition, Mol."

"Yes, indeed."

Nordland and Molly stopped and let the train of guests pass. Nordland tested two of the doors and found a third unlocked. It was an unused office. Molly followed Nordland inside. He closed the door and drew close to her, opening her parka and pushing it down over her shoulders. She allowed him to kiss her and pull at her knee-length skirt. She liked the executive. He was passionate, yet gentle and considerate. He had few expectations, though he was not shy about asking for what he wanted. He never rushed, and in the empty office, as he pressed her against the steel bulkhead, a fear of discovery added a thrill. The glimpse of a past life the previous day through the observation telescope was nothing more than a wisp of memory for Molly. Her focus had returned to her present and her future. Thoughts of Bill were as far away as the *Aganippe* from Pole Station.

Molly was content, and she compared her orgasm to the gentle waves that lapped against the pylons floating on the sea below. Nordland kissed the palm of her hand, and Molly adjusted her coat to return to the promenade. Her client and business partner opened the door, and he bowed as a signal for her to lead the way. She felt the cold breeze brace the skin of her face and neck and stepped through.

Bill stood before her. His shock of recognition was instant. His eyes widened, and he tried to speak. He mouthed something, but no sound came out. Molly's lips parted, the crimson lipstick framing silence. She stared at her old lover, her ex-husband, the father of her child, and she saw the added years to his hair, his face, and his careworn eyes. Her reaction was anger and annoyance, though she kept every muscle in control. She would not allow an unexpected distraction to send her off-course. *How is it possible that he could be here, now?*

Molly pushed past Bill, her hand in Nordland's. "Kristian, we need to return to the lounge for the ceremony."

"Molly?"

Bill's voice was not quite as silken as it was when he was twenty-one and fresh aboard the ship-rigged bulk-carrier *Chelsea* with his able-seaman's papers. Nordland touched Molly on her elbow, and she pressed forward, leaving Bill's question unanswered.

"Molly!"

Yes, that's Bill, all right. A question turns into a demand and a demand turns into a shackle.

The executive opened the lounge door for Molly. "Sorry to keep you waiting, ladies and gentlemen." Molly slipped off her parka and gave it to the servbot. Champagne glasses were lifted and scattered applause greeted her. All the chairs on the dais except two were filled with reps from government and private firms. The nations ringing the Arctic Ocean were ready to sign the contract: Canada, United States, Russia, Denmark, and Norway. CEOs from mining companies, timber and lumber syndicates, construction companies, fishing conglomerates, and tourism companies waited. Nordland took his seat as rep for the shipping firms. A human rights NGO was a witness the contract. Molly took her seat at the center chair. "Ladies and gentlemen, I know that many of you are on a tight schedule. I suggest we dispense with further ceremony and move forward with signatures. I will be last to sign. Agree?" Molly called for the official copies, and Ginny supervised as aides circulated the paper.

Bill and his companion entered the lounge. *That's Micah Panang. How is this happening?* The pair edged toward the bar, though Bill kept Molly in his sights. He had no idea what to make of the gathering, and something in Molly tripped, like a relay. As the last national representative initialed and signed the document, she cleared her throat.

"Ladies and gentlemen, thank you so much for participating in this historic hour. I feel the need to have a least one small ceremony. I'd like to propose a toast." She raised her glass, glancing at Bill. "To leaving the past in the past, and to making new futures."

Bill's eyes darkened as she swallowed the last of the champagne.

The lounge emptied within minutes, leaving Molly and Ginny to gather the documents. Molly urged Nordland back to his ship. Bill started for Molly, and Micah made a weak attempt to hold him back. He shrugged her off. Molly's mouth went dry, but she treated him as if he were another guest.

"Molly," he said.

"Hello, Bill. What a surprise to see you. Micah, nice to see you as well."

"Same here, Mol." Micah smirked, thoroughly enjoying the encounter. "How's tricks?"

Molly ignored the remark.

Ginny messaged Molly via her minds-eye: Do you want me to call security?

Molly glanced at the secbot stationed near the lounge door. No, Gin. Bill won't hurt me.

"I'm surprised, too." Bill scanned the now empty lounge. "What just happened here?"

Bill wore a white cable sweater that had faded to a gray-yellow with a hundred washes, jeans threadbare and frayed at the edges, though clean and well-tended in the proud way of the frugal poor, and flex-sole boots with new laces. He also wore a parka, stained by the rain from countless storms and bleached by the Arctic sun's harsher ultraviolet. The contrast to Molly's formal business wear was stark.

"A contract signing, an important one."

"I gathered that much."

"Molly Bain is President and CEO of the Cyprian Association." Ginny measured Bill, her skepticism in full view.

"'Cyprian,'" Micah said. She put a finger to her lips. "That's a fancy word for prostitute, right?"

"Our association is something like a union, Micah," Molly said.

"A union? Of whores?" Bill struggled to comprehend. "These people signed a contract with you to be a whore?"

Molly heard the judgmental tone before from many people. Bill's was nothing new. "The Arctic is a new land. We're offering a new way of thinking about a very old institution. It's good for everyone."

"I don't understand. What's happened to you?" Bill's shock was palpable, as if someone had popped a balloon. *He's discovered that I am not what he thought I was. I never was that person.*

Molly studied Bill's gray-green eyes, part of her screeching against the rising feelings of decades past, like half-seen ghosts in the heart of a twenty-two-year-old, free-spirited, intelligent woman with three circumnavigations to her credit, and she remembered how he melted her defenses with his eyes, like a secret weapon.

"You haven't changed at all, Bill," Molly said. "Older, but not different."

Bill straightened in offended annoyance. "How would you know? You haven't spoken to me or Anne in fifteen years."

What about Anne? The mention of her daughter's name opened an old wound. Her pregnancy was a mistake. After she agreed to marry Bill, ending the pregnancy seemed impossible. Her marriage to Bill was the worst decision of her life.

"Do we have to discuss this now? Let me buy you a beer on the *Aurora*. I've worked for this day as long as I can remember. Let's celebrate it and get reacquianted."

"Reacquain—we were married for three years. The beer here is just fine." Bill indicated the lounge's bar. "Luxury liners aren't my thing."

"I'm sorry, Bill, but it's time for Ginny and I to go." Molly gathered her portfolio and headed toward the elevator. Ginny followed, glancing back at Bill and Micah like a rear guard.

"What happened at Algid, Molly?" Bill called it out, like an announcement. "I want to know."

Are you sure you don't want me to call security?

He's torturing me. Molly kept this thought to herself. Instead, she texted: He's angry and hurt, Gin, that's all.

"I have a right to know. Anne has a right to know. Why didn't you come back?"

Why did I get pregnant? I didn't want children, but Bill was so kind, so gentle and caring while I expanded into an ugly whale. The birth was a relief, and Bill was instantly in love with his daughter, and I did what I could to be the doting mother, but it was not what I wanted. Bill had found a way to tie me to him as surely as a prisoner chained to the wall of a dungeon.

"You know what happened, Bill. The whole world knows what happened."

"I didn't hear what happened from you. I was your husband."

Molly returned to the bare table, cleared of decoration and the linen cloth. *I don't want to hurt him, but he needs to know.* "All right, Bill. You want the honest truth? The Spike was a disaster affecting the whole planet, but it was my chance for a fresh start. I loved you for a while, but I shouldn't have married you. You were a father to Anne in a way I could not be her mother. It was better for her that I stayed away. I had other, more interesting things to do."

Bill was slack-jawed. "You abandoned us, deliberately."

Micah pulled at Bill's arm. "I think we should go, Bill."

"Who the hell are you?" Bill's hands became fists.

"I made myself into something, Bill Penn. You're still a topman on an antique floating truck." Molly marched at a quickened pace to the elevator, Ginny trailing. The elevator closed, but Molly heard Bill's voice, screaming:

"You're a whore, a fucking whore. You fuck men for money. I hope you rot in hell."

CHAPTER 18

Bill took his trick at the helm, and he watched the strobe lights of Pole Station in *Aganippe*'s wake. The wind was lackluster, and the tedium broke down his effort to repress his anger at Molly's declarations. He directed the anger inward, and his mood reflected the flaccid sails on *Aganippe*'s masts. *I am the stupidest man who ever lived.*

Micah came into the wheelhouse with two coffees and set one down in front of Bill. "It's fresh. Sugar, no cream."

Bill glanced at the cup. The black liquid was as still as the air around the ship. He didn't touch it.

"Molly Bain was trouble from the beginning, Bill. You know that."

"I don't want to talk about it."

It was easier to stay silent while he worked out his feelings. Women didn't like this, but that's tough. Of one thing he was certain: Molly was wrong. He had changed. Living with a child on a parched piece of land in a warming planet forced a person to adapt, perhaps in subtle, unseen ways, but adapt nonetheless. He backed off a tad: One thing hadn't changed until now, Bill agreed. His image of Molly was frozen on the day fifteen years ago when she took the job on Project Algid. That image had now melted away, like the ice that once covered the earth above the Arctic Circle year round. Molly was not the woman he thought he married.

Maybe that's why Anne hates her. She sees what I refused to see.

Micah propped herself against the door post. "Look, I don't want to live with a moody sailor who has a festering sore on his psyche. It makes for a miserable passage."

Bill said nothing. He replayed the first time he saw Molly and their talks and meals together and the languid moments after lovemaking over and over in his mind, as much as he remembered two decades later. If there was any pain or twinges of doubt, they were evanescent at this stage of his life. *What did I miss? How did I screw up? I guess I shouldn't have called her a whore.*

"When you guys started seeing each other, I thought it was just another one of Molly's flings."

Micah's statement punched through his mental haze. "What do you mean by 'flings'?"

"I knew Molly before you met her. She was a thrill seeker, maybe an addict."

"I don't get it."

Micah was uncomfortable. "I'm not sure how much to say. I probably should've told you this when you met her. We had one long job together, on the tramper Poet. Molly'd dress up, go ashore, and hang out in the lounges in the luxury hotels. Don't ask me why. She met some... interesting people." Micah checked herself from adding to this observation.

"Why didn't you say anything?"

"Because I thought there's was something nice between you, and it was none of my business. I'm not an expert on relationships." Bill couldn't recall Micah with any long-term lover. "I wasn't surprised when you told me back in Port Simpson that you broke up."

Was I the only one surprised? Perhaps I was too busy with Anne or the ranch to notice.

Micah ducked out of the wheelhouse, giving Bill a mouthed "Later" when Captain McMadden charged in, chewing on an empty mist stick. He glanced at the electronic slate showing the ship's status.

"You're off course, Penn," McMadden growled.

"I haven't had steerageway my whole watch, cappy. The guy before me had none either. We can only drift, unless you want to power up the motors."

"Fuck it to hell." McMadden spat out the stick. "We used up too much of the batteries keeping station with *Aurora*. We'd never make it to Bežat."

"Where?"

"Bežat, damn you. Have you never heard of it?"

Bill shook his head. "I thought we were going to Dudinka."

"We are."

"But—"

"Shut up. You'll find out soon enough, that is, if I don't kick you off my ship sooner."

Bill thought better of challenging McMadden on the point. The captain had saved his neck once before, and Bill's presence put his ship in danger of another boarding by a BES agent.

McMadden growled again as he punched up the weather forecast. "No change for at least twenty-four hours." He scratched his red-bearded chin. "Any radar contacts, Penn?"

"No, sir. Nothing out of the ordinary."

"Any sonar contacts?"

"Sonar?"

"Are you deaf?"

Bill was surprised. "I didn't realize I was supposed to monitor the sonar set. I didn't even know we had a sonar set."

"Stubbs!" McMadden roared. "Get your ass in here."

Stubbs poked his head in the door. "What's up, skip?"

McMadden pointed at Bill. "This man says he hasn't been watching for sonar contacts."

"I, uh..."

"Never mind. You're both idiots." McMadden pounded on the console. Bill watched over his shoulder as he scrolled through a report, which listed fish schools and pods of whales.

McMadden grunted. "Nothing, but that don't mean shit."

"I don't understand," Bill said.

Stubbs searched his pockets for his box of mist. "Submarines or drone submersibles. Not that we can spot them anyway, if they have stealth capabilities."

McMadden grinned, but with no humor. "Sneak right up on you and grab you by the ass."

"Why would some naval vessel—"

"Navy?" McMadden spat. "Fuck the navy" He lowered his voice. "Ever heard of the Tiger?"

Bill mouthed "No," embarrassed at his ignorance. *Wait one. The crazy derelict in Yesler City said something about a "Tiger."*

"He, it, bosses the worst lot of thieves and murderers since the Somalis on the Horn of Africa. Worse even than the Malays in the Strait of Malacca. They make the buccaneers in the Caribbean look like pre-schoolers."

"Are you talking about pirates?"

Stubbs found a mist stick and chewed on it. "What the hell did you think he was talking about?"

"I heard rumors, but..."

"No rumor, son." McMadden's voice dropped to a whisper. "No rumor."

For the first time since boarding *Aganippe*, Bill saw fear on McMadden's face. Not even Kilel had fazed him. *Bežat. Where have I heard that name before? A legend?* The flashing strobe lights of Pole Station dipped below the horizon, leaving *Aganippe* alone on a sea that had darkened. Molly's luxury liner had long ago continued on its way. From this point on the earth, everything headed south. Bill remembered an old sailor's superstition. The damned soul of a fresh-dead sailor always flies in the direction of hell. That direction is south.

CHAPTER 19

A €20 NOTE FELL INTO Martin Scribb's bowl, and the green rim shone. It was an old note folded in quarters. It was the first gift since Martin arrived in Churchill, Manitoba. The supercapacitors in Harry and Millicent's truck had given out three kilometers from town, and the monk walked in. Looming over him was a disheveled man, a mirror image of himself, at least in terms of height, weight, and clothing. He was younger, bearded, and intense, with dark, gentle eyes. A beanie covered his head.

"Thank you and God bless you," Martin said.

"No need to thank me. I know what you're going through."

No, that's not possible. You can't know what it's like not to exist.

The visitor lowered himself to the ground, sitting cross-legged. "Mind if I sit with you?"

Wary, Martin said nothing. A breeze off Hudson Bay stirred the dust in the strip mall's gravel parking lot.

"How long have you been in town?"

A robber chatting me up first? I don't see a gun or a bulge that might be a gun. "A few hours."

"Where are you bound?"

Bound? "I'm not certain." *The colonel told me to come here and wait.*

The visitor held out his hand. "My name's Reason."

Martin considered whether to take Reason's hand. He decided the gesture was genuine. "I'm Scribb. Martin Scribb."

The breeze blew on the hair behind Reason's ears. "Are you hungry?"

Martin's stomach growled. "Yes."

"Come with me and you'll get a hot meal at my place. You'll be with friends."

Why was this stranger being so kind? On the other hand, what choices do I have? Martin studied Reason's face, and believed he saw a sincerity that eased his anxiety. "I don't know. Trusting others is difficult for a man like me." Martin pointed to his brand.

"Understandable. Perhaps this will help." Reason touched the brim of his beanie and peeled it off his scalp. On his forehead was a brand: three links of a chain. The raised welt on the man's forehead, just below the hairline, was at least as old as Martin's. He had never seen this style of brand before.

Reason sighed. "You see, I do know what you're going through."

Martin swallowed. "How? I mean, what did you..."

"What did I do to deserve disidentification?" Reason shrugged. "It's a long story. I'll tell you over supper." He stood up, brushed off his faded jeans, and returned the beanie to his head, covering the mark.

Martin didn't move.

"Well, are you hungry or not?"

Rising, Martin pocketed the €20.02 in his begging bowl, and he slung his knapsack over his shoulder. The pair followed a chip-sealed road that bordered the docks and wharves of Churchill's industrial zone. Floodlights illuminated the exteriors of the elevators, warehouses, the open holds of bulk carriers, and the decks of container ships loaded by automated vehicles. The only humans Martin saw besides Reason were at the guard shacks. Reason beckoned Martin toward a group of neglected structures clustered around a parking lot. Reason climbed a short flight of creaking steps. He knocked, and opened the door. Again, he beckoned Martin to follow.

Reason raised his hand in greeting as he entered. "I've brought a new friend." Wiping his feet on the mat on the landing, Martin offered a quiet hello to the occupants of the front room, two well-muscled men wearing coveralls, who appraised him as if he were a truck.

"Come in! " The female voice came from the kitchen. A youngish woman smiled with whitened teeth as she wiped her hands with a towel. Reason removed his beanie and coat, hanging them on a peg. Martin followed Reason's lead.

The woman extended her hand to Martin. "I'm Jill, Reason's wife. Are you hungry, Mr...."

"Scribb. Please call me Martin."

"You look hungry, Martin. I've got some spaghetti on the stove. It'll be ready in ten minutes."

Jill kissed Reason on his lips. The act mesmerized Martin, though a piece of him made note of its tentativeness, signaling tension between husband and wife, or maybe playacting. The gesture elicited an old fantasy, or rather, a memory of a fantasy. Molly Bain's sexual dominance in the Project Algid office was exceeded by her intellectual brilliance, but company males let hormones cloud their judgment. Martin never acted on his fantasy, playing the part of the good CEO, but the impossibility of its fulfillment after her betrayal made it all the more painful.

Jill waved her hand. "Wash your hands and come into the kitchen, Martin. The rest of you come too. We're going to eat in a minute."

The group squeezed around a kitchen table, and Jill soon set down a plate of steaming spaghetti with marinara sauce. He held back from diving into the meal like a ravenous dog. The two men from the front room had no such qualms; they scooped the food into their mouths as if they hadn't eaten for days. Reason's table manners were more restrained. Jill ate with the delicacy of a gourmand. She sprang up from the table. "How could I have forgotten?"

She produced five wine glasses and a bottle of red wine. She'd already pulled the cork. Martin eyed the bottle as if it were a long-lost historical artifact. He didn't recognize the label or the winery, though the wine came from Canada. The country wasn't known for its wines until the Warming had taken hold in the 40s, and the higher average temps in northern latitudes made viticulture possible. It was one of the rare benefits of the Warming and even the Spike, although older wine-producing regions had suffered, especially in France and Italy. Martin loved a good bottle of wine in his previous life.

Reason was a practiced conversationalist who drew information out of Martin without prying. The wine had loosened Martin's tongue; he skipped over much of the story of his role in the Spike, adding that he had joined the Penitents of St. Francis to atone for his sins. When asked why he had traveled to Churchill, he replied that he was on a pilgrimage as part of his penance. He noticed the glances between Jill and Reason at his answers, but Martin's alcoholic repose and the satisfaction at a filled belly weakened his emotional walls.

"I'd like to know more about you." Martin sipped from his glass. "People avoid me like the plague, but you've been so generous. Are you often this kind to non-persons?" Martin surprised himself with his impertinence. *No more wine for me.*

"I know what life is like for you, more than most people." Reason reflexively touched his brand.

"Reason's dissing was unfair and unwarranted." Jill's voice was harsh. "The punishment did not fit his... mistakes." Her face eased. "We don't like to see injustice done to anyone. We have to keep a low profile, like you. A hearty meal among friends and a warm bed for the night is the least we can do."

They're going to give me a place out of the cold. Has God answered a prayer? "Aren't you afraid the police will harass you for helping me?" Martin did not want to be the cause of any trouble.

"What more could they do to Reason?" Jill tore at a piece of bread. "Churchill is a tolerant place, as long as we keep to ourselves."

"I've been able to provide services to local businesses," Reason said.

"Services?" Martin was intrigued. *A dissed with a job. Unheard of.*

"Related primarily to personnel issues. Workers are sometimes difficult to find for certain jobs, particularly in a growing port like Churchill."

"I thought the government was encouraging unemployed people to move to areas with labor shortages." Many coastal cities had never recovered from the inundation from sea-level rise. The old cities teemed with the unemployed and their families.

"Some have moved to northern Manitoba, but there are still some jobs they won't do." Martin glanced at Jill and the two men from the front room, who had kept silent through the evening, apart from grunted acknowledgments when Jill served second helpings. "I try to fill those jobs."

Martin's heart leaped. He was depending on the colonel to fulfill his promise of a return to society, but perhaps he no longer needed his conditional benevolence. *I could make a new life for myself by working here in Churchill with Reason.* Martin reflected that the jobs Reason filled might not be the easiest or the most pleasant, given his underground life, but Martin had learned to tolerate pain and suffering. Any job was better than wandering the continent begging. "Is it possible you might find a job for me?"

Reason smiled. "Let me see what I can do. In the meantime, you're welcome to stay the night."

"I'm blessed by your generosity. Thank you so very much. May we talk in the morning about a job?"

"I like your eagerness, Martin. I'll have to speak to my contacts."

Reason's fleeting looks at Jill and the two silent guests troubled Martin, but he was too content to heed the questions that gnawed at his subconscious. He finished the last of his meal and swallowed the final drops of wine in his glass.

Jill got up from the table. "Coffee, Martin?"

"Oh, yes, please." Martin's conviction that his life was somehow taking a turn for the better grew stronger.

"Martin, I have to make a private call," Reason said. "Will you excuse me?"

"Of course." The monk reached for the final slice of bread as the other men followed Reason into the front room. Jill set a cup in front of Martin and poured the hot, dark liquid. She also set down a creamer and a bowl of sugar. Martin's mind flashed to happier days before the hydrate disaster, when he ate almost daily at fine hotels in New York West and San Francisco.

Reason returned to the kitchen. "Martin, I've put a sleeping bag in the front room for you. I have to leave for an appointment, and I won't be back until very late. Jill will be here in case you need anything."

Martin shook his host's hand. "You don't know how grateful I am for your generosity."

Martin awoke to darkness and jostling. He was no longer in the house on the Churchill waterfront. The room was small and close, and he smelled bodies and heard moaning. Feeling water sloshing against his leg, he sat up. He found his wrists bound and he lost his balance, falling against another body. "Watch yourself, asshole." The voice was unfamiliar and despairing. Martin shook his head to push out the last cobwebs of sleep, but his mouth was dry, and his stomach heaved. Nausea threatened to explode. He was in a vehicle, but it moved with an odd pattern. The movement slowed, and it swayed from side, yawing and pitching as if it were at sea. The slap of water against the walls of the room confirmed it. The boat slowed to a stop and Martin felt a nudge, as if the boat had bumped against something.

A rusted metal on metal grind pierced the silence. The noise came from overhead. Martin saw pinpoints of light within a square of blackness. A shape blocked the stars, and the muffled click of rubber on metal told Martin someone was descending a ladder or stairway. "Everyone! If you speak a single word or make any noise, you're dead." It never crossed Martin's mind to say anything; he had no idea what was happening, and darkness obscured everything. "Someone will place night-vision glasses in your hand. Put them on."

Martin heard the rustling of clothing and muffled jangles he couldn't identify. Someone took his wrist and placed an object in his hands. With his wrists bound, he had trouble orienting the glasses, but he managed to put them on. His eyes adjusted to the soft green glow. He counted six bodies on the floor with two men standing over them; Martin was the seventh captive. The two men were the silent guests at Reason's home. One of them carried an automatic rifle, and the other was handing out the glasses. Another man supervised, holding a handgun. Martin recognized him.

"Reason, what's happening?"

"Shut up or I'll put a hole in your neck." His voice was restrained but threatening.

What now, dear Lord? What have I done?

Reason pointed his gun at a woman, who flinched. "You. Get up the ladder. Quick!" The woman wobbled toward Reason, unsure of her footing in the unfamiliar room and artificially enhanced light. Reason grabbed her by her torn jacket and pushed her at the ladder. "Get up on deck, or I'll shoot you where you stand."

The woman climbed, and as she reached the opening, ghost-like hands pulled her out of the hold. The other captives followed the first one up the ladder, until one man, tall and heavy, halted next to Reason, his head down. He raised his head, peering at the sky in his goggles, and then spat in Reason's face.

The captor exploded with rage, and he pistol-whipped the captive, who sprawled on the deck, goggles flying. Reason grabbed the guard's automatic rifle and beat the defiant captive until blood poured from his nose and mouth in a black stream. The captive's blood spattered Reason's trousers with black stains.

"You." Reason pointed first at a petite woman, and then to Martin. "Take this piece of shit above."

Martin was frozen in place. Hours before, he had shared a meal with this man.

"Move, or you'll get worse."

"Our hands…" The petite woman showed her bound hands in an odd gesture of supplication, made all the weirder by the goggles resting on the bridge of her nose.

Reason growled and reached for a knife. He cut her bindings and then Martin's. "If you so much as think about running, I'll cut out your eyes."

"You take him by the shoulders," the woman said to Martin, who obeyed for lack of any other excuse to act. He was emotionally paralyzed, though his body carried out the commands of others. The unconscious rebel was slick with blood, and Martin struggled to pull him up the steep stairway. The petite woman held the victim by the knees and followed Martin. As Martin reached the opening, other hands reached down to haul up the unconscious captive. More hands took Martin aside and pushed him into the group of captives that had already climbed out. They huddled together, green and unsubstantial. He was joined by the petite woman and the beating victim, who was thrown at their feet.

A bank of low clouds had crept in, obscuring the stars. The night was moonless. The boat was tied against a narrow black object in the water that stretched away into a bank of fog. A short walkway connected the boat to the object, and

Reason ordered the captives across. Martin noticed an opening in the floor of the object.

"Get down there, through the hatch." Reason ordered. "Keep silent." A rubber-like coating muffled Martin's steps on the deck. The bound captives climbed down the ladder through the hatch. Martin and the petite woman carried the injured captive, still unconscious, down the ladder. Reason pointed to another opening. Martin removed his goggles, and the light swapped from green to red, emanating from fixtures in the ceiling and walls.

"Down." Reason poked the barrel of his gun into Martin's arm. He descended another ladder, and then a third. The air temperature rose, along with the humidity. Martin lost his orientation, but he was surrounded by pipes, valves, switches, panels, and warning labels, some of which displayed the universal symbol of a radiation hazard. The group reached a filthy room with bunks that stank of sweat and urine. Martin saw a half-dozen other people in the room, and he guessed they were also captives. With the petite woman's help, he laid the moaning rebel in a bunk.

The light switched from red to full-spectrum LED, and all the captives squinted or lifted their hands to block the brightness. "Out of the way." Reason shoved Martin aside and brandished his knife. A guard waited at the door. Reason cut the bindings of the other new arrivals.

"Reason." Martin shaded his eyes in the harsh light. "What are you doing? Why are you doing this? I thought you were going to help me find a job."

Reason smirked. "I kept my promise." He departed, and an idea came to Martin. It explained why Reason was disidentified.

Before he called out again, another person entered the room. Each captive, including Martin, stepped back, and some gaped. A creature unlike anything Martin had ever seen stood before them. He had the height and build of a man, but he was a chimera, not a man. His face and neck were covered with yellow and black hair, arranged in stripes. His hands were also furred. Narrows slits of irises surrounded by golden borders studied each captive. When his gaze landed on Martin, a shiver of terror crawled up the monk's spine.

The creature smiled, and showed the teeth of a carnivore, with tearing canines and slicing incisors. When he spoke, it came out as a low growl, but with a soft edge. "I am Kapitan Gore. Welcome to *Extinction*." He stepped forward, taking in the faces of each captive. "Listen carefully. Work hard, and you'll be treated as my loyal crew." Martin puzzled at Gore's odd accent as he continued. "Slack off, and you'll be treated worse than the damned." He turned, and at the door, he stopped. "Mutiny, and I'll kill you myself. With this." He raised his hand and showed razor-sharp claws.

"Mr. Nelson?"

A voice came from the corridor. "Aye, sir?"

"Take her down. Set your course for the Arctic Ocean."

CHAPTER 20

KILEL TOUCHED THE STYLUS TO her tablet, closing the classified report from the informant at Pole Station. Rain from a rare summer shower streaked the window of her Eugene office. The report confirmed what she had suspected: Bill Penn was aboard the *Aganippe*. Kilel had circulated an image of the suspect to all the BES agents and environmental police agencies across the Arctic. The informant spotted Penn when the ship stopped for a minor repair and he went aboard the station with another crew member to collect a part. By rights, she could send a patrol craft to arrest Penn and bring him back to Eugene for interrogation, but Kilel hesitated. He was a thread, that, if pulled, might unravel something bigger and perhaps more important than a species extinction. Carbon smuggling was rampant, especially petroleum, because it was so easy to hide. The end of a species was a devastating event for life on earth, but the Carbon Age had devastated a entire biosphere. *We have to reduce the carbon load in the atmosphere at all costs. Burning even a thimble-full of oil is suicidal.*

Still, the investigator needed information. Where was *Aganippe* going? Intelligence gave her a few ideas, but the shore of the Arctic Ocean was teeming with new settlements, some not yet mapped. Kilel had only one viable connection to Bill Penn and *Aganippe*: Anne. It was time to speak to her again.

Kilel prepared herself with a few notes. She pinged Anne, then remembered that the young woman could not afford video conferencing capability via her minds-eye. *Damned com companies. Everyone hates them.* The call would have to be voice only.

"Hello? Who's this?" Anne's voice was as clear as if they were in the same room.

"Janine Kilel."

"I have nothing to say to you."

"I've heard from your father." Kilel dressed her tone in sympathy.

"You're lying."

"He's aboard a cargo ship. He's healthy, as near as I can tell."

"Why should I believe you?"

I can hear her wanting it to be true. "You'd know it if I was lying. I keep telling you we have a common interest in seeing him home with you."

An indicator in Kilel's minds-eye told her Anne had muted the audio. "Anne?"

A few seconds later, the audio un-muted. "Well, thank you for letting me know. Goodbye."

Kilel added a note of command. "Don't hang up."

"I don't know anything more. What more do you want?"

The audio was muted again. *Someone's with her. Mike Schmidt?* Kilel gambled. "Mike is welcome to listen in if you want, Anne." Kilel's minds-eye showed Mike's avatar conferencing in. *Maybe I can play him against her.* "Welcome, Mr. Schmidt."

"Inspector." Schmidt's tone was confident, if wary. *If she and Anne aren't a couple, I'm a dog catcher.*

The inspector turned up the pressure. "Anne, your father's in the Arctic on a ship called *Aganippe*. Its last known course was toward any of several Russian ports. Where would he go in Russia?"

"I have no idea."

Kilel decided another shock to Anne might jog the truth out of her. "Your father may be involved in carbon smuggling, specifically crude oil, aboard *Aganippe*. Do you know anything about that?"

Anne sounded distressed. "No, that can't be true. You're making that up. He wouldn't break the law. He's a good man."

"I beg to differ. He's destroyed an entire species. A man like that is capable of smuggling illegal fuels and precursors."

Mike spoke up. "You can't just go around accusing people—"

"I believe Mr. Penn's ship is carrying illegal oil to a port in Russia. I want to know which one. Do you want to be an accessory to carbon racketeers, Mike?"

"How... No, of course not, but—"

Anne cried, "I don't believe it. It's not possible. He would never—"

"He is, and I will find him, and he will be punished." Frustrated by Anne's intransigence, Kilel paused to reign in her fury. A thought occurred to her. She called up an image in her minds-eye.

"Inspector? It's Anne. Are you there?"

Kilel studied the holo-pic. The image was familiar, but it was faded and grainy. "Who is this?"

"I'm sorry, I can't see—"

Dammit! "I'm sending you an image file. I'll put it in your public folder. Take a look at it."

Kilel transferred the file, and she saw the indication that Anne opened it.

Anne cooled down. "My mother. Colonel Penn asked about her. Remember?"

Kilel absently tapped the tablet stylus on her desk. She had no interest in the conversation between the colonel and Anne in the detention center, imagining it to be unimportant family business, and she'd left Anne's holding cell to let them talk. *That was a mistake. The woman in the image may be the key to finding Bill Penn, and I've seen her before.* "What's her name?"

"Molly. She and my dad divorced when I was little."

Kilel heard pain in Anne's voice, but Molly elicited something... "What was her name?"

"Molly Penn." Anne said the name as if Kilel were dense as stone.

"No, her maiden name."

"Bain."

The answer hit Kilel like a punch. She called up the BES database in her minds-eye, and the answer came back almost before she finished composing the query. The photo in the database wasn't the same as the holo-pic, but it was an image of the same person taken a few years later at the trial. "Your mother is Molly Bain."

"That's what I said. What are you getting at?"

"Molly Bain is an environmental criminal. She was convicted of crimes related to the Spike. She escaped disidentification by turning state's evidence against Martin Scribb."

"You're wrong!"

Again, Kilel felt she had Anne where she wanted her. She drilled the next words home. "Molly Bain, formerly Mrs. William Penn, with one child, Anne Penn, was an AI researcher who programmed the drilling robots that failed on all the Algid Project methyl hydrate sites, causing a massive release of methane. The release started a cascading failure of the entire methyl hydrate bed in the Barents Sea, releasing millions of metric tons into the atmosphere, doubling its capacity to retain atmospheric heat for a decade. Your mother killed twenty percent of the wild species on the planet. Your mother caused the worst mass extinction in sixty-five million years."

"Stop it," Mike interrupted. "You have no right to talk to Anne like that."

The inspector shook with anger. A primal part of her wanted to arrest Anne merely for the traits of Molly Bain in the young woman. She wanted to visit punishment on Anne for the sins of the mother for her environmental genocide.

"Anne was a baby." Mike picked the tone Kilel guessed his father used at a traffic stop. "She had nothing to do with the Spike or what her mother did."

To keep from laughing with contempt, Kilel breathed in and closed her eyes. "You're correct, Mr. Schmidt. Anne had nothing to do with the Spike or her mother's crimes. Unlike her father, she's not responsible for the fire that wiped out a species. She is, however, her mother's daughter, and her father's daughter." Kilel recalled the snag with the magpie nest. "That much is clear."

Anne voice dripped contempt. *Why hide it from me?* "I'm going to close the connection, Inspector." Now her voice quivered. "I love my father. I'll never help you again. You and your kind can go to hell."

"Is it true?" Anne sat next to Mike on a bench her father had made from scrap wood. The confrontation with Kilel had exhausted her, and she rested her head on his powerful shoulder. "Is it true my mother caused the Spike?"

Mike was uncomfortable, but Anne did not want to move. "I was in pre-school when the Spike hit. All I remember is that my parents were worried. I'm sure Kilel was just trying to scare you so you would tell her where your dad is."

"I'm afraid. Maybe I said something I shouldn't have."

"You're afraid? It's a good thing it was a audio call. If Kilel were here, you would've slugged her." Mike rested his forearms on his knees. Light from a camping lamp illuminated his face. "Don't listen to her. She's a bully, and it's the bullies who are afraid."

Anne's constant anxiety since her father's escape broke into panic. She'd never been so fearful for Bill's safety or her own. The longer he was gone, the more she worried he'd never come back. Would he be like her mother? *If Mike weren't here...* "I don't know where Dad is. I don't have any idea. Kilel knows more than me."

"Try to relax, Anne." Mike held out his hand. In his palm was another camera. "The stores always sell these in packs."

Encouraged, Anne managed a thin smile.

"Come on."

Mike led the way to the snag. His strong shoulders tapered to a sturdy waist she hadn't noticed before. Since their lunch in town, he had visited her at the ranch every day, bringing supplies and news. He had volunteered to stand watch with her over the magpie eggs. On the path, she stopped, aware of something unconscious and intangible, until Mike halted.

"Something wrong?" he said.

"No." Anne reached out her hand to Mike, not really sure what she wanted. He took the fingers of her hand, intertwining his, and pulled ever so gently, returning to the path. The angle of his arm was awkward, and after a few steps he let go, an act that caused Anne a different kind of pain, and she almost reached for his hand again to soothe it away.

They reached the snag, and Mike climbed the ladder. He reinstalled the camera, and the video feed returned to their priv-chan. Back at camp, Anne lit the stove, and they ate a supper of baked beans, bread that Mike had brought from the Feed and Seed, and a surviving jar of Anne's blackberry preserves from the previous season.

Anne watched Mike pump fresh water for Maxie. "There's something else, something that happened in Eugene that I don't think Kilel knows about."

"While you were in detention?"

The dog slurped his water.

"Remember I told you that an old BES guy there said he was my uncle? He gave me a video."

"What kind of video?"

"I'll share it with you." Anne sent the commands to her minds-eye to share the holo-vid in Mike's public folder, but "permission denied" errors popped up. "That's weird. It won't let me share it out."

"Have you looked at it?"

"It's from a few days after I was born. It has Dad, me, and my mother in it."

"Maybe he wants you to keep the video private."

"It's so odd." Anne stuck her hands in her jeans pockets. "Why would he give me a video he doesn't want me to share? He doesn't know me."

Mike looked puzzled as well. "You're family."

"Barely. It's crazy. I can't get it out of my head that he's my uncle, my dad's brother. How can one word like 'uncle' stir me up so much?"

"He's probably got more than one reason for giving you that file." Mike wiped a plate with a dish towel. "Cops playact to get what they want, usually information."

The thought disappointed Anne. "You think it's a trick?"

"Bessies are all the same."

As darkness fell, Anne rearranged the items she had salvaged from the fire. The holo-vid from Colonel Penn seemed salvaged as well. Anne played it two or three times, and it had missing frames and a few glitches, like it had been corrupted and recovered.

Mike poked his head into her tent. "Who has the first shift with the eggs tonight?" They had come up with a way to keep vigil on the magpie eggs for as many hours of the day as possible.

"I can take it," Anne said.

"I figured you'd say that." Mike grinned. "It'll go fast."

Anne cocked her head, perplexed. "Why?"

Mike beckoned. Anne followed him to the coop, and he opened the back door to the nesting box where the eggs waited, bathed in light the color of ripe crabapples. Anne peered in. One of the eggshells had a wide crack, and Anne heard a tiny peep.

CHAPTER 21

COLONEL PENN DISLIKED THE FROWN on Dr. Pierson's face. The screen she studied showed a video feed generated by the robot control interface, aka the controller, placed in the colonels' right forearm. It resembled a smaller version of an arm guard for an archer, but placed closer to the elbow. A green lamp, no bigger than a pinhead, glowed near the corner of the controller nearest the colonel's thumb. The controller communicated via an induction mechanism with the millions of nanobots that coursed through the colonel's bloodstream.

Pierson's feminine scent contrasted with the lab's whiff of solder and burnt flux. Days had passed since the colonel last spoke to the researcher, and Raleigh felt as if his life was as ephemeral as the doctor's perfume. A large, blood-engorged blob filled the screen. "My tumor can't have grown that much, doctor. That doesn't look right."

Pierson breathed out—*Disappointment?*—as she manipulated the image of a disorganized jumble of tissue and blood vessels in the colonel's brain. The colonel saw pulsing clumps of cells and, as the magnification and image contrast increased, individual neurons, some pale but alive, others on the verge of death, their dendrites and axons withered like the fingers of an arthritic hand. Other cells, as misshapen as goblins, were the mutated cancer cells. The colonel noticed dark dots, some tiny as pinheads, some splotchy and irregular. *My saviors, Mother willing.* Magnified further, the objects swam in the intercellular fluid like animal plankton. The pinheads were individual nanobots.

"The clumps!" The colonel pointed at the hologram, excited as a child. "The robots are swarming on the cancer cells, working together, just like you programmed them."

Again, Pierson did not respond, instead focusing her intense concentration on one group of robots attacking a cancer cell. The monster squirmed in its death throes, then disintegrated, the mitochondria, ribosomes, and diseased nucleus spilling through a huge tear in the cell membrane. The nanobots, as if exulting in victory, scattered in search of another cell to attack and destroy. The colonel watched until his eyes hurt, and Pierson's unexpected reticence alarmed him. The gloom intensified with the thickening rain and clouds as late morning turned to early afternoon.

"I have some preliminary results." Pierson was downcast. She folded her hands. "I'm sorry, Colonel, but the experiment is producing mixed results at best."

The colonel pursed his lips.

"The glioblastoma is growing slower than before, but it has not stopped growing."

Relief filled the colonel's mind, though his intellect reminded him that the reprieve was temporary. "That means we have gained some time."

"True, but how much is hard to say. It could be a day, a month, or a year."

"The robots are working. They are killing the cancer cells. I saw it happening."

"Yes, they are, but very inefficiently. The attack you saw was unusual. The logs we downloaded from your controller show fewer successful attacks than we anticipated, and there were far more unassigned robots than we hoped." The colonel recalled the drifting robots, aimless with no instructions. "They might even behave in your body in ways we're not sure about. The logs are unclear on that score."

"You mean they're attacking healthy cells?"

"There's no direct evidence of that." The doctor turned away.

The colonel's face grew flush. He had endured enough, but he stopped himself from lashing out at Pierson.

"We haven't solved a problem that has troubled us from the beginning," the doctor said, frustration in her voice, as if she wanted to shake her fist at an un-cooperative medical gremlin. "We know how to tell the robots to find and kill specific types of cancer cells. That's what we've done with your glioblastoma."

"It's not working." The colonel sighed.

"Coordinating millions of robots is far more complex than we thought at first. Managing their self-replication and disposing of expired robots adds to the trouble. We've written software—" she glanced at the colonel's implant—"that can anticipate and act on all the variables, including ones we can't even imagine. We're convinced our theory and design is sound, but there's something wrong with the programming, something we can't find."

"You mean there's a bug?"

"You could call it that. It's a problem with one of the AI algorithms. I've sat up for days with the programmers in the lab looking for it, testing patches and rewrites, but as soon as we think it's fixed, the problem pops up again."

"What are you going to do now?"

"Keep trying to find the problem." Pierson looked as if she had been beaten at a game of cards. "Once we find it, we can update the software in your con-troller, and give the robots new instructions."

"Maybe you need to call in some other expert, someone who can look at the problem with fresh eyes." *Someone who knows what they're doing.*

Pierson blinked behind her glasses. "No one is doing this kind of work. We're on the bleeding edge, as someone once said."

The colonel pressed Pierson. "Even if you find this bug and fix it, there's no guarantee it will even get the results we want, correct?" The colonel wondered if Pierson thought of his case as a chance to cure a terminal disease, or just an experiment that may or may not succeed. The colonel was too exhausted to raise the question, but he did not believe Pierson had all the answers. "I know someone who could fix your bug in the blink of an eye, if I could find her."

"Who could that be? There's no one else with our expertise."

"Her name is Molly Bain."

Pierson grew indignant. "Colonel, her reputation... We're all working as hard as we can. We're perfectly capable—"

The colonel brushed off Pierson's objections. "I don't even know if she's alive or dead. If I find out, I'll let you know."

As he donned his raincoat and departed the Maynard Center, the colonel gambled more chips on Martin Scribb. Protecting him from interference was proving to cost more than he expected, though the lives of the couple that kidnapped Scribb in British Columbia were a trivial price to pay. *If I'm not willing to make such decisions, I'm a dead man, in the old sense of the phrase.*

CHAPTER 22

Martin Scribb awoke to a low thrumming that wiggled the drops of condensation collecting on the steel slats above his head. The drops' rhythm meant *Extinction* was still prowling the depths of the Arctic Ocean. He closed his eyes in anticipation of the next sound—*CLANG CLANG CLANG*. He imagined blood leaking from his injured eardrums as Reason pounded the metal in a deafening reveille.

"Get up, you ass-fucking dogs. Get up now, or I'll stuff you into a torpedo tube along with all the other human waste."

His tormentor dished out threats as if they were the greasy slops fed to *Extinction*'s damned, but Martin was slow out of his bunk.

"Move, asswipe. You're the goddamned slowest of the whole stinking lot." Reason poked Martin hard with a steel pipe, raising a welt. The monk yelped in pain. "Shut up!" Reason barked, "or you'll be the first in the tube." He exhaled in Martin's face. His breath stank of stale beer and spent mist. "Do you know what happens to a human body at this depth?"

"You've told me a dozen times." Despite the daily humiliation, Martin feared Reason and the other bosses less and less as the days passed. *Extinction* needed Martin and the other cursed men and women who lived above the bilge.

"You're crushed like a bug until there's nothing left but a grease slick, spreading out until you disappear into nothingness." Reason snarled. "Would you like that?"

Martin understood nothingness. Out in the normal world, he lived in a kind of social hell, a paradox of existence without substance. At least the tortured souls in the popular conception of hell had demons to keep them company. Each poke and prod with a firebrand was an acknowledgment that the soul existed and deserved attention, however unwelcome. The disidentified's hell consisted of unending indifference by others, except when they felt threatened. *Extinction* was closer to a purgatory than a hell. People, even if they were psychotic like Reason, spoke to Martin as if he were human.

Martin swung his legs to the deck and slipped on his flops. He occupied the lowest bunk in a tier of five. The other three dozen or so anathematized in the compartment climbed out of their bunks, as the bosses continued poking and prodding everyone. Reason and his colleagues drew blood most days with their clubs, but beatings were rare, and serious injuries few. One of the damned had died since Martin had been shanghaied, but the poor devil was sick to begin with. The bosses preferred not to kill, because the dissed and other unfortunates were difficult to replace. Still, fear was as rampant among the crew as the lice that infested their bodies and the open sores that dotted their exposed skin.

The damned—the word they used to describe themselves—filed through a hatchway past another compartment where each bunk was filled by a snoring wretch, exhausted by eighteen hours at his or her station. Martin's group lived in the lowest tier of the crew quarters, which was also home to most of *Extinction*'s population of non-human vermin. Colonies of rats scurried on the deck, disappearing when the bosses showed up for a security check, or to drive the crew to their stations.

Underlying every human or vermin-caused smell was the stink of petroleum. A microscopic film of crude oil covered everything, and a rainbow of micro-slicks floated on the puddles of condensation that collected on the deck plates. Martin conjured in his mind the droplets of oil that made the air thick and heavy, and he imagined it coating the alveoli of his lungs. *It's a matter of time before my lungs become reservoirs for the molecules that were once dinosaur bones.*

Reason herded Martin's group into the crew mess. Benches lined each side of an aluminum table covered with stains of all colors and crawling with cockroaches. The shit-colored insects ran up to each bowl of cornmeal mush like puppies eager for scraps. New crew refused to eat the gruel. Hunger forced them to dip their unwashed spoons into their food, which varied in consistency from watery chunks covered with an oily sheen to thin papier-mâché. Experienced crew valued the submariner insects as protein, and they swallowed the unlucky bugs who slipped into the gruel and drowned. Some were eaten before their legs stopped wriggling.

Martin savored his meals, remembering the days in the hot sun of the eastern reaches of Pacific West when a drink of water was all he expected for days on end. He relished chewing on a piece of gristle or a sliver of carrot. Moldy crusts of bread were thrown on the table. The damned devoured them in seconds. The scraps came from the bosses' mess, or the captain's cabin. As Martin sized up his shipmates, he noted that none were starving, though none were thriving. The cook—an unseen psychopath—was adding nutritional supplements to the gruel, maybe antibiotics as well. Ranchers once did such things to cattle and sheep. Why not do the same thing to the damned?

Martin had made the acquaintance of a bunkmate who went by the name "Osco." He also had a brand on his forehead. They whispered to each other at meals to avoid the bosses' wrath. Martin always started the conversations.

"How long?"

"How long for what?" Osco picked at a roach carapace between his teeth.

"That." Martin pointed at the brand.

"Seven years." Osco slurped at his spoon, a drip of sweat falling into the bowl.

"For what?"

Osco scratched the gray stubble on his head. Enough dirt was packed under his fingernails to grow a small vegetable garden. "Does it matter?"

"Just making conversation."

"You're a strange one, Scribb." Osco stared at Martin with black eyes. "You're talkative for a dissed man. You could lose your tongue for talking too much."

Martin swallowed a bite of gruel.

"I killed thirty-eight people," Osco said. "One by one, with a knife. A serrated knife."

Martin and three or four others paused their eating. "Impressive," said a young man with a missing ear.

"I ate them," Osco added.

"A gourmand, eh?" The man with the missing ear wiped his bowl with a finger to capture the last lumps.

Martin forced back a gag. Others chuckled, careful not to draw attention.

Osco pointed his spoon at Martin. "What about you?" He already knew the answer; Martin had told him.

"I killed millions."

"What's that you say?" Osco enjoyed teasing Martin.

Martin cleared his throat. "I killed millions upon millions." *That's what the tribunal said, though it's not true. It was Molly that killed them. I found the emails and the minds-eye logs, but she struck a deal with Raleigh Penn. Me for prison. For once the powerful leader, the money man, instead of the cubicle drone, would go down. It was a lie. Blood, even the blood of in-laws, is always thicker than water.*

"Did you eat all them millions?" Missing Ear grinned. His skin boiled with oil folliculitis. Pus dripped from one of the pimples.

Osco smirked. "No, but they cooked. Every one. In the Spike. Right, Martin Scribb?"

A boss ordered silence. Each crewman and woman at the table scrutinized Martin with equal measures of hate, disgust, and indifference. He was a celebrity, of a kind, on the boat. Martin did not feel threatened by his fame. That was the paradox of *Extinction*. They were already dead; no one wasted the energy to kill for revenge.

Martin had another motive behind his garrulousness. He still hoped to find Molly Bain in Bežat, though he had no idea where it was, or even if it existed, despite the colonel's assurances. Bežat was in or near the Arctic Free Economic Zone, and Kapitan Gore's order to set course for the Arctic Ocean was evidence that Bežat was at least nearby. Ever since the incident with the couple in Alberta, Martin believed the colonel was watching over him, perhaps even getting him the berth on *Extinction*. Martin was confident that he was heading in the right direction, though he never expected to conduct a search from the lower deck of a corsair submarine. He decided the risk of revealing something more than his background as a mass murderer would help his cause. "I'm looking for someone. Her name is Molly Bain."

Osco and the others ignored Martin.

"There might be a reward if I can find her." Martin had no idea if the colonel would honor a promise to pay a reward.

"Never heard of her," Osco said. "Who is she?"

Who is she? The most beautiful, most intelligent, sexiest woman I've ever known. She was my Athena, and it's because of her that I'm here. Martin shrugged. "A friend of a friend. I promised I'd find her if I could."

"If you need a girlfriend, I'm available." A young woman with matted hair gazed at him with mocking eyes.

Martin was repulsed. "No, I'm not looking for Molly Bain in that way."

"Smart." Osco winked at Martin. "That's Lizzie Castrata. She's trouble."

"Castrata?"

"Her real name. Killed ten married men. She cut off their dicks and sent them to their wives in a box marked 'special delivery.'"

"They weren't very nice to me, so I had to punish them." Lizzie Castrata laughed. So did Osco, who choked when Reason shoved a club into his ribs.

"Enough. Meal's over. Get to work."

One at a time, the damned filed out of the mess into the engine room. The thrumming that welcomed Martin on his waking came from the steam turbines driving shafts that spun twin propellers at the stern of *Extinction*. A nuclear power plant, ancient but serviceable, generated the steam that drove the turbines. Martin was happy when he heard the bosun assign him to the engine room; he had studied nuclear power engineering in college, and he had visited a plant before the post-Spike environmental protection frenzy restricted nuclear energy to the military. The loss of year-round ice in the Arctic brought a hundred years of tension to a head, resulting in the Three Degrees North War, a brief but violent naval conflict which ended in a stalemate and the creation of the Arctic Free Economic Zone. Submarines and submersibles fought much of the war, and a number of subs were never accounted for and presumed lost with all their crews in the Arctic Ocean's depths.

Martin discovered on his first day aboard, however, that one of the boats had reappeared. All the markings, from numbers on the bunks to labels on the miles of pipes, were in Cyrillic script, though the crew supplanted some of the labels with English. In the engine room he found a faded but readable plaque on a generator. He knew enough Russian to make out the boat's name: *Yuri Dolgorukiy.*

"You keep an eye on these pressure gauges. If they get to this mark," an engineer in clean overalls pointed to a daub of paint on the gauge, "let me know."

"What happens if I don't notice?"

"You're scalded to death when the steam pressure breaks the seal." The engineer stuck his stylus in the air, indicating a joint in the overhead pipe. "And this old Russian self-propelled coffin takes us and her ghosts to the bottom."

"Ghosts?"

The engineer scratched on his tablet. "Five hundred of them. All Russian sailors. All suffocated to death. All except her captain."

CHAPTER 23

BILL DELIBERATED HIS OPTIONS ALONE on the maintop cross-trees, thirty meters above *Aganippe*'s deck. An ancient satellite phone lay in his hands, like a drug he dare not take. Micah's warning rang in his ears: Bessies, corsairs, or other unruly elements might hear and hone in. Micah's warning came in a whisper during a hurried discussion about *Aganippe*'s true cargo, whether a topman's job was worth the risk, and whether they should jump ship. *I'm already accused of one environmental crime. I don't want to be part of another.*

Bill heeded Micah's warning for a day, but separation from Anne drove him toward taking dangerous chances. He and Anne had spend time apart in the past, but never at such distance and difficulty of a check-in. Bill doted on his daughter, he admitted, but how many fathers are on the run from the BES, and how many children are witnesses to an unfair accusation of environmental crimes? Bill had to know that Anne was okay.

McMadden gave Bill permission to climb to the cross-trees below the main t'gallant yard. Bill enjoyed the solitude on the tiny platform. It offered a moment of tranquility in a tense ship. McMadden may be a cranky, profane man, Bill thought, but he was a crack seaman. The ship glided so smoothly over Arctic Ocean that Bill felt as if he floated in mid-air.

The captain didn't know he had the phone. Bill found it by accident when he was sent for batteries in the electronics locker. He noticed the phone's data encryption and electronic masking capabilities. *Maybe I could speak with Anne for a minute or two before anyone realizes what's going on.*

Bill looked down to the deck. Stubbs leaned on the rail and flicked a spent mist stick into the sea. He did not look up.

His hand trembling, Bill linked into the global com system and dialed Anne.

Loop failed. Setup may have failed. Tampering with factory settings may void the manufacturer's warranty—

Bill cleared the screen. *I shouldn't be doing this.* He dialed again.

Loop failed. Setup may have—

Stopping himself from cursing, in case it drew Stubbs' attention, Bill rebooted the phone. He ran the setup routine, hoping—

Initialized. Satellite located. Number to call?

He dialed a third time. Excitement drowned out his unease. A series of clicks indicated a search.

"C'mon. C'mon," Bill whispered to himself.

"Hello?"

The voice was a young woman's, but the signal had traveled so many tens of thousands of miles that it was barely understandable. "Anne, is that you?" *It could only be her. I dialed her unique identifier.*

"Who... Dad?"

"Anne, it's your father."

"Dad? Is that you? Where—"

The signal strength dropped away, and Bill feared he'd lost her. "Anne!" He cupped his hand over the mouthpiece, while keeping one eye on Stubbs, who sipped a cup of coffee. "Anne, it's your dad."

"Where are you? I can barely hear you. Are you coming home?"

How much I want to say Yes! Bill reflected, however, on the course of *Aganippe*, away from his daughter and his life.

The elapsed time on the call was already fifty-three seconds. *Is someone listening?*

"Listen to me, Anne. I only have time to see if you're okay."

"Tell me where you are, Daddy. It's so good to hear your voice."

"You sound good to me too. Are you home?"

"Daddy... Da..." The poor signal fragmented Anne's words. "I can only hear a little of what you're saying. Are you on a ship?"

The question startled Bill. *Should I tell a lie, in case Kilel is there?* "Are you alone?"

"Mike Schmidt is here. He's helping me with——." The signal dropped away.

Mike Schmidt, the cop's kid? Is he spying on her? Bill shook his head, disbelieving his own conclusion.

"Dad, I have to tell you something. Inspector Kilel detained me. I had to tell her that you might have gone to Port Simpson, that you might find work there."

Anne's report set Bill's blood to boil. *Kilel will do anything to track me down, including preying on Anne.* His anger was tainted by guilt for having put Anne in Kilel's sights.

"I'm sorry, Dad."

Bill thought he heard crying. *Or is it just static?* "No, sweetheart. You did nothing wrong. Bessies are stupid and thoughtless."

The elapsed time on the call was one minute, forty-eight seconds.

"Anne, I have to go. I can't talk any longer."

"No, don't go." Anne pleaded with her father. "Kilel said something. She talked about——" The signal dropped out again. "——afficking——"

Bill guessed at the missing words. Carbon trafficking. *Am I closing my eyes to the obvious?* "Anne, I can't hear you. The signal is very poor. I have to go."

"Dad, are you there? Are you ever coming home?"

Christ. How many times had he asked that question of Molly in the months before she disappeared? After two weeks went by without a call, he left Anne with an older woman who sometimes cared for the toddler. A half-dozen checks at her Seattle apartment and the local Algid office turned up nothing. He returned home and the divorce papers arrived the next day. For a month, the documents sat unread, because he didn't want to accept the contents. Call after call, ping after ping to Molly went unanswered. She had abandoned her daughter and her husband. It was years before Bill stopped waking up each morning wondering why.

"I *am* coming home. I promise, sweetheart. I love you."

"I love——"

Link failed. Reinitialize?

Bill turned the phone off. The final elapsed time was two minutes, fifteen seconds. *Long enough to be heard by practically the whole planet.*

"How come I feel worse, not better?" he said to himself. Bill rested his head against the mast, wondering if he'd done something stupid. *Aganippe* was watched day and night by a half-dozen governments and international agencies, Bill assumed. *No one is unwatched these days.*

Running figures caught Bill's attention. Sailors were climbing the shrouds.

"Aloft there! Penn!" McMadden's voice pierced Bill's funk. "We're adding canvas. Cast off the gaskets on the main royal."

Bill pocketed the satellite phone and scrambled up the royal yard. From nearly the highest point on the main mast, he loosened the ties that bound the sail and let it fly. He had a few seconds to scan the horizon. The sky was a white-blue color and the sea a matching gray. His chest tightened when he saw a dark shape under the surface slip around *Aganippe*'s bow. Another fast-moving shape surged underneath the ship. He never served in the navy, but he'd seen the weapons before. Their skippers liked to stalk cargo ships as training exercises. Despite his safety harness, he gripped a hempen line as if his life depended on it. He realized a nightmare was coming true.

I'll never see Anne again.

CHAPTER 24

THE ENGINE ROOM OFFICERS ON *Extinction* learned about Martin's engineering background, and as he performed his duties with the most efficiency of all the damned, he was given more responsibility as a kind of trusted inmate. He learned that the sub was lost in the last hours of the war for the Arctic, but not to enemy action. A mechanical failure took out her buoyancy systems, and she sank onto the continental shelf a hundred meters above her crush depth. With her communications systems dead, her crew had one hope: a dash for the surface in a submersible with a message begging for help. The captain, Gorov, and a pilot set off, never to be heard from again. The Russian Navy, embarrassed by its failure in the war, covered up the loss of *Yuri Dolgorukiy*.

Extinction was *Yuri Dolgorukiy* reincarnated. The chief engineer gave Martin nominal authority over a team of the damned assigned to one of the reactor's backup cooling systems. The equipment was jury-rigged and obsolete, and Martin struggled to keep ahead of the continual problems. A pockmarked man, strong but weak-eyed, took Martin's previous station.

"Captain on deck!"

Gore maintained a quasi-military posture among his crew, and he made surprise visits to the engine room. The bosses and engineering chiefs came to a loose attention while the damned continued monitoring the boat's systems. Martin heard Gore before he saw him.

"Where's that son of a bitch Kerensky?" Gore's boots clonked on the metal grate of the deck. His fearsome face, covered with yellow and black hair, entranced and frightened Martin. His eyes had the indifference combined with wildness that Martin guessed kept cat owners wondering when the animal would slash the hand that fed.

"Here, sir." The named officer stood at attention, shaking. Gore pushed him into the compartment, closing the door behind. The bosses regarded each other in unspoken expectation.

Martin heard a loud bang and a scream, but it didn't come from the compartment. The pockmarked crewman crumpled to the grate, holding his arms above his head as scalding water and steam poured down on him. Alarms sounded and another man screamed. An engineer ran past Martin, parboiled flesh dropping off his back. More alarms sounded. *Extinction* lurched and Martin felt a sensation similar to a dropping elevator. The boat was going down. Gore emerged from the compartment. "What in the devil's name..."

Martin was already moving. He pushed Gore aside and crawled behind an instrument panel. The monk switched a patch cable that routed electronics to a key valve in the cooling system. He yelled an order, and one of the wretched crew closed a valve, stopping the flow of scalding steam. The alarms stopped, the instrumentation returned to normal, and the slow downward drift of *Extinction* halted. Martin kneeled next to the pockmarked man, whose skin was like boiled cabbage. Martin said a prayer over his body.

A shape hovered. For a split second Martin thought it was the colonel.

"You. What's your name?" Gore said.

"Brother Martin Scribb."

"Scribb." Gore's cat eyes revealed nothing, but Martin sensed he was weighing a decision. "Come with me."

Glancing around and wiping his hands on his filthy singlet, Martin followed the captain out of the engine room.

Martin sweated it out in the captain's great cabin. *Extinction*'s air was kept at a low humidity to resist corrosion, but in Gore's living space, the humidity had to be one hundred percent. Tropical plants lined the walls, some with huge flowers with exotic scents that matched the thickness of the air. Mixed with the moisture and perfume was a whiff of decaying leaf litter. It was the smell of slow death. The thing missing was the cacophony of insects mating, killing, and dying in a true jungle. The metal walls and deck were clear of the rust Martin would've expected in a humid environment. *A special paint or coating must fight off the inevitable oxidation.*

Gore tapped at a tablet keyboard, his fingers dexterous despite their thickness and covering of tawny hair. The curved claws that the creature showed on Martin's arrival were retracted. Gore's green-yellow eyes bored into Martin. "Well, Mr. Scribb. It seems you have saved *Extinction*."

"Please, sir." Martin picked up on the military forms of address favored on the sub. "I'm a brother of the Penitents of Saint Francis."

"I see... Brother Scribb." Gore grimaced, which Martin took as a kind of smile, though the teeth were that of a carnivore, not an omnivore. "Allow me to say thank you. You are the hero of the hour."

"If I had not acted, everyone on board might've died, myself included."

"Indeed. You are responsible for enough death, aren't you?"

Gore's remark stunned Martin, until he realized that Gore knew everything about him. "I cannot imagine allowing any more people to suffer, even if they are dissed or murderers."

Gore grunted and rose from his chair. "I have not eaten since this morning. Do you mind?"

"No, of course not."

"May I get you something?"

Despite Gore's fearsome appearance, and his ability to kill him on the spot in a horrific way, Martin was calm. Perhaps this is how prey felt when they were in the jaws of the predator. "A cool glass of water?"

Gore removed to an adjacent room, and returned with a tray containing a glass of water dripping with condensation, along with a large bowl of raw meat.

Martin sipped the water. "You act as your own steward?"

"Luxuries are few on *Extinction*, even for me, and stewards in my service don't last very long."

Martin did not want to know what Gore meant, but he was by turns fascinated and terrified when Gore took a piece of bloody meat, placed it in his mouth, and tore at it. He worked it not like a ravenous beast, but as if he were a wild predator with table manners worthy of royalty at a state dinner. He wiped his bloody hands and mouth with a cloth napkin.

"Forgive me if I do not offer you a share of my little snack, Brother Scribb," Gore said. "I've not eaten cooked meat for many years and I have none in my larder."

"I'm not hungry."

"I know you want to ask me questions, Brother Scribb. Please, don't be embarrassed."

"Well, sir, I must admit that... Well, your appearance..."

"...is unusual."

"To say the least, sir."

"I've always felt, even as a child, that I had the heart of a tiger. That was one reason I went into the military. When I was a midshipman, I had a large bengal tiger tattooed under my right arm. Not regulation, but enforcement was lax in those days."

"The Russian Navy?" *Damn me, that was presumptuous.*

If the captain was annoyed, he hid it. "I think you already know part of my story."

"You rose through the ranks to become captain of a nuclear attack submarine named *Yuri Dolgorukiy*. She disappeared at the end of the Three Degrees North War. The Stavka presumed the submarine was lost, along with all her crew, but they were wrong. The captain survived."

Gore wiped a drop of watery blood from his lip. "I volunteered to risk my life to bring help. Rising through the depths to the surface, I realized that my life was over, my career ruined, because the loss of the boat would be blamed on me, even if I managed to rescue those men and women. The war's end meant that the Arctic Ocean would have to be shared, not the best outcome for a military man, in my view."

"So you killed the pilot and disappeared, leaving your crew to suffocate." Martin avoided sounding judgmental. He was in no position to wag a finger.

"Desperate times, and so on," Gore said. "I was lucky. I found myself in an isolated settlement on the Russian Arctic coast. No one found me or... what is that wonderful American phrase?"

"Ratted you out?"

"Just so. After a time, I realized that *Yuri Dolgorukiy* was salvageable. Before the war, I was assigned to a task force searching out and destroying pirates along the Russian coast. I had made a few contacts among the criminal classes and offered to bring *Yuri Dolgorukiy* to them in exchange for an investment in a risky but lucrative enterprise."

"What might that be?" Martin asked, though he was ready to speculate.

"You will learn all about that shortly."

"Is that why you brought me here?"

"Originally, you were just another crewman on *Extinction*. Crew is hard to come by, but the policy of disidentification, rather than execution, created a class of humans desperate to escape a fate worse than death."

Martin had to agree. In a twisted way, he had found a renewed purpose to his life, less powerful than his desire to be welcomed back to normal society, but nonetheless an incentive to survive for another day. He was shocked to feel a sense of loyalty to *Extinction* and Kapitan Gore creeping into his consciousness.

"We were kidnapped, not invited."

"Yes, but you may find it difficult to believe that almost no man or woman leaves my ship once they are aboard."

"Are you serious?'

"Look at yourself, Brother Scribb. Are you in shackles? Are you abused?"

Martin kept his opinion of the bosses to himself. "I'm several hundred feet underwater."

"You may leave the boat at any time, though I cannot vouch for your safety once you step off her."

Martin saw Kapitan Gore's self-delusion. He failed or refused to understand that he and all the people on *Extinction* were in a kind of prison, despite their freedom of the seas and their stealth. The question was: For what purpose?

Gore tore at another piece of meat. "Let me tell you something, Brother Scribb. You're unique among the disidentified. The vast majority are animals. You, on the other hand, are an intelligent, quick-thinking man who recognizes an opportunity and seizes it, even if it means the deaths of millions."

"I didn't plan on the deaths of millions."

"Come now. You knew the risks. They'd been known for a century." Gore shifted in his seat, preparing for something, and Martin soon learned what it was. "I'd like you to join me. I need intelligent men like you. Let me show you the opportunities. Freedom and wealth. Or wretchedness and social non-existence. You decide."

The idea of joining Gore repelled Martin at first. *He's right, though. What other choices do I have? The colonel's promise to restore me to society could be empty. He may not even have the power.* "I'll have to think about it."

"Take your time." Gore was finished with the interview. "If you'll excuse me..."

Martin remained seated. "I still don't understand something." He gestured at Gore with an open hand. "This... change. The look. How?"

"Have you not heard of DNA tattooing?"

Martin shook his head.

"Ah, as a religious, you have been cloistered to some degree. It is a procedure, very expensive, very dangerous. Think of that tiger tattoo I mentioned. Something like it has been tattooed on my DNA."

"A chimera."

"A 'chimera' is a fire-breathing creature from Greek mythology with parts of a lion, a goat, and a snake." Gore chuckled, adding a growl for color. "I'm not that."

"A... mutant?"

"'Hybrid' is more benign, though still not quite accurate. I have a self-image to protect."

"Why?"

"Fear is a powerful weapon. Human beings are obsessed with the surfaces of things. They see a tiger, and they see cunning, stealth, and a painful death. I have to deliver on that promise occasionally."

In the end, the decision to accept Kapitan Gore's offer of "freedom and wealth" came easily to Martin. He had known plenty of the alternative since his

J.G. Follansbee

disidentification, and although he still held hope of finding Molly Bain and the possibility of redemption in the eyes of the larger society, Martin saw *Extinction* as a way to hedge his bets. Gore would extract some sort of price for his generosity, though Martin had no idea what that price was.

So much had happened since he left the monastery. He lost his begging bowl in Churchill, but he was getting one solid meal a day, so he didn't miss it. He prayed less and less, though he was unsure why. Gore moved him to another compartment, cleaner and less crowded, with bosses whose brutality ended with verbal viciousness. Unspoken was a threat of returning to the deepest bowels of *Extinction*, and Martin knew a good thing when he saw it.

He retained his job in the engine room, overseeing the same group of common criminals and other misbegotten who had been at the wrong place and time when Reason's press gang came round. Martin recommended changes to reactor procedures to the chief engineer, which reached the ears of Gore. The captain invited Martin to the control room, where every officer, male and female, greeted him with contempt. Martin recognized Nelson, whom Gore introduced as his executive officer. Lurking near a holo-console was Reason, Gore's tactical officer and well as chief thug.

Just when Martin thought he was going mad from *Extinction*'s endless wandering, the crew was ordered to action stations. The submarine's watertight doors were sealed. Gore had removed the escape pods from the crew compartments. If *Extinction* were disabled or sunk, the dissed and others who were not on duty would die. Martin's compartment, in contrast, had a lifeboat, though he had no idea whether it would function if and when it was deployed.

Nelson's voice came through the intercom. "Martin Scribb to the control room." Afraid he had done something wrong, the monk clambered through companionways and up ladders to the brain of the boat. Gore, Nelson and other officers hunched over a monitor table.

"Brother Martin, do join us." Gore was ebullient. "I was beginning to think our hunt would be fruitless, but one of our drones has found a target."

Martin approached the tactical table, uncertain. Numerous images and readouts, updated every few seconds, filled every inch of the surface. Martin recognized sea temperature, salinity, speed, course, and the chemical formulae

for various hydrocarbons. Images were shown in infrared, normal, and intensified light with its characteristic green tones, though it wasn't necessary in the
24-hour day of the Arctic. The "target" was a sailing ship.

Gore spoke in a kind of gurgle. "Ladies and gentlemen, the sensor array is
giving us a strong green signal. I propose we investigate. Objections?"

No one said a word.

"Very well. Mr. Nelson, stand by to deploy countermeasures. Mr. Reason,
standard boarding procedures. Mr. Scribb, would you care to join me in the
gig?"

"I don't understand. I don't know anything about—"

"I want you to know what we're about, what I'm about. Follow me, if you
please."

Martin, Gore, and two other crew with stasers and ordinary pistols crawled
into a submersible. Gore himself sat in the pilot's chair. The submersible un-
docked from the mother boat and glided downward into semi-darkness. Gore's
handling of the submersible was so smooth that the sensation of floating was
soporific. The jarring note was Gore's constant back and forth discussion with
another submersible, which was out of view.

Light filtering from above increased. Martin's ears popped and Gore turned
to the pair of armed crew. "Stand by," Gore said. His lips pulled back, revealing teeth dripping with saliva, as if he were ready to pounce. "Three, two, one,
GO."

Martin was blasted with freezing air that smelled of sea salt. The armed
crewmen bounded out of the open hatch, and he glimpsed a rust-streaked wall
and lettering that spelled out *Aganippe*. The hatch closed and Martin felt his
stomach lurch; the submersible was sinking. Martin gripped his seat, his gorge
rising, and the sensation of falling stopped. Semi-darkness enveloped the submersible, and Martin realized they were under the sailing ship, perhaps hiding
from defenses. Martin heard Gore whisper something into his mic with the
word "secure." He brought the submersible back to the side of the ship and
surfaced.

Gore loosened his crash web and slipped out of the pilot's seat. "Let's go
see what we've found, shall we, Brother Scribb?" The hatch opened a second

time and Gore handed Martin a heavy jacket. Gore climbed a rope ladder with the dexterity of a monkey to the deck of the ship. Martin followed, aping Gore's technique, though it took one of the armed men to lift him over the rail.

After the relative stability of *Extinction*'s deck, the lurching deck of *Aganippe* threw Martin off balance. Gore and his men took no notice. Martin reveled in the fresh air, unlike the filtered air of the submarine, and his eye was drawn upward to the complex of ropes and fabric that hung from the ship's masts. The vessel was huge, though Martin had to revive his thinking when he saw a long black shape, like a snake with *rigor mortis*, on the sea surface a half-mile or so from the sailing ship. *Extinction* had risen.

Three armed pirates from the other submersible held stasers over a group of men and women of various ages and nationalities, all of whom were bound and seated on the wooden deck. One of the captives, a large, red-haired bear of a man, argued with a guard. As Gore approached, the bear-man's face drooped as if he had suffered a stroke. He also cried in terror when Gore stopped inches from him and addressed the guard.

"What's happening here?"

"Sir, this man claims to be the captain. He's refusing to cooperate."

"That's not true." The bear-man blubbered like a child. "I was trying to explain. We're on a mission of mercy. We're going to Bežat. To help the refugees."

"On your feet," Gore said.

"Listen to me. I know who you are, what you want." The bear-man struggled to obey Gore's command, until he was helped by one of the guards. "We can trade."

"Your name?" Gore bared his teeth.

"McMadden." The man shivered from fear.

Gore drilled a look into McMadden's eyes. "I'm going to ask you once. Show me all the access points to your cargo. I want every drop."

"Listen to me. I know where you can find ten times what I have." McMadden nodded like a madman. "I can tell you, but please let me deliver my cargo to the refugees at Bežat."

"A mission of mercy, you say?" Gore let slaver drip from his fangs. "Oh, yes, you'll deliver your crude to the refineries there, at ten times what you and your backers paid for it."

McMadden held out his hands. "It's business. We're delivering a product the refugees need. We have to cover our risks. You know what it's like."

"I'm a businessman, too, captain. I steal from everyone and sell to the highest bidder, and I have an insatiable appetite for oil." Gore relaxed. "However, I'm not averse to a trade. What do you have that I would want, besides your crude?"

McMadden explained, the words cascading out of his mouth in a torrent. Gore was impressed, Martin saw. The corsair glanced at Nelson, who acknowledged an unspoken order. He returned his attention to McMadden. "Thank you for the information, Captain."

McMadden grimaced, breathing easier.

"For the last time," Gore continued, "show me the bungholes for your oil tanks."

McMadden shook his head in disbelief. "You agreed to a trade."

"I agreed to nothing, and you don't seem to understand how serious I am." Gore hissed like a deranged cat. "You." He pointed at a chunky woman wearing an apron. Martin noticed food stains. "Get up."

The woman, her face stricken, didn't move. The guards lifted her up, stepping back, as if they knew what was coming. Gore stepped toward the woman and raised his hand so that it was parallel to the deck. Martin blinked, and missed the hand's lightning fast swipe, but he saw the result: The woman's abdomen was sliced open, her intestines sliding out of the multiple openings like spaghetti through a colander. Her scream was unbearable, but Martin did not avert his eyes. Gore's claw swiped across her throat, ripping flesh as if it were rice paper, and the woman slumped to the deck, twitching. Blood spurted from her neck for a second or two, then stopped, flowing in rivulets over the side of the ship.

Out of nowhere came a small robot that resembled an upside-down cooking pot. It started cleaning up the blood.

Gore turned to the bear-man. "Captain McMadden, where are the bung-holes for the oil tanks?"

McMadden burbled, his terror absolute, tears streaming down his face.

"Show me," Gore growled. McMadden stumbled toward the bow. Martin and a guard followed the pair. McMadden stopped about midway to the bow, and pointed at the deck. Gore glanced at the guard, who said something into his headset.

Extinction eased closer to *Aganippe*, close enough for crew to throw ropes across the narrow chasm separating them. The submarine was three times longer than the sailing ship, and Martin imagined it extended below the water far deeper than the hull of the captured ship. *Extinction*'s crew hauled on the lines, which were attached to hoses. With a hammer and chisel, one of the crewmen knocked off wood on the deck that covered a cap, which was pulled off. The hose was lowered into the hole, followed by the vibrations that signaled suction. Oil was transferring from *Aganippe* to *Extinction*. Another hose was pulled over the *Aganippe*, and the process repeated. Within an hour, Nelson announced the operation complete.

With *Aganippe*'s remaining crew gathered in the waste of the ship, Gore addressed them. "I am Kapitan Gore of *Extinction*. I have taken that which does not belong to you. Your mission of mercy is a sham. McMadden and his backers care only about profit. The Bureau of Environmental Security probably knows about you and what you're doing. Consider yourselves lucky to have met me first."

Gore shifted. "Unlike your captain, I'm prepared to offer you a share of what we earn when we deliver to Bežat. Yes, I'm going there, too, with your cargo, once my tanks are full. You are all criminals, even if you claim you knew nothing about the smuggling. You can guess what will happen to you when you are convicted of violating the carbon laws. I need crew. Experienced men and women, even if you have not served on a submarine. Your skills at sea are valuable. You can take your chances here, or with me."

Gore searched the silent faces. "You there. What's your name?"

A strong, well-built man, perhaps in his forties with longish, graying hair glanced to his left and right.

"Yes, you," Gore said, pointing his paw at the man.

"My name is Penn, Bill Penn." The man said it as if embarrassed.

"What do you say, then? Wait for the bessies? Or join me?"

Penn searched the face of a leather-skinned woman next to him. "I'm with you."

"Me, too," the woman said.

Three others in the group of thirty or so stepped forward. "Very well, then. I wish the rest of you luck."

The new *Extinction* crew members walked past Martin, and it struck him. *Penn. William Penn! Could it be?*

Extinction retrieved the oil hoses and the deployed submersibles. Gore, Martin, and the new crew members crowded into a small boat, which shuttled them toward *Extinction*, now about three hundred meters distant from *Aganippe*. Martin marveled at the drifting ship's grace, even with the sails slack.

"Nelson," Gore said.

"Aye, sir?"

"Execute."

"Done, sir."

Martin heard a low rumble, and *Aganippe* disintegrated in fire and debris. When the smoke cleared, the ship was gone.

CHAPTER 25

THE MONTAGE OF IMAGES JERKED and jumped for Janine Kilel like a crippled dancer. In the chair next to her was a lab technician with the name "Portunes" on his badge. His white coat was clean but rumpled. Colonel Penn recommended him as a crack forensic scientist. In a mobile lab near Port Simpson, they watched the video footage of the pier that once hosted the brigantine *Aganippe*. The quality of the video irritated Kilel. "Is this the best you can do?"

"It took me a week to recover this much," Portunes said. "Whoever destroyed this video did a thorough job."

Kilel glanced at the man's dense analysis on her tablet. "Put it in simple terms for me. What are we looking at?"

"The video shows a series of passenger vehicles arriving at the pier over several hours. The vehicle drops off individuals, who then board the boat."

The ship took up about a third of the screen, with the vehicles moving in and out of the frame.

"What's interesting are the gaps in the data stream," Portunes continued. "If you examine the time codes, you can see that there's a large jump in time after the passenger exits the car, sometimes as much as ten minutes."

"I see."

"The question is, what is the car doing during those gaps?" Portunes paused the video. "You'll recall on page four of the analysis of our results from the micro-sample sweep. Droplets of crude oil were found on the bollards positioned closest to the ship."

"The pier is old," Kilel said. "Perhaps they were left from pre-ban days?"

"The amount of water and other signs confirm that the droplets were fresh, a few days old."

"Perhaps they came from other vessels that had used that pier?"

"We examined all the boats at that pier since *Aganippe*'s departure. None of them had oil with the same signature. None of it was crude oil, for certain."

Solid logic on thin evidence, Kilel thought. "You also located a suspect in another investigation I'm running."

"Yes, ma'am." Portunes touched keys on his terminal. Another video image displayed on the screen. "You can see a man and woman boarding the ship about an hour after the last crew arrival. They come on foot, not by car. The man has been identified as William Penn. The woman is identified as Micah Panang."

"They boarded *Aganippe* together on the same night I attempted to arrest the man. It's not a coincidence. Who is she?"

Portunes touched his personal tablet. "She's listed in the employment and social welfare databases as a licensed merchant seaman, but there are gaps in her record."

Kilel let the question of Panang go for now, but William Penn was connected to the oil smuggling. She was sure of it. If he hadn't been before, he'd learned of it when he boarded *Aganippe*.

"We should discuss the vehicle now, Inspector."

Kilel and the scientist exited the mobile van, which was parked thirty meters up a forested track that branched off a two-lane secondary road out of Port Simpson. Kilel's car was parked next to the large van, its security bot stowed. The mobile investigation crew's secbot watched over the scene as the pair of BES agents approached the burned-out hulk of another car.

"Local police found this a few days ago," Portunes said.

Kilel sniffed petroleum. "What happened here? An accident?"

"The police don't think so." Portunes' voice was euphonic. "There's no sign that it lost control or hit anything before it was destroyed. The local police speculate that it was stolen, then abandoned."

"You believe otherwise."

"Yes. The license plates are missing. The license and registration transponder was deactivated and the memory wiped. Most of the other identifying characteristics have also been removed or altered."

"That would be typical of thieves, probably a ring, with some sophistication," Portunes said.

"I've also identified the cause of the fire. A flammable liquid that was heated or sparked. The leak came from an area of the vehicle normally clear of such fluids. A closer examination found a series of sealed and connected spaces in the frame. One of the seals leaked, and the fluid came in contact with a heat source. Thus, the fire."

"Any trace of the fire's fuel source?"

"Crude oil," Portunes said, proud of his discovery. "The traces we found match the traces found at the pier in Port Simpson. A calculation of the amount that could be transported by the car—about a hundred twenty litres..."

"...a barrel of oil," Kilel said almost to herself.

"...and the number of cars seen in the data streams give us an approximate amount of oil transferred to *Aganippe*," Portunes added.

"Excellent work. Anything else?"

"Yes, Inspector." Portunes paused. "The supercapacitor pack was damaged in the fire, but the trace elements in the device's electrolytes pointed to a particular manufacturer."

"And?"

Portunes glanced back to the van and the security robot. "I'm afraid you won't like what I've found, Inspector."

"Go on."

Portunes sighed. His pride gave way to apprehension. "The supercapacitors are installed in vehicles supplied exclusively to the Bureau of Environmental Security. No one can purchase these capacitors on the open market, which means the car has to be BES in origin."

The implication of this discovery was not lost on Kilel. The smuggling ring was sophisticated and extensive, but was there a connection to the government? Kilel found the idea hard to accept, but she was not naive enough to dismiss it.

She crossed her arms. "Have you connected this car to any of the images from the pier?"

"Not yet." Portunes sighed again. "The fire badly damaged the vehicle, but we think the traces of oil serve as a connection."

"Not good enough." Kilel was skeptical of whether an Environmental Crimes Tribunal judge would accept Portunes' hypothesis. *That's a question for the prosecutor.* "Let's say this car was transporting crude oil to the ship. How was it transferred?"

"I found an access port in one of the tanks, Inspector. The oil could've been loaded and unloaded from there." Portunes perked up as he speculated. "A simple system of hand-pumps or small electric pumps and hoses could have connected the car to the boat."

"That's not shown in the video images," Kilel said.

"Of course, Inspector. It's the key piece of evidence the smugglers would need to hide."

"You're sure no images exist."

"Yes. A very sophisticated malware worm was let into the system. It knew what to erase."

Kilel turned to walk back to the mobile lab. She stopped, eyeing the burned-out hulk of the smuggler's car. *The pieces fit.* "What about the oil itself? What have you learned?"

Portunes cleared his throat. "The smugglers took some pains to mask the oil's chemical signature, but we've narrowed it down to northeast Pennsylvania, near the shore of Lake Erie."

"Those wells were closed by the Carbon Acts," Kilel said dismissively. "They were all capped and all the pipelines and infrastructure torn out. Even the towns were evacuated."

Portunes put a finger to his lips. "Perhaps one or two of the wells is still producing in secret."

Could it be possible? The Carbon Acts included severe penalties for producing oil without a license, and military units guarded the old wells day and night. Banning oil had, ironically, made it even more valuable than before. Smuggling and illegal production happened, but never at the scale Kilel had discovered. If the government were somehow involved...

The lab technician and the inspector stood next to her BES vehicle, which gleamed, even in the dull light of the overcast sky. "Good work, Mr. Portunes. I'll make a note of it in my report." Kilel detected a hint of a smile in Portune's otherwise dour face.

Kilel ordered the car to return to the BES offices in Eugene. She touched a button, and the passenger side seat redeployed into a flat, plain divan without arm or backrests. She removed her shoes and suit jacket, thankful for the stretchy fabric of her trousers. She assumed the Padmasana Yoga pose, her back straight, her visage serene, her heart rate slow and steady. She embraced the intrusion of her surroundings into her consciousness, and let it go, as if dropping a handful of rose petals.

Images, thoughts, emotions, sensations drifted in and out of her mind. Unbidden, the shadow of Anne's angry countenance at the ranch passed over Kilel's motionless body. *For an instant I was afraid of her.* The inspector wasn't accustomed to defiance; Everyone she encountered outside BES was deferential at least, if not groveling or submissive. Anne was intimidated at first, but she lost her fear at some point. *How?* Kilel remembered the interrogation when Anne spilled the fruit on her tunic and she almost struck the girl. *I lost my temper. She found my weakness. She found my fear.*

"Colonel Penn is dying."

The voice in Kilel's imagination was Anne's, though she had no idea about the state of her uncle's health. For that matter, neither did Kilel. *Is this an insight or a mirage?*

The sun peeked through the overcast, and a shaft of light penetrated the car. Kilel's heart filled with regret. Raleigh Penn was as close to a mentor as she had experienced in her career. A psychologist might call him a father figure, but the analysis was cheap. He was a hero. He had built the institution she served, and he created the values she internalized. If he was dying, the loss was lamentable. *Anne would lose an uncle, a good man she never knew.*

Kilel set aside her emotions as she brought herself out of her meditation. She decided her next moves on the smuggling investigation and the search for William Penn.

CHAPTER 26

MARTIN WATCHED THE GUARDS STRIP Bill Penn and the woman Micah Panang, looking for weapons or valuables. Kapitan Gore ordered *Extinction* to get under way, and the wreckage of *Aganippe* was still burning when the sub submerged. Gore called his officers together to discuss his next move. Gore opened and closed his paws/hands like vises.

"Captain McMadden gave me intelligence that I think we will all find useful." Gore bared his teeth, a sign he was not satiated with the petroleum pilfered from *Aganippe*. "A cruise liner, *Aurora Borealis*, is carrying a cargo of crude oil."

"A passenger liner? That's ridiculous." The skeptic was Reason. "Who would take such a risk?"

"Who would suspect that a new passenger liner, one built with government green subsidies, would smuggle oil?" Gore grunted. "It's a perfect cover."

"It's a perfect trap," Reason said.

"McMadden had no reason to tell us what he knew, other than to save his own skin."

The incident with the chunky woman replayed in Martin's mind.

"Perhaps he was lying to save himself and his crew."

"The insanity of his claim lends truth to the tale," Gore said. "It fits with the other intelligence we've gathered over the past few weeks."

"Rumors, you mean."

"Someone is conducting a major oil-smuggling operation. I believe *Aganippe* was part of that operation, and McMadden knew enough about the other players to make a credible claim about a seemingly innocent cruise ship."

"We're walking into something that smells like shit." Reason readied a lipful of spittle for the deck, but he held back.

Gore had a feral look in his eye, though, that showed he would not be denied. "I abhor competition. I intend to intercept the liner, take her cargo, and deliver it myself to Bežat. Do you have a problem with that, Mr. Reason?"

Martin had trouble wrapping his mind around the concept of thieves stealing from smugglers, but he was focused on Colonel Penn, who might be the key to his social salvation.

"I never have a problem with making a profit," Reason said, "but I'd like to stay alive to enjoy my profits." Seeing Gore would not be budged, he threw up his hands. "What choice do I have?"

Gore put his furry hand on Reason's shoulder. The man gaped at the paw. "This is why I like you, Mr. Reason. You're a born skeptic, but you know when to give in to a persuasive argument."

Reason grinned sourly.

Gore announced: "Our next problem, ladies and gentlemen, is finding this glorified yacht."

Bill sat the mess table stirring his soup with a crust of bread. Each meal on *Extinction* brought back the grisly image of the cook lying on the deck of *Aganippe*. Each meal reminded him that he had survived her death and the deaths of McMadden, Stubbs, and the others only because he was on the run from BES and needed an excuse to get off *Aganippe*. McMadden didn't want him there in the first place, but Bill cursed himself for not knowing her cargo. He cursed himself twice for volunteering to join the crew of a renegade submarine tanker designed to carry an immoral substance. He was in the uncomfortable company of two monsters; one the master of *Extinction*, and the other a disindentified monk who had unleashed forces that killed tens of millions. The hypocrisy of his behavior embarrassed him. *How will I explain this to Anne?*

One of the murderers sat across from him. Martin Scribb's face was recognizable, even a decade after the Spike and the trials. He was leaner and shabbier;

the photos of Scribb that Bill remembered always showed him in the styles favored by New York West financiers. Bill ignored Scribb at first, but he soon understood the ridiculousness of obeying the law forbidding anyone from communicating or interacting with the dissed. Everyone on the ship wore a brand. Bill might soon have his own. Like it or not, he and Scribb were now shipmates.

"I've done some research on you, Bill." Scribb's voice still had that smooth, salesman-like quality he remembered from the trials. It made Bill sick to his stomach. "We have something in common."

Micah laughed at Scribb's assertion as she pushed a half-eaten bowl of yellowish gruel away. "That isn't possible, unless you mean your connections to the bessies."

"That is true, Ms. Panang, but that's not what I had in mind."

"He means Molly," Bill said. "She worked for Scribb at Algid."

"Small world."

"Indeed," Scribb said. "We have more in common than that."

"If you've done your research," Bill informed him, "you know that I've been accused of an environmental crime. But I'm not responsible for the destruction of that bird species, whatever the law might say. You, on the other hand, are a genocidal maniac." Bill regretted his statement when Scribb grimaced. *Was that guilt? Could he have a conscience?*

"I suppose you wouldn't believe me if I said the Spike was not my fault."

Micah laughed. "That's what every criminal says. 'I was framed!'"

Bill was curious, though, to see what the man had to say. "If the Spike wasn't your fault, then whose fault was it?"

"Molly Bain's."

Enraged by this accusation, Bill grabbed Scribb's stained shirt and pulled him close. "You're a liar. You killed millions through negligence and stupidity. Molly was just a programmer."

"That's what Raleigh Penn wanted you to believe."

"Raleigh?" Bill was taken aback by the nearly-forgotten name. He had trouble recalling what his older brother looked like. "What's my brother got to do with this?"

"Who's Raleigh Penn?" Micah said.

"The man who prosecuted me," Scribb said. "The public wanted blood, but a lowly coder wasn't enough. Molly supplied Raleigh all the evidence, maybe even doctored some of it, and they crucified the big, bad CEO."

Micah's mouthed dropped. "The prosecutor was your brother, Bill?"

"You're raving, Scribb. Molly was my wife. I knew her. She's not a backstabber."

Scribb was doubtful. "You're sure about that? She abandoned you and your daughter—unexpectedly, I imagine. Don't forget, I was on the other side of that divide."

Bill had no answer. He once thought he knew Molly, but the revelation of her new career—high class whore—astonished him. They were married, for Heaven's sake. *What other secrets did she keep from me? What else have I refused to see?*

"It doesn't matter, Scribb." Micah pointed a finger at the man. "You were the head of the operation. You made the decisions. Eighty million, ninety million people died within months of the incident, and another billion had their lives changed forever for the worse. They—we—are still suffering."

Scribb plead his case. "I suffered a social execution. I paid the ultimate price. I don't exist, officially, and no one acknowledges my physical existence, unless pushed." Scribb's distress increased. "Listen, Bill. Would saving one human being from an unnecessary death redeem a mass murderer? Resurrection is possible, don't you think?"

Bill wasn't giving him any succor. "I thought the government wiped everything about you out of everything, databases, public records, all that stuff."

"What is done can be undone."

"Tell that to the dead millions," Micah said.

Scribb was not going to let up, though. "You believe in redemption, don't you, Bill?"

"I'm not a philosopher, Scribb," Bill sighed. "I just want to go home to be with my daughter."

"Maybe I can help you to achieve that goal."

Again, Scribb insisted on barging into his personal life. "I don't want your help."

"Molly can help us. I need to find her. Do you know where she is?"

"No." It wasn't a lie, strictly speaking. Bill did not know the position of *Aurora Borealis*.

"She has a particular skill set that I'm looking for."

Bill recalled her at Pole Station. *Molly is a madam, the owner of a bordello, remade into something more acceptable with corporate terminology that makes it sound like she's peddling family entertainment.* His bitterness surprised Bill. He'd get depressed sometimes, and frustrated, but despair was unfamiliar. "You're a pervert, Scribb, aren't you?"

"Come again?"

"Don't give me that. I did some of my own research. She's a whore in everything but name." *On the other hand, she's doing what was always her thing, being on her own, making her own rules, taking chances in places no one else dared.*

Scribb was puzzled. "I don't know what you're talking about. I'm interested in her programming skills. She's one of the world's foremost experts on artificial intelligence software, and I have a… friend who is in need of her expertise."

"A friend?" Micah's question was more than inquisitive.

Bill flicked a roach off the table. "AI. That's why you hired her in the first place, back before the Spike. She's still doing that work?"

Micah smirked. "You want her for more than her programming skills, Scribb."

The monk's face flushed in embarrassment. "I thought I made clear I'm uninterested in her talents as a personal entertainer."

Bill was still trying to figure out Scribb's angle. "You want revenge, don't you, Scribb? Revenge against my wife?"

"Justice is a better word," Scribb fired back, "and she's your ex-wife, divorced fifteen years ago. Still carrying a torch, Bill?"

Bill lunged for Scribb, grabbed him by the neck, and smashed his face into the table. Scribb turned his face in time to avoid a broken nose.

"I think you are, Bill," Scribb mumbled as Bill banged him into the table top a second time. "She's the genocidal maniac, not me."

Bill released Scribb at last, and the dissed man rubbed a new contusion on his cheek. "You're not only sick, Scribb, you're delusional."

Scribb stuck to his earlier point. "She knows more about artificial intelligence than anyone."

"I'm not interested in helping you, dissed man."

"It's your brother that needs the help. I was sent by him to find Molly."

"Really small world," Micah said, intrigued.

Bill couldn't care less about that connection. "I haven't spoken to Raleigh in twenty years. He and I are strangers." Bill knew that Raleigh was high up in the BES hierarchy, which disqualified him from any kind of relationship. "I don't care what happens to him."

Martin begged to differ. "If you help me help Raleigh, he might help you."

"A tangled web," Micah said.

Bill was more interested by this prospect. Raleigh did have the power to call off that BES dog Kilel. "I've seen Molly once since the trials, and that was by accident."

"When was this?"

Bill told Scribb about the encounter at Pole Station.

"Do you think she's still there?"

"Doubtful. She's probably on the ship that brought her there."

"Which is?"

"*Aurora Borealis*. It's a new passenger liner."

Martin's face lit up. "That's amazing. That means she's near. Are you sure?"

"That's the kind of boat she would travel on, given the people I saw her associating with. It was the only ship in the area besides ours."

"Do you know where she might be headed?" Scribb's voice pitched up. He was excited.

Scribb's eagerness puzzled Bill. "There are several ports where *Aurora* might be headed."

"Ah." Scribb narrowed his eyes. "I believe I can get you what you want, to go home and be with your daughter, if you share your information—or rather, informed speculation—with Kapitan Gore."

Bill studied Scribb's face. During the Spike trials, Martin Scribb's defense team had lauded him as a model citizen, who had never had trouble with the law, apart from the occasional carbon overusage fine. The man before him didn't seem like he was capable of having a hidden agenda. "I will tell Gore myself."

"Agreed." Martin smiled and rose from the bench. "I can take you to him now, if you like."

Bill was uncertain about the turn of events, but he followed Scribb to the control room, where they found Gore and his officers poring over a map. Micah asked to come along. Bill shrank back from the spectacle of a man who had tattooed his DNA with millions of base pairs of an animal, but then again, he had seen many strange things over his lifetime. After Scribb's introduced him, Bill weighed whether to show his cards or dicker with Gore, but he was not the best card player. He decided to play out the skein.

"My guess is that *Aurora Borealis* is heading for Dudinka, because that's the site of a new port facility owned by the same man who owned the ship."

Gore estimated aloud the distance *Aurora* might have sailed since Pole Station. "By my reckoning, the liner may have already arrived at Dudinka. That means our opportunity has been lost. Still, Gore ordered *Extinction* to put on best speed. "Let's just see what progress she has made."

CHAPTER 27

THE ORDINARY FRAGRANCE OF BOXWOOD consoled Anne as she re-potted bedding plants in the Thomasburg Nursery. With Bill gone, she needed the routine of her part-time job to anchor her days, even if it meant more time away from the hatched magpie chicks than she wanted. A dozen times she replayed the record-ed call from her father—*Yes, it was him, not a BES trick*—to reassure herself that he had not abandoned her, though his absence nagged her like a stubborn insect pest. Mike, on the other hand, was becoming a bulwark against a new random-ness of life that upset her. She hoped the instability wasn't a new normal, though she didn't want Mike to go back to the status of mere acquaintance.

Anne was ten minutes into her watering routine when a shadow near the fruit tree saplings caught her eye. Her uneasy mind connected the human um-bra to a sleek black sedan she had noticed in the parking lot among the normal collection of pickup trucks and autonomous delivery vans. The visitor was camouflaged by shelves of paving stones. "Can I help you find something?" she said.

The gaunt figure of Raleigh Penn emerged. "Hello, Anne."

Her hand went to the crucifix hanging on her neck, as if touching it warded off evil. Anne's encounter with her uncle at the detention center came back to her from time to time, as if it had happened in a distant country a hundred years ago. Here he was again, but dressed like an ordinary businessman, instead of a paramilitary officer. He reminded her of an underfed lion, weak but still capable of killing.

"I hope I'm not bothering you, Anne."

What is that in his face? Longing? Desperation? "No, you're not. I mean, do you live around here?"

Raleigh grinned. "I'm not looking to replace my dying ficus, if that's what you mean." He glanced at the saplings.

Anne's heart quickened. "Is something wrong? Did something happen to my father?"

The colonel fingered a sapling's label. "No, Anne. Not to my knowledge anyway. He's somewhere in the Arctic on a ship, probably off the coast of Russia."

Anne's mind jumped to the magpie chicks in the coop. *Does he know?* "The refuge biologists still haven't contacted me about—"

"That's a problem, but that's not why I'm here."

Anne shifted her weight to one foot. "I don't understand—"

"I want to talk to you."

An unintelligible announcement blared over a nursery loudspeaker. "Now's not a good time." Uncertain, Anne resumed her watering, hoping her uncle might get the message that he was unwelcome. *He's a bessie, always up to no good.*

"I know this is awkward, but I would like to talk to you. Please."

Raleigh's tone confused Anne. *A request, not an order.* Everything about his presence unsettled her. *I don't trust him.* "I'm sorry. I've given all my information to Kilel. If you need something, talk to her."

Her uncle's shoulders had a bent, almost broken air. "I see. I've made a mistake. I'm sorry, Anne. Excuse me." He slipped past Anne in the narrow aisle. He had a vaguely medicated smell.

Despite her mistrust, she sensed a wound. *Maybe cooperation will help Dad.* "Wait, um, Colonel. I'm due for my break." *I'm going to regret this.* "There's a picnic table behind the main building. It's supposed to be for mist users. I'll meet you there in five minutes."

Fifteen minutes later, Anne found Raleigh waiting for her at the table. He was alone.

"I thought you had forgotten about me," he said.

"I'm sorry. I had a customer to deal with." She did not like lying, even a minor fib, but she needed time. She debated whether to run home or text Mike that the colonel had come looking for her, but she hesitated. *If he were angry or wanted to arrest me, it wouldn't happen this way.* "What's this about, Colonel?"

"You're welcome to call me Raleigh, if you like." He pushed an unopened fruit drink toward her. "It's hot out here, even in the shade." He'd already emptied his drink box.

A peace offering? "I suppose you'll want me to call you 'uncle' too?"

"Don't you believe I'm Bill's brother?"

Anne cocked her head skeptically. "I believe you. I just don't think you're deserving of a word like 'uncle.' That's someone I would love. I don't like you."

"What do you know about me?"

The question took Anne unawares. Until she met him at the detention center, his existence was like a fable. The main thing Bill imparted to her about Raleigh was a hostility. "All I know is that you work for the BES and you did something awful to my grandparents."

"Whom you've never met."

"Are you calling my father a liar?"

His face took on a quality of contrition. "What actually happened is more complicated than you think."

"I'm not interested." Anne folded her arms. "You still haven't told me what you want."

Raleigh brought his fingers together. He was having a hard time finding the words to say whatever was on his mind. The little blood in his face drained away.

"You're sick, aren't you, Colonel?" Anne resisted an impulse to touch his arm in reassurance.

"I'm dying unless I can conjure up a miracle." He related the story of his glioblastoma, the failed conventional treatments, and the uncertain experimental treatment.

Anne felt sorry for him in the way one feels about a victim in a news reports. She thought his story was incomplete. "At the detention center, you asked me about my mother."

"You told me you had no idea where she was. I believe you, of course."

"You didn't explain why you wanted to find her. Does it have something to do with her AI work?"

"Yes, indeed." Raleigh regarded Anne thoughtfully. "Well done. A fine insight on your part."

Anne shrugged. "It's not hard. You told me the experimental treatment depended on nano-bots. Everyone knows the only way to control hundreds or thousands of them is complex machine learning. That's AI."

"I'm still impressed, Anne."

"If you're trying to make me like you, it's not working. I still can't help you find my mother." Anne rose to leave. "I have to get back to work."

"Wait, Anne." Raleigh lifted his hand, and Anne feared he might touch her. She stared at his hand as if it were a poisonous snake. He pulled it away. "That's not the main reason I came. You barely remember your mother, just like you barely know me. I'd hoped..." His voice trailed off.

Anne sat down, despite a quiet voice that told her to run. "What did you hope?"

He interlaced his fingers. "Anne, you and I share many things, 'values' you might call them. We both care about saving nature, preserving it against stupid behavior by ignorant human beings, restoring it to a purer state." As he spoke, the jacket of his suit opened a few centimeters, and Anne glimpsed the grip of his service automatic.

"I don't agree." *He still wants something from me, and it's making me cringe.* "I don't believe in harassing people for things that aren't their fault."

Unbidden, a fantasy flashed in Anne's imagination. She snatched the pistol from the colonel, and he ran. She leveled the weapon, aiming in the way her shooting coach instructed. She squeezed the trigger and dropped her uncle. *Where did that come from?* She blinked in an effort to concentrate on the real Raleigh Penn in front of her.

A flash of impatience crossed Raleigh's face. "Anne, I'm asking you to listen to me. You probably want to know why your father hates me so much."

"He doesn't hate you." *Yes, he does.*

"I accept his feelings about what happened between my parents and I, and how it affected him. I regret it sometimes, more these days than in the past, I have to say. I was very young, younger than you, and young people don't always foresee the consequences of their actions."

Anne felt her blood pressure rising. "You did something to your parents."

"I didn't do anything to them. I merely turned them in."

Anne was incredulous. "For doing what?"

The colonel stretched out his hands in supplication. It was an odd thing to see from a man of power. "Dad—your grandfather—was a brilliant software engineer. He didn't follow the rules. He *made* them. Your grandmother was his equal, a poet with a vision that, well, very few people appreciated, apart from her husband." Raleigh's face wrenched at the memory. "They had a son that didn't measure up to their standards and expectations. I wasn't particularly creative or iconoclastic. I preferred structure and predictability."

"But I found something I believed in." Raleigh's visage turned firm, and his eyes lit up. "Saving the earth, ridding it of the exploitation and abuse that had brought on the Warming. People had to change, everything had to change, and I wanted to be part of the solution." The colonel's hands balled into fists, as if readying himself for a brawl.

Anne wasn't afraid. "I don't understand. They lived on a dairy farm."

"Many people responded to the Warming by returning to the land, thinking they could heal it. Jack and Eunice Penn thought working close to the earth was a way of redeeming bad behavior, but it was just arrogance and naiveté." Raleigh relaxed his fists, and he sighed. "I understood the value of the new rules. I wanted to help enforce them. I told my parents I planned to join the new military units with environmental protection missions. They told me rules were for the dull-witted. They said a new kind of fascism was rising. They wouldn't sign the documents allowing me to join the Army cadets. They blocked access to com tribes I wanted to join. They thought I'd lost my mind." Raleigh was scornful.

"They did something you couldn't accept."

The fire returned to his mien. "The Warming was getting worse. The government, with the blessing of the people, decided to attack methane emissions, and one target was cattle. Dairy farmers and cattle producers were told to cut down. Jack Penn did all he could to reduce methane—feed, additives, new strains—but it wasn't enough."

Anne was struck by her uncle's reference to his father by his full name, as if Jack Penn was a suspect in an investigation.

Raleigh continued, "Jack wasn't meeting the methane quotas and the inspectors issued warnings. He was desperate to keep the farm and his dream. He hacked the monitoring system to show the cows producing less methane than their actual output."

"You found out, didn't you, Colonel?"

"Why did he do that, Anne? Why did he lie? He betrayed everyone, me, his family, every human being."

Anne thought she saw tears in his eyes, but it might have been age or his illness.

"An inspector questioned Jack's reports. I went to the inspector and told him what I saw."

"You went behind your father's back and reported him."

"What else was I supposed to do? He was a part of the problem, not the solution. He was doing everything I hated." Raleigh cupped his face with hands and exhaled. "The government levied huge fines. One thing I didn't understand was how close to the edge we were, financially. The fines destroyed the business. That's probably what the government wanted. It broke his spirit. Two years later, he sold out, and I joined the military when I turned eighteen. Dad died a few months later."

"Where was my father during all this?"

"He was only four when the government prosecuted Dad. The last time I spoke to Bill was the day I left for the Army."

"Dad told me that you disappeared. You didn't even come to your mother's funeral."

"I guess I couldn't face her. Maybe the same was true with Bill. I was in the midst of the life I'd chosen. I put aside the values I was raised with. I had my own values. I hardly heard anything from my mother or Bill, except when he sent me word about your birth." The tension on Raleigh's brow relaxed. "I remember that day like it was yesterday."

My dad tried to reach out, but it was lukewarm. Anne thought of the video in her private com folder. *Is my uncle trying to make amends?* The revelation that her uncle, her only living relative apart from her father and mother, had destroyed his own family in the name of saving the biosphere, struck her as twisted and hateful, like the fanatics that had burned heretics in the name of the "true faith." She could not imagine doing the same thing to her father, even if he were to blame for the refuge fire and the near extinction of the magpies. *I would defend him until my last breath.* At the same time, Anne knew of families in the valley with their own tensions. Mike and his father did not always get along. Gary Schmidt expected Mike to be near to help care for his terminally ill mother. Though he loved his mother, Mike wanted to pursue his own dreams.

Would I defend my mother, if I could, even though she abandoned us?

"Colonel Penn, I still don't understand why you're telling me all this. It happened before I was born."

"I'm telling you because I have no else to tell, Anne. I still believe I did the right thing, but I regret it all the same, and I wish I didn't hurt my parents, or Bill. I couldn't see it then, but I see it now. When death is staring you in the face, it's hard to ignore your mistakes."

"I would never have done such a thing."

"That's why I had to talk to you. You have something which I don't understand."

"What's that?"

"Compassion for the sinner."

A part of Anne despised a man who took revenge on his father and mother by turning them into the government. On the other hand, she knew the history of humanity's careless disregard for its home, and how it still faced its ultimate destruction, even with the Carbon Laws and everything people were doing to save their future. *He was trying to do good.*

He has no one. Anne remembered Kilel at the detention center, how she deferred to him and how he was a little afraid of her. Kilel was not his friend, at least not in a way he needed, that every person needed. *He's afraid of dying alone.* Anne was his last chance at connecting with anyone who didn't see him as a heartless government functionary or a traitor to his family. *The truth is, he's both to me.*

"If you want my forgiveness, Colonel, you won't get it from me."

"I understand. But I have another request."

Anne's wariness reasserted itself. "I don't—"

The colonel hesitated again. "If I survive this illness... If I find your mother and everything... Will you let me come and visit you?"

He's afraid I'll say No. "Colonel, I don't know. I'm not... My father wouldn't..." *What would I ever say to him?*

"I promise not to intrude. Just once or twice a year, maybe? A text or email now and then?"

It would be easy, Anne grasped, to reject the colonel and inflict the same kind of pain the bessies had inflicted on her. However, she couldn't say the words that would hurt her uncle. *Like it or not, he and I share blood.* Anne licked her lips, torn between a habit of aversion for this man who had wrecked her father's family, and pity for a man utterly alone who craved human contact. "I'll have to think about it."

"That's good," he grinned. "That's very good."

For the first time in the conversation, Anne saw happiness, even joy, in the colonel's face. She half-expected him to ask for a handshake, or even a kiss, and the thought of touching him repelled her. He asked for neither, and behind him, the black sedan was guided by its AI to a spot a few meters from the table. He rose from his seat and the door of the car opened for him. The gun disappeared from view.

"Thank you, Anne. I hope to see you again soon."

Anne said nothing more. As she watched the car pull away, she couldn't escape the impression of it as a hearse, bearing a corpse to the grave. What surprised her was a sharp pain in her chest, which could only be a feeling of loss.

CHAPTER 28

MOLLY BAIN ACCEPTED KRISTIAN NORDLAND's invitation to join him on the bridge of the *Aurora Borealis* as the liner turned on the final leg of its trans-Arctic voyage. The ship reached for the mouth of the Yenisei River at the southern edge of the Kara Sea, but it hesitated, slowing as the wind died to a whisper.

Molly was impatient to reach her destination. "The electric motors would be useful right now."

"I want to enter Dudinka in grand fashion, and it wouldn't do for us to arrive behind a tug because our batteries were depleted." The white-haired Nordland glanced at the pair of uniformed men standing by the ship's mahogany wheel. A helmsman held the ship on course. The master, taller of the two, wore a close-cropped beard and cap festooned with gold braid.

"I understand your need to make an impression, Kristian, but I have business to attend to."

"Don't worry, my dear friend." Nordland brushed a bit of dandruff off his suit coat. "The current is in our favor, and a freshening wind is forecast. Our sails will soon be full again."

Molly examined the horizon and the sky, and old instincts reawakened that led her to trust her eyes, the motion of the deck, and the fragrance of the air. High clouds and riffles to the east suggested the forecast was correct, once *Aurora* cleared Vize Island to port.

Something about the birds bothered her. The gulls and terns that ranged over the water flicked about as if nervous, hovering for a few seconds over the waveless face of the sea, and veering away. They were confused, as if discovering an error at the last second before alighting on the water. For an instant, Molly saw shapes moving under the long swell. It was a shoal of herring, or a pod of whales, or her imagination.

One of the navigation consoles chirped. A dry-voiced AI intoned, as if announcing the evening's dinner menu. "Attention, please. An unidentified sonar contact." The AI gave a bearing, depth, course, and speed.

Molly frowned. "What could that be?"

Nordland wasn't worried. "Submerged log. Transient temperature inversion. The sea is full of mysteries."

The captain gave the AI a number of orders. Though she almost saw the code running, Molly missed much of the meaning. *I've spent too much time away. The mariner's world has moved on. Aurora* continued her slow glide southward.

"Attention, please." The AI's voice was insistent this time, as though the computer had rising anxiety. Molly projected its nervousness on the executing code. "A second unidentified sonar contact." This time the captain ordered the two contacts plotted on a screen. They moved in courses parallel to *Aurora*, but they were equally distant from her.

"Those aren't sunken logs, Kristian," Molly warned.

Taking more notice, Nordland edged closer to the captain. "Security Condition One?"

The words were not an order, but the captain responded. "Agreed. Navcom, Security Condition One. Deploy defense drones."

A light shudder shook *Aurora*'s hull. Lights and readouts changed on the consoles, showing more detail and parameters Molly didn't recognize. The helmsman tensed.

"Molly, I think it would be a good idea if you returned to your cabin. If this turns out to be something unpleasant, you'll be safest there."

Her experience at sea kept her from arguing. She pushed the down button on the elevator. As she waited, a tremendous spout of water lifted itself in front of *Aurora*, like a pillar blocking her path. The helmsman turned *Aurora*'s head to port to avoid the obstacle.

The AI voice came through the console. "Security drone number two is no longer responding. I have also detected insertions of viruses into the data storage systems."

"What are the viruses looking for?" Nordland said.

"Ship's schematics and blueprints."

"Navcom, Security Condition Two." The captain didn't wait for Nordland's suggestion. A pleasant, if urgent, alarm sounded over the ship's public address system. The voice was male and commanding, repeating: "All passengers return to their cabins immediately."

Molly's apprehension intensified as Nordland took her by the elbow to the stairs. "The elevators shut down in this situation. We're in danger here, Molly. The AI security bots can handle things, and we should get to safety on the lower decks."

As the pair reached the door to the stairwell, the sea around *Aurora* boiled. Two submersibles emerged from the water and accelerated toward *Aurora*, skipping over the waves like flying fish.

Nordland was alarmed. "Security Condition Three!"

The officer repeated the order, and the helmsman took a station near the captain, leaving the helm for the nav AI. *Aurora* was dead in the water, the proverbial sitting duck. The crewman's hands flew over the consoles, abandoning the slow back and forth of voice commands. The bridge, located near the stern, gave an unobstructed view over the entire length of *Aurora*, and Molly saw two pods emerge from the deck amidships. The pods bristled with antenna and missiles.

"*Aurora* is armed?" Astonished, Molly pulled away from Nordland. "She's a passenger liner."

Nordland's eyes were hard. "The Arctic is a dangerous place. The war may be over, but battles are still fought in the Wild North. Only a fool would walk into a crime-ridden neighborhood unarmed."

Molly watched a missile launch from one of *Aurora*'s pods, but she didn't have a chance to see its effect. Nordland pushed her through the door to the stairwell, and he followed. They scrambled down the stairs, Molly thanking the heavens for wearing flat-soled shoes. As the door latched behind the pair, an explosion shook *Aurora*'s command deck, and Molly glimpsed the reflected orange glare of flames on the walls. The lamps dimmed. Nordland and Molly found themselves blind. The emergency lighting came on, changing every color to blood red. Screams, muffled by the carbon fiber walls, drove the couple to the promenade deck, where they emerged near the casino.

Passengers ran past them toward the stern carrying luggage, as if frantic to catch another ship. The ship's com network was overwhelmed with messages as friends, lovers, and family tried to locate one another. A text came through from Ginny Magante: Smoke is filling up the passageways. I'm fine. Take care of yourself. A security bot fired two shots from its staser before the mechanical beast exploded into a thousand pieces. A kiosk announcing the evening's floor show disintegrated as a projectile blew it into shrapnel. Molly and Nordland ducked behind a sofa and fell to the floor. The armored legs of a biped robot were followed by two pairs of black-booted human legs. The humans shouted and another explosion rocked the lobby. One of the humans fell to the floor, headless.

Nordland tugged at Molly's dress. He pointed to a darkened passage. They crawled over the all-weather carpet and got to their feet, racing athwart *Aurora* to a companionway that ran the entire length of the ship. They collided with other passengers, but Nordland pushed against the tide.

"Where are we going?" Molly demanded.

"The first-class observation lounge," he yelled over the pandemonium. "It's armored."

They hugged the wall as if it were the bank of a raging river, and the water was the panicked passengers. Molly had never encountered pirates at sea, but curiosity in her first years under sail led her to the back alleys and wharfside taverns in ports from the Barents Sea to the Southern Ocean. She met disidentified, scarified, deformed, limbless, sociopathic men and women who answered her queries as to their living with "independent entrepreneur" or "opportunistic business owner." She met Gregori Ilyenevich Gorov on one of these jaunts.

The other side of the walkway was all window, and Molly spotted one of the attacking submersible-cum-hydrofoils rushing in the same direction as their run. Tiny spouts of water made by bullets chased the craft. The craft turned ninety degrees, and a missile exploded. As Nordland and Molly reached the lounge, the targeted craft emerged unharmed from the falling spray.

The lounge was ahead of the mainmast. A missile or shell struck the mast above the course yard, severing it. The upper half of the mast pitched overboard, a thin splinter of carbon fiber holding it to the stump. The masthead sank, dragging the hull into a 15-degree list. The foremast had also been severed, but the remnant was missing. The mizzen remained intact, but its yards were askew. Molly knew the ship was lost to the invaders. She faced Nordland. "Do you think someone got out a mayday?"

Nordland scanned the damage. Fire poured out of the bridge, puffing as if it was a breathing monster. "The automated systems would, but it will take hours for anyone to get here." Another explosion sent a shudder through *Aurora*. "*Aurora*'s defense systems weren't designed for such an attack. They're overwhelmed."

The starboard missile pod slew toward its quarter, attracted by movement. The sea bulged, as if pushed up by a water-breathing demon, and a bulbous black shape burst through the bulge's center, pushing upward at high speed, imitating a breaching humpback whale engulfing a stomach-full of krill. As the sub settled, a billow of condensation puffed from its deck, flying toward *Aurora*'s missile pod, blowing it to scrap. Molly ducked as a melon-sized chunk of metal smashed into the lounge window, leaving a jagged crack. The wound distorted the dagger-like shape of the submarine, and Molly observed small craft emerging from its flanks. They sped toward *Aurora*'s broken hulk.

Molly turned to Nordland. "What do we do now?"

The white-haired shipowner sat on a stool at the bar, dazed. Molly knew the signs of despair and resignation when shipmates were lost at sea. "Kristian, were you expecting this?"

Nordland shook his head.

"I'm sure Mr. Nordland was expecting us, but hoping we would not find him." The growling voice came from the door, and a shiver went up Molly's spine when she saw the face of a tiger with its tawny, black, and white stripes, and the incongruous pink of the tip of its nose. Its canine teeth were long and sharp, and shiny with saliva, but the shape of the face was human, the eyes intelligent and probing, as if looking for weakness.

"Gregori Ilyenevich," Molly whispered. A strange mix of terror and excitement surged through her body.

"Mrs. Bain." Gore bowed his head, and he pointed a pistol at *Aurora*'s owner. "Mr. Nordland, you know what I want. Let's make it easy on both of us, and no one else will die."

Nordland said nothing, avoiding Gore's gaze.

Gore stepped toward the shipowner. A masked, armed guard followed Gore and took up a position that would allow no escape from the lounge. "I wanted to kill you last time we met." Gore grinned. "I'm not an impulsive man. I knew we'd do business together. We have mutual business acquaintances. A network of competitors, you might say, of which we are a small part."

"You're a monster," Nordland said. "You're a thief, a liar, and a murderer."

"I plead guilty as charged, though monster is a rather intolerant thing to say," Gore hissed in Nordland's face. "Enough games. I want what you have. Show me where it is."

"Kristian, tell me what this is about." Molly said.

Gore wasn't going to wait for long. "Very well, Nordland. I shall have to find a way to be more persuasive." He glanced at the guard. "Take both of them to the fantail."

The guard lifted his automatic rifle, a signal for the captives to precede him out the door. Nordland led the way. Molly glanced behind her in the faint hope of a rescue. She was at a loss, and did as she was told. Gore followed the guard, and a second armed man, his rifle ready to defend the party's rear, took up the last spot. They followed the long hall along the ship's centerline that opened into broader spaces. Severed arms and legs, blood stains, and destroyed robots littered the points where the ship's crew and security systems had battled the invaders. Molly retched at the cloying smell of congealing body fluids, but kept her composure as she worried about her friend Ginny. Nordland put a silk handkerchief to his mouth. Nothing was alive, apart from her party. A black robot patrolled a side corridor.

The group passed through a splintered mahogany door into bright sunlight. Hundreds of men, women, and a few children huddled on the fantail deck, a narrow area over the stern meant for outdoor activities. A few white-uniformed *Aurora* crew members were scattered among the passengers. The sun shone onto the deck, warming the air to a tolerable temperature. Many passengers wore night clothes and shivered next to loved ones. Ginny waved at Molly, blowing a kiss of reassurance. She wore a cashmere coat and a diamond bracelet. Molly ached to embrace her, but she was in thrall to Gore and his goons.

Passengers nearest to Molly gasped, and a few whimpered, as they spied Gore. Their faces displayed disgust, curiosity, terror, and resignation, as if the corsair would be the last sight of their lives. Gore relieved the frustration of the shorter passengers when he climbed a few steps on the staircase leading to the ship's restaurant. The crowd quieted down, save for the muffled crying of a baby.

"I am Kapitan Gore, master of *Extinction*, and this ship has something I want, though none of you have it, save one." Gore's growl carried well over the crowded deck. "Many of you know Kristian Nordland, the owner of this vessel, the first of her kind and hopefully many more. Mr. Nordland, step forward, if you please."

A guard poked his rifle into the small of Nordland's back. He lurched a step, away from the crowd.

Gore extended a paw-hand toward Nordland. "Mr. Nordland is a skilled businessman. He has many revenue streams to protect his company. He doesn't put all his eggs in one basket. He has one line of business that many of you have heard of, but would never imagine such an upstanding citizen participating in, particularly after the Warming and the Spike. Can you guess what that line of business might be?"

The crowd was silent and sullen.

Gore continued, "That would be carbon, ladies and gentlemen. Specifically crude oil, and its transportation."

The crowd inhaled, Molly included. She glanced at several faces, some of whom she recognized from the parties leading up to the signing of the agreement with the Cyprian Association. Shock at the invasion had turned to disbelief.

Murmurs rose into shouting. "Why are you telling us this?" said one. "We don't have any oil," said another. "Take what you want and leave."

"I intend to," Gore responded. "We know the oil is aboard, but the ship's data protection measures are quite good. I need Mr. Nordland's cooperation to avoid further unpleasantness." He was impatient with polite talk, and he became more direct. "Let me put this another way. I can find the oil on this ship by myself, and then I can sink it, with all aboard. You'll drown in the freezing water like rats. Or Mr. Nordland can show me where the oil is, save me time, and save your lives. It's up to you."

Shouting in the crowd died down to muffled conversations. Molly was drawn into a knot of people uncertain what to do next. A stout man, wearing a dressing gown, walked up to Nordland, who stood at the foot of the staircase, like a condemned man at the gibbet. "Is this true, Nordland? Is there oil on this ship?"

Nordland lifted his head, but said nothing.

The stout man considered Gore. "Whoever you are, whatever you are, give me five minutes with this... man, and I'll get what you want."

"Be my guest." The wolfish grin on Gore's face raise goosebumps on Molly's arms.

The stout man searched the crowd, and two large companions emerged. They took Nordland by the arms into the corridor. The crowd stood stock still as Molly listened to grunts and a muffled scream from behind the doors. Two minutes later, Nordland emerged, supported on each arm by the large men, who escorted him to a network console. Nordland's face was black and blue, and blood trickled from his mouth. The stout man approached Gore, who remained in his spot on the staircase. "Are you linked into the ship's network?"

"I am."

"Nordland." The stout man barked his orders. "Show this creature what he wants to see."

Nordland lifted his right hand to the console. The small finger of the hand was bent at a painful angle. Molly wanted to feel pity for Nordland, but no such emotion came. She saw the screen update.

"Excellent," Gore said. "My com is receiving the information. We will soon be on our way."

A woman in the crowd yelled and pointed. Molly spotted the black torpedo shape of the submarine, which had edged close to the drifting *Aurora*. The two hydrofoils stood watch on the seaward side of the mother ship. With an efficiency Molly admired, the submarine's crew deployed hose and pumping gear, and they scrambled to points on the ship. They tore through thin coverings to access ports. One of the ports was at a spot that the repair bots had clustered around days before. She chided herself for not recognizing the black stain as oil.

As the submarine crew sucked the crude out of *Aurora* like a leech taking blood, Gore stepped off his temporary pulpit and padded to the ship's rail. Passengers parted before him as if he were toxic. He scanned the skies. He was at his most vulnerable here; taking the noxious liquid left him almost defenseless. *If we rushed him and his guards, we could retake* Aurora. One look at the terrified passengers argued against an attempt. Nonetheless, Gore's momentary weakness let Molly's curiosity run rampant.

"Kapitan Gore, why do you want the oil? No one has built a carbon-fueled submarine for decades. Yours must be nuclear-powered. Oil is no use to you."

Gore turned to Molly. "My, you are an enchanting creature, Mrs. Bain. Quite ambitious as well, transforming a profession reviled for centuries into a legitimate enterprise. From the moment we met, all those years ago, I knew you were special. I thought we might be partners, one day."

Molly gulped. She had kept her relationship with Gorov/Gore, if not a secret, as clandestine as possible. She had pretended he was an acquaintance, like an old school contact. Any hint of a stronger association with him was a threat to her plans.

"I don't understand, Kapitan."

"We are alike in many ways. I am continuing a tradition going back centuries as well, though not quite so far as yours." Gore touched a claw across Molly's cheek. She felt its razor sharpness, but it did not cut her skin. "Like you, I bring warmth to human beings who need it." Something caught Gore's eye on the deck of the sub. "Excuse me, Mrs. Bain. I need to attend to a few details before we depart."

Molly's eyes followed Gore as he walked along *Aurora*'s rail, speaking *sotto voce* into his com. Her physical closeness to Gore and his touch electrified her. It dredged up passions from risk-filled days when she had no ties and no responsibilities. They had encountered each other weeks before she met Bill, and he had some of Gore's strength. Nights with Bill reminded her of nights with Gregori. That was before the Russian's metamorphosis, but his animal attraction now was as powerful, perhaps more so, than the early days. Gregori's charisma balanced his pathology. Bill had neither, but their bond was strong, if fleeting. Molly was about to break up with Bill when Anne turned up. Mistakes piled on mistakes, and Project Algid was a way out. Molly's face grew pale when she spotted Bill Penn—in the here and now, standing on the deck of *Extinction*. Alongside him was a man she hoped never to see again.

CHAPTER 29

THE RAMP SECURED TO THE deck of *Aurora Borealis* swayed as Bill climbed aboard.
The weeks of working aloft on the doomed *Aganippe* had inured Bill to the crisp
air of the Kara Sea, and he wore a light jacket. Scribb followed him up the ramp,
having scrounged a tattered parka. Micah, ever adaptable, remained aboard
Extinction, accepting her new role. Bill's skin crawled when he imagined that
anyone would associate him with the rogue submarine, but then again, if he had
stayed with his shipmates on *Aganippe,* he would've died with the others. *What
would have happened then to Anne?* The hoses sucking the petroleum from *Aurora*'s
hidden tank vibrated, slapping the liner's carbon fiber hull. Bill seethed at this
latest offense: a new "green" passenger wind ship carrying thousands of barrels
of illegal, planet-killing oil.

Bill let Scribb take the lead as the monk sought out Gore. A dense crowd
of passengers on the fantail encouraged a sense of dread. Molly must be among
them. *Was Scribb right? Am I still in love with her?* The terrorized passengers, leaning close to each other to keep warm, parted as Scribb pushed through. They
recognized the tulip brand and turned their backs to him, figuratively and liter-
ally. The dissed man didn't notice their contempt, or didn't care. He spotted
Gore and set a course, straight and true.

"Kapitan Gore," Scribb said. "May I have a word?"

"Mr. Scribb, what are you doing here?" The growl of Gore's voice magnified
Bill's apprehension. "I ordered non-essential people to stay aboard."

"I needed to see you, sir," Scribb said, obsequious in the extreme. "It's about
a passenger on this ship."

Gore hissed. "Military units are probably on their way. We could be attacked at any time. We have no time for visits. Why are you here?" The captain glared at Bill.

"There is someone aboard you should know about," Bill said, feeling as if he were betraying a friend. *She might be my ticket home.*

"Her name is Molly Bain," Scribb added.

Gore looked annoyed. "I've already spoken to her, Brother Martin. She runs the Cyprian Association."

"She is Bill Penn's wife."

"Ex-wife," Bill said.

Gore laughed, a breathy chuckle. He thought he knew what was up. "Family scores are none of my concern. Get back aboard *Extinction*."

"Let me explain, captain. She has skills and knowledge you might find useful," Scribb informed him. "She is the world's most renowned expert on artificial intelligence."

"What is that to me?"

"She could be a valuable hostage, or perhaps she could even be persuaded to join your crew. Her skills are incomparable."

Gore considered Scribb's point, and applied it to his enterprise. "Very well, I'll speak with her."

Scribb turned to Bill. "Mr. Penn, do you see her?"

For an instant, Bill was indecisive. *What if I'm sending her to a different death or worse, by calling her out? Perhaps Gore will let* Aurora *go.* Nevertheless, he walked into the crowd, Scribb close on his tail. She was not hard to find. Her oval face, highlighted by the animated tattoo that was as enchanting as it was distracting, signaled her fear, though she fought hard to hide it with poise and confidence. The silk shawl draped over Molly's shoulder covered a modest, if curve-hugging outfit. The pale green color of her blouse reminded Bill of a shallow tropical cove. *No wonder I fell in love with her.* He felt an urge to kiss her, but he pushed the preposterous thought away. *Remember what she did to Anne.*

Scribb called over Bill's shoulder. "Molly, it's so good to see you again after so many years. You're as beautiful as ever."

Molly's hand was entwined in the hand of another woman, almost as beautiful, in a white cashmere coat. The companion cried, "You can't take her. She's nothing to you."

Bill and Molly locked eyes for a full second. Her expression was blank, but she switched her focus of attention between him and Gore. *Is she nothing to me?* If the time were a week ago, Bill might have agreed.

With feigned politeness, the guard pointed the way for Molly through the crowd. She drew herself up, kissed the female friend on the cheek, and walked ahead of Bill and Scribb until she was standing in front of Gore. Bill was surprised at her quiet compliance. Gore's tawny face was almost unreadable, though Scribb was pleased.

"What do you want, Martin?" Molly kept her attention on Gore.

Scribb turned to the pirate, obeisant. "Kapitan, may I suggest some privacy?"

Gore's cat's eyes remained on Molly, and Bill again tried to get a read on him. "The restaurant, upstairs," the captain ordered.

The passengers watched them climb as if the group were abandoning them.

Inside the restaurant, Scribb directed the group to a cloth-covered table, mocking the behavior of a maitre 'd, and his three guests took a seat. The table was large enough for ten, and each took a place some distance from the other. That suited Bill fine; he didn't want any part of any of them. Scribb found four glasses and a bottle of wine, and removed the cork like a sommelier, pouring just the right amount in each glass. No one, except Scribb, took a sip. His hand trembled, from either fear or anticipation.

"Please, my friends, drink." Scribb's tone was oily. "There's always time for a glass of wine, even on difficult days."

"Enough with the boot-licking, Martin." Molly touched the glass, despite her disgust with the monk. "Tell me what you want."

Scribb consumed the wine audibly. "You have valuable skills that our business—"

Gore jerked his head at Scribb. The dissed man noticed.

"...that Kapitan Gore, er, can make use of."

"If you think—"

Scribb interrupted. "I'm referring to your AI skills. Ships like *Aurora Borealis* have very sophisticated defenses. *Extinction* needs someone like yourself. We could do great things together."

Molly had no interest in this proposition, Bill saw. *Could I say something to persuade her?* "You haven't changed at all, have you, Martin?"

"I'm sorry?"

"Still selling dreams, I mean. The last dream you sold nearly destroyed life on this planet."

Martin spat his response. "You, as I recall, were a willing participant. Weren't you, Mol? And for your efforts, you got off with a couple of years of prison, while I paid the ultimate price. Or did you forget?"

"Enough," Gore growled. "Scribb is correct, Mrs. Bain. I have need of skills such as yours. *Aurora*'s defenses were formidable, if inadequate. I believe you should join us."

Molly hissed. "You 'believe'? What is that supposed to mean?"

"Let me put it this way, Mrs. Bain. You have a choice: Join me or I will destroy *Aurora* and kill all aboard her."

"You're a maniac," Molly said, the edge in her voice sharp.

Bill protested, more for the principle than for any residual feelings for her. "That wasn't the deal, Captain. We're supposed to persuade her to join us, not coerce her."

"Mr. Penn, I can understand now why she left you. You cannot read her as I can. She has no love for Mr. Scribb, and will not follow him again, but I reckon she is valuable, and I want her on *Extinction*. For a woman as decent as Mrs. Bain, life or death for her fellow human beings is a powerful incentive. I have no such qualms." Gore's amber eyes returned to Molly. "Well, Mrs. Bain, what shall it be?"

Molly's face twisted with anxiety, a sight that surprised Bill. *When had that ever happened?* "If I agree to go with you, will you guarantee the safety of everyone aboard *Aurora*?"

"I give you my word."

"What good is that?" Molly's fingers gripped the edge of the table.

Gore wasn't going to split hairs. "You'll have to take that chance. I believe you know that I *will* kill everyone on *Aurora* if you do not agree. That includes Mr. Penn, by the way."

Bill recoiled at Gore's threatened betrayal. "Wait, what are you doing? I helped you."

Molly slumped in her chair. "I guess I have no real choice, do I?"

"I disagree, Mrs. Bain." Gore sniffed at his wine. "We always have choices. Some choices are easier than others."

I'm sitting at a table of monsters, Bill thought.

Gore stood up and motioned the guards to the door. "I'm informed that the petroleum transfer is complete. Shall we, my friends?"

"Kapitan, your wine. You haven't touched it," Scribb pointed out.

Gore was eye-to-eye with Scribb. "Wine makes me ill." The corsair bared his teeth, and Scribb shrank at the sight.

The group emerged from the restaurant and trooped down the stairs to the fantail. Gore stopped at the same place where he had made his earlier announcements as Bill, Scribb, and Molly entered the companionway. Bill heard Gore make another announcement, though the exact words were difficult to make out. When Bill reached the deck of *Extinction*, he noticed activity on an upper deck of *Aurora*. Hatches opened and a dozen or more blaze orange boats were lowered to the water.

As Gore drew near, Bill tensed, but he wanted to know what was happening. "Kapitan, what did you say to them?"

Gore turned to the *Aurora*'s hulk as the orange lifeboats pulled away. "I gave them a choice. Die on *Aurora* or live on a lifeboat."

The creature's depravity was endless. "You are all about choices, aren't you?"

"He who has the power controls the options." Gore scanned the gunmetal sea. "I said the passengers would live," he clarified. "I said nothing about the ship. She's worthless now anyway. The oil she carried has corrupted her."

The last of *Aurora*'s lifeboats moved away from the dead hull, and Bill heard muffled explosions. Unlike *Aganippe*, *Aurora* did not die immolated. Instead, she steadily settled lower and lower in the water until she slipped under the waves like a coffin lowered into the ground.

Molly descended a ladder into *Extinction*. Tattered men and women jerked aside as the guards escorted her forward, led by Kapitan Gore. The air was a miasma of sweat, machine oil, and unease. Competing with the trauma of living through the capture and destruction of *Aurora Borealis* was the Gordian knot of feelings toward Bill. The shock of seeing him at Pole Station hadn't worn off, and now he'd brought her aboard a vessel that could become her tomb. Gore had reappeared in her life as well, as unlikely an event as Bill's resurrection. No, there was a difference, she thought. Embers from her love for Gregori Ilyenevich smoldered, while ash was all that was left of her marriage. That's why it was so easy for Molly to say yes to Gore, in spite of the threats. *I may have just thrown away everything I've worked for, but I'm like a moth careening into a flame.*

The dogs tightened on a watertight door, a klaxon sounded, and the scratchy announcement "Dive. Dive. Dive." blared over the intercom. A shudder ran through the boat's steel hull. Molly braced herself and the deck tilted toward the freezing depths of the Arctic Ocean. *At least Ginny and the other passengers have a chance once the local coast guard finds them.* The guards disappeared, a further sign that she had nowhere to run. She had no idea what to do if the boat was attacked and sunk. In the shallow Kara Sea, if the pressure hull weren't breached, *Extinction* would settle on the bottom, and she would suffocate with the rest of the crew as the oxygen ran out. The world would not rescue a crew of dissed.

They passed through a hatch into a large room with metal tables and benches. The Spartan atmosphere suggested a military vessel with a dearth of discipline: chipped cream paint on the steel surfaces, signs of rats and roaches, and a thin film of grime on the LED lamp coverings. Martin invited her to sit, and her former boss set a cup of something in front of her he called "coffee," although the provenance of the greasy liquid was unclear. Martin's hairline had retreated like a shrinking glacier in the years since she had seen him last. Despite his unctuous behavior toward Gore, his brown eyes had lost much of the innocent sparkle that had attracted her to his methyl hydrate enterprise so long ago. She never once thought of him as a potential lover. She wanted to loathe him, because of what he had done to the planet, but her complicity in the disaster mitigated her hatred. She had helped him, but she had escaped his own fate by the slimmest of margins; she saw in him what she might have become. Unlike Bill, he had changed as well.

"Martin, I don't remember you as a religious man," Molly said.

"My mother was a devout Catholic," Martin said. "My mother insisted on baptism, catechism lessons on Sundays, and confirmation. It gave me a certain respect for the church as a moral institution, but I didn't believe in the dogma."

Molly rested her chin in her hands as she anticipated a boring lecture, though the information might be useful. "Something changed?"

"The day Father Gonzales found me, I felt as if I were dead. As a social outcast, I was spiritually dead. Spirituality may be an individual experience, but it happens within a social setting, else why would religions exist in the first place? This may sound silly, but Father Gonzales resurrected me."

"You were still disidentified. He didn't change that."

"Let me put it this way: He gave me hope that all was not lost."

"Hope of redemption?"

"No, that came from another quarter, which is why I have sought you out."

Molly noticed Bill's attention rise. "Hope from where?"

"You know the man. He's Colonel Raleigh Penn, Bill's brother, your former brother-in-law, the man who prosecuted us and oversaw my disidentification."

Bill's face twisted in disgust. "He's an officer in the Bureau of Environmental Security. That's why I left my ranch. BES has accused me of a crime that was not my fault. The fact that he's my brother means nothing. I haven't seen him since I was a child."

"I believe he has a certain feeling for Molly," Martin said. "He was the one who prevented your disidentification. He saved your life, in a sense."

The same system that had executed Martin's social persona had spared Molly's. Of the dozen or so sentences to disidentification, only Martin's sentence was confirmed. "What does Raleigh want from me?"

Martin explained the illness killing the colonel and the failure of the experimental treatment.

Molly didn't get the connection to her. "He's dying and he wants me to fix his problem? Why should I?"

Martin raised his brow in surprise. "Because you owe him something."

"I don't owe him anything."

"As someone who has experienced disidentification—the contempt, the rejection, the isolation, the physical and emotional violence—I believe you owe him a great deal. He prevented that from happening to you, and he's Bill's brother."

"Don't help Colonel Penn on my account, Molly," Bill reiterated.

Martin edged closer to Molly. "The colonel is also Anne's uncle."

What about Anne? She was always part of the conversation, but it was like talking about a celebrity you've never met.

"Bill, I heard you have a holo-pic of Anne," Martin said. "Pull it out and show us."

"Why should I...? I guess it doesn't matter." Bill removed the device from his pocket and set it on the table. It projected a moving image in three dimensions above the table. Anne wore the cap and gown of her high school graduation. Bill touched a corner, and it spoke: "Hi Dad. How do I look? Thanks for everything." She waved her diploma. "Valedictorian! I love you. You're the best dad ever..." Despite the grim surroundings, tears wet Bill's eyes.

The image of the happy young woman transfixed Molly. Physically, Anne was a younger version of her, but with lighter hair, maybe a little taller. She was beautiful and intelligent. Molly couldn't help feeling admiration for Bill. *He did a good job of raising her.* It confirmed for Molly that leaving all those years ago was the right thing to do. *I had no time for mothering.* Molly laughed at the odd confluence of feelings. "That's not enough for me, I'm afraid."

"Then do it to help me, Molly," Martin said. "You were the most brilliant person on my staff. I admired you for your intellect. I was even a little afraid of you."

You were in love with me. "You've done nothing for me, Martin. In fact, you destroyed me when you destroyed the world."

"I accept responsibility for what happened, but the one thing that Father Gonzales taught me was that there's always a chance at redemption. That chance comes when we can help a fellow human being. I have a chance to save a man's life, and so do you."

Bill begged to differ. "Colonel Penn represents everything that's gone wrong in the world since the the Spike. The Bureau of Environmental Security is as bad as the Gestapo in Nazi Germany or the FBI after New York was nuked by the Judgment of God. We're better off if he's dead, if you ask me."

"I agree with you, which makes helping him all the more meaningful," Martin said. "Jesus said to love your enemies. At another time, I'd have rejoiced at the painful death Colonel Penn faces, but hatred destroys those who hate."

Molly heard the noble words, but Martin's motivations were more self-ish. Helping Colonel Penn was a means to an end, that is, social restoration. What disidentified person wouldn't take that opportunity? Plus, she wasn't sure she had the skills to solve the AI problem Colonel Penn and his doctors faced. Martin admitted he knew little of the technical details. She needed to hedge her bets.

"All right, I'll help you." *I won't help Martin, but I will help Bill and Anne.* "There's one condition: You must see that Bill and I leave this ship unharmed. If anyone else is here against his or her will, they must be freed."

"That may be difficult," Martin said doubtfully. "Gore has trouble recruit-ing crew. He kidnaps and enslaves the disidentified."

"That's not my problem, Martin. If you want my help, you agree to my terms."

Martin crossed his arms. "Very well, Molly. I agree. Let me talk to him."

CHAPTER 30

KILEL SAT IN HER CAR at the top of a hill in Pennsylvania about two hundred meters from a gate. Rain was falling in sheets, camouflaging her from the guardhouse. A faded, tumbledown road sign further screened her car from scrutiny. The sign read, "Welcome to Titusville: Birthplace of the Oil Industry." The rain cut both ways: It obscured her vision as well. She lifted her binoculars, which enhanced the dull gray light of the early morning to show a patrol with robotic dogs arriving from its latest circuit of the grounds. She set her own secbot to autonomous mode and started the car.

The young men of the Eastern Pennsylvania Militia gaped as she slowed at a striped barrier in front of the gate. One of the guards approached her, and she cracked the window enough to show her personal identification. Kilel was never denied access to any facility, government or private, if she was on an investigation. Her research on the 28th Infantry Division, Special Assignments Unit showed a stellar record since it had been assigned security duty in the third North American sector established by the Carbon Acts. Her evidence for the security breach was explosive, and she had to confirm the details for herself.

A sign on the lawn in front of a modest building announced the headquarters of the local environmental security region, which covered part of the old oil and gas producing areas of the northeastern United States. Its commander, Brigadier General Rex Gill, was a thin, compact man, with a hawk nose and hazel eyes. His uniform looked tailored to conform to his muscular body. He greeted Kilel and invited her into his office. "Coffee, Inspector?"

"No, thank you, General."

"No vices in the BES, eh, Inspector?" Gill chuckled.

"I had a large cup with my breakfast." Kilel called up her notes on his service record in her minds-eye. Gill's affect suggested irritation and nervousness, but he controlled his emotions well. She turned her internal attention to her security bot's monitor. It was well inside the region's perimeter, and it had already visited some of the old wells. It had found nothing unusual.

Addressing Gill, Kilel folded her hands on her lap. "I hope you don't mind that I've come unannounced."

"We're always ready to accommodate Bureau personnel... May I call you Janine?"

"Inspector Kilel will do."

Gill held his breath, even as he spoke. "To tell you the truth, it's a busy time for us, Inspector."

"How so?"

"Is our conversation on the record?"

"If you prefer off-the-record, I can arrange it." *He's guessed why I'm here.*

Gill exhaled. "We've seen an increasing number of security, ah, issues in recent months."

"What sorts of issues?"

"Inspector, you must understand. We're understaffed here. Recruitment is difficult, and my area of responsibility covers the entire eastern third of the state."

"Perhaps I can be of help." Kilel already knew what Gill was talking about, but she wanted to see if he would try to hide something, if pressed.

"Maybe so. We've suspected for a long time that someone or some group is extracting and removing petroleum from the area. We're adjusting our security patrols and adding some new automated capabilities to determine what's going on."

"You're saying oil is disappearing from the old wells that you are supposed to guard?"

"We have thousands of wells to monitor, Inspector." Gill's voice had an edge that didn't fit with a man having ordinary trouble doing his job. "We have the best monitoring systems in place, besides the standard physical checks by humans and robots." He appeared ready to admit a truth. "There's evidence in the sensing systems' logs and physical evidence that oil has been pumped from certain wells. I've seen it myself. I've *smelled* it myself. That sweet smell is actually in the air when you visit the site, but I can't explain what's going on." Gill averted his eyes, a gesture Kilel noted.

Kilel lifted a hand. "Have you mapped the wells that you say have been tapped? Where are they?"

Gill touched keys on his tablet and a two-dimensional map of the immediate area emerged over his desk. The Lake Erie shore curved along the left edge of the map. "Do you see the red and orange dots? Not many, but they are within a short distance from some of the old roads in the area. Those roads were abandoned where the area was evacuated after the Carbon Acts took effect. Some of the roads are still in good condition."

"So you're saying that someone is taking the oil out on those roads."

"That's the most logical explanation, Inspector. We haven't noted any unusual visits by aircraft, and the wells are too far from the lakeshore. It's possible that the oil could be packed out by animal, robot, or even humans. The amount suggests vehicles, even a small train of vehicles."

Gill was following the script so far, Kilel thought. She glanced at the map over his desk and ordered her minds-eye to overlay her map of the wells suspected as the source of the oil she found at Port Simpson. It was not a perfect match. Her attention switched to her security bot, and she ordered it to the nearest well on her map that did not appear on the general's map.

"I'm surprised that you haven't picked up odd vehicles or other behavior on your remote sensors."

Gill scratched on his tablet. "That's another thing. My techs think someone's tampered with the systems, probably the logs themselves, or the data streams."

"An inside job?"

The officer straightened up. "I run a clean operation, Inspector. My men are loyal and committed to upholding the Acts."

Gill's pronouncement did not ring true for Kilel. "Of course, General. I meant no insult, but the pattern is troubling, agreed?"

Kilel was distracted by a message in her minds-eye. Her security robot had found the well that was the most likely origin of the oil sample at Port Simpson, and the well was not on Gill's map. Kilel ordered the robot to take a sample.

Gill sighed. "I'm conducting my own investigation, but I've found nothing conclusive."

Kilel stood up and went to Gill's office window, which was streaked by the driving rain. A forlorn spider plant was drying out in the air-conditioned room. Kilel had the urge to tell Gill to water it.

"General, I reviewed your personnel file and service record this morning before coming here."

"What does that have to do—"

"You grew up in this area, didn't you?"

"Yes, ma'am." Gill licked his lips.

"As I recall, the local people resisted direct government control of this part of the state for years after the Carbon Acts were passed."

"That was a long time ago. I was a child at the time."

Isn't that convenient for him? "Your grandfather was a leader in a local resistance force, was he not?"

"Inspector, I don't see what that has to do with your investigation."

"Nothing, General," she said, enjoying herself. "I just have a fondness for history, especially environmental history."

"Will there be anything else, Inspector?" Gill's voice grew cold.

"Yes, General. Another question." Kilel approached his desk, wanting to get right in his face. "Right after the Three Degrees North War, you were a military attaché in the U.S. embassy in Moscow, correct?"

"Yes."

"Much of your job revolved around implementing an agreement by which the world's militaries would transition away from carbon-based fuels for ships, airplanes, and so on. You made a number of good contacts who knew much about the logistics of moving fuel, including ways to move it in secret.'

The General assumed an offended dignity. "Inspector Kilel, if you are accusing me of something, come right out and say it. Yes, I know about clandestine transportation of fuels, but that doesn't mean I'm involved in a conspiracy to smuggle oil out of my area of responsibility. What would I gain?"

"You're the one using the word 'smuggling,' General." Kilel grinned. "As to gain, I can think of a hundred ways you would gain, or anyone, for that matter. Money, power, perhaps even prestige. Rebellion is in your blood, but carbon-based fuels are now illegal, and for good reason." Sweat beaded on Gill's forehead. "I'm sure you understand that, General Gill."

Kilel exited Gill's office and drove off the compound into the wet hills of Pennsylvania.

Colonel Raleigh Penn rode the elevator to the fifth floor of the Interior Ministry building, grieved that he couldn't take the stairs. If it were a year ago, he would've done so without thinking twice. These days, by the time he walked the flights of steps, he'd be out of breath, and he couldn't risk appearing weak to the Minister. His semi-annual meeting with her was too important for the Bureau and himself.

The elevator door opened to a long hallway with a double set of faux-mahogany doors at the far end. He self-consciously smoothed down his BES uniform, checked the placement of his ID badge, and tucked the tablet under his arm. The dark green biopolymer case was indistinguishable from kid leather. He waited for the biometric scan to confirm his identity, and he heard the click of the lock.

A young male receptionist greeted Raleigh without getting out of his chair. He gestured toward the Minister's closed office door. Raleigh noticed an alcove near the reception desk. A security bot, one of the latest models, was stowed in the alcove, a tiny green light glowing below the housing of its camera. It faced the Minister's door. Raleigh knocked twice, aware of the bot's eye on his back. It recorded and monitored every twitch, changes in body heat, certain pheromones, and other metrics that predicted aggressive behavior. The algorithms approached 100 percent effectiveness, though the media made much of the occasional error.

"Good morning, Colonel Penn. So good to see you." The Minister greeted Raleigh warmly, her handshake firm. Women in power never saw the need for a crushing handshake, the colonel reflected. She was dressed in the dark suit preferred by female executives, with fabric covering her entire body, from the tight collar to her shoes, with a suggestion of curves. Raleigh had learned to be careful in her presence.

"It's a pleasure to see you again as well, Minister." Raleigh bowed as he released her hand. She directed him to a sofa and chair set near a coffee table with two cups, a pot, and cream and sugar. Though the pot was full, Raleigh knew they were for decoration only. The Interior Minister was not chatty.

"I must say, Colonel, you look a little thinner than when we last visited."

I've lost ten kilos in the past six months. I had to have all my uniforms altered. "Thank you for noticing, ma'am."

"I hope all is well? With your health, I mean."

How much does she know? Probably everything, though it's none of her business. Check that, it is her business. That's how she's survived, politically. "I have some minor issues, ma'am. Nothing to worry about."

"I see." She studied him with that x-ray vision of hers. "What do you have for me today?"

She says it as if I'm a waiter in a restaurant. "We're making progress on several fronts, ma'am, but I must also report some difficulties."

"First, the good news, if you don't mind."

"We've broken up an extensive illegal fishing operation in the Gulf of Alaska. I think that problem will remain under wraps for several years to come."

"Yes, I read your report on that. Excellent work. Please convey my compliments to Inspector, ah..."

"Kilel."

"Yes. I hope you're considering her for a promotion sometime soon?"

"Of course. She's near the top of the list for the next round."

"Very good."

Raleigh went down a brief list: New protections for the remaining rainforests in New Guinea, the discovery of tropical fish species in the waters of Tierra del Fuego off South America, the efforts to reverse desertification in the Texas Republic. He briefed the Minister on each, and she asked probing, thoughtful questions.

The Minister glanced at her jewel-encrusted watch, and Raleigh idly wondered if all the diamonds were legal.

"I'd like to go back to one thing, Colonel."

"Yes, ma'am?"

The Minister pitched forward. "It's about Inspector, ah..."

Raleigh watched her feign ignorance. "Kilel?"

"Yes, of course." The Minister locked eyes with Raleigh. "She's very active, isn't she?"

"Active? I don't understand."

"Persistent, thorough."

Raleigh could think of a few more adjectives that were less flattering. "She's one of our best investigators."

"Colonel, as you know, I'm a great supporter of the Bureau and the Carbon Acts. I was among the first to support their amendments in the Assembly after the Spike."

"The Bureau has always appreciated your support." *What does she want?*

"Would you agree that even in the cause of environmental protection, zealousness can sometimes be overdone?"

"I'm sorry, ma'am. I'm not following you."

The Minister showed a rare hint of irritation. "I read your introductory report for our meeting, Colonel. I saw that you and Kilel are investigating a minor case of carbon smuggling. Something to do with shipping across the Arctic Ocean.'

Minor? Did she actually read the report?

"In my personal opinion, Inspector Kilel's time is better spent elsewhere. Do you agree?"

"I'm not sure." *What is she talking about?*

"You know what's best for your agency and the inspector. I'm not one to micromanage."

"No, ma'am." *She's warning me off. Why? What is Kilel doing?*

"Excellent. I have complete faith in you, Colonel. Your service continues to be stellar. Speaking of promotions, the newest promotions list from Personnel crossed my desk today." The Minister cleared her throat. "I was disappointed to see that your name was not on the list."

"That doesn't surprise me, ma'am. I'm not due for consideration until next year." *Lieutenant General would be a nice cap on my career.*

"Bureaucracy is so tedious." The Minister crossed her legs. "I have the authority to award promotions in the case of meritorious service, and I believe you qualify."

"I'm flattered, ma'am."

"It's true, Raleigh. You're a true patriot for the earth."

She's exposing herself and me to charges of attempting to obstruct justice. "Thank you, but I'd rather follow the normal procedures."

"Nonsense, Raleigh. I'll start the paperwork right away. I owe you. Do we understand each other?"

No, it's me owing you, and I'd better pay up. "Perfectly, ma'am."

"Excellent." The Minister was cheery. "And I hope whatever health issues you have clear up very soon. Let's have dinner together sometime. My treat." The Minister held out her hand, a signal that the meeting was over.

In a moment, Colonel, soon to be Lieutenant General, Raleigh Penn, against his will, found himself in the reception area facing the security bot. Its green light was steady, an implacable threat. In spite of that, he smiled inwardly. *If my guess is right, Anne is my insurance against failure.*

CHAPTER 31

THE TEXT AND VIDEO ON Janine Kilel's tablet displayed as clear as the Oregon sunshine, but her concentration failed her as she wrestled with Colonel Penn's newest demand. Under normal circumstances, she took her orders and moved on to other priorities. That's why she checked out a car from the BES motor pool and told it to drive to the Penn residence in Brier Valley. She had made up her mind what to do next with Anne, but the instructions from the colonel gnawed at her like an injury.

The scene played over and over again in her mind. She was sitting in her Eugene office, answering email and com queries, when Colonel Penn came up in the queue.

"I'd like a concise update on the oil trafficking case, Inspector." Colonel Penn's skin was sallow, his eyes rheumy, and the skin hung on his facial bones like a draped cloth. His hands, though, were still powerful; he might still best her in the jiu jitsu matches the agency arranged as morale boosters. *A man at death's door.*

Kilel wasted no time with pleasantries. She summarized her last *pro forma* activity report. "The trace evidence points to a very old oil field in Pennsylvania protected by the local environmental guard force. It seems—"

"What's the bottom line, Inspector?"

"Sir?"

Penn sighed. "Have you drawn any conclusions?"

"Sir, it's too early to draw conclusions. I'd need to—"

"You're an experienced investigator. Give me your informed speculation."

His testiness disconcerted Kilel. The colonel was methodical and patient. She worked in a similar way; that's why they got along. "I've formed the outline of a hypothesis. I don't have any proof yet that would stand up before the Tribunal."

"Go on."

"Sir..." *How much of what I say might hurt me?* "I believe there may be elements in the government that are involved in this smuggling operation." There, she had put her foot in it for good now. "The chemical analysis of the oil samples, as well as the ownership of vehicles involved in transporting the oil, point to a government connection."

Colonel Penn's pallid face turned gray. "Do you realize what you are saying, Inspector?"

Kilel shifted in her chair. "You asked for speculation, sir. The evidence is thin and circumstantial. I have a few other ideas..."

"What's your next move?"

Careful. "I've spoken to the general officer in charge of the sector where the oil comes from," Kilel said, more comfortable on this ground. "I'm not satisfied with his answers. I'd like to bring him in for further questioning."

Colonel Penn's silence unnerved Kilel. She detected a slight narrowing of his eyes, and for an instant, he appeared indecisive. She had never seen that in him.

"Janine, I would like you to postpone your interview with the witness."

"Sir?"

"Postpone your interview."

"May I ask why, sir?"

The colonel's face turned stony. "Information has come into my possession related to the case."

"With respect, sir, may I see that information?" *Is he holding out on me?*

Penn lowered his eyes. "That's not possible. It's classified at the highest levels."

He's lying. Why?

"Furthermore, Inspector, I'd like you to place your investigation on inactive status, at least for the time being. Understood?"

Penn's order stunned Kilel. He had never halted one of her inquiries before. The implications of his order, after she had laid out her speculation, solidified her suspicions that a person or group deep inside the government was running the smuggling operation. *He's saying, "If you get too close to this, you'll get burned."*

"Sir, I need to tell you that your brother may be involved."

"What evidence do you have?" The colonel said, astounded. "How is that possible?"

"Surveillance at Pole Station shows him boarding a launch that belonged to the *Aganippe*. I suspected he might be aboard the vessel. He disappeared soon after, along with the ship itself."

"Perhaps he was aboard her when the boat vanished."

"It's possible," Kilel said. "The boat's disappearance is still a mystery, though my hypothesis includes the possibility that it was attacked by some sort of off-the-radar force."

"You mean a marauder?"

"Rumors of pirate activities are strong in the Arctic. The Russians tried to stamp them out for years."

Penn's face was blank. "I find it difficult to believe that our remote sensing technologies can't find a pirate."

"Unless he has help."

"From whom?"

Don't go there. "I don't want to speculate further, sir, but outside help would explain why he or they are eluding us."

Kilel knew that family relationships were powerful, and people would protect their blood. Yet the colonel had told her, in so many words, that he was indifferent to his younger brother. *What about Anne?* Until this moment, Kilel hadn't considered the possibility that her boss might harbor emotions for his niece. *Does she have a connection to the smuggling?* The inspector shook off the idea as wild and unfounded. The girl was far too guileless. Instead, Kilel gambled that loyalty, however weak, might persuade the colonel to continue the investigation. "I also think it's possible that your brother may have thrown his lot in with them."

Penn considered Kilel's point for about a second. "That's irrelevant, Inspector. Please suspend your investigation until further notice."

Damn, but what's the real reason he wants me to stop? Her long experience in bureaucracies argued for compliance, not because of some need to be submissive to a higher authority, but for the need to bide her time. *What if the colonel is at the center of the ring?*

"Yes, sir," she said.

Penn ended the conference without so much as a thank-you. In her car on the road to the Penn ranch and the wildlife refuge, she turned his words over and over, like a puzzle, and her conclusion was always the same: powers above him wanted Kilel to back off. A thought crossed the inspector's mind, and she called up the colonel's public schedule for the past few days. He had traveled to the Capital, and his meeting schedule put him at the Interior Ministry for most of his stay. He had regular meetings with the minister to maintain a friendly, if distant relationship. The information in the calendar entries was far too general to mean anything, but the implication was inescapable.

The Interior Ministry oversees the special military units protecting the oil fields from poaching. Mother in Heaven, is someone at Interior running this show?

Anne Penn and Mike Schmidt disbelieved what the video feed of the remaining Klamath magpie nest showed them, and they climbed the ladder to the hole in the snag. Green sprouts of early colonizing plants—salal and poison oak—poked through the ash of the scorched areas of the refuge, despite the bone-dry soil. Mike was first up the ladder and he peered in, letting a hand mirror reflect the dim scene at the bottom of the hole. Dread seized Anne when Mike shook his head. He stepped off the ladder, allowing her to see the nest for herself. Among the downy feathers was the single chick, motionless. The lack of defensive behavior by the parent birds confirmed its death.

Anne climbed down and reclined against a basalt rock heated by the incessant sun. A pair of field glasses hung on her neck. Maxie panted in the rock's shade. In previous seasons the mortality rate among the magpie chicks had been high, but enough survived to maintain the population. The fire had changed everything, and with the death of the chick, the species was one step closer to extinction. Anne missed her father more than ever. He always knew what to say or do to help her feel that life was not spinning out of control. "We did what we could."

"It wasn't enough."

"We've got the chicks in the coop." All but one of the eggs had hatched, and they kept the human foster parents busy feeding them an insect mash with tweezers.

"What if they die? It'll be our fault."

"No, it won't," Anne said. "They're all healthy. They're all eating."

"It could change in a heartbeat."

Anne stood up to talk to her friend face to face. "Mike, you're not helping. I don't need you telling me that I'm going to fail."

"I didn't mean—"

"If Dad were here, he'd say something to me. He'd say, 'It's going to be all right. You're doing fine.'"

"It's just that—"

"No, tell me that I'm doing the right thing. Tell me that this isn't stupid."

"It's not stupid." Mike's voice was quiet, almost shy.

Bird and insect sounds filled the atmosphere with competing melodies.

"I want to fix this, but the goddamn chicks dying on me isn't helping." Anne swept her hand across the burned refuge. "How come this had to happen? It was an accident. I've got to fix it so Dad can come home."

"Look, shit happens."

Anne turned on him. "Oh, fuck off. Use your brain. The species is dead, Dad is going to be dissed, and there's nothing I can do about it. You're the same as everyone else. You're just like the other idiots around here."

Mike's face was stricken with hurt. He pushed himself off the rock and stumbled to the path leading to the ranch.

Anne realized what she'd done, and she hurried after him. "Mike, I'm sorry. I didn't mean you're an idiot."

"No, you fuck off." Mike turned on her, angry. "I came up here because I wanted to help you."

"Wait," Anne cried. "You are helping, but I was mad about the chick. I didn't think the chick would die."

Mike's anger subsided as well. "I came up here because I wanted... to be friends."

"We are friends."

Mike took a step closer to her. "I thought... No, there's no point."

"What?"

"I thought maybe we could be more than friends. I came up here, because if I didn't, it might be weeks before I saw you again in town. I didn't want to wait that long."

Mike's admission stunned Anne. He was attractive and kind, to be sure. With her dad gone, though, it never crossed her mind that Mike was any more than a male acquaintance. She remembered the moment when he took her hand before they installed the camera. *Am I not seeing what's right in front of me?* She was grateful he had watched over the chicks. *I could do what I'm doing alone, but he makes it easier.*

Anne took a tentative step toward Mike, and then a puff of dust on the road leading to the ranch caught her eye. Mike noticed her attention shift and followed her gaze. The sun glinted off the chrome of a vehicle. Anne raised her field glasses, and she spied the BES shield on the door. "Christ, it's Kilel."

Anne and Mike raced down the path, Maxie trailing, and they reached a short rise, which gave them a closer view of the ranch buildings. Kilel was at the coop, fumbling with the latch. *The chicks are noisy. She's curious.* A thin copse of cottonwoods marked the edge of the Penn property. With Mike close behind, Anne punched through. "Inspector!"

Kilel's head snapped around. "What is happening here? What are you doing with these chicks?"

The dog snapped at the officer.

"Maxie! Down." Anne stopped a few meters from the coop. "Wait, Inspector. I can explain," she gasped, winded from her sprint.

"There's nothing to explain. Do you realize what you are doing?"

"I'm trying to save them."

"You have no right, no right whatsoever."

"It's the birds' last chance. Please, Inspector."

"That is not for you to say. That is not for any human being to say." Kilel glanced at her car, and the security bot trotted over to the three humans. "Anne Penn, you are under arrest for willfully interfering in a natural process without authority, and that's just the start of things."

The security bot stiffened, and Mike stepped forward. Kilel repressed a scream at this surge of adolescent loyalty. "Stay out of this, or I will arrest you as well."

Anne lifted her hands, as if warding off danger. "Inspector, please wait. Let me explain. If we don't help these chicks, the species will die out."

"That process was set in motion by your father," Kilel charged. "Interfering with it makes it worse. It's that kind of thinking that has brought the earth to her knees."

Anne couldn't believe how petty the officer was. "You don't understand."

"We must restore a balance. Human beings have interfered too much with the natural order. That means we stop putting our nose where it doesn't belong." Kilel removed one of the magpie chicks from the nesting box. The delicacy of her motion confused Anne. She held the chick in her open palm.

"What you have done here was not meant to be," Kilel said. "The Mother did not intend this."

Kilel closed her fingers over the chick, as if her hand were the mouth of a predator.

The move terrified Anne. "Please, Inspector. Don't do this. It's the last one."

Kilel tightened her grip on the helpless chick.

"Its brothers and sisters are the last ones." Anne's voice was low and firm. She had to get through to this insane woman. "If you kill it, you'll be just as guilty as the criminals you hunt."

Anne heard the chick's plaintive peeps through the fingers of Kilel's closed hand. The inspector was in a trance, as if working through something in her mind, trying to make a decision. When she spoke, her voice was distant. "I've sworn an oath to protect the earth from the depredations caused by greed and indifference, and my own agency is committing those sins."

What is she talking about? "Inspector, I know you came here looking for justice." Anne stepped forward, keeping an eye on the security bot. "We both want the same thing. We have more in common than you realize." Anne pointed toward the copse. "The chick in the last magpie nest, out in the refuge. It's dead. We've just come from there. The chick in your hand is the last hope for the species. Without us, the magpies will disappear."

Through Kilel's closed fingers, the chick pecked and pushed back with more urgency, as if aware that its death was near, and it fought for its life.

"Let it live, Inspector Kilel. We have a chance to fix the mistakes. We have to try."

Almost like an automaton's, Kilel's fingers opened, and she returned the chick to the nesting box. She took a deep breath as she closed the latch and rested her hand on the plywood wall.

"Inspector?" Anne reached out and touched her arm. "What's wrong?"

Kilel glanced sternly at Anne's outstretched hand and let her breath out. "Nothing is wrong, Miss Penn." She exhaled, as if practicing a breathing exercise. "I'd like your help."

"You'd like... I don't understand." *She's talking nonsense. Is the woman unhinged?*

"I need to find your father, and I know you want to find him as well."

Steel came back into Anne's voice. "I've already helped you all I can."

"There's something more you can do." Kilel faced Anne. "We do have something in common: your father. We both want him alive and back home. There's more at stake now, more than a species of bird." Kilel paused. "I've lost track of your father, but I have an idea where he might be."

Anne wanted to cheer at the news. "Where?"

"A place called Bežat in the Union of Russia."

She was incredulous. "Russia? How is that even possible?"

"Anne, I believe he is in personal danger, far beyond what he imagined after the refuge fire."

This was starting to sound like an awful political drama on the chans. "Why should I trust you?"

"If I go to where he is on my own, he might run again," Kilel explained. "If you are with me, perhaps... but I can't compel you to accompany me," she said, rigid as always with her self-imposed rules. "It's dangerous, but we can do it."

Mike put in a word of his own. "Anne needs to stay. We need to care for the chicks."

Kilel studied Schmidt. "It seems to me that you're capable of taking over for your girlfriend."

"My what?"

"I can't help you," Anne said. This new dilemma tortured her. Nothing ever stood still long enough for her to understand it. First the fire, then Dad runs away—*He had no choice!*—my uncle wants to be friends, and now Kilel wants my help based on a crazy guess. "I don't know anyone in Russia. I've never heard of—"

"This may be the only hope you have of seeing your father again alive."

Damn you. Will you never stop hurting me? "I don't speak Russian. I don't—"

"You don't need to do anything. You're my bait. If your father is at Bežat, you'll draw him out. Then we'll bring him home."

She needs me, Anne realized. It dawned on her: She had leverage over this bizarre BES agent. "If I go with you, you have to agree to drop the charges against my dad. The fire was an accident."

"I don't have the authority—"

Anne wasn't having it. "You said something about your agency committing sins. I don't know what that means, but I think something's going on that scares you, and you need me to get to the heart of it."

Kilel's acknowledgment was stiff, as if it were painful. "I don't make promises I can't keep, but I'll... do what I can."

In Anne's mind, the inspector's reluctance meant Kilel really did know where her father was. The risk was worth it, if it meant reuniting with him. Anne grasped Mike's hand and squeezed it. "I have to go," she said, committed to her new course. "I have to try."

CHAPTER 32

Bill never felt farther away from Anne and the life he'd built in Brier Valley. The escape to Port Simpson, the voyage to the Arctic Ocean, the unexpected encounter with Molly at Pole Station, even the sinking of the *Aganippe* and *Aurora Borealis,* struck him as otherworldly events. Simple geography proved the point of his isolation. He sat in a seat of a pilot car on the shore of the Gulf of Ob, a Russian coastal inlet he'd never heard of before *Extinction* surfaced in its midst. The sub offloaded her contraband crude, leaving the trucks—fifty-odd lumbering, autonomous tanks with wheels and motors following one another like elephants in a parade—to drive a twisting, rutted, unmarked military road in a remote region called Krasnoyarsk Krai. He longed for a bath and a meal that didn't taste like paste.

In the seat next to Gore, Bill monitored the nav systems. As the captain's captive in all but name, Bill was bound to follow his orders or risk a nasty death like the one he witnessed on *Aganippe*. Bill had no friends within ten-thousand kilometers, apart from Micah. He was trapped with only one chance of reuniting with Anne: Find a way to link Molly with Raleigh Penn, the brother he knew about as a well as he knew Russian, which was not at all. His brother's AI problem presented Martin Scribb with an opportunity to keep his part of the bargain with Molly: freedom in exchange for helping Raleigh. In the hours and days after Molly came aboard *Extinction*, Gore rarely let her out of his sight. She was with Gore and Bill in another seat of the cramped car, a holo-terminal emitter on her lap. Gore's executive officer, Nelson, served as guard and backup driver in case the AI failed.

In some ways, Molly's presence was worse than Gore's or Scribb's. Gore was easy to understand; he wanted power and wealth. It was unclear to Bill how Scribb benefited from finding Molly, though Bill didn't care. The man's history as leader of the disastrous Project Algid was enough for Bill to form an opinion. *They're both slimy as hagfish.* His opinion of Molly was tougher to nail down. He'd loved her once, but not now. She was the mother of his child, though she had abandoned her and him. She was the same intelligent, adventuresome woman that had captured his heart as a young man, but she had gone in a strange direction.

"Why?" Bill asked the question as Molly manipulated a subroutine on the 3-D code editor.

"I assume you mean, why did I choose my profession? That's what moralizers always ask." Molly sighed. "After the trials, I had nowhere to go."

The answer made no sense to Bill. "You could've come home. Anne needed her mother."

"You mean to Brier Valley? No, that was in my past. Motherhood and domesticity were not what I wanted. I knew you'd take good care of Anne, so I choose other things."

"Like becoming a whore."

Molly ignored the condemnation. "A female relative back in the 1850s moved from Ohio to a new settlement in the west, set up a bordello, and within twenty years owned most of the town. Her name was Louise. She financed an opera company and built a women's hospital. She left her money and property to the town's schools when she died."

Bill was unimpressed by the family genealogy.

"A great-grandmother of mine researched public records and found some letters Louise had written," Molly continued. "The town tolerated her, but she was never accepted. The moralizing preachers and upper-class women who arrived after her kept her from investing in legitimate businesses she couldn't finance herself. Other men and women set up their own bordellos, with standards far lower than hers. She prospered, but she was in a social cage. She called it a 'jail with invisible bars.'"

These rules exist for a reason. "She died a rich but unhappy woman."

"She believed she was doing the town good by offering a place for men to blow off steam in safety and privacy."

"You decided to follow Louise's example," Bill said acidly.

"I was out of money. No one would hire me. I escaped disidentification, but I might as well have been dissed. Louise showed me a way to start over. Another woman from Algid had the same idea. Ginny Magante and I became business partners and started the Cyprian Association."

Ginny? Molly's friend on Aurora's fantail. An idea came to him. Molly had gained something from her experience at Project Algid, despite its depravity. Gore confirmed it when he purred, "It seems to me that Martin Scribb was nothing if not a classic entrepreneur. His risk-taking attitude rubbed off on Molly. I can certainly understand that manner of thinking."

Molly kept talking as she scrolled through a section of code. "I handled the technical and operational end and she had contacts in the mining and shipping industries, which were first in line as the Arctic opened up for trade. Right after the war, we saw the Arctic Free Economic Zone as a chance to take our ideas to a new level."

The pilot car lurched over a pothole. Scratching the week's worth of stubble on his jaw, Bill still didn't understand the purpose of a union for prostitutes, but he remembered the scene at Pole Station. Molly was surrounded by rich and powerful people, none of whom were ignorant or stupid. *Maybe she's doing some good, though I can't figure out what that might be.*

Molly eyed Bill. "How did you come to work for Kapitan Gore? You're not the pirate type."

"I had to stay a step ahead of the bessies." Bill told Molly a brief version of the fire, his voyage on *Aganippe*, and his decision to volunteer aboard *Extinction*. "I had no idea that *Aganippe* was carrying oil, though I ignored the signs, looking back on it."

"So you weren't coming after me?" Molly said. "I thought you were trying to find me when I saw you at Pole Station."

Bill rolled his eyes. "No, that was pure coincidence."

"You came after me later."

Does she still have feelings for me? He laughed at the irony. "That was when Scribb said he might be able to get BES off my back. He needs an AI expert, and I thought of you."

"You aren't trying to rekindle something that's long dead?"

Bill caught Gore's glance, but the sailor answered, wearily, "Don't flatter yourself, Molly. I stopped loving you long ago. You abandoned Anne and me. That was the end of it."

A pained look shadowed Molly's face. Bill's statement hurt her more than he expected, but it left him unaffected. *It's her own fault.* "If I hadn't met Scribb, we wouldn't be here."

Molly changed the subject. "Why is he so interested in helping your brother?"

"Beats me. Probably because Raleigh is high up in BES. He's been there a long time. I imagine he can pull a lot of strings."

"It may not matter because I'm not sure I can help Martin with whatever problem Raleigh has." Molly entered a few keystrokes, and code changed color from red to green. "I still work on artificial intelligence, but it's more of a side-line than anything else."

Bill hadn't considered that Molly might fail. "Scribb is my best chance to get home to Anne and back to a normal life."

"Is she doing well?"

Bill wanted to spit out the words, *Why should you care?* But he held back. "She's beautiful and intelligent. You'd be proud of her." *Spoken like the father who adores her.*

Molly tapped a few keys and paused. "Will you tell her about me, when you see her?"

"If you like," he said sharply. "Shall I tell her everything, including your career choice?"

She agreed, too quickly for Bill's taste. "She should know. She'll make her own decisions about what she thinks of me."

"She's already decided what she thinks of you."

Molly's curiosity was piqued. "What is that?"

"She hates you."

"Hates me? Why?" The revelation stung Bill's ex. "I'm an independent businesswoman with friends at the highest levels. I'm what every ambitious woman aspires to be. I'm proud of what I've accomplished."

Bill could not resist mocking her. "Apart from running a business that degrades women, you abandoned us, remember? You never wrote. You never contacted us by com. Nothing for fifteen years. How do you expect her to react? The only reason I don't hate you is that you gave me Anne. I'm proud that she's everything you're not."

Molly faced Bill, her voice quiet. "Believe it or not, I am interested in Anne." She broke her gaze with him for a second. "Maybe more than I realized." She returned to Bill, and said, "If she is as loyal and persistent as her father, and if she's inherited some of my intelligence and spirit, she must be an incredible kid."

The praise took Bill aback. It was self-serving and egotistical, but it was genuine. Perhaps Molly did care about Anne, despite her despicable choices. The possibility confused Bill, but he was not so rigid that he couldn't accept that Molly had found a way to rationalize her thinking and behavior toward him and Anne. The edges of Bill's resentment toward his ex-wife dulled as he considered her point of view, though he could never agree with it.

The convoy trundled on, and by the afternoon of the third day, Bill's eyes smarted and watered. At first, he thought one of the tankers had sprung a leak, but the monitoring system reported nothing. Outside the pilot car, as the convoy moved south at a brisk pace, the relentless green of tall shrubs and stunted trees continued on each side of the road, a living wall that blocked the view beyond a few feet. The land extended into an expanse of low rolling hills, and the pilot car's navigation computer recorded a slow gain in elevation. The stinging in his eyes waxed and waned, as if the convoy passed through invisible clouds of chemicals.

On the fourth day, Gore halted the convoy, and Bill emerged from the pilot car. Molly stood by. "Why are we stopping?" Martin joined them from one of the trucks carrying Gore's thugs.

"We've reached our destination, Bežat," Gore said.

Bill repeated the word, though it did not roll off his tongue as it did for Gore.

"'Run,' in English," he said.

A broad valley stretched before them. The floor was smooth and feature-less, until Bill realized the "floor" was the top of a cloud the color of a grilled pancake. Tendrils of smoke lifted off the cloud like dust devils on a desert plain. Mechanical sounds drifted up from the true floor of the valley, which Bill picked out through breaks in the smog. Reflections of sunlight suggested bends of a river, though the colors were bent in odd ways, as in a funhouse mirror.

Gore growled. "Back in the car. We have an appointment."

Within a few minutes of descending from the top of the rise, the pilot car was enveloped in the brown haze, which thinned and thickened with a rhythmic progression. The trucks followed like a train of pack mules.

The tiger-man issued orders and monitored a map of the sprawling city. Despite his fearsome appearance, and his status as a prisoner, Bill had lost some of his fear of Gore. However, Molly was the most relaxed of all in the car, as if she was on familiar ground. *This isn't her first time with him.* "You asked me how I met Kapitan Gore. What about you?"

"I've known the captain for a long time, Bill," Molly hummed. "The intro-ductions he had made while I visited the darker corners of harbors from Prince Rupert to Nagasaki proved valuable twenty years later when I reinvented my life."

Gore grimaced, but Bill was incensed. *Gore was a lover.* "You slept with him."

The captain snarled, and Bill regretted his outburst.

"Calm down, boys," Molly clucked. "It was a long time ago, Bill, before we met. Believe it or not, I was faithful to you, but I admit I was a little randy before then." Molly clicked a key and smiled at the pop-up. "I've missed you, Gregori."

Gore glanced her way, but his cat's eyes were impenetrable. "You've done well for yourself, Mrs. Bain."

"Thank you. Business is good for you?"

"I'll know once I've delivered my cargo."

One thing Bill remembered from his early days with Molly: She never talk-ed about her previous lovers. The sailor was grateful for her silence on that score. He tended toward jealousy, holding onto relationships tight enough to strangle them. In all the years since Molly left him, only one woman in Brier

Valley interested him beyond a furtive night or two. Her name was Daphne, an auburn-haired, chatty woman, and she owned a sprawling ranch on the other side of the valley. Her husband had run off, fed up with all the hard work. Bill met Daphne at a farmer co-op meeting, but he jumped too soon to talk of marriage. She stopped returning his calls and texts, and blocked him from her network contacts, and stopped coming to co-op meetings. Bill didn't understand why she was frightened of him. He later heard she had left the valley to find her old man. Anne was about nine at the time. He reflected on his constant worry about Anne's well-being. *Am I clinging to her?*

The pilot car emerged from the haze into a clearer layer heavy with particulates. Dwellings cobbled with found wood from pallets or crates, or sheets of rusted steel, lined the road. Tarps draping the slapdash hovels lay limp in the dead air. The pilot car rolled close to one shanty. A young woman sat in a doorway, the door missing. Her vacant eyes bulged, her cheeks sank into her skull, and her threadbare clothing hung on her bones. A listless boy child put his head on her shoulder.

The column skirted a square surrounded by more substantial buildings rising three or four stories, remnants of an older town. Dozens of merchants in a market of ragged shelters offered rotting fruits, moldy vegetables, and hand-sized loaves of dark bread. Huddled men and women haggled, their mouths muffled by the car's armored windows.

"Who are these people?" Bill said.

"Victims of our grandparents and great-grandparents," Gore said. "Their lives are the result of decisions made in the Age of Coal and the Age of Oil."

"They're refugees, but from where?"

"Have you observed their dark skin?" Gore's amber eyes burned. "How did someone with skin and eyes the color of onyx come to this place, do you suppose?"

As the planet's atmosphere heated, the marginal lands of Africa, the Indian subcontinent, and other regions for thousands of miles on either side of the equator could no longer sustain agriculture. Rising sea levels pushed humanity from the coasts. Rainfall patterns changed, and from south Asia, millions moved north, pushing into the Hindu Kush and the Himalayas. The ice and snows of the mountains disappeared, leaving nothing but stony desert. The displaced millions continued north. In the chaos of those times, governments disappeared, and whole nations vanished.

"How many are they?" Molly said.

"In Run? Perhaps a half-million. In other settlements, two or three million more. No one has counted them. It is not important."

"Not important?"

"To them. They care about surviving until tomorrow, and keeping their loved ones warm. A population figure is something an academic, or a tax collector, cares about. There are none of those here."

The convoy trundled down a narrow street and passed a group of warehouses, coming into a broad tract of land ten or fifteen hectares in size. The tract was pitted with two dozen black pools, resembling the footprints of gigantic round-footed monsters. Rubber sheets lined each of the pools. Each had oil, most less than half-filled. The pilot car drew near enough to the edge of a pool to allow a view of the bottom. A black sludge oozed between the high and low points of the uneven floor, interspersed with the iridescence of watery petroleum. The acrid air made Bill's skin itch. Gore directed Nelson to shacks at the far end of the tract. "Our destination," he said over the hiss of the tankers' brakes.

A group of ragged, barefoot men walked single file on a path between the pits. On their shoulders they carried lengths of ten-centimeter hoses, rope, and other gear. Two vehicles resembling tractors that towed aircraft on a tarmac road led the group. The workers hooked the tankers to the back of the tow trucks, and the trucks maneuvered the tankers down the paths between the pits. The first tractor and tanker-in-tow halted next to a pit, and a pair of workers scrambled underneath the tanker, hooking up one of the wide-mouthed hoses to an spigot in its belly. A worker opened a valve, and a thick liquid the color of dark chocolate gushed from the hose's mouth into the pit. More tractors and workers showed up, and one by one they rolled a tanker to a pit and repeated the procedure. The workers spoke little, and moved in a measured manner, as if they had done the task a thousand times and took no joy in it.

"Our delivery is complete," Gore said soon, appearing next to Molly and the others outside the pilot car. "We've been invited to dinner at Run's City Hall. I'd like you to join me."

"Do I have a choice?"

"What about us?" Martin said, Bill beside him.

Gore maintained his geniality. "You may come as my guests."

"How gracious of you," Martin said. "I'm looking forward to it. Friends turn up in the most unlikely places. Perhaps you'll know someone, Molly."

Gore motioned everyone back to the vehicles. The pilot car lurched forward before making a wide turn to the pit farm's entrance.

"What happens to it?" Bill said.

"To what?" Gore said.

"The oil. These vehicles are electric. I don't see any others, except for the tractors. What do the people do with the oil?"

"The internal combustion engine is not dead, despite what governments may tell you," Gore said, keeping his gaze trained on the windshield. "Heat is a precious commodity in the northern latitudes, despite the Warming."

"What about your oil?"

"It is no longer mine. I've sold it to the mayor of Run."

"What does he do with it?"

"She."

Gore's opaqueness infuriated Bill. "I asked you a simple question."

"Why do you want to know?"

Bill was simply curious, but Molly answered the question. "Bill's a species killer. I'm a convicted carbon felon. Our curiosity is part of our twisted thinking."

Gore laughed. It was raspy, like the tongue of a cat. "Very well. Nelson, let us take our colleagues to the lower circles of Hell."

Nelson touched a screen, and the car turned left down a potholed street. The khaki haze thickened, but Bill made out the walls of a narrow canyon on either side of the road. The shoulder clung to the edge of a desultory river. The canyon walls vanished behind a smog that thickened further to zero visibility. The car's air filters kept out most of the cloying smell of petroleum, but Bill's eyes watered again. Nelson wiped his eyes as well. Gore opened a small locker near his feet and removed four respirators. "You'll need one when we arrive."

The pilot car pulled off the road and halted. The four passengers exited, respirators on. The smog hovered on the ground like a blanket, obscuring everything but the outlines of buildings and dead trees. Bill heard human voices in the distance beyond the brown air. He heard a *whoosh*, like the sound of a lighting match, except much larger. Gore led the way up a trail. Nelson cocked his pistol and clicked the safety off.

The volume of the voices increased in number and intensity. Another *whoosh*, and Bill felt a blast of heat and saw flares of orange and yellow light. As if they crossed an invisible boundary, the smog lifted, though not wholly. A dozen fires burned, each engulfing home-made contraptions of barrels, lengths of tubing, frames of twisted steel, all coated with tar the color of coal. Men, women, boys, and girls, oily from sweat and petroleum, carried makeshift containers holding a few liters of a viscous substance resembling watery jelly. None of them paid attention to the visitors. A boy approached an open fire and poured the crude oil onto the flames, which flashed. From two tubes, a blond liquid flowed into large plastic containers.

"This is a refinery," Molly said through her mask.

"Indeed," Gore said.

None of the workers wore respirators.

Bill tightened the respirator's straps against the poisonous air. "I've seen photos of the old refineries before the carbon laws banned them. They don't look anything like this."

"Refining crude oil is simple. You boil the petroleum and capture the vapors. You cool the vapors with water and they condense." He pointed at the blond liquid. "That's diesel fuel. It's taken to the market and sold."

"I didn't see many vehicles in the town."

"Diesel also works as a heating source."

"Why don't people just use the solar grid or wind generators?"

Gore's laugh had no mirth. "Let me explain something, Mr. Penn. Even after a hundred years of solar power and wind power for the masses, it still takes technological poise and financial resources to deliver it. Oil requires no such investments, as you can see. The poorest man or woman can use it, though the environmental costs are high, and they know it. Freezing to death, however, is not an option."

A boy pushed past Bill carrying a jug of diesel fuel. *Hell is too kind a word for this place.* Persecution by Janine Kilel was a blessing, compared to the life these children led. Was Gore performing a service to these people, or was he perpetuating a cycle of poverty and poison started by generations in the past? Whatever the cause, this was the price of carbon, borne by the weakest of the earth.

CHAPTER 33

MOLLY INHALED AS IF SURFACING after a dive. The air inside the drab concrete building was cleaner than the Arctic air at Pole Station, without the dry, tangy smell of recycled atmosphere in *Aurora Borealis*. The scent reflected a time before the Warming, when the countryside around Run was a humid mixture of pine needles and rushing water.

"So good to see you again, Kapitan Gore. Welcome back to City Hall," said a crisp man with the black pushed-in nose of a pug dog. "Your usual room is ready."

Gore gestured toward Molly. "This is Mrs. Bain."

The reception clerk's face displayed the characteristic blank affect of com access. "Of course." He touched a keypad. "Mayor deMayer is expecting both of you in the Tsarina Alexandra Ballroom at 19:00. The servbot will show you to your rooms."

A robot, as shiny as the day it left the factory, came up next to Gore and Molly. The three took an elevator to the eighth floor, and by habit Molly touched her right forefinger to the door. The lock clicked; the hotel had already learned her DNA ID print. Gore followed her into the room, a clean, if standard hotel-style two-room suite.

"My room is next door, Mrs. Bain. The mayor is the fastidious type, and I've asked the concierge to make certain arrangements for you. You'll find an appropriate wardrobe in the closet. I'll see you a few hours."

Gore departed, and Molly walked over to the curtain-shrouded window. The fabric was for looks only; steel plates had replaced the window glass. With a sigh of gratitude, she opened the faucets in the bathtub and touched a button for salts. After a half-hour soak she wrapped herself in a hotel robe and lay on the comfortable, if squeaky, bed.

A soft tone awakened her. The time was 18:20 by her minds-eye. She select-ed a low-cut dress of carmine satin. She hung the gown in the dressmaker, then touched the "measure" key as she slipped out of her robe. A green laser swept across her naked body, taking measurements in three dimensions. A readout asked her to turn 180 degrees. The laser measured her again. By the time she slipped back into the robe, the "ready" light on the dressmaker glowed. The altered gown hugged her in a flattering way. As it happened, the cosmetic studs in her ears set off the design.

Molly adjusted her auburn hair without a brush or comb. *A girl can't have everything.* She heard a soft knock at the door.

Kapitan Gore greeted her in an old-fashioned uniform. His face was a mask, but she sensed his arousal at the sight of her. "You are very attrac-tive this evening, Mrs. Bain. Are you ready to accompany me to the council meeting?"

"Nearly. Won't you come in?"

Molly made a show of fine-tuning her attire in hopes of getting Gore to talk. "Gregori, you are the only person who calls me 'Mrs. Bain.' Why?"

"I consider our relationship a professional one."

"It also keeps you distant." She pitched her voice at a level she knew relaxed men. "I haven't been married for almost twenty years. I want to know you again, as we did when we first met. Do you remember?"

A guttural sound emerged from Gore's throat.

"You look very good, Gregori." Molly drew near to her former lover. "Your uniform is familiar, but from a previous era?"

Gore lifted his furred hands to Molly's bare shoulders. "It is a replica of the uniform my great-great grandfather wore in the Soviet Navy, the old Russian Navy of 1950 or so."

"It suits you."

They kissed. Gore's lips tasted as human as any man's, though the fur on his face felt like a cat's, finer than a man's beard.

"I admire you, Gregori. You've remade yourself. You've found your path in your own way."

"You have done the same, Mrs. Bain. We saw the opportunities a new world offered and exploited them."

"Gregori, I'm more than someone who can make your tankers follow one another like ants. Let's you and I be partners, business partners..." Molly pressed against him and lifted her face to his. "...and partners in life. We could conquer the Arctic together."

Gore brushed Molly's check with the pads of his paw. "The offer is tempting, but we are no longer twenty years old. I have little tolerance for partnerships, beyond a brief encounter." The corsair brought a claw to Molly's neck and she felt the scratch, too light to be a caress, heavy enough to tear the topmost layer of her skin. It thrilled her and frightened her. *I won't take No for an answer. He is a monster, but I still love him.*

The worst thing about the room assigned to Bill was sharing it with Scribb, but thoughts of the dissed man melted away as Bill showered and shaved. The closet's tailoring AI adjusted the semi-formal clothes for him, and though he wasn't used to dressing up, he felt refreshed and ready for an evening out. Except for his forehead welt, Scribb was almost unrecognizable in his getup.

An empty belly reminded Bill he hadn't eaten in nearly a full day. "Scribb, I'm going to find something to eat."

"They'll have tons of food at the soirée, I'm betting."

"I'm not waiting." Bill scanned the hallway for a kitchen he spotted earlier. Spotting the auto-chef on a counter next to the open door, he reached for the device's menu selector, noticing, but not reacting to a man sitting at a table. The stranger's plain clothes hung on him as on a skeleton.

The man croaked, "Bill, it's good to see you again."

He looked familiar to Bill, but out of place. "I'm sorry, I don't know—" In a flash, he recognized him. "Jesus fucking Christ."

"Divine I'm not, though I have some influence in high places."

The shock hit Bill like a staser blast. "Raleigh? How?" Bill's hand was poised over the auto-chef, as if frozen.

"Perhaps you could order me a coffee?"

Bill forgot his hunger and let his hand fall to his side. "Raleigh—" Bill's body swayed with disorientation. "Anne! Is something wrong?"

"She's fine."

The assertion failed to reassure Bill. "Kilel, is she here?"

"No, Bill."

Bill couldn't focus. He half-heard Raleigh as his emotions caught up with his perceptions. He hadn't seen his older brother since he was eighteen. They exchanged a total of a dozen words since Anne was born. *A few pictures, maybe.* Bill rarely talked about him to anyone, even his daughter. *It's like he materialized out of thin air.* Thoughts of the girl reoriented his mind. He stepped toward his brother, voice menacing. "If you've hurt Anne or done anything—"

"Relax, Bill. I told you she was fine. I saw her not long ago. She's healthy, at home, and worried sick about you."

Watchful, Bill slid closer to the door, preparing to run. He was buffeted by a sudden squall of emotions, which surged from deep in memory into the present, breaking through and swamping all other feeling, even worry about his daughter. Waves of memory pounded him, beginning with the fear and hurt transferred by mother and father to a four-year-old who absorbed them like a sponge but could not understand them, succeeded by confusing, frightening experiences a six-year-old articulated with tears as a brother announced his betrayal and people in uniforms shut off the dairy farm's water and electricity, ending with flashes to a funeral first for the father and then for the mother, but no brother anywhere near. A decade of hurt compressed into an explosive moment. Bill clenched his fists then opened them, raising them to Raleigh palm out as if blocking him from sight. Bill's voice was low and calm as he struggled to control the maelstrom in his heart and mind. *He wouldn't come all this way after 20 years just to inflict pain.* "Seeing you makes me want to kill you for what you did to mother and father."

Raleigh studied his pale hands. "I wouldn't blame you if you did, though I don't think you're capable of it."

The truth of Raleigh's statement loosened the tension. "I'm not, but I think you should get out, just the same, in case the truth is different."

Raleigh's eyes hardened. "I can't just now, Bill. I need to find someone."

His brother's resistance enraged Bill, as if the older man was preparing to betray him again. "Who are you chasing now?"

"I need to find Molly, your wife."

Ex-wife, Bill wanted to say, but he remained silent as the storm in his heart calmed and he grasped Raleigh's meaning.

Turning to Bill, Raleigh was calm, direct, even warm. "How much do you know about my situation?"

Bill repeated what Scribb detailed in the *Extinction*'s mess hall. Raleigh's near-death appearance corroborated the story for Bill.

"Molly is my last hope for survival. Will you take me to her?"

Bill thought of calling out to Scribb, but didn't. "Why me?"

"I'd rather it'd be you than that cretin." Raleigh sneered in Scribb's direction.

The early emotions subsided, and cold rationality ruled Bill's mind. Raleigh was desperate, and he needed his younger brother to save his life. He'd probably already attempted to find Molly with the usual network surveillance, but Run was no ordinary city. Bill guessed that Raleigh had few options but to make contact with him and with Scribb in order to locate Molly. Bill made his calculation. "I want something from you, and you're going to give it to me."

Raleigh had an air of expectation. "You want revenge? Payback for what I did to Mother and Father?" He made the suggestion as if ready to bargain.

"No, Raleigh. Revenge would do me no good. Or Anne."

Raleigh lifted a corner of his mouth. "An intelligent conclusion on your part. Anne is a beautiful young woman, smart, gifted even." He hung his head a little. "I'm sorry that I didn't take the time to get to know her better. Or her father."

Is he trying to soften me up? "You took the road you took, Raleigh. Own up to it."

"I have, but it's too late for me to do anything about it."

"There's one thing you can do. Scribb said you might be able to get the charges against me dropped. Can you?"

Raleigh considered a moment. "Yes, I can do that."

"Can you guarantee that Anne will never be touched by anything related to the refuge fire? I don't want her future tainted by it."

Raleigh was thoughtful, as if a new idea had occurred to him. "Yes, I'll protect her any way I can."

Another thought came to Bill. "How can I know whether to trust you?"

"I'm a professional, Bill. You may hate me, and I may deserve it, but I believe in what I do. I don't make promises I can't keep." Raleigh sighed. "Apart from that, all I have to offer as a guarantee is my regrets. I'm sorry, Bill, for everything."

The sight of Raleigh's shoulders lifting a millimeter or two, as if the words were waiting to be said for a lifetime, convinced Bill that his brother was sincere. *Have I made a mistake, hating him all these years?* "Very well. I think I should bring Molly to you. This is what we'll do."

A pillared City Hall corridor overflowed with people in formal, if festive dress. South Asian traditional fashions influenced most of the garb, Molly noted, with flowing drapes of fabric in colors that ranged from a grapefruit yellow to deep saffron. Many of the men wore turbans, and the women graced their heads with a simple drape of sheer fabric. The exposed faces, arms, and feet of one couple intrigued Molly. Each of the pair was a hybrid of human and birds of paradise, the sensational iridescent colors of their faces and necks broadcast by hundreds, if not thousands, of feathers. The feathers grew out of their skins, the shafts growing in the same way as a true bird's.

Molly's elegant stride complemented the aristocratic bearing of the uniformed Kapitan Gore, who greeted guests here and there. The music's volume increased, as did the press of people, who moved on the dance floor as if choreographed. Gore stopped at a table and bade Molly to sit. A tuxedoed human server set golden champagne and a selection of mist sticks in front of the new arrivals. The sticks glowed with colors indicating their potency: from red, which would generate hallucinations, to no color at all, which elicited a few minutes of pleasant warmth.

With the nonchalance of the practiced courtesan, she surveyed the walls and ceiling, which were covered with frescoes worthy of the grand ballrooms of Paris or old New York. On the crowded mezzanine, she spotted Bill and Martin, cleaned up, but dressed plainly. Micah Panang rested on the railing, beverage in hand. Molly inferred a pecking order: elites on the main floor, middle classes on the mezzanine.

A large woman in a muted suit decorated with an intricate broach reached out to Gore. "Kapitan, it is so good to see you again." Her Delhi accent matched the caramel color of her skin.

Gore inclined his head in salute. "Mayor deMayer, I'm honored by your invitation. May I present Mrs. Molly Bain."

"The president of the Cyprian Association. We've read about your work in the AFEZ. Pioneering, in many respects."

Molly offered a friendly smile.

"An expert in artificial intelligence as well. A renaissance woman. What brings you to our city?"

"Mrs. Bain is my guest," Gore said. "She was instrumental in getting my latest delivery to Run without serious problems."

"I'm pleased to meet you, Madame Mayor," Molly said, extending her hand.

The mayor's grip was confident, her gaze, measuring.

"Thank you for inviting me to your party," Molly added.

"Party? What is she talking about, Kapitan?" The mayor grinned. "Of course, you're not familiar with our government in Run, are you, Mrs. Bain?" A chime interrupted her conversation. "I'm being called to the council dais. Please excuse me."

The mayor made her way toward the raised stage on one end of the rectangular hall. Eight of the nine places on the platform were occupied. The mayor took a seat at the empty high-backed chair in the center. As if on cue, the throng of three or four hundred guests took chairs at tables around the edge of the ballroom's dance floor, now empty. The crowd on the mezzanine stilled.

Mayor deMayer banged a gavel. "The meeting of the Great Council of Run will now come to order. We have a blessedly short agenda this week, though a grave one. The clerk will call each item."

An aged man stood at one end of the dais at a rostrum. "Madame mayor, honored council members, our only agenda item concerns the matter of Citizen Harunah."

"Yes, of course. A grave matter indeed."

The crowd shifted in its seats, uncomfortable.

"Let's get it over with. Bring in the citizen."

Two security robots dragged in a half-conscious man, his torn and dirty clothing saturated with dried blood. A few in the crowd averted their eyes as he was taken to the center of the dance floor. Gore's eyes widened with anticipation. The bots forced the prisoner to face the mayor.

"Citizen Harunah, you stand accused of..." The mayor picked up a tablet and scanned it. "...of various crimes, all of which are in the public record. I won't bore the council by reading them. You have been determined guilty by the gendarmerie. Do you have anything to say before sentence is passed?"

The prisoner moaned and his head lolled on his chest.

"If I may, madame mayor." The receptionist with the pug nose spoke from his place on the dais. He was one of the nine councilors. "The accused is a resident of my ward. I have been asked to speak for him."

"Very well. What can you say in his defense?"

"Well, madame mayor, that's the problem. I was asked to speak up for him, but I can't think of anything useful to say. I did want to place on the record my statement that I tried to speak up for him."

"Very well said, councilor. You're a credit to your ward and constituents."

The other councilors agreed.

"I move and second that Citizen Harunah be dealt with, according to the law." The mayor glanced down each arm of the dais. "Is there further discussion? No?" The mayor addressed the semi-conscious prisoner. "It is the sense of the Great Council that you deserve the maximum punishment for your crimes. I assume you have nothing further to add that will move the discussion forward. Therefore, you will be disposed of."

The condemned prisoner's mind cleared, and he screamed in a language Molly did not comprehend. Urine flowed down his leg, puddling on the floor.

The mayor put her mouth closer to her microphone to overcome the noise. "Security, execute."

One of the bots deployed its staser and placed it at the back of the prisoner's neck. Molly heard a click. The prisoner's body stiffened, and slumped. The security bots lifted the lifeless man and carried him away. Within seconds, a cooking-pot-sized bot rushed onto the dance floor to clean up the dead man's piss. The acrid smell overcame the perfume of flowers and artificial fragrances.

Gore bared his teeth. "Justice in Run is rough but dependable."

The mayor clasped her hands in front of her. "If there is no further business, I'd like to adjourn the meeting." DeMayor lifted her gavel and brought it down like a thunder clap. The orchestra leader lifted his baton, and the orchestra played a waltz. Couples twirled on the cleaned dance floor as if nothing had happened. Molly glanced up to the mezzanine. Bill, Martin, and Micah were gone.

The wildness of Run attracted Molly, despite the execution. It was the same feeling of opportunity that drew her to the Arctic Free Economic Zone after the Three Degrees North War. Run draped a veneer of legality over an obvious lawlessness, like the gun-toting marshals of Old West Arizona. People in the streets of Run remained trapped in dependency on the very thing that had destroyed them: oil. As in all human upheavals, some profited and thrived in the midst of disaster, Kapitan Gore among them. Molly believed all people had a choice: be a victim, or a victor.

Molly's reverie was interrupted by a movement on the mezzanine. Bill waved at her and mouthed something. Molly scanned the com channels, but found nothing labeled "Bill Penn" or "William Penn." *Why doesn't he use his com?* He pointed at the door to the main floor. He showed up at the door's scanner. The security bots prevented his entry.

"Gregori, Bill Penn would like to speak with me. May he be allowed in?"

Gore peered at Bill. "I don't see why I should."

"Because you are a gentleman, sir." An appeal to vanity always worked when Molly needed something from a man.

Gore wasn't happy about it. "I've asked the mayor's permission, and she's consented."

Molly rose from the table and met Bill at the door. The scanner glowed green and Bill walked through. He was as handsome as any on the main floor.

"Mol, I need to talk to you."

"Let's dance." She took her ex-husband's hand. "You remember how to waltz, don't you?"

The couple glided around the floor with the others. Hesitant at first, Bill soon found his rhythm as Molly led.

"Someone is here to see you," Bill said.

"Who?"

"You need to come with me."

She wasn't going to play guessing games. "I'm with Gore. He'll want to know why."

"Say you have business with me," he said, a touch coldly.

"Business?"

"You know what I mean. Please, Molly."

Bill was not interested in her services, that much was certain. She searched Bill's entreating eyes for a clue as to what was going on. She left him in the middle of the dance floor. The other couples and triples swirled around him as she conferred with the master of *Extinction*. He assented.

Anxious to fulfill his promise to Raleigh, Bill directed Molly to the council chambers' main door. He led her to a stairwell and they walked down two flights.

"Where are we going?" Molly said.

"It's near."

Bill hurried through a concrete tunnel, Molly trotting behind him in her fashionable shoes. Until the encounter at Pole Station, and now at this brutal, absurd party, he hardly imagined her in gaudy clothes. She'd adapted to a new life in which he didn't belong. He pressed his ear to a steel door and opened it, taking Molly through. The room was large and lit with overhead lamps. Rivulets of condensation stained the concrete columns.

Martin Scribb stood next to a seated man at a table loaded with unfamiliar equipment.

Martin brightened. "Molly, I'm so glad you decided to come."

"What's going on, Martin?"

"Molly, may I present Colonel Raleigh Penn."

Bill's brother pivoted. Molly's reaction shifted from shock to pity. She saw what Bill saw in the kitchen; Raleigh Penn was nothing like the prosecutor who had sent her to prison after the Spike.

"So pleased to meet you again, Molly. I apologize for my appearance. I normally wear my uniform when I'm in public, but I'm here incognito."

"Molly," Bill said, "It's like we discussed on the sub. Raleigh needs your help."

"You are the only person who can help him," Martin said.

"It's simple, Mol," Bill said. "If you can help him, he will help us and Anne."

"You're not making sense."

Raleigh's voice was reedy, and he took an extra breath before each sentence. "Let me explain, Molly." A glioblastoma was killing him. An experimental treatment with nanobots was his last hope. The programming was based on her ideas. The treatment was failing. "In exchange for your help, I will use my influence to dismiss the charges against my brother and my niece, your daughter. I have also promised Martin to restore his identity."

The monk-cum-entrepreneur broke in. "You must help him, Molly."

"The equipment on the table will give you access to the nanobots in my bloodstream," Raleigh said. "All the software is loaded. Everything is ready for you to begin."

Molly stared at all three men. "Why should I help you? What do I get out of this arrangement?"

Bill was ready to stop her if she tried to walk away. *I won't let go of this chance easily.*

"Nothing, Mrs. Bain," the colonel said. "If you chose not to help, Bill and Anne will go to prison. I guarantee that. As for Martin, he's already dead, so he has nothing to lose."

"I'm disidentified," Martin said. "It's worse than dead."

Bill shook his head. *Why has Raleigh included Anne in his threats?* "Anne had nothing to do with the fire or the birds, Raleigh. I'm the one charged with the crimes."

The corners of the colonel's mouth lifted. "I happen to know, Bill, that Anne is suspected of interfering with the natural progression of a species through its evolutionary cycle. Inspector Kilel is very thorough, and she is relentless. She reports to me. I make the final charging decisions in these cases."

"You and your regrets," Bill hissed. "You're an extortionist."

"I'm dying. I want to live."

Martin picked up the appeal. "Molly, you must understand what I've gone through. I have a chance to live again, a real life, among people. Please help me... and the colonel."

"You are all insane," Molly said. "You've dragged me away from my future to save your own. I'm not the person you knew, any of you. You seem to think that I'm suspended in amber, that I'm the same sailor or programmer or woman of the past. I'm none of those things. I'm inventing the future after all of you destroyed it."

Molly turned her back on Bill and the others. Before Bill could grab her, Raleigh spoke. "You may be inventing the future, but Gore is not part of any-one's future, least of all yours."

"What do you mean?"

"My brother, Martin, others, all know that you want him."

"It's not true."

"Perhaps they're wrong. Perhaps they're right." Raleigh lifted himself out of his chair. A wave of fear crossed Molly's brow, as if after more than a decade, she recognized the prosecutor of the Spike trials, the fanatic who cut a deal with her that condemned Martin. "I can squash Gore like a bug, and I can squash you."

Raleigh leveled a hard glare at her. "My agreement to let you go free was kept secret from the world. That can change overnight, Molly," he snapped his fingers with unexpected energy, "and what would happen to your dreams then?"

Molly glanced at Martin, whose lip was lifted in a triumphant sneer. He had cornered Molly with the threat of exposure. "The Spike was your fault, Molly, not mine. You programmed the robots, and it was your command that set them to work, and they failed." His voice had been steadily rising in anger, but now he relapsed into his usual servile whine. "Look at it this way. You have the privilege of helping the prosecutor again, and helping me."

"And you'll help yourself, Molly," the colonel said. "In gratitude for saving my life, I'll see that Bill and little Anne have a life untainted by the shame of killing a small part of the earth."

"Molly, please," Bill said. "If you don't care about me, help for Anne's sake."

Molly waved her hand at the equipment, still not willing to give in. "I've never seen these devices before."

"I wouldn't have sent Martin searching for you if I didn't think you were up to the task, Molly," the colonel said. "I've grown familiar with your work. You are my last hope."

Bill offered one last plea. "Does your daughter deserve to go to prison? Ask yourself that."

Molly scowled, but her former husband was right. Anne was an innocent. *If I do nothing, Raleigh will make her another victim. Her life will be over.* "What do I need to do?"

Colonel Penn rolled up the sleeve of his right forearm, showing the plate embedded in his skin. He lowered it to the reader, and a series of lights blinked in rapid succession: red, yellow, a steady green. Molly picked up a tablet, larger than a standard office tablet, and the screen brightened. The colonel named the application behind each icon, and Molly touched them. She recognized a common interface to AI programs, modified for medical use. Other icons on the tablets linked to a standard AI development environment. The network lights indicated a live connection, the data encrypted. Molly thought of using the tablet to send a call for help, but to whom? Gore? Her future was tied to the colonel's.

The system's complexity daunted her. Yes, the structure was built on some of her ideas, as well as other researchers' ideas. She struggled to recall her college organic chemistry to grasp the highlights. The best place to start was the error logs. A few ideas came to her, but not a solution. She found three small bugs, and modified one of the program objects that played a role in how the nanobots interacted. She dived deep into the core logic, and her habitual focus morphed into a tunnel vision. She didn't care about Colonel Penn, but Anne mattered more than she expected.

As the minutes dragged into an hour, Martin brought out food and water. Bill paced the cavernous room, as if he walked the deck of a ship. In some ways, the AI framework wasn't much different than the oil tankers talking to one another as the oil convoy drove to Run, keeping each other at a distance to avoid collisions. *Maybe, just maybe.* She decided this was her best hope of making the system work for the colonel, without taking the whole thing apart and rebuilding it. After a few rounds of debugging, she compiled the additions, linked them to the main program, and restarted the hardware. "Colonel, I'm going to upload the changes to the nanobots."

Like a child in a hospital bed, the BES officer complied. "How will you know if it's working?"

Molly said nothing as she watched the monitors, noting the status messages flash on the screen as the cradle changed the bots' instructions. The gloom of the concrete walls pressed down on her. "I'll have to look at the logs again tomorrow."

"I can't wait until tomorrow." The colonel grew irritated. "I need to know now."

"I can't deliver an instant fix," she fired back. "It's taken years for you to reach this state. Do you expect some sort of miracle?"

"Can't you give me a preliminary judgment?"

A child in more ways than one. "Let's wait an hour, and I'll check the logs."

"Very well," the colonel said. "We'll wait."

The time passed with excruciating slowness. The four were silent. Martin sat on the floor hunched against a wall. Bill continued to pace, and the colonel seemed to age another ten years. Music from the council chambers filtered through the air ducts, and Molly imagined Gore waiting for her. *They're right. I do want him.* She had rebuilt her life, accomplishing her goal of making the Cyprian Association into an economic and cultural force in the AFEZ. What was next? Her future was bright, but murky. *Will Gregori have me? Together, we'd be unstoppable.*

The colonel's voice gurgled. "Please check the logs now."

"It hasn't been a hour."

"Check the logs," Raleigh thundered.

Molly relented and tapped the tablet into life. Bill and Martin watched over her shoulder. "The error logs are clear," she said. "The service logs show plenty of activity, though I don't understand some of the medical terminology."

"Let me look." The colonel studied the readout, but his face was impassive. "I need your professional opinion. Are your modifications working?"

"I don't know. They need more time."

"Give me your professional opinion!"

My professional opinion? You're dead, Raleigh Penn, and no amount of fiddling with this experimental treatment will save you. What happens if I tell him the truth? He wants good news. He wants me to tell him his life is saved. He'll know if I'm lying. I want to get out of this place on one piece.

"I believe there is a strong chance that the modifications are working, but without more facts, I can't say anything more."

The colonel considered Molly's statement. "You are correct, of course. I've been sick a long time, and I've gambled everything on this. Forgive me my impatience."

"What do we do now?" Bill said. After keeping calm for all this time, Molly could see how anxious he was. Anne really did mean everything to him.

"I have a room in a nearby hotel," Colonel Penn said. "We wait, together."

THE FIFTEEN-HOUR TIME DIFFERENCE BETWEEN Bežat and Brier Valley drained Anne's energy. In counterpoint, Kilel's vigilance in the City's Hall's reception area sharpened. Anne imagined the inspector sniffing mist or liters of coffee to keep her going after the BES jet landed at Dudinka or during the long drive to the refugee city's outskirts. Anne never saw the officer take or drink anything, though she snatched a few hours' sleep as the AI driver ticked off the kilometers.

Gut instinct told Anne her father was near, a feeling she feared that Kilel shared. *She's like a hunting dog that's caught the quarry's scent.* A change in the inspector's appearance tempered Anne's distrust. Swapping her BES uniform for civilian clothes, she had metamorphosed from martinet paramilitary officer to a striking, if prim, privileged-class woman who happened to pack a staser. Anne had teased out some of Kilel's personal story: She grew up in the Palouse Grasslands. Her father was an ecosystem restoration scientist whose work was wiped out by the Spike. Her mother died when she was ten. Kilel served in the military under Anne's uncle.

History Anne did not share with Kilel included the existence of a protected file in Anne's private com folder. Her awareness of the file itched like a bug bite. Her uncle had entrusted her with its safe-keeping, Anne thought. *Would telling Kilel betray him? Would it matter if I betrayed him?*

The hours dragged by in the cathedral-like lobby of City Hall. The two spent little time out-of-doors, both distrustful of the sticky grime that had streaked the building's exterior and settled on the unmarked police car the inspector borrowed in Dudinka. Kilel, her eyes red with irritation, dug into her travel bag and handed Anne tissues infused with antihistamine. The com signal was strong, but Anne's c-tribe was unreachable, and most important for her, Mike was unreachable. She feared that Mike would lose interest in her and their plan for the magpie chicks. She needed to be there with him—for the birds' sake, and for her own.

As afternoon turned into evening, the quality and numbers of people arriving at City Hall changed from ordinary to strange and wonderful. The cavalcade was at once a zoo and a high-fashion show. One couple was naked, their skin was painted in a kaleidoscope of color that shifted with every stride. One gentleman was dressed in a military uniform from a century or two in the past, except that his face was that of a tiger. A beautiful, dark-haired woman in a skin-tight red gown accompanied him, but Anne missed her face in the busy crowd. Anne scanned the public com channels, hoping to see her father's signal, but IDs, video, and text chatter overloaded the system. Kilel had problems as well, even with her powerful filtering tools.

The crowd thinned around 19:00. Latecomers hurried down a corridor that led to the council chambers. The doors closed, and the com signals died off; the room was protected by an anti-snooping system. The inspector was unable to penetrate the security. With a sigh Kilel suggested something to eat, almost as if Anne were a friend sharing a travel adventure, and Anne admitted she was hungry. The hotel cafe was empty, and the two women ordered a simple dinner.

The bass of music echoed from the council chambers as the walls of the building transmitted the low-frequency booms. They died off for a time, then came back. Kilel had gambled she would spot Bill as he came in the main entrance, and the gamble had not paid off. The inspector's disappointment did not deter her. *If anyone can find my dad, she can. I have to respect that.*

A shift change resulted in a new reception clerk on duty. With Anne in tow, Kilel approached a young woman who would not be out of place in New York West or San Francisco.

"May I help you?" The woman was chirpy.

"We're looking for someone, a relative," Kilel said. "May I show you his photo?" The inspector shared the photo of Anne's father over the hotel reception com channel with the clerk. "Have you seen him?"

The clerk regarded Kilel closely. "We are obliged to protect the privacy of our guests, Ms..."

"Kilel. The young woman with me is his daughter. It's rather urgent that we find her father."

"Your relationship?"

"A friend."

Anne wanted to alert the clerk to the truth, but she held back, in part because she again felt her father's proximity. *Give the inspector a chance to find him.*

Kilel set a €10 bill on the counter in front of the clerk, who eyed it without touching it.

"If you leave a message, Ms. Kilel, I will see if I can forward it to him."

"He's here?"

"I'm sorry, but I cannot answer that question."

"Miss, if you would be kind enough to let Mr. Penn know that we are anxious to find him, I'd appreciate it."

"I would be happy to help." The clerk glanced to her left—twice—as she pocketed the bill.

As one, Anne and Kilel followed the clerk's gaze to an elevator. A man in a plain business suit escorted the woman in the red gown into an elevator. Just as the doors closed, the man showed his face in profile. Anne gasped and said, "Dad" *sotto voce.*

Kilel bolted toward the elevator doors. They shut before she got there. Kilel punched the elevator button and sent call requests to the elevator through the hotel com. A full sixty seconds passed before it reappeared at the hotel lobby, empty.

"Get on." Kilel's order came out as close to frantic as Anne had ever heard.

"Up or down?"

Kilel hesitated. "Down." The inspector did not explain why as Anne punched the button for the lowest level. The world shifted; Anne had become an ally of the inspector, instead of a prisoner.

The elevator door opened to a dingy concrete hall festooned with pipes dripping with condensation. Lights in the ceiling cast deep shadows every few meters. Anne stepped out of the elevator, but Kilel halted. The elevator doors slid toward closing, but Kilel put her hand out to keep them open.

"What's wrong?" Anne said, eager to explore. "You saw him. My father got on the elevator. He's here."

"I don't like it," Kilel said.

"What? Are you claustrophobic? Or scared? Dad is here."

Kilel sniffed. "This is a perfect place for an ambush. They could be waiting for us."

"For you, you mean."

Kilel showed a tight smile. "We're in no rush." She motioned Anne back into the elevator.

"No, I want to go find my father."

"What if I left you down here? How would you find him?"

The distant echoes of a metal door banging shut made Kilel's point. Anne returned to the lobby with Kilel.

"What now?" Anne said, dismayed by the inspector's dithering. *What if that was my only chance?*

"We wait."

Kilel sat at the same sofa they had claimed in the morning, and Anne reluctantly joined her. If her father had gone to an upper floor, it did make sense that he would come back down. At 02:00 local time, the inspector decided that Anne's father would not appear, at least in the town hall lobby.

They returned to their hotel room. Kilel took a chair near the window and closed her eyes, not to rest, Anne thought, but to think. Kilel entered a meditative state. Anne watched, at once fascinated and intimidated by the inspector's inner calm and strength. Her breath came steady and even. Her facial muscles relaxed. Anne had learned these techniques in high school yoga classes. She needed to take up yoga again. After a few minutes of stillness, Kilel opened her eyes. "He's coming here."

"My father? How do you know?" Anne cried. "Are you psychic?" *She's lost it.*

Kilel moved without haste to the window, which overlooked a public square. "I'll forward you the image. The receptionist sent it to me."

That was more solid, Anne thought. Her minds-eye notified her of a new message. The attachment was a security camera view of her father and the woman in the red dress exiting a back door. Anne recognized her. "It can't be."

"It's your father."

"Yes. The woman is..." The word stuck in Anne's throat. The encounter was so unexpected, she had trouble accepting it as real.

"Let's go," Kilel said.

"You said they were coming here." Anne slipped her shoes on.

"Colonel Penn is staying in this hotel. They are either running from him or to him. I'm betting it's the latter."

The women passed through the hotel's front entrance and halted near a kiosk with broken glass and graffiti in Russian. A few pedestrians wandered in the square. Anne saw the borrowed police car parked in the hotel's driveway. *She must've told the car's AI to move it.* Kilel scanned the courtyard, her hand near her staser. Its ready light signaled full power. "There." She indicated a man and a woman about fifty meters away, and Anne recognized her father. Before she called out, Kilel ordered, "Quiet. You'll get your chance to speak to him."

Anne wanted to disobey, but she knew how single-minded Kilel was. At a basic level, Anne trusted the inspector, if only for her consistency. She knew this world. Anne didn't, and she didn't want to start something while the maniac beside her held a staser.

"Come, Anne. He's unarmed. Neither is your mother."

Kilel's use of the word overcame Anne's final doubts. She stared at Molly and let the fact sink in. Her mother was just twenty feet away, next to her father. Curiosity, anger, and terror swirled in Anne. Molly Bain was beautiful and elegant in her gown, though she had hints of circles under her eyes. She was tired, and not just from a late night. Anne's father was dressed in a business suit, incongruous in itself, because he never wore anything other than jeans and a t-shirt. A casual observer might mistake them for a couple, but they hadn't been together since Anne was a year old. A quiet fury pushed aside her other emotions. Her father was often lonely. *I won't let that woman cheat him of his heart again.*

The inspector walked straight toward the pair. Bill spotted her and stopped, alarmed. Molly said something Anne couldn't hear.

"BES agent." Kilel announced herself with firm authority. She broadcast her credentials on the com network. "You are under arrest for crimes against the environment."

Anne's attention was on her mother, who shared the same fascination. Molly mouthed the word "Anne" and inclined her head as if asking a question. Anne answered with a nod. A man behind the couple distracted Anne. He was also dressed in a suit, which hung on him better than her father's clothes fit his frame. Anne noted the disidentification mark on his forehead. What was her father up to?

Kilel repeated her instructions to Bill and drew her staser. The pedestrians nearby scattered, except for the dissed man.

The courtyard got more crowded when Colonel Penn stepped out from behind a row of withered vegetation. He was wearing civilian clothes, which confused Anne. The strange place, people dressed wrong, dissed people with her father and mother. Nothing made sense.

"Inspector Kilel, may I have a word?" the colonel said.

"Sir, remain where you are." Kilel kept her weapon on Bill.

Kilel's warning to the colonel startled Anne. *What is she thinking?* The girl's palms sweat as adrenaline coursed through her body.

A ping popped up in Anne's minds-eye. It was from her mother. Get ready to run.

"Don't, Anne." Kilel was monitoring Anne's com traffic.

The colonel raised his hands. "You're to be commended, Inspector."

"Sir, I..." Kilel sounded as if she wanted to make a declaration, but changed her mind. "What are you doing here?"

"The smuggling operation," Raleigh said. "I received a tip. A trusted source, and I had to follow up myself."

Kilel lowered her voice. "Sir, you're ill. I can see it from here." Anne registered his gaunt appearance as well. He looked worse here than at the nursery.

"Inspector, I know you are investigating the endangered species case against my brother." The colonel's hands trembled like a chittering bird. "You must trust me. The smuggling case is far more important. I was about to take him and Mrs. Bain into custody."

Bill growled. "You back-stabbing..."

He's lying, Anne, Molly texted. He needs my help with his illness.

Anne didn't understand what her mother meant. A part of her wanted to bolt, if not to her father, then somewhere, anywhere, to get away from Kilel. The woman was unhinged.

Kilel held her weapon steady. "Sir, I must decline your request. I've come a long way for Mr. Penn, and I intend to take him into custody."

"Inspector, I appreciate your dedication and focus, but as your superior, I am ordering you to allow me to arrest Mr. Penn."

Tension wound Anne's muscles like a spring. No one was arresting her father if she could help it.

"Colonel Penn," Kilel said, "why did you order me off the smuggling case?"

"Orders, Inspector. From above."

Anne worked up the courage to text Molly. What are they talking about?

Molly's emo-sigs were active. They displayed a mixture of pride and shame.

"I understand, Colonel," Kilel said. "I'm sorry, I cannot let Mr. Penn out of my sight. Or you."

The colonel took a step forward. An aluminum case hung heavily on his left arm. He did not want to let go of it. "Janine, don't risk your career on this. I'm... close to retirement. I can recommend you for promotion. I've often thought that you would be a perfect candidate for my position... when the time came."

Anne, you must believe me when I say...

"Colonel Penn, I'm placing you under arrest." Kilel's weapon ticked. "Please move next to Mr. Penn."

The colonel was astonished. "You're making a mistake, Janine. Let me continue my investigation... and I'll forget this happened."

...I did what I thought was best.

"Colonel, move closer to Mr. Penn, or I shall be forced to discharge my weapon."

Anne did not comprehend her mother's words, even as Anne listened to the conversation between Kilel and the colonel. *Is she talking about her abandonment of my father and me? Is she talking about the smuggling?*

"Inspector, let me continue with my plans, and I will tell you all I know."

Kilel remained cagey. "About the carbon operation? Colonel, I want to know who is running the operation in the capital, and who told you to halt the investigation."

"Yes, Inspector. Telling you is the least I can do, but I believe you already know the answers."

Kilel angled her head. "The traces of oil at the Yesler City pier, the burned-out car, the behavior of the general in Pennsylvania, your orders to me, your lies to me just now. The rot is seeping down from the top, from the minister's office itself."

"Yes," the colonel said.

"And in the Bureau?" Kilel was incredulous.

The conversation made little sense to Anne, except that the mention of a minister raised further alarm. *Powerful people are involved in this, but all I want to do is go home with my father.* Kilel took her eyes off her quarry as she parleyed with the colonel, and Bill and Molly began to inch away. Kilel kept talking to the colonel, discussing some case. An awareness dawned on Anne that Kilel knew what her father was doing and she was letting it happen. *She wants us to run. She's really after the colonel.*

"I don't know for sure, Janine, that our agency is involved, but it seems likely. Believe me that I'm not involved."

Anne sent this text to Molly: I'm ready. In a sudden burst Anne ran to her father. Even as she sprang forward, he and her mother were running to one side, and Anne angled her pounding feet to match their trajectory. Any moment she expected to be struck by Kilel's staser.

A puff jumped from the pavement at the colonel's feet. A gun's report echoed in the square. The colonel raised his hand to shield his eyes. A bullet entered his chest, and he dropped in a heap. Anne heard a second shot. Colonel Penn came to rest on his left side. A third shot rapidly followed. The rifle was on semi-automatic. Anne knew the sound and the effect. She once fired a vintage M-16 rifle during her marksmanship class.

Anne, Bill and Molly ducked behind a concrete planter, its flowers withered. The dissed man joined them, and Anne fought her instinct to ignore him. "We have to get out of here," the man said.

"Shut up, Scribb," Bill said. "We know that."

The electronic whine of a staser on full power preceded its release. Kilel crouched and fired, and a section of hotel wall shattered. Yet the gun gave a fourth report, and Kilel fell to the pavement.

Rather than being relieved, Anne was alarmed by the fallen officer. As hateful as Kilel was, no one deserved to be shot out of ambush. "The inspector's hit," Anne said.

A look passed between father and daughter, the tilt of the head and the set of the jaw a silent communication both grasped. How many times had they talked about helping a shipmate or a neighbor, even one you despised, when a life was in danger? He or she might be on a passing vessel while you were drowning, and you prayed that he would return the favor when the time came. *You may hate that person and everything about him, but he is a human being same as you*, her father taught.

Bill pushed his companions aside and ran to Kilel. He lifted the unconscious, bleeding police officer onto his back, as a soldier might on a battlefield. Anne's feelings alternated terror with pride as he waddled into the hotel's entrance.

Anne expected him to be shot too, but the rifleman apparently only wanted the BES officers.

"What do we do now?" the dissed man said.

Anne had only one thing in mind, to go to her father, but he was now in the hotel. She noticed her uncle bend his leg. "The colonel is still alive."

"Molly, look." The dissed man pointed at an approaching figure. "It's Gore, and…"

Anne missed the name of the other person, because she was transfixed by the vision of a bipedal orange cat, dressed in a historical uniform. *I saw him at City Hall.* Anne's com displayed his avatar, a stylized face of a bengal tiger. A woman, tanned and wiry, carried a sniper rifle as if she had shot it a moment ago. The cat-man left his conversation channel open to the public, perhaps by accident. Anne monitored the conversation.

Well done, my lovely Micah. Our partners will be pleased.

CHAPTER 35

BILL'S ANKLES AND CALVES PROTESTED at carrying Kilel's unconscious deadweight. He fought up the hotel's flights of stairs and directed Molly to push open the fire door. "Molly, the door lock," Bill huffed. While Anne and Scribb looked on, Molly entered the room lock code given to her by the colonel. Bill laid Kilel like a sleeping child on the double bed. The inspector's blood soaked her blouse.

"Scribb, watch the hall," Bill ordered.

Molly's eyes lingered on Anne. *See*, he thought, amid the whirl of thoughts in his mind, *that's what you gave up.*

Bill found a thick towel in the bathroom. He tore Kilel's blouse at the wound and grimaced. He pressed the towel against it. "Someone needs to get a doctor."

"Why did you rescue her?" Molly said.

"I saw her lying there, bleeding," Bill said, exchanging a glance with Anne.

"You could've just left her there."

"She needed help," Anne said.

"That's what we do, Molly. We think of others, not just ourselves," Bill said. "Someone needs to find a doctor."

"I will," Scribb said.

"Well, go on. Go!" Bill said.

Martin settled on Kilel, as if he wanted to ask something.

"What are you waiting for, Scribb?" Bill said.

"Is she going to live?"

"How the hell should I know?"

The monk's face twisted in resignation, and he left the room.

"Bill, your brother is still moving," Molly stood at the window. "He's still alive."

Kilel groaned, and Bill refolded the towel, looking for another clean patch to compress the wound.

"Go to him," Bill said. "He needs help."

"I'm not going out there." Molly said. "I don't want to get shot."

Anne, at her father's side, regarded Molly with distaste. "I can do it."

"No, it's too dangerous. Molly should go. I've got to stay here with Kilel."

"I'm not dressed for rescue work," Molly said.

Anne started for the door.

"No, Anne," Bill shouted, fighting a wave of panic.

"The shooters don't care about me. And he's my uncle."

"Anne!"

She dashed into the hall.

"Dammit." Bill wanted to watch for Anne in the courtyard, but he needed to hold the towel and stop Kilel's bleeding. "Molly, get over here."

"What? Are you kidding me?"

"Fuck it, woman. Think of someone else for a change and hold this towel."

Molly growled, but she followed Bill's order. They switched places and he peered between the steel plates in the window. A jolt of anxiety subsided when Anne appeared and kneeled next to the colonel. The officer's arm slid over the pavement. Anne rested her hand on his. Bill was struck by the tenderness of her gesture. His mouth moved, and she moved her ear closer to hear. Colonel Penn's arm relaxed. Anne lifted her hand from the colonel's and gazed up at the hotel, as if looking for reassurance. She trotted back to the hotel entrance. After a moment, she showed up at the room door, her face white.

"What did he say?" Bill said.

"He died right there in front of me." Anne buried her face in her father's chest. "Your brother is dead."

Bill held his daughter in his arms. *How can a man miss his child so much and not go insane?* "It's all right, sweetheart. He and I, we didn't know each other very well. You and I have to get through this, then we'll talk about it. Okay?"

Anne cleared her throat. "He had a message for Kilel. Something like, 'Don't give up' or 'Don't worry.'"

"What else?" It was Kilel, half-conscious. "What did the colonel want?"

"Take it easy." Bill returned to the inspector, edging Molly aside. "You've been shot. You're bleeding. We're getting a doctor."

"What else did he say?" Kilel was insistent.

Anne brought a cup of water to Kilel. "He said, 'Interior Ministry' and 'Protect yourself.'"

Kilel blinked at the ceiling. "We need to get him out of Run."

"Inspector, I'm sorry," Anne said. "He's dead. I'm sure of it. Blood was everywhere."

Kilel closed her eyes. Bill wondered if she was saddened by his death, but he didn't have time or the energy to ask her. "Where's Scribb and a doctor?" he said to no one in particular.

"They won't come." Scribb slid back into the room. "There's a clinic next door, but the doctors are too scared to treat a bessie."

"What do we do now?" Molly said.

"We could leave her," Scribb said.

"No, we shouldn't abandon her," Anne said.

"The hotel might find a doctor."

"No one's going anywhere." Kilel propped herself up on the bed, reaching down to her holster. She pointed her staser at Bill. He cursed himself for failing to disarm her.

"Inspector." Scribb's eagerness bordered on desperation. "The colonel promised..." He pointed at Molly. "She's part of the smuggling ring. I did nothing. She helped Gore get the oil here. She's..."

Molly hissed, "You're a liar, Martin. I was a hostage."

Scribb's agitation grew. "She fixed the AI programming for the convoy. She was with him at City Hall with Gore. They might be lovers..."

Kilel pointed her staser at Scribb's head. "I know who you are, dissed man. You're dead. Get out."

Scribb's face flushed. Bill knew the look. The man wanted to scream at the injustice done to him. He was nothing more than a ghost. He kept himself in check, though, and backed out of the room.

"Maybe Martin's right," Molly pointed at Kilel. "In the shape she's in, she can't follow us."

"You'd abandon her like you abandoned Dad and me?" Anne's tone dripped with bile. "I won't leave a person who is injured, even if she wants to put us in prison."

Molly turned away, uncomprehending.

"If we leave her, someone's likely to finish the job," Bill pointed out. "Bessies aren't popular in Run."

"I'm your way out of Run. I can protect you, even if I'm hurt." Kilel winced. "Mr. Penn, can you see a blue and silver car on the hotel driveway?"

Bill scrutinized the plaza and the entrance. "I see it." It was five meters from Colonel Penn's body.

"The police car you got in Dudinka?" Anne said.

"We need to get to it," Kilel gulped. Her skin was growing pale.

"What if the sniper is still out there?" Molly said.

"We'll have to risk it."

"Wait," Bill said. All of this was too convenient. Kilel still pointed the staser at him, and he remembered her threat the last time she did so, back on the dirt road near Thomasburg. "How do we know you're not lying? Maybe we should leave you behind."

"Dad, we couldn't," Anne said, disbelieving.

Kilel was breathing heavily, weakening by the moment. "You're tainted by your association with me. You're all marked for death by whoever shot the colonel. I'm your best chance for survival. Like you, I could walk out on my own, but I also need you. You have information that I want to break up the smuggling ring. I'm willing to trade. You help me, and I'll help you."

Bill glanced at Molly and his daughter. "Anne knows nothing. You're bargaining with me only, Kilel. Molly knows what she saw on the road here, nothing more. She was a prisoner." Kilel panted slightly, losing color in her cheeks, and Bill pressed his advantage. "You have to drop the species destruction charges against me or I won't cooperate. Is that clear? All I want is my daughter and my life back."

"Agreed."

Kilel's lack of hesitation, given her determination to find him, raised Bill's suspicion. "Why should I trust you?"

"You don't have to trust me, Mr. Penn. I'm being pragmatic. We both win by surviving and delivering on the bargain."

"We don't have many choices," Anne said, although Bill could see that she feared the woman, despite the wound. He saw no other way. *I'll have to hope that Kilel is as rigid about keeping her promises as she is about enforcing stupid laws.* "Let's go," he said at last.

Kilel holstered her staser. She tried to sit up, but she moaned in pain. Bill lifted her good arm over his shoulder. Kilel whimpered, but got to her feet. Bill led her out the door, glad for the strength he gained aboard *Aganippe*.

The four marched down the stairs, through the lobby, and out in the open to the car. Bill cringed, waiting for the shot that didn't come. The few pedestrians ignored them, passing the colonel's body as if unattended corpses were a common sight. His eyes stared up into the smog. Bill wondered what would happen to his brother's body, but he did not feel any great loss, apart from the regret that comes from wishing he had tried to know his brother better. He reached out to him when Anne was born, but he never followed up. It didn't occur to him then that Anne deserved to know her uncle, if only because he was family. Keeping her from him was cruel. *Perhaps Raleigh could've offered something good to her, if not to me.* Bill also remembered his brother's words at the hotel: *"I'm sorry that I didn't take the time to get to know her better. Or her father."* They once had common ground—Anne—but it was too late to share it.

The scissor doors of the police car lifted, and they slipped inside. The fit was tight and uncomfortable. Kilel croaked a command in Russian, and the car's controls woke up. The doors slid shut. She spoke again, and the car accelerated.

The police car jostled Janine Kilel and the three passengers as it avoided the ruts and potholes in the gravel road leading out of Run. Despite the pain in her shoulder, she reached into a compartment labeled with a water droplet and the Cyrillic "X2O." Another compartment contained a well-stocked first aid kit. Bill Penn helped her with an injection designed to kill pain without dulling the senses. Next to the first aid was a larger, unlabeled compartment. Kilel queried the car's AI and found two automatic pistols. Each had two clips and she loaded a clip and a shell into the chamber of each gun. As her strength returned, she updated the AI's instructions with spoken Russian.

"What did you tell it to do?" Molly Bain pushed her auburn hair away from her face. Even disheveled and bleary-eyed, the woman was alluring. Envy was an unfamiliar emotion for Kilel, but she felt like an awkward teenager beside her.

"I told it to go to Dudinka without stopping." The car swerved to avoid a chuckhole. "We'll arrive tomorrow."

"How many languages do you speak?" Molly said, sounding curious.

"Why do you want to know?"

"Just making conversation," she sighed. "We have a long drive ahead."

"I took a year of Russian in college." Kilel did not want to engage with the woman, whose history Kilel knew, at least as far as the Spike was concerned. *She may have paid a debt to society, but she can never repay the debt to the earth.*

"How did you join the BES, Inspector?"

Kilel directed her gaze out the window at the opaque wall of vegetation. "Your former brother-in-law recruited me."

"Raleigh?"

"I was in graduate school, studying environmental history and public policy. I had submitted my master's thesis on the early air quality policies of the old U.S. Environmental Protection Agency. My adviser sent it to Colonel Penn." Kilel flashed on Penn's body lying in the hotel square back in Run. Emotion rushed into her, led by a feeling of sorrow she hadn't known since her mother's death. "That was before he became a colonel."

"Were you close to Raleigh?"

Was I close to him? Was he more than my boss? "He supervised me on several cases. He is… was my lead on the oil-smuggling case." The sorrow was almost uncontrollable, which embarrassed the officer.

"I'm sorry if these memories are painful," Molly said.

"It's my wound," Kilel said gruffly, glancing down at her injury. *I'll show no tears in front of this woman.*

Molly edged closer. "Let me see." She lifted the bandage. "I'm not a nurse, but I don't see any fresh bleeding. You'll have a nasty scar if it isn't sewn up soon."

Bill stirred from the backseat. "Something to tell your grandchildren."

Kilel didn't realize Penn was listening. The idea of grandchildren had never occurred to her.

Molly returned to her place in the car. "Is there someone in your life, Inspector? Your non-professional life?"

Kilel paused. The last person to ask her that question was her father. They spoke infrequently now. "No. My work is very demanding." Kilel closed her eyes. "I'd like to rest now." She doubted her three prisoners would attempt an escape.

The car drove on in silence, though Kilel stole a glance now and again at the family, though the word applied only in a descriptive sense. Anne Penn and her father were close as parent and child. The relationship between mother and daughter was a different story. The young woman stared out the window, attempting to ignore Molly, whose face begged for acknowledgment. *She wants to connect with the girl, even after twenty years of absence, or perhaps because of it.* Molly lifted her hand to her daughter's tousled hair, as if to stroke it.

The girl flinched and rumbled, "Don't touch me."

"Anne, I want to tell you…"

"Are you going to say something melodramatic, like, you're sorry? You abandoned me and Dad, just like you were ready to abandon someone else." Anne pointed at Kilel, who feigned sleep.

"I'm not proud that I left you and Bill to follow my dreams."

"You ought to be ashamed."

"I'm not ashamed either." Molly's voice firmed. "I did what I thought was right for me."

Anne hissed. "You are the most selfish woman I have ever known."

Bill was attentive, Kilel saw, as he let the drama play out.

"Maybe I made a mistake. Maybe I should've come home, or found a way to work away from Algid."

"You're every child's nightmare." Anne returned to the window.

Molly was unfazed by Anne's hostility. "I see you here, now. I saw what you did back in Run, how brave you were. I saw you go out to your uncle. I see you are better than me, more than I deserve in a daughter. I am who I am, Anne. I've made my own way, in my own way. No one's choices are ever perfect." Molly reached out to Anne again, but she cringed.

"You can't escape your responsibilities to others because it's inconvenient," Anne said. "I was not a barrier to sidestep." Anne struggled to hold back tears. "All my life, I saw other kids with mothers who showed up at school events, who explained how to be a woman to their daughters, who picked them up from camp. I sometimes imagined what it would be like, to have two parents instead of one. You say you're sorry. Don't be. You got what you deserved."

Anne's response hurt Molly. Kilel measured the sting of the words in how she clasped her hands and interlaced her fingers. Kilel's mother was a vague memory, except for the sorrow. She died of cancer when her daughter was ten, though her father claimed that the Spike had killed her. She was one of tens of millions of victims, real and imagined, of Molly Bain and Martin Scribb.

The inspector edged toward the police car's dash and peered at the gravel road. It cut through a series of sandy ridges. Instead of following the contour, the roadbuilders sliced into the ridges to keep the road flat. For a few seconds, walls of scree rose on either side of the car, before falling away until the car came to the next ridge. The car's AI attempted to maintain the speed ordered by Kilel, but it slowed to avoid damaging the undercarriage.

The travelers left the smog of Run behind, but dusk had fallen, and visibility was limited. Kilel kept the headlights off; the car's radar saw obstacles long before a human and its GPS systems kept the car on course. No other vehicles came near. Kilel spied a wide curve ahead, with the exit hidden behind another cutting. Her anxiety surged. She checked her staser: ninety percent charged. "Mr. Penn, can you handle a weapon?"

"Yes, but..."

A thud against the armor plating of the car interrupted him.

"What—"

Kilel ducked when another thud hit the car. She peered over the dash, and she switched on the car's night-vision enhancements. The windshield flashed green. Kilel made out the contours of the road, the vegetation, and heat signatures of...

"Mother," she said. "Get down!"

A series of thuds raked the armor on the car's left side so hard the car swerved to the right. The AI recovered, but slowed the car, making it an easier target. An object smashed into the armored roof, but didn't shatter it. Kilel addressed the car's AI in rapid-fire Russian, and it crossed and recrossed the imaginary center line in the road. The car slowed further to perform these maneuvers, and more shots hit home.

"What are we going to do?" Molly said, her voice high-pitched.

"The car is built to withstand high-velocity rounds," Kilel said. "We just have to get past the shooters."

An alarm sounded from the dash, but before Kilel and the others reacted, a loud bang lifted the vehicle's right side a meter off the roadbed, and it crashed into the ditch between the road and the rising scree wall. The explosion tossed the occupants like dolls, but the reinforced roll cage of the car prevented shrapnel from turning their bodies into mincemeat. The power systems failed, and the dash, as well as the night vision, dimmed to nothing. Kilel smelled smoke. The scissor doors opened. "Everyone out. Get down into the ditch. NOW."

Bill was the first out, crawling between the door and the crumbling wall of the road cut. Kilel heard more thuds. The destroyed car offered a measure of protection, if they stayed out of sight. Anne crawled after her father. She was followed by her mother. No one was injured. Kilel handed the pistols to Bill, safeties off. She felt his fingers grasping the weapons as she held them out. Then she herself scrambled outside.

Molly and Anne huddled together at the bottom of the ditch, which was filled with fetid water. Bill fumbled with the pistols. "Give me the other pistol," Kilel ordered. Anne's eyes followed the weapon. Above them, the *pop* of rounds coming from the assailants sounded like large drops of rain, though the sky was clear.

"What now?" Bill said.

Kilel assessed the situation. They were pinned down by an unknown enemy, though the list of candidates was short. She had a staser and a police-issue automatic pistol with twenty rounds. She flicked off the safety of her staser. She was uncertain about Bill's abilities to handle a weapon. *Did he set up this ambush? No, he has more to gain by siding with me.* The area was so remote, even her powerful com detected no towers. Her com found the BES satellite overhead, but she stopped herself from sending a call for help, wondering if the ambushers were monitoring. "We'll have to see what they want."

"You mean, negotiate?" Molly said. "With whom?"

A distant female voice called out. *"Inspector, are you all right?"*

Kilel said to her companions, "Get under the car." All four crawled underneath the smoldering vehicle, which protected them from attackers above. The car sat with its rear half above the point where the roadbed pitched down into the ditch. That gave Kilel a view up and down the road for fifty meters. Bill took a position next to Kilel. A half-moon rose above the horizon, scattering muted light on the scene.

"We don't want anybody else hurt."

"That's Micah Panang," Bill whispered. "I think she's the one who shot you, Inspector. She's got a rifle. Gore is probably with her."

Kilel was unsure who Gore was, although Martin Scribb had used the name too. "The fire that hit our car was automatic weapons. They've got help, but they don't know whether we're dead or alive." Kilel considered their options. "Mr. Penn, when I say 'Go,' fire a few shots toward the voice. Got it?"

In the half-light, he nodded.

"Go!"

Bill lifted his pistol above the level of the road and fired five shots in rapid succession. At the same time, Kilel lifted her head and her staser above the road edge. She spotted movement and discharged the weapon twice. Nothing happened; no ping, or scream, or anything that told her that she hit something. The discharges reduced her staser's reserve to thirty percent.

"That'll keep their heads down for a little while," Kilel said.

"*Fighting us is pointless. We only want you. The others can leave.*"

"Don't believe them, Bill," Kilel said. "You and your family will be just as dead as I will be if we give up."

"How do you know that?" Molly's fright was telling. "They might let us go."

Bill shook his head. "Kilel is right. I saw Gore murder thirty of my shipmates on *Aganippe*. He'll kill us without thinking twice about it."

"What are we going to do?" Molly said. "They have more guns than us, and more people. We'll never get out of here."

"Where would we go, Inspector?" Anne said. "We're a hundred miles from anywhere."

The pain in Kilel's shoulder screamed, despite the painkiller, and she felt the sticky wetness of fresh blood. "We have one chance of surviving more than a few hours. We'll have to draw them out and take out as many as we can. Maybe we can drive the rest under cover for a time. We'll make for the bush and head east. I might be able to call for help if we can get into range of a com tower. My com battery is getting low. I don't want to risk draining it on a satellite call."

"What if it doesn't work?" Molly was terrified.

"We have to fight them," Anne said, defiant. "We can't just wait to be slaughtered."

Anne, Kilel noticed, had stayed calm, like her father.

"Follow my lead, Bill. Get ready to shoot anything that moves but stay on the ground. We won't have a second chance."

A hail of bullets slammed into the broken vehicle.

Bill's face twisted in the gloom. He was terrified, despite his calm. "What if they shoot you where you stand? They want you dead."

"Thugs like to gloat before finishing the job. At least I hope that's true." Kilel crawled out from underneath the car. "I'm coming out!" Kilel got to her knees as she yelled into the darkness. "I'm giving up!"

"*Put your staser on the ground.*"

Kilel complied. Her heart pounded, but the pistol in her waistband offered comfort.

"*Go to the center of the road and come forward ten meters.*"

"You understand what will happen if you kill me?" Kilel said. "You'll be caught and dissed."

"*Shut up. Now stop.*"

A female figure came forward out of the darkness. She wore night-vision glasses.

Bill called out from the wrecked police car. "Micah! It's me, Bill. Anne is with me. You have to let us go."

Another set of bullets pocked the ground near the car. A female voice cried. Kilel couldn't tell who it was.

Micah said sadly, "It's too late, Bill."

Kilel saw her chance. In a motion as smooth as a cobra's strike, she reached behind her and pulled out the pistol. Micah, distracted by talking with Bill, flinched, then dropped as Kilel's first bullet struck her through the left eye. Kilel turned to her right, but saw no one else in the darkness. Pain tore through her calf, and she fell on the gravel road, her wounded shoulder grinding into the packed rock. The fall knocked the pistol from her hand. She reached out to it, but a boot kicked it away. She followed the leg up to the face, and she gasped, in pain and in shock. Even in the faint light, Kilel saw the assailant wore no night-vision glasses. It didn't need them. It had the eyes of a cat, the pupils dilated, ready to kill.

"I commend you, Inspector, on a brave effort," the tiger-man said. "But you've failed."

"Who are you?"

"I was called Gorov many years ago. I am Gore now."

The pain in her leg and shoulder overwhelmed Kilel, but she wanted to know why she was about to die. "Tell me... tell me who..."

"Who is running our little enterprise?" Gore's tongue licked his distorted mouth. "Someone in power, high up, but I don't know who, specifically. The information is... What's the English word? Compartmentalized. I don't care, as long as I know where to find the oil and how I will be paid."

Kilel laid her head on the dusty road. The creature confirmed what she had suspected, but she doubted if she had time to make use of the information.

Gore growled. "I also have instructions to kill you, and I know how to follow orders. Good-bye, Inspector. It was a pleasure to meet you."

Gore raised a pistol to Kilel's head. She could distinguish the individual hairs on Gore's hand silhouetted in the starlight. She had no idea her natural night vision was that good. Perhaps it was the heightened senses she heard accompanied the experience of death. It would have been an interesting discussion with Colonel Penn.

A tiny movement caught her eye, paired with a *pop*. Gore's gun dropped to the ground. He roared with pain and raised his arm, spraying blood from the severed artery in his wrist.

"Gregori!" Molly sprang from the damaged police car, followed by Anne. Kilel felt as if she was slipping into a void. Bill was prone on the ground, bleeding. *Hit by one of the last rifle rounds.* Anne held her father's pistol before her. She was on one knee, both hands aiming the gun. "I'll kill him," she shouted to anyone who was nearby. "Any more shooting and I'll kill him."

Molly folded her hand over the mangled paw of the tiger-man. "No, Anne. I'll take him away. Go home with your father. Go home now." Molly lifted her voice. "He's shot. The captain is hurt. I'm bringing him to you." Molly pushed the creature ahead of her, leaving the lifeless body of Micah behind.

Kilel's mind cleared a little, and Anne kneeled next to her. She laid the pistol on the ground. "You've been hit again. Dad is hit too. He might be dead."

Anne's touch confused Kilel. The young woman stroked the inspector's hair. Perhaps it was the same touch she offered the birds. Bill was a lucky man. Mike Schmidt was a lucky man. The darkness around Kilel confused her. *Is this the end of my life? Or are the stars just the stars?*

"Take care of the birds, Anne."

The half-moon slid into her field of vision. A crunching sound entered her consciousness, the sound of feet on gravel. Anne backed away, and Kilel's physical pain was magnified by the separation. She heard a second pair of feet on the road. The gait was regular—and inhuman. She thought of Gore. The sounds stopped centimeters from her. She reoriented her head and saw a shape, black as death, outlined against the cliff. It absorbed light as well as blocked it.

A new sound. A helo, coming from the east. It was low on the horizon, approaching on an attack vector. The noise intensified, and Kilel recognized a second helicopter of a different type. It switched on a floodlight, and the rotor wash turned the calm night into a storm. The glare blinded Kilel for a few seconds. Anne covered her head with her arms. A black security robot stood over Anne. A second robot guarded Bill. The rotor wash blew dust into her eyes and mouth, but not before a helmeted man with a red cross on a white field on his shoulder stooped over her. On his lapel was a gold pin in the shape of a tulip.

CHAPTER 36

WHEN IT BECAME CLEAR THAT the helicopter was landing at the BES detention facility's helipad in Eugene, Anne resigned herself to spending years in custody. She was too tired to fight and argue, though she regretted the fact that she might never see Mike again, never know the fate of the magpies. She prayed her father would be jailed near her. She also said a prayer for her uncle. Inspector Kilel said his last act was sending a call for help to the BES.

It was his last act, but it was not his last request, Anne knew.

Her release came without warning. Inspector Kilel instructed Anne and Bill to stay close as they exited the helicopter. They approached a drab building with narrow windows next to a fence topped with barbed wire. A short hall connected the building to the outside world. Kilel opened the door and stood aside.

"Technically, you're still under arrest, both of you," Kilel said. "You're my prime suspects for numerous environmental crimes, but… I don't see a reason to hold you further. Stay close to your ranch."

Anne nearly hugged Kilel, but the inspector's manner was chilly, as if she were doing something against her better judgment. Anne remembered her words on the gravel road: "Take care of the birds."

Anne's new freedom brought with it unrestricted access to the com networks. She checked in with her c-tribe first, and she was disappointed that Mike's status was unavailable. *Same damned rural service.* However, Kilel's public profile was available, and Anne made her decision. "Inspector, when we were in Run, and the colonel was dying, he asked me to give you something."

Kilel raised her eyebrows in surprise. "A gift?"

"I don't know what it is. He said to give it to you when I thought the time was right." Via her minds-eye, Anne sent a ping to Kilel's public profile, and Anne transferred the video file the colonel had given her after her interrogation. Unlike the time she tried to give it to Mike, no errors occurred. "Are you able to open it?"

Kilel concentrated for a moment before her eyes widened. "Do you understand what this is?"

"Like I said, I don't know. I couldn't open it, and I couldn't transfer it to anyone else."

Kilel stepped away from Anne and her father, absorbed in the gift. She halted and took a breath. "Anne, Bill, it will take me several days to go through everything in this archive, but trust me when I say your uncle, your brother, is a man whom you should admire."

Anne and Bill parted from Kilel, who struck Anne as a woman transformed by a new discovery, or a new understanding of something she thought she had grasped before. Bill summoned a cab, and they soon arrived in downtown Eugene. They ate at one of the neo-carnivore restaurants, but they said little to each other. Bill pushed around the remaining neo-beef on his plate.

"What's wrong, Dad?"

"I was thinking about your mother."

The simmering anger Anne reserved for her mother surfaced. "She abandoned us again. She's despicable. I wish I could've told her so."

"I don't think it's that simple, Anne."

"I saw her run away with that monster."

"I think she saw her future with him, and not with us."

"All the more reason to put her out of my mind."

Her father gave her one of his measured looks. "You're more like her than you realize. I see it, even if you don't."

Could that be possible? Anne turned over the idea, appalled by its potential truth.

Her father grinned, and he placed her hand over hers. "You're obstinate, independent, and resourceful."

"I could not choose her life." Anne sipped her coffee. "Dad, I think your brother was the same way."

"Kilel said I should admire Raleigh, but I don't think I can forgive him for what he did to our parents." Bill reconsidered his statement. "Maybe I just need some time. He was certainly intelligent and ambitious. Does forgiving the dead count for anything?"

Bill called a public trans-car, which would take them to Thomasburg. Anne's thoughts turned to Mike. She imagined him staying up late to tend the magpie chicks, and sleeping in his tent next to hers. It was something she'd have to explain to her father, but she knew he wouldn't mind.

When she and her father arrived at the ranch, her heart thrilled when she saw Mike's pickup near one of the outbuildings, the rear hatch open. Tools and shingles lay in the bed. The tents and outbuildings were still in place, as was the chicken coop, including the glow from the heat lamp. The returning vegetation in the refuge offered a promise of health by the burning heat of summer.

Deputy Gary Schmidt, out of uniform, emerged from a shed, and Anne halted, unsure of the reason for his visit. Maxie followed Gary and barked his recognition of his mistress and master. Behind the dog walked Mike, dust in his hair. Anne ran to him, stopping short of a full-speed collision. She saw her excitement reflected in his eyes.

"Anne," Mike said, "thank God you're back. When..."

"This morning." Anne related the events of the last days. "We came home as soon as we could."

"Anne, I..."

Anne kissed him. *You waited for me.*

Mike blinked.

"Well, then." Gary scratched his scalp. "You're not going to kiss me, are you, Bill?"

Anne's father lifted the corner of his mouth in a knowing way and shook the deputy's hand. "What in blazes is going on here, little girl?"

Anne didn't answer, because she wasn't certain, except that she knew her heart, when it came to the things she cared about. *Mike is as much a part of my home now as this place and Dad.* She had to check one thing: She found the English woodcut in her tent, clutching it to make sure it was real.

Mike pulled Anne in the direction of the coop. Her heart leapt when she saw seven tiny pin-feathered bodies bob their heads and peep when she opened the access door. "I've been busy with a project while you've been gone." Mike lifted the flap of his tent and brought out an object made of cloth. He put it on his hand.

"What is it?" Anne said.

"I read about this on the nets. We can't let the chicks bond to us, so I made this magpie puppet." He opened and closed the puppet's beak, and made a weak chirping sound. "I need to work on the parent call."

All four of them laughed.

"Let's try it," Anne said.

Mike found a plastic bag of dead crickets. Reaching in with the puppet's bill, he grabbed some of the food. He put the puppet inside the nesting box, and the chicks peeped energetically. Mike fed an insect to each of the chicks.

"I also discovered the nest with the missing second pair of magpies," Mike said. "We've got a second healthy brood."

Anne let herself think about the future. She and Mike had given the Klamath magpie a chance to survive. She and her father were back home. It would be hard, but they could start again. She took Mike's free hand in hers, and drew close to him.

Martin Scribb sat cross-legged in the middle of the dusty town's plaza. The sun's heat hammered his head and shoulders, intensified by his wool habit. In his time away in the north, he had lost his deep tan. It showed signs of returning as his sunburns healed. Martin had accomplished his mission, to find Molly Bain and bring her and Colonel Penn together, but the colonel's unexpected death occurred before the officer fulfilled his promise to restore the monk's social identity. Martin's failure was as painful as his disidentification was permanent.

After his customary four hours in the plaza, Martin's begging bowl sat empty. Father Gonzales, upset that Martin had not kept his vow to continue supplying the monastery with income while he traveled, increased his daily income target to make up for lost time. Martin rose, knees and ankles stiff, and he trudged down the main street toward home and his cell. Shopkeepers tolerated him less than before, and the local police kept him away from public water fountains. Taking a shortcut down a narrow alley, he enjoyed the relief of the shadows cast by the buildings.

"Brother Martin."

Martin cowered. A figure stepped out from a doorway.

"I'm glad that I found you."

Martin peered into the semi-darkness. "Do I know you?"

A serious, handsome woman in the uniform of the Bureau of Environmental Security approached Martin. "We've met, though I remember very little. It was in Run, in Krasnoyarsk Krai."

Martin recalled the face, pale and drawn when he last saw it. "You're the BES officer who tried to arrest Bill Penn. You were shot."

"I'm Janine Kilel."

Unwelcome memories from Run flooded back to Martin. "Ah, Inspector Kilel."

"It's Colonel Kilel now."

Another colonel to torture me? "Congratulations." Martin lowered his eyes. "If you'll excuse me, the abbot gets angry if I'm late."

"You look thirsty, Brother Martin. Here." Kilel held out a bottle of water, a gesture that amazed Martin. Kilel was breaking the law by acknowledging his existence. Giving him a gift was a felony, but bessies were immune to a charge under the social death statutes. On the other hand, accepting a gift was not illegal for the disidentified. Dead men cannot break the law. Martin sipped the water rapturously. "Thank you, Colonel."

"Not at all."

Martin bowed and edged past Kilel.

"Don't you want to hear what happened after we met?"

The suggestion revived his sense of loss. "I suppose you will tell me."

"You ought to know. Please walk with me." Kilel related the story of the ambush and rescue. "I have a question, Martin. Why do you think Bill Penn saved my life?"

"Why don't you ask him yourself?"

"I want your opinion."

"Perhaps he's just a good person who sees you as a fellow human being, not just a bess—an environmental security officer."

Kilel smiled. "No need to protect my feelings, Brother Martin. My mission is more important than my ego."

"Your mission?"

"To protect the earth."

"What happened to Molly Bain? There was a young woman as well."

"Anne Penn." Kilel's brow creased. "Molly Bain has disappeared. None of her business associates have seen her since she was in Run. I was wondering if you might have heard from her."

Martin shook his head.

"Hmm." Kilel mused. "I'm impressed that you managed to cross two continents and an ocean to get back here."

"The doctors who put on this brand," Martin pointed to his forehead, "didn't remove my wits."

"How—"

Martin interrupted. "I suppose you handed Bill Penn and his daughter over to BES Corrections as soon as you could."

"If I had wanted them remanded into custody of the Environmental Crimes Tribunal, I would've done so in Dudinka," Kilel said.

"I don't understand, Colonel."

"I brought them back to Pacific West and I let them go."

Kilel's statement shocked Martin. "You let them go? I never would've guessed that you would do something like that."

"Why is that?"

"I haven't known you long, but you are one of the most single-minded people I've ever met. Bill and Anne Penn, and Molly Bain for that matter, are environmental criminals, as I understand the law," Martin said. "I have some experience in these things."

"Make no mistake, Brother Martin. Bill Penn is still under investigation for his crimes against an endangered species. Anne Penn is an accessory to those crimes. Molly Bain should be charged with aiding and abetting carbon smugglers. They are all felons, as far as I'm concerned."

"They saved your life."

The pair stopped in front of a marked BES car. Kilel was distant. "As a professional, I have to stay objective, but I can't ignore that fact."

"Mercy is one of humanity's greatest qualities," Martin said.

Kilel clasped her hands behind her back. "Mercy has nothing to do with it. The law says I can take into account mitigating circumstances. A citizen provided life-saving help to a police officer. That kind of thing should be recognized, encouraged."

"Of course." Martin shuffled in place.

"You, however, did not help me."

Martin straightened and choked back his fear. "What will you do now?"

"I'm continuing to look into the carbon-smuggling ring, though it's far more extensive than I imagined. I'm treading lightly, you might say."

"Your life is in danger."

"It goes with the territory," Kilel said. "Justice will be served on everyone in due time." The door on the BES cruiser clicked and opened. "Won't you please step into the car?"

Terror washed over Martin, but the words of protest stuck in his throat. *What have I done now? What did she discover?*

"Please, Brother Martin. Let's not make a scene."

Martin complied. He was a dissed man, a nothing, with no defenders, no allies. Father Gonzales might say something on his behalf, out of duty, but no one else would.

The door closed, but the ritual of arrest didn't go as Martin expected. Kilel did not restrain him with cuffs or drugs. She relaxed at the cruiser's controls, and the ready light on the security bot glowed red. The bot was off. Light jazz came from the sound system.

The car made its way through the baking streets. Martin stayed silent, fearful more words might make his situation worse. He knew the town well from his daily begging, and they weren't headed toward a police station or the small BES office on the outskirts of town. After a few minutes, the car stopped in the visitors parking lot of the town's medical clinic. Kilel stepped out of the car and bade Martin to follow to the clinic's entrance.

"This is yours, Brother Martin." The inspector handed him an electronic document.

Martin unfolded the document, which connected to a com channel and loaded. He read it, and his knees buckled.

"Brother Martin," Kilel said, "I went through Colonel Penn's papers and notes on the smuggling ring. I learned that he promised you re-identification if you helped him. You did so." Kilel kept her eyes on the clinic's facade.

"I would never offer such a trade. You committed genocide against nature." Kilel paused. "I also know about the deal Molly Bain struck with Colonel Penn to pin the full blame of the Spike on you." Her voice lightened, as if she was capitulating in an argument she had lost. "People are afraid of the Bureau, and that fear is useful. Yet we also believe in justice, and that means keeping promises, even those made by dead men. This document reinstates your identity as Martin Scribb."

A thrill flowed through Martin like a lightning bolt. His dream had come true. "I never imagined the day would come. I don't know what to say. Thank you? Why are we at the clinic?"

"Page six," Kilel said.

When Martin found the order, he sat down on a bench in the shade of a tree. Tears filled his eyes, and the world blurred around him, as if he were dying. In fact, he was reborn.

"Don't be late, Martin." Kilel directed him toward the clinic entrance. "The surgeon is waiting to remove your brand."

EPILOGUE

THE CONCUSSION FROM THE DEPTH charge added insult to injury. The damaged *Extinction* lay still, three hundred meters down in the underwater trench where Kapitan Gore hid her. The pressure hull groaned, protesting the strain of pushing it beyond its design limits. Gore knew his boat; the groaning was more like a sailor's gripe than a signal of danger. He sat at his desk in the captain's cabin, the condensation dripping like sweat down the carbon fiber walls behind the tropical plants. The entire submarine was as silent as a tomb, appropriate, given that the sub-chasers on the surface had a good chance of finding her if a crewman so much as coughed. He had survived an attack once before, and he would kill the bosses and the damned on his boat to survive again, if necessary.

Molly Bain was beyond their possible fate. Her gray skin did nothing to mar her beauty as she lay prone in his bunk. The first depth charge had thrown her down a companionway. The bruise on her temple confirmed the injury. She breathed for an hour or so before dying. Under normal circumstances, Gore disposed of bodies, but the option didn't cross his mind for Molly Bain. He loved her once, many years ago. She watched over him while the injury to his wrist healed. He was cruel but not heartless, so he brought her aboard as his personal steward.

Gore saved his cruelty for those who betrayed him. He finished the final entry in what he called his "vengeance log." It was an informal document, not required by any regulation (not that he cared) or any maritime tradition, except perhaps among thieves and extortionists. It contained details of every transaction: the who, what, where, and how much of his criminal life. As a military man, he was prepared to die. As a criminal, he was prepared to take everyone with him, even those whom he had never seen. He didn't know their names, but anyone with basic problem-solving skills—perhaps that BES inspector—could unravel the entire petroleum operation with a few details from his log.

His repaired wrist ached from the strain of tapping the tablet. He pushed through the soreness to record the details of his betrayal. First, communications with his contacts dried up. Next, he followed the news chan stories of the disappearance of the North American Interior Minister. Gore sniggered when her body was discovered at a museum dedicated to the outlawed oil industry. The pundits blamed reactionary terrorist groups who never adjusted to the Carbon Acts, but Gore guessed that his fellow conspirators had decided to plug a hole in their leaky enterprise.

Gore knew it was only a matter of time before the rest of the ring was rolled up, and he lay low. He believed *Extinction* was too valuable for the true leaders of the ring to give it up, but his hopes were dashed when the first depth charges and hunter-killer torpedoes entered the waters above him. His countermeasures were as good as the world's best navies, but he was running out of time and resources.

Gore finished the entry, archived a copy in the boat's digital storage, and sent a third copy to a device attached to *Extinction*'s outer hull. Another concussion rocked the submarine's pressure hull, and Gore wondered for the first time if escape was worth it. With an international naval force circling above him like vultures, he would be caught and dissed. Or perhaps "accidentally" killed in a firefight. He had loved his life as a corsair, free from every authority, save his own. Death on his own terms was preferable. One emotion dogged him: loss. Micah Panang had gone through the second course of DNA tattoo treatments days before the BES inspector shot her through the eye. Micah promised to become his mate, sacrificing much of her humanity for him. Life had been less interesting for Gore since her death.

The master of *Extinction* armed the device. He touched the key that released it, and the panel glowed green, signaling success. Once it broke the surface, it would transmit the vengeance log in all com frequencies, telling everyone on earth about his work. He growled with satisfaction at the irony: As the device floated upward, depth charges and torpedoes sped down to meet *Extinction*. No one heard his laughter when the pressure hull collapsed.

AUTHOR'S NOTE

THANK YOU SO MUCH FOR reading *Carbon Run*. I sincerely hope you enjoyed it. Writing is a challenging and rewarding experience, and I'd like to hear your feedback. Please take a moment to review my book on Amazon, Goodreads, or your favorite book review site. You can follow me on Facebook (@AuthorJGFollansbee), Twitter (@Joe_Follansbee), and Instagram (@jgfollansbee). You can also follow me on my personal blog. Tell your friends!

Carbon Run is the first full-length novel in my dystopian thriller series, *Tales From A Warming Planet*. Watch for the second and third full-length novels, *City of Ice and Dreams*, and *Restoration*. You'll also enjoy the novelette *The Mother Earth Insurgency*, published in 2017. I will also publish a collection of stories under the title *The Mother Earth Insurgency* in 2018.

Thank you!

— Joe Follansbee, Summer 2017

◆ ◆ ◆

Twenty-three months since I last knew my name. Twenty-three months since I could say where I'm from. I'm a nothing, but these people expect me to tell them whether they'll live or die.

The repetitive shriek of the klaxon frightened the *inmigrantes* crowding the ship's passageway. Sento had no answer to their questions, even if she allowed herself to speak to them. *I don't know why the warning sounded.* Hundreds of hands, black, brown, and white, old and young, brushed her as she trod the *Kildare's* decks. The pleas implicit in their touches tensed her powerful shoulders and arms. In her flak jacket and pistol, she was a symbol of order in the chaos, despite the fact she was there to protect the ship, not them. Like them, however, she was scared, but she couldn't show it for fear of stoking their worries.

Except for the boy. *He said his name was Koi something. Nahim.* His touch was different. It distracted her from her isolation.

Sento paused a few seconds under an air vent. The cold Antarctic air dispersed the thick smell of unwashed bodies choking the passageway. Stray tawny hairs drifted in front of her eyes as she avoided arms and legs jamming every corner. A misstep in her trail boots, the soles almost worn through, would be painful for the stepped-on victim. She flicked the hairs behind her right ear. Someone once said she had the face of Aphrodite but the jaw of Hercules. *Who said that to me? I wish I could remember.*

The *inmigrante* questions were alike in English, Spanish, or Portuguese. "Have we arrived early?" "¿Por qué nos detenemos?" "Será que estamos afundando"? She kept silent, pretending to ignore the immigrants while watching them. The ship had stopped, but she saw no point in stating the obvious. Though her instincts called on her to offer a word of reassurance or share a food pack, her job required wariness toward the families huddled into tight balls of fear. In Punta Arenas, the shipowner admired her buff upper arms and shoulders, and when she rejected an offer to sponsor her in the local blood sport, he hired her as security for the trip to Nordenskjöld.

It was a convenient way for her to follow a dream.

Her boots clicked on the deck plates, the sound muffled by the prone refugees passing along rumors and rumors of rumors about the trouble with the ship.

"The engines have failed."

"The Chilean Coast Guard ordered us to stop. Everyone will be arrested."

"We're lost."

Booms and groans rumbled through the vessel's belly, as if it had a painful case of indigestion. In Punta Arenas, Sento overheard stories of mothballed derelicts purchased by criminals, refurbished just enough to get their engines working, and sent off to Antarctica overloaded with passengers. No water. No food. No safety gear. Many of the ships came back for another load. Many disappeared without a trace. Sento convinced herself that her ship's owner had more scruples. He offered her cash on the spot. *It's safe, he said, like rowing across a pond.*

She halted in front of an unraveled middle-aged woman huddled alone under a companionway. She was familiar, but not in the way a friend or colleague is familiar. She was a disidentified. Like ghosts, the disidentified inhabited a place between society's light and dark. They were living husks, legal non-entities, socially dead, without names, with all data about their existence expunged from every database and document that might have stored facts and figures about their lives. Sento's eyes lingered on the tulip-shaped welt on the woman's forehead. The law required indifference to her, but Sento did not feel bound by this rule. As if absently attacking an itch, Sento raised her fingers to her hairline, expecting to find a similar welt of disidentification. Nothing was there, but the younger woman shared something with the dissed woman she couldn't explain. Whenever she encountered a non-person, she gave in to the connection, instead of fighting it.

"Are you okay?" Sento whispered, sitting on a locker stenciled with "100 chalecos salvavidas."

"Go away." The voice was muffled behind a gauzy cloth.

Sento nodded, but she removed a food pack and lay it near the woman's bare, calloused foot.

The ragged woman's shiny eyes stared at the food pack. "They'll report you. They'll put you in jail."

Local authorities didn't always look the other way from illegal acts of compassion, but Sento wasn't worried. "I don't think there's any bessies on this rust bucket. We're fifteen hundred kilometers from the nearest police station." Sento readied to leave the dissed woman.

"A little water, maybe?"

Sento handed the woman a sealed pouch of fresh water. She carried plenty. She wanted to ask, *What crime did you commit?* The tulip signaled an environmental crime of the worst kind, but the woman wouldn't know the answer to Sento's unspoken question. Dissing not only erased all official traces of life, it permanently damaged parts of the brain that held memory important to identity. The woman probably didn't know her real name.

Sento felt a kinship with the dissed, because she remembered nothing about her life prior to the day she woke up in Valparaíso. *Twenty-three months, one week, five days ago.* Sometimes, she thought she'd been dissed, but the lack of a welt argued for another explanation for her amnesia. No other explanation presented itself.

The dissed woman tore open the water pouch with hands that belonged to a skeleton. "Do you know why the ship has stopped?"

"No." The three-man crew had barely spoken to her since their departure from Punta Arenas. They kept to themselves behind a heavy gate Sento was not allowed to pass. Her job, though, was clear: Keep the *inmigrantes* away.

"Iso." Koi Nahim, the migrant, 11 or 12 years old, dropped to his haunches near Sento and the woman, his mop of black, curly hair in need in a comb. "Isorropia."

"Go away, boy," the dissed woman croaked.

"I've heard that word before," Sento said. She dreamed it before she heard it spoken by refugees on the road south. It was a lodestone, a myth, an abstract concept, all equaling salvation for them. *Maybe for me.*

"At least he pronounces it correctly," the woman said. Sento wondered if she was once a teacher. In the dissed, accents or mannerisms from a prior life often persisted. "Idiots say 'I so.'" She dropped the gauze cloth, which hid sores on her lips, to bite into the food pack. "Isn't that right, boy? It's the way moronic dreamers talk about Isorropia." She said the first syllable like the "e" in "equal."

"Isorropia," Sento repeated with the correct pronunciation.

"Roll the 'r' if you want to impress your betters," the woman said.

"Iso." Saying the word, Koi regarded Sento with curiosity, as if evaluating her.

Uneasy with Koi's gaze, Sento focused on the dissed woman. "What do you think it means?"

"It's a place that doesn't exist." The woman relished the chewy food. "Think Shangri-La or Eden or similar nonsense."

"Iso." The youth nodded to add emphasis.

"Why does he keep saying it?"

Koi reached out to touch the creamy skin of Sento's cheek. The corners of his mouth turned up. If he were anyone else, Sento would've have pushed his delicate fingers away, but his touch was like a warm breath.

"He thinks he's going there." The woman addressed Koi. "Child, Isorropia is about as real as the million euros in my hip pocket." She rasped and dismissed Koi. "Go back to your rat hole and dream your dreams."

The youth lifted his head in defiance and marched off.

I believe in Isorropia too.

"Harmless little son." The dissed woman sighed.

Sento studied the wretched woman. "You're dreaming about something. That's why you're here."

"Everyone wants a new life, sooner or later. That's Antarctica's promise, now that the West Antarctica Ice Sheet is practically gone."

Immigrants gave Sento a dark look as they shuffled past, their pace impatient. "Everyone's restless." Sento stretched and rose.

"Don't... I mean..." The woman stopped herself from reaching out. Touching a non-dissed made the recipient a law-breaker. "Thank you for your kindness."

Sento shrugged, safe in her knowledge that *Kildare* was out of reach of the law. "I'll check on you later."

Sento stepped over and around packs and bags and bundles. The passengers cursed the cargo ship's cranky wireless network, which went dark as soon as the engines spun down. Without a tie to the global net, they felt cut off. In Sento's case, her minds-eye apparatus hadn't worked since they day she woke up in Valparaiso. Isolation was her world. She didn't share the same dream as the *inmigrantes*. They sought escape; she sought home. All she knew for certain, however, was that it had a name: Isorropia.

To escape the stale air and reek of desperation rising from the *inmigrantes*, Sento stepped out of doors. The dawn was red like cayenne pepper. The sun trudged on its low-angled climb to its solstice peak barely more than the breadth of both Sento's muscled hands from thumb to pinky. A cranky, demanding *Arf! Arf!* reached her. Sea lions had gathered on the nearby shore, below a sheer rock cliff that knifed into the Weddell Sea. Behind the cliff rose mountains crowned with glaciers. The lions' yap brought her up short, and a spike of anxiety ran up her spine, signaling another unpleasant crumb of memory. Like a submarine's periscope, the feeling meant something dreadful lay below the surface of her consciousness.

She dismissed the fear with a shake of her head. Refreshed by the bracing breeze, she encountered a tall man with skin the color of milk chocolate, wearing a tattered parka. Sento marked him as a leader. *Given-name Hosea, like the Jewish prophet.* When he spoke with others, they nodded in agreement or affirmation as he spoke. *A possible threat.* His wild-eyed wife was pregnant. *Awilda. A strange name.* When Sento first met him, a day out of Punta Arenas, he was with two children, his own, Sento guessed. All were *inmigrantes*.

Sento nodded to him in thanks as he held open the door.

"Do you know where we are?" Hosea said.

A tinge of frustration bothered Sento. "No, I'm in the dark, just like you."

"Some of us believe we're close to Nordenskjöld."

The town was a dot on the east coast of the 1,300-kilometer Antarctic Peninsula, as scoured by inlets and fjords as the country of its Norwegian explorer namesake. Sento and the *inmigrantes* boarded *Kildare* 10 days earlier, enduring the passage across the Southern Ocean to Nordenskjöld. Another 20 kilometers south and they'd cross the Antarctic Circle.

A commotion broke out on deck. People poured out of the cargo and passenger spaces, chattering like birds, excitement in their steps. The desperation of the immigrants swam beneath the surface of their dirty faces and worn-out clothes. Sento knew these people, as a group, if not individually. Fear and sorrow turned to hope and back again as she hiked beside them on the road from Valparaiso. Some had traveled more than a year, walking or hitching rides across half the globe to escape political chaos, police persecution, thousand-year droughts, or crop failure after crop failure as the Warming's effects accelerated. Sento shared one thing with them, the drive to go south.

She was different, however. Sento was outside their mass, like a tiny moon that traveled with an eccentric asteroid in space. Unlike the dreamers, the seekers for a new life, she obeyed the constant pressure in her heart to push south. Whether Isorropia was a myth or not didn't matter. Only moving relieved the pressure. Once, when she and thousands of other refugees were stopped at a border crossing for weeks, she fell ill. When the border was finally opened, she was as strong as ever within days. Sometimes, she substituted the simpler concept of "south" for the internal obsession that drove her like a pack animal, but south ended at the Pole, and the answer to her identity—as well as Isorropia—was somewhere between here and there. *Would I know it if I saw it?*

The deck plate hummed as the electric engines spun the propellers. The crowd on the main deck cheered as *Kildare* crawled around a headland, but Sento spotted the whitecaps. *Kildare* emerged from the lee of the headland, which blocked the winds coming from the other side. The breeze was strong enough to take the top off one or two of the waves in the bay beyond. *Kildare* rocked a few degrees as the wind struck it. Sento, keeping an eye on the crowd, saw parka hoods go over heads as wind-chill cut the temperature. Many had endured mountain blizzards during their journey. Sento's gut churned, though, and not from the boat's movement.

They entered the bay. The wind lessened by degrees, but waves crashed on the stony beach below the town, which clung to a rocky shelf. Like the immigrants, like Hosea beside her, she felt the pull of the land, but the voice of the waves on the cobbles said *home* to her, not hope for a better future. *What home?*

Sento did not expect the other settlement. To the south, about two kilometers distant from the town, a collection of tents, shacks, and lean-tos sprawled on a narrow expanse of sand. It had a semi-permanent look, unlike the frame and stone structures of the town. *A refugee camp.*

"I like you," the shipowner said to Sento, back in Punta Arenas. "Let me give you some advice. Come back to P-A and work for me. There's nothing on that beach or in that whole continent. It's an empty waste, and it kills you by surprise. No human was meant to live there, and the ones that do will slit your throats in your sleep."

Sento believed the owner, but the pull of Antarctica was far more powerful.

◆ ◆ ◆

The Mother Earth Insurgency: A Novelette
City of Ice and Dreams (Winter 2017)
Restoration (Spring 2018)
The Mother Earth Insurgency: A Collection of Tales from a Warming Planet (Spring 2018)
To get early information about release dates, visit my personal blog, http://joefollansbee.com, and sign up for my reader newsletter.

ABOUT THE AUTHOR

J.G. FOLLANSBEE IS AN AWARD-WINNING writer of thrillers and science fiction stories with climate change themes. An author of maritime history and travel guides, he has published articles in newspapers, regional and national magazines, and regional and national radio networks, including National Public Radio. He's also worked in the high-tech world. He lives in Seattle.

www.ingramcontent.com/pod-product-compliance
Lightning Source LLC
Chambersburg PA
CBHW031028260626
47153CB00016B/341